The Haunting of
Drearcliff
Grange
School

Also by Kim Newman and available from Titan Books:

The Haunting of Drearcliff Grange School

KIM NEWMAN

TITAN BOOKS

The Haunting of Drearcliff Grange School
Print edition ISBN: 9781785658839
E-book edition ISBN: 9781785658846

Published by Titan Books
A division of Titan Publishing Group Ltd
144 Southwark Street, London SE1 0UP

First edition: October 2018
1 3 5 7 9 10 8 6 4 2

A CIP catalogue record for this title is available from the British Library.

Printed and bound in the USA.

For Grace

Contents

Primus

The Great Game

1: Re-Enter: Kentish Glory

AMY THOMSETT OF the Fourth Form could float, but not fly. She was becoming expert in the use of what Light Fingers called her 'mentacles'. Amy thought of the phantom limbs as bendy tubes with thick gloves at the ends. Her party piece was gripping smallish items, then moving them. With fists in her pockets, she could turn a key, strike a match or stop a clock. For a grand finale, she'd wobble a pot off the table and pour. She always sloshed tea into the saucers. Her friends were mostly too impressed to complain.

With a little less confidence, she could take mental hold of her body, lift off the ground, then shift *herself*. It was *very close* to flying.

Tonight, she floated thirty feet above a plane of churning khaki soup. The air was clear up here, but cold enough to freeze the truncheon off a brass policeman. Fog humps over recognisable cathedrals, towers and bridges gave her a rough idea where she was. She had a rolled-up map with her, but knew better than to fish it out. The cruel wind that flicked city grit at her face would whip the map from her numb fingers.

She had come to London to play in the Great Game.

She'd worried pigeons would be a hazard, but sensible scavengers of the skies were tucked up in nests out of the weather.

The same went for the paladins who patrolled these airways. The Aviatrix and Dr Shade must be snug in their eyries, pasting press cuttings into scrapbooks or honing crime-battling skills.

Before Amy learned a measure of self-control, her 'light spells' were often inconvenient or embarrassing. Many girls were rebuked by parents for not keeping their feet on the ground or their head out of the clouds. In her case, that old tune was tiresomely apt. Mother was misguided, though – wrong about Amy's 'problem' and wronger still about the school she'd sent her to.

At Drearcliff Grange, Amy learned not to be ashamed of her Talent.

Her tutor Miss Gossage, familiarly known as the Sausage, favoured psychical jargon. Preferably involving long German words. According to Miss Gossage, Amy was a *poltergeist*. More precisely, 'a locus of *poltergeist* phen-*omen*-ah'. In olden days unquiet spirits got the blame when girls levitated or teapots floated. *Poltergeist* meant something like 'noisy ghost'. Amy's best friend Frecks had issued a standing invitation to haunt her ancestral home. She wanted her spendthrift brother Ralph driven potty with looming candlesticks and rattled chains.

Shivering, Amy fondly recalled the comfort of draughty, leaky Walmergrave Towers.

The quilt of fog muted street sounds. Amy heard faint car horn toots and saw funnel-shapes of light crawl through murk. Other ghostly glows came from shrouded streetlamps or brazier fires. It wasn't a fit night to go out on the town. Occasional snatches of song rose as pub doors opened, then quieted as they were slammed to keep the weather out.

Amy began singing to herself.

'One thousand and one green bottles hanging on the wall, one thousand and one green bottles hanging on the wall... and if one green bottle should accidentally fall – *whistle whistle whistle* kerr-*ASH!*' – it was Drearcliff tradition to include sound effects – 'there'd be one thousand and *none* green bottles hanging on the wall...'

The weather made the Game more challenging.

Miss Gossage was awfully enthusiastic about challenges. She had supreme confidence in Drearcliff Spirit. 'Boldness,' she would say, 'always *boldness*.'

Amy was supposed to serve as an observation balloon, relaying intelligence to teammates on the ground. For all her enthusiasm, the Sausage was not a mistress of tactics. Up here in the arctic blast, Amy was in no position to gather or relay intelligence. Much more of this and her brain might turn into a lump of ice. If she lost concentration, her floating became unsteady. No one would be impressed by a paladin who wobbled in mid-air. If she blacked out altogether, she'd plummet and that would be the end of her story.

At Drearcliff Grange she had special lessons to develop her Talent.

'Attributes and Abilities are not enough,' Headmistress said. 'An Unusual Girl must cultivate *Applications*.'

During outdoor training, Amy was tethered so as not to be swept off by strong gusts. Miss Gossage beat time with a baton as she executed slow aerobatics, trailing lengths of gauze from her wrists. 'Elegahnce, Thomsett, e-leg-ahnce,' shouted the Sausage. 'You are a sprite, a fay... Swirl your streamers with *panache*!' Amy usually got in a tangle with her tether and gauzes, dashing dreams of a ballet career as the only swan who wouldn't need hoisting in the *pas de deux*. She'd have to fall back on haunting homes to order.

Nevertheless, she no longer flapped like a broken kite. Miss Gossage had her adopt a diving pose to cut down wind resistance – legs straight, arms out, hands open. She felt silly, but could propel herself like a dart. The posture was murder on her back, especially when she had to float with books perched on her head.

'Talent is well and good, Thomsett, but Talent alone does *not* make up for shockingly poor deportment. Straighten that spine, gel!'

Her landings were woeful. More often than not she pranged and sprained an ankle. The Sausage insisted Amy spend hours on boring earthbound calisthenics, pushing against a solid (and smelly) gym mat. She must grow strong and stay supple to cope with the stresses and strains of being a Moth Girl... of being Kentish Glory.

Paladins had colourful handles. It was a tradition. Some hid their real names and faces. Everyone knew the Aviatrix was Lucinda Tregellis-d'Aulney – a Drearcliff Grange Old Girl! – but Dr Shade's true identity was a mystery. According to *British Pluck Weekly*, that was to stop nemeses nobbling him by going after his loved ones. Should she pretend Kentish Glory was not Amy Thomsett to protect *her* loved ones? At present, the nearest thing she had were her friends in the Moth Club. They could all pretty much look after themselves. It would be a brave nemesis who dared try anything on with Mother.

For the Great Game she wore the mantle of Kentish Glory.

Her kit was a thick wool leotard, tennis skirt, riding boots, flying helmet and goggles, and a fisherman's waistcoat with useful little pockets. The double-layered mothwing cloak was tarted-up salvage from the theatre wardrobe. Light Fingers sewed all the Moth Club costumes. She'd troubled to make Amy's wings the authentic Kentish Glory (*Endromis versicolora*) colouring – orange undercape with brown markings, brown overwing with white markings.

The natty get-up was at once uniform and disguise, though most of the school had a fair notion of the true identity of the flier in their midst. Flapping at the end of a line over the cricket pitch was a bit of a giveaway.

She shared *all* her secrets only with her closest chums. To commemorate survival into the Fourth Form, the Moth Club swore a dire oath of loyalty, sealed with pinpricks of blood. Amy, Frecks, Light Fingers, Kali – to the grave, and beyond! Thomsett, Amanda; Walmergrave, Serafine; Naisbitt, Emma; Chattopadhyay, Kali: Desdemona House, Fourth Form,

Drearcliff Grange School. To bowl straight and bat square. Spirit – always Spirit! Kentish Glory, Willow Ermine, Large Dark Prominent, Oleander Hawk – by day and by night, in lessons and after Lights Out, firm in any just cause, till the end of time.

'Nine hundred and twenty-two green bottles hanging on the wall,' she went on, 'nine hundred and twenty-two green bottles hanging on the wall... and if one green bottle should accidentally fall – *whistle whistle whistle* kerr-*ASH!* – there'd be nine hundred and twenty-*one* green bottles hanging on the wall...'

She imagined bottles plunging into the fog – and the distant *kerr-ash* of glass breaking on paving stones.

Last year, when but lowly Thirds, the Moth Club rallied the Remove – the school's stream for Unusuals of all forms and houses – to best a hooded conspiracy. They pit Talent and Spirit against trespassers from another plane of existence intent on turning the world into a colony of human ants. In the summer term, Kentish Glory and Company saw through the sheikish good looks of the Reverend Rinaldo and the lamia charms of his 'wife' Ariadne and saved a coven of Sixths from fates worse than death. Unaccountably, the victims were in two minds about the rescue. Still, the Moth Club asked for no thanks. Struggle in a just cause was reward enough. Except for Light Fingers, who sulked unless she got at least a *little* thanks.

This year, as sophisticated Fourths, the Moth Club's epic battle was with Drearcliff Grange's stringent rules against cosmetics. Like generations of schoolgirls before them, and doubtless generations yet to come, Amy and her friends seethed at a cruel regime that denied them warpaint. Shopgirls their age striped themselves like birds of paradise. Magazines were full of testimonials from actresses who owed their success to the transformative products of Max Factor. But Drearcliff girls must show bare faces to the world, exposing every blemish to mockery – rendering themselves so hideous no fellow would ever clap eyes on them without a shudder. It was a conspiracy to condemn them to lives of sad spinsterhood. Women died of melancholy because of such unjust strictures.

Only the most daring girls tried to get round the rules. Frecks – Serafine Walmergrave – made a Clara Bow beauty mark with a soft pencil, and passed it off as the last surviving freckle from the plague that earned her undying handle. Kali – Princess Kali of Kafiristan – maintained her caste mark with blood-red paint she would sometimes lightly dab on her relatively rosy lips.

Shivering in the air, Amy no longer gave a heaped teaspoon about beauty make-up. She wished she'd thought to lather her face with protective grease like a Channel swimmer. She wrapped her cloak tight about her, more like a cocoon than wings. Her jaws ached from clamping them shut to prevent chattering teeth. This cold didn't suit moths. As she inhaled, hooks of ice formed in her lungs. Her breath came out warm, though – dampening the scarf wrapped around her lower face.

The bright-mauve muffler didn't really go with Kentish Glory colours. The smitten Laurence knitted it for Frecks last Christmas. When her idol casually lent the scarf to Amy for the duration of the Game, the Ariel Third's eyes glinted with tragic pain. 'Her need is greater than mine,' said Frecks, bestowing a heartening thumbs-up on her admirer. 'Our gratitude flows like the proverbial wine. We couldn't pull this jaunt off without you, Young Pocket.'

That was the honest truth. Drearcliff Grange strategy relied on Larry's singular Talent – putting objects temporarily out of reach of mortal grasp in an aperture in space she could open and close at will.

Ever since Frecks let slip about the Moth Club, Larry burned to join. Amy didn't think of herself as unkind, but baulked at bestowing even associate membership on a person who didn't understand how moth names worked. They were supposed to be appropriate to home territory. Amy was from Worcestershire, where – perhaps against expectations – the Kentish Glory was most commonly found. Larry wanted to call herself Scarce Forester, because a cloak with that species' iridescent blue-green colouring would be glamorous. The Laurence family homes were in Belgravia and Berkshire, where *Jordanita globulariae* was yet to be sighted. Larry was an Ariel. It was typical of that most well-heeled of houses to assume rules would be waived for their convenience. Amy wouldn't have been surprised if she'd wanted a *butterfly* handle. Larry needed something better than Pocket, though. It gave away too much. Mademoiselle Marsupial would be subtler. Or the Purple Pixie.

'Eight hundred and fifty-three green bottles hanging on the wall, eight hundred and fifty-three green bottles hanging on the wall, and if one green bottle should accidentally fall... *Whistle whistle whistle* kerr-*ASH!* – there'll be eight hundred and fifty-*two* green bottles hanging on the wall!'

Even Amy was getting tired of the crashing bottles.

For all she knew, the Drearcliff team could have been captured or disabled by their arch-rivals, Lobelia Draycott's House of Reform. The Great Game's defending champions. Also known as the Disapproved School. Repository for the Worst Girls in England. Girls weren't sent there; they were sentenced there. Mrs Draycott's staff were prison warders sacked for brutality and Magdalen Sisters defrocked for excessive use of the tawse.

Bad blood ran between Primrose Quell, the Draycott's Captain, and Prima Haldane, Drearcliff's Head Girl. Quell, formerly of Goneril House, was expelled from Drearcliff Grange last term. Headers Haldane set aside the Code of Break and tattled to Dr Swan. Queenie Quell ran what Kali called a protection racket, collecting thruppence out of every shilling spent on black market tuck, make-up or sundry contraband. The moral defects that got Quell booted out of Drearcliff Grange suited her for advancement at the House of Reform.

Kali wondered if Quell might ditch the Game and just use fog cover to get even with Haldane. The daughter of a Kafiristani bandit chief and well up on the gangs of Chicago, Kali understood the concept of *vendetta*. She said the team should keep a wary eye out for pigmeat hung from a shrub. 'It won't be no bacon tree, mugs... it'll be a *ham bush*!'

Amy looked down and wondered if she saw red traces in the fog.

Between Drearcliff and Draycott's, it was always personal.

At the Off, Quell's she-imps had made mocking, grunting sounds at the Drearcliff Grange girls.

There was a sad story about that.

If it came to a punch-up between rival schools, neither would win. Clever Dick's Brain-Boxes – Cadet Branch of the Splendid Six – would scoop the tobies and go home for cocoa. Amy worried a battle was fought and lost while she was freezing her proboscis off in the stratosphere. Even the weeds, wets and dims of Humble College – fully, St Cuthbert's School for the Sons of the Humble and Pious – could hardly participate less than a person bobbing about like a rudderless Zeppelin.

'Five hundred and ninety-one green bottles hanging on the wall, five hundred and ninety-one green bottles hanging on the wall, and if one green bottle should accidentally fall – *Whistle whistle whistle* kerr-*ASH!* – there'll be five hundred and *ninety* green bottles—'

Miss Gossage's high sing-song *buzzed* in the back of Amy's mind.

'Mawther Hein to Kentish Gloreah, Mawther Hein to Kentish Gloreah, come in, come in, ovah...'

The ungainly, lopsided teacher was herself an Unusual. A Drearcliff Old Girl (Class of '11), Clemency Gossage returned to the fold after a Disappointment. Assiduous collectors of staffroom gossip had not discovered whether the Disappointment was in love or another field of human endeavour. The betting was on a punctured romance though. The Sausage was the sort of google-eyed, pre-emptively apologetic goose who'd let some rolled-stockings vamp waltz off with any swain not nailed down and golly-gosh-what-a-rum-do about it rather than use her Talent to get her chap back or put her rival out of the picture.

Chemicals in Miss Gossage's brain made her a living telegram service. She could transmit brief messages directly into the minds of pupils she had a fix on, and receive curt responses. A Talent as close to mental telepathy as floating was to flying. The party piece had Applications in the field, even if – or *especially when* – the field was thirty feet above a fogbound city.

'Mawther Hein to Kentish Gloreah, what is your – ahh – position? Ovah.'

Amy concentrated. The Sausage could pick up short sentences, formed in the mind but not spoken aloud. It helped to mouth the words.

'My position *is* over… over Fitzroy Square or thereabouts.'

She tried to think an 'over'. A full stop formed in her mind – Frecks' beauty mark.

'EC3 and E1 parcels collected… ovah.'

Good news. They'd been sure about the EC3 site, but iffy on the E1.

'Parcels collected… and posted. Pillah box ain roowt to WC1. Postmein sent to SW2. No developmeints on W1. Ovah.'

Pillar Box was Larry Laurence. Another dud handle.

WC1 was 'Helen's Hole', the Troy Club. The easy one.

Before the Off, Amy saw Haldane's reasoning in not collecting the WC1 parcel until after the team had tackled some real puzzlers. It was like having a match in hand. Now, with the fog, she had a notion 'the easy one' wouldn't be as easy as all that. The Great Game wasn't famous for gentle warm-up rounds. It was, in fact, known for fiendish trickiness from the Off to the Finish.

Amy's antennae tingled. Well, her eyebrows itched – which was still equivalent to a moth becoming alert to danger, food or a change in the weather. A more *specific* intuition would have been preferable, but – as Dr Swan said – 'we must find Applications for the Talents we have.'

Miss Gossage *buzzed* again – a zizzle of irritation, unlike any sound issued from a human throat… Not strictly a sound at all, since it was all in the Sausage's mind and Amy's. It was like an ice-cream headache.

'Oh, noodles,' said Amy, aloud.

She had lost count of those precariously-placed green bottles and couldn't be bothered starting all over again. No matter how many of the blessed things were hanging on the wall – and why anyone would want to hang bottles on a wall was beyond her! – they'd just have to jolly well stay put and *not* accidentally fall. All that broken glass was bound to get underfoot and be a nuisance.

Fitzroy Square or thereabouts. North of Oxford Street.

Not as insalubrious as Soho, according to Light Fingers, but not exactly respectable either. Denizens called this Fitzrovia. Anywhere with denizens rather than residents was decidedly suspect. Light Fingers' larcenous parents, who once moved (very fast) through the demi-monde, fleeced many a mark in the clubs of Fitzrovia… watering holes famous for cocktails, gambling and other vices.

The Troy Club was the only seedy salon in town to waive cover charges for Drearcliff Grange girls. If Mother found out places like 'Helen's Hole' were on the itinerary of a school trip, she wouldn't approve.

Amy wasn't sure this was where she should be hovering either.

This was not getting them home in time for tea and buns.

There were three more 'parcels' to be 'collected' and 'posted'.

There was but one thing for it.

She extended thin, jointed mentacle spines. Spreading her cloak like wings, she fanned a hole in the fog. She saw wet rooftops before the hole filled in.

Taking a deep, clear, stinging breath, Amy began to sink.

The ground was calling her. Loud and clear. Over and out.

Her nose stung. The goggles kept fog out of her eyes, but she couldn't see worth a toffee.

'Noodles,' she said again, for extra emphasis. 'Soggy noodles!'

II: Nine Hours Earlier: On the Road

'THE OFF IS at sunset,' insisted Headers Haldane. 'It's in the rules.'

Girls groaned. Amy, like everyone else, was fed up with rules. Sunset was hours away. And the Off was in London.

Rattletrap, the school motor charabanc, was barely past Andover.

Joxer, the Drearcliff Grange Man of All Work, mumble-grumbled as he bent over the steering wheel. By his lights, Rattletrap – spanking new, and a proud purchase for the school this term – was an instrument of Satan. With many a lurch and backfire, the vehicle veered across the road, searching for ruts to get stuck in. Joxer scorned irresponsible mechanisation. Horse and cart had served the school since Founding Day and he saw no need to abandon tried and tested conveyance. 'What be next,' he muttered, 'a *nairy-plane*? T'ain't a natural thing, and no good'll come of 'ee!'

After two hours' bouncing on a hardwood pew, Amy was beginning to agree with him. That ancient cart at least had upholstered seats – though faithful Dauntless might not have got this far without conking out by the roadside, no matter what secret formula Joxer added to the nag's oats. Rattletrap was built for excursions to the seaside on sunny Bank Holidays.

A canvas roof could be wound up to keep off the worst of the rain, but open sides left passengers at the mercy of wind, smuts, petrol fumes and small boys throwing stones.

'Stuff the rules,' said Frecks, risking a Major Infraction for impudence to the Head Girl. 'Stuff 'em with walnuts. You know who we're playing. Draycott's Girls don't give a fourpenny whoops for the laws of Great Britain, let alone the rules of the Great Game. The Brain-Box Brats think cheating's clever, not wrong. Even the Humblebumblers will have opened the envelope by now. Unless you crack on, those sooners'll collect the tobies double-quick. We'll end up holding the wooden spoon. Again. That'll sit ill with the assembled throng on our return.'

Last year's result fostered a fierce sense of injustice. Amy hadn't been selected for the team then, but shared the wounded pride. A pall of humiliation settled on the whole school.

Before the Off, a Draycott's girl with a Talent for pocket-picking sidled up to Miss Gossage and switched envelopes. Thus, Drearcliff Grange were packed off on fools' errands. Lucretia Lamarcroft, the Amazonian Captain, was duped into 'trying out the famous echo' in the Quiet Room of the Diogenes Club. Apparently, under the bylaws of that institution, you could be shot for coughing – but she gave out a war-whoop that'd have startled a herd of stampeding buffalo. Aconita Gould, the Scots Wolf Girl, followed a false trail to Battersea Dogs' Home and was subjected to a flea bath. Janice Marsh, the aquatic American, was lured to a slab in Billingsgate Fish Market and barely escaped gutting. Moria Kratides, the undersized Sixth, led a party into the sewers of Hampstead on a hunt for the fabled Black Sow whose brood of flesh-eating swine terrorised Under-London. That was a put-up job too. The Kratides Expedition got beastly lost in unsanitary tunnels.

With their main rivals sabotaged, Draycott's romped to victory with four out of five tobies. Apparently, their 'unorthodox tactics' did not violate the rules Haldane set so much store by. Dr Swan made several speeches in assembly to steel the school's resolve. For over a year, the message from Headmistress had been unambiguous. Drearcliff must win the next Great Game.

Which was not to say they were limited to 'orthodox tactics'.

'Initiative is encouraged,' Dr Swan told them.

They should interpret that how they wished, Amy presumed.

Haldane gripped the oilskin document packet. Its provenance was beyond reproach. Even Headers saw sense in taking custody of the envelope early in the day. The Sausage handed it over before the team trooped aboard Rattletrap. The black wax seal was imprinted with the skull sigil of the Undertaking. The sombrely dressed fellowship, known for their discreet presence at sites of mysterious occurrences, had overseen the Great Game since its beginnings in the reign of James the First and Sixth.

The first teams to compete were the Homunculi, apprentices and acolytes (not all strictly human) of the occultist John Dee; the Sea Eyasses, buccaneer cabin boys and rigging rats; the Weird Sisters, the sly fey lads who played the witches in the original production of *Macbeth*; and the Daughters of Annwn, urchin vixens who filed their teeth and worshipped Old Blood Goddesses. Rhyming riddles set by Francis Bacon led to the hiding places of the pickled heads of five Spanish sea captains. Whoever claimed the biggest bag of bonces won the day.

The outcome of the first Game was hotly disputed. The longed-lived survivors – an Admiral of privateers and a High Priestess of Agroná – married each other, but never put the quarrel to bed. Seventy years on – despite the pleas of children, grandchildren and great-grandchildren – they determined to settle the matter with a clash of cold steel. Tragically, the duellists ran each other through and expired in each other's arms. Heirs and adherents divided into factions to keep the fight going. Somewhere, the Disagreement of Eyas and Annwn raged still. Over the centuries, the death toll has been equivalent to a medium-sized war.

The Armada noggins served as prizes for a century or so before they flaked to bits. Reluctantly, the Undertaking replaced the heads with toby jugs.

Those who did well in the Great Game frequently went on to figure in the *Shadow Chronicle of Britain* – the record of wars, feats and crimes too disturbing for ordinary history books. Those who did poorly in the Great Game seldom figured in the Chronicle of Anything.

Amy closed her eyes and imagined the seal crumbling.

'Lay off that hocus-pokery,' said Headers, voice rising an octave. 'Whichever of you *Unusuals* is casting the fluence, cut it out. I'm on to your wicky tricks. One thing you'll find about me is that precious little can be got past my nose.'

Everyone repressed smirks.

Haldane's most prominent feature was her hooter.

'But, Headers—' began Frecks.

'You're on notice, Walmergrave,' Haldane told her. 'Any more talk of *cheating* and it's a Major Infraction.'

Frecks threw up her hands in despair.

Amy drew in her mentacles.

The rest of the team slumped and slouched.

Rancour and resentment stewed.

Prima Haldane had risen through assiduous creepery. As Chief Whip, she marked down more Infractors than any five prefects put together. As Head Girl, she was a stickler for School Rules. If it were up to her, she'd make up more of the beasts so more girls could be marked down for infractions of them. Her honker was perpetually poked into places it wasn't welcome.

When Headers was a Third, her good-hearted cellmates Byrne and di Fontane got it into their noodles that her problem was a sad, shy inability to make friends. On her birthday, they surprised her with a midnight feast. Haldane refused to budge from her cot and reported the whole corridor to the whips. Infracted for After Lights Out Activity, her would-be benefactors ended up scrubbing the Heel – a traditional Drearcliff Grange punishment – and cursing her name.

Unpopular with her peers, Haldane secured her current position – which entailed being Team Captain in the Great

Game, among other honours and responsibilities – by toadying to beaks and tattling on potential rivals. Susan Byrne, jolliest girl in school, easily lived down the After Lights Out Black Notch Haldane put in her Time-Table Book and seemed a natural for elevation to the post of Head Girl. However, her tenure as Fifth Form Ariel Captain was tainted by scandal – a persistent fug of perfumed cigarettes in her cell, a sixpenny-a-trick whist ring, letters arriving from boys she claimed never to have met which (upon examination by Keys, the school censor) referred to licentious escapades off grounds. So Haldane was left as the only viable candidate.

Whisper had it that the Selection Committee debated breaking the tradition that Head Girl should be an Ariel. Likely candidates among the athletes of Goneril or the terrors of Tamora were considered. The Suggestion Box was stuffed with recommendations for Rose of Viola, whose particular qualifications for office were being startlingly fair of face and completely without voice. When Headers began assembling dossiers on Sixths of other houses, the Committee gave in and advised Dr Swan to pin gold braid on the pest and be done with it. After all, it was only for a year, and what harm could she really do? It wasn't as if she were another Antoinette Rayne or Ariadne Rinaldo. She was no *Unusual*.

Talents were tolerated – encouraged, even – but unspoken convention reserved the position of Head Girl for what Light Fingers contemptuously referred to as 'an Ordinary'.

Last year, she could not have imagined anyone worse than Sidonie Gryce, the witch who was Head Girl when Amy first came to Drearcliff. But Gryce could be bribed or otherwise got around.

'One thing you'll find about me,' insisted Haldane, 'is that I cannot be bribed or got around.'

'That's two things,' said Light Fingers quietly.

'I cannot be tempted, gulled or—'

'Led by the nose,' suggested Frecks.

Giggles were not stifled.

Before Headers could share another thing they would find about her – that she was not to be sneezed at? – Miss Gossage rapped a bench. At the same time, without meaning to, she *buzzed* in Amy's head.

'Leviteah is fine in its place, gels,' said the Sausage, 'but this is no light matter. Remembah, we are a team. We represeint School Spirit. We must prevail. Our honour is at stake.'

'Who, me?' said Honor Devlin humorously.

'Yes, you, missy my gel,' said Miss Gossage seriously. 'Yes, all of you. Not oneses and twoses, but youses and usses. Fortitude, gels!'

'Fortitude, attitude and pulchritude!' said Frecks.

Devlin – known as Stretch because of her rubbery bones – saluted, slapping elongated fingers against the brim of her boater.

'Boldness…' the Sausage said.

'Always *boldness*,' the whole team chimed, though more than one thought it was waggish to pronounce it 'always *baldness*'.

'Dr Swan has made space in the trophy cabinet,' said the Sausage. 'Space enough for five jugs. Those who disappoint Dr Swan do not prospah.'

Miss Gossage was talking about herself, not just the team.

However wary they might be of Draycott's felons in skirts, everyone in the charabanc was more afraid of Myrna Swan. Headmistress had subtle ways of wreaking revenges.

Miss Gossage set an example with Character, but lacked Guile. Were Miss Borrodale – the Science teacher – in her place, Drearcliff Grange might be better placed for a quick victory. Fossil Borrodale had recipes for irresistible toadstools treats. Come the Off, Quell's myrmidons might be wracked with mystery tummy upsets.

The Silly Sausage was above such tactics. Worse luck.

Yesterday afternoon, Dr Swan invited the team – *sans* Miss Gossage – to her study for a word of advice and encouragement.

Surprisingly, Headmistress had the girls hold hands as in

a ring-a-rosy. Then, she said, 'Do not trust *anyone* not in this circle. Show no mercy, for none will be shown to you. Do not *play* the Game, *win* the Game. You all have Abilities, whether Unusual or not. Use them. Look askance at easy opportunity. Become mistresses of *mistrust*.'

That sank in, though Amy felt strange about it.

Dr Swan didn't hold any hands – was she telling them to *mistrust* her?

Haldane nodded as if taking it in, but was holding Nancy Dyall's hand so the straight talk might be corkscrewed in her mind. Dyall's Talent was radiating discombobulating waves.

Headers turned the sealed packet over and over in her lap.

Did she realise she was picking at the Undertakers' seal as if it were a scab?

Frecks' wooden spoon talk was getting to the Team Captain. A poor showing would reflect badly on her. Even Haldane wouldn't prize a commendation as the most rule-abiding loser in the Game. Lamarcroft, last year's Team Captain, lived out her final term at Drearcliff Grange as a Fallen Heroine. After a poor showing in exams, she enlisted as 'Private Jane Noone' (Noone for No One) in General Flitcroft's no-questions-asked Regiment of the Damned. They were currently fighting in the Nejd-Hashemite War. No one was sure on which side.

Piling into Rattletrap after a hearty breakfast, the Moth Club had bagsied the back bench. Amy, Frecks, Light Fingers and Kali could turn round and peer through the isinglass window in the canvas, once-overing dishy motorists.

Early in the excursion, Amy and Frecks played Light Fingers and Kali at pub cricket. When they passed an inn or hostelry on the left, they scored runs equal to the number of legs on the sign. The Cow and Chandler in Mere scored a Six, the Goose and Trumpet in Zeals a Two, and so on. Light Fingers and Kali batted the right side of the road. When Rattletrap passed the Duke of York's Regiment in Ratfyn, the right-handers claimed a match-sweeping Twenty Thousand. Argument arose as to how many of the Duke's well-remembered ten thousand men were actually depicted on the sign. Amy declared before things got too heated. It was a Little Game. Not one that mattered.

Larry Laurence had tried to squeeze onto the Moth Club bench. Even if the Fourths bunched up, no room could be found for her. The titchy Third settled for a position of expectant adoration in front of Frecks, bony knees on the seat, sharp chin on the backrest. Long after the match was abandoned, Larry pointed out legs on the left. Even an impressive Thirty from the Coach and Six at Goodworth Clatworth – counting the coachman and two painted passengers – was too little too late. Larry took the rout personally. If she were at Frecks' side (instead of Amy), she'd have magically detoured Rattletrap past a pub on the left called the Million Millipedes.

'On the right,' said Larry, at Sutton Scotney, 'the Star! A duck!'

'A duck has two legs, but scores no runs,' said Frecks. 'An answer begging for a riddle.'

Larry brayed with laughter, and footnoted how clever and amusing that was.

'Lay off, Young Pocket,' said Frecks fondly, tousling the younger girl's hair.

That shut the Third up, and made her glow...

Thinking about it, Amy reckoned trifling with the mite's affections was a smidge unfair. If Frecks were wearing her silver coif, it might tarnish. Passed on by her uncle, who flew with Pendragon Squadron in the War, its mystic protection thinned if the wearer's purity of heart wavered. The Lady of the Lake held her knights to moral standards so high it was hard to maintain them and still breathe.

Amy diagnosed a spark of something not unlike jealousy in her own breast. Crushes should be treated kindly... but Frecks was *her* best friend. She should know better than to encourage Laurence.

Serafine Walmergrave, a girl with countless admirable qualities, was possessed of a confidence that could – if unchecked – verge on big-headedness. If Frecks ventured a *bon mot*, she needed the honest, proportionate response only a friend could give, not the uncritical, seal-flapping applause of a smitten disciple. Or else she'd lose perspective. Pendragons had fallen for less.

'Here, have some sweeties,' said Light Fingers, offering a bag of all-sorts.

Larry politely declined – as if suspecting the tuck were poisoned. Believing Frecks' friends conspired to cast her into outer darkness, she was suspicious of everyday courtesies. Even the offer of an all-sort.

'Please yourself,' said Light Fingers, flipping a liquorice wheel into the air and catching it with her mouth.

Light Fingers was Amy's *Unusual* best friend. Her Talent was swiftness. Emma Naisbitt was fleet of foot and quick in thought. She inherited it from her parents, who were convicted (if romantic) thieves. Conjurer and glamorous assistant in the evening, cracksman and lookout after midnight. Where Frecks was confident, Light Fingers was cautious. Frecks had a dramatic ginger mop… Light Fingers' hair was of no particular colour. Light Fingers sometimes worried about the things that made them Unusual. 'They call us *flukes*,' she was eager to remind Amy, 'no matter how nice they are to our faces.'

'You should hear what they call *me*, kittens,' Kali would say at that.

Amy and Light Fingers didn't know what the girl meant.

'On my first day at school, Arbuthnot asked me if it washed off?'

'Your forehead dot?'

'No. The soot. Girls used to stick fingers in my face and see if they came away black. I asked Peebles if she got her pasty fizz from chalk powder. She didn't get it then. She don't get it now.'

Amy didn't either.

Kali was a moderniser. Her father was a silent-strangle or cut-throat sort of bandit. The Princess favoured the rat-tat-tat of tommy guns, the squeal of getaway car wheels and the explosive statement of 'pineapples' tossed through windows. She'd learned English from magazine stories about American gangsters and molls. She chewed gum, daring whips to make up a rule against excessive mastication.

'Everyone's a fluke,' Frecks usually said, thinking that settled forever.

'But some can take their helmets off and be Ordinary,' Light Fingers would think or whisper, setting it all off again.

Only best friends could have this conversation over and over and still be best friends.

Amy wondered whether Light Fingers disapproved of Larry, an Unusual, choosing to bestow worship on an Ordinary? The Third wasn't at all taken with fellow Talents like Amy or Light Fingers.

Or Honor Devlin and Charlotte Knowles.

Stretch and Miss Memory sat together, playing cat's cradle. With extra joints and pliable bones, Devlin had an unfair advantage, but Knowles had crammed a thousand or so string configurations into her mind. Devlin and Knowles were Fifths, veterans of the Remove.

Haldane was next to Miss Gossage, on the backwards-facing bench behind Joxer's cushioned seat. She proudly wore the double braid of Head Girl and Chief Whip on boater, blazer and overcoat. She looked like a rear admiral from a landlocked country whose navy made up in pomp what it lacked in ships. Kali said Headers was a sap for not unpicking the trim. Excess glitter would let Draycott's know she was coming from a mile off. A good way to get gunned down in the gutter.

Sitting as far from Haldane as possible without moving to another bench was Hjordis Bok. The Goneril Sixth was school hop, skip and jump champion. She was hard to please, sinking into wordless gloom while girls she'd just beaten rallied round to clap her shoulder in good-humoured congratulation. Amy often saw Bok on her own in all weathers, practising – golf, discus, weight-lifting. Wybrew, her House Captain, insisted the team include a girl from Goneril, the sport house, otherwise it was dominated by the uncategorisables and Unusuals of Desdemona. The Great Game was not a sport in the sense Goneril understood it, but house pride must be satisfied. So Bok was with them.

The last of the team had a bench to herself. Nancy Dyall – Poppet – was a secret weapon, liable to blow up before deployment and wipe out the battalion. The Desdemona Third's odd, uncontrollable Ability made her difficult to be around – all the more so when you forgot she was there, which she could make you do.

The team was a mix of Unusuals and Ordinaries. They represented the whole school, not just the Remove. Frecks was a fringe Unusual, by virtue of that ensorcelled chainmail balaclava. And it took an elastic definition of Ordinary to include Kali, heiress to a criminal empire. Haldane, with her methodical sneakiness, and Bok, made near-perfect by practice, might be as much use in the field as Stretch, with her party piece of reaching tall shelves, or Miss Memory, who could shove reams of rote learning into her mind but would eventually fall asleep and forget it all.

This was the Drearcliff Grange team.

Amy trusted Frecks, Light Fingers and Kali – the Moth Club – and saw the use of Larry, Bok and Knowles. Devlin was a good sort. Her cheeriness was more valuable to the side than her ductility. Morale was key, particularly when play went against the school. Haldane was no Lungs Lamarcroft, but – despite one or two of the things she would tell you about herself – she could be got round. And, in the end, Dyall was terrifying. A tactic would be to let Draycott's collect the tobies, then have Poppet walk up and scramble their brains so they didn't remember who they were and what they were doing, then take away the prizes and waltz home with them. Amy hoped it wouldn't come to that but a decent showing for Drearcliff Grange was required.

Revenge must be had.

The Draycott's team must have a leaf.

If it was there, she would see it.

It was something she'd discovered on her own and talked about with Light Fingers. Her friend had a similar knack, and was excited that they shared it. Nothing to do with their Talents, but a way of thinking, of approaching situations, of sizing up people. It worked on anyone, but was especially useful for Unusuals.

Spotting the leaf.

It was Amy and Light Fingers' private term for a fatal weakness.

When mighty Siegfried bathed in dragon's blood, an unnoticed linden leaf stuck to his heroic back so his skin wasn't unpuncturable all over. A rotter eventually stuck a dirk into the tender spot, putting a tragic end to Siegfried's saga and kicking off further trouble in the next opera.

The moral was that mighty heroes all have leaves.

Captain Adonis, who ran about in a circus outfit battling gang bosses with flat heads or iron teeth, drank a patent medicine that rendered him invulnerable to bombs, bullets and knives but deathly allergic to strawberries. If he accidentally ate one, he'd explode. Were Amy advising the American overman, she'd have suggested he keep quiet about his leaf – but he let it get in the papers. Duke D'Stard invented a tommy gun that sprayed strawbs instead of slugs. The Captain was splattered, but got out of dying somehow and dumped his nemesis in Sing Sing.

Amy was up on the leaves of her schoolfellows.

Pinborough of the Sixth, the boxing champion, tossed her fringe before delivering her roundhouse knockout. An opponent who knew that could duck under the blow and clip her glass jaw with an uppercut. Frecks' charm depended on an abstract notion of 'purity of heart' that wasn't always realistic. Knowles could know everything about a subject but not *understand* any of it. Even Light Fingers had a leaf, which Amy couldn't explain to her. Hotly aware of the unjust treatment of Unusuals, she mistrusted Ordinaries even when she shouldn't.

Fearsome as the competition was, they would have leaves. Amy hoped she would spot them.

But battle couldn't be fought until the envelope was opened.

'It's so overcast it *looks* like sunset,' Amy declared.

'One thing you'll find about me is that evasions—'

'Get right up your nose?' Frecks suggested.

While everyone was laughing, Amy leaned over and told Poppet to go and sit by the Captain.

Poppet was reading the *Girls' Paper*. She folded over the corner of a page to keep her place in 'Sally the Stowaway' and handed the periodical to Amy. Dyall insinuated herself into a spot on the front bench between Bok and Headers. She slid slowly closer to Haldane, staying beneath her notice – *under her nose!* – and seeming to shrink within herself.

Amy waited a few minutes. Haldane's face grew slack.

Rattletrap hit a bad patch of road. Girls slid along benches, bumping into each other. First accidentally, then on purpose. Devlin's arm got bent in the wrong places. She snapped the extra elbows straight, eliciting groans and yucks.

'Can't be helped,' she said, unashamed.

Swift as a hummingbird, larcenous as a magpie, Light Fingers took advantage of the distraction. She vaulted over bench backs, plucked the envelope from Haldane's grasp, and leaped back to her place. Only Amy was close enough even to notice she'd moved.

'We should open the envelope,' said Amy. 'Hang sunset.'

Light Fingers handed it over.

Haldane's countenance betokened forthcoming rage at 'the wicky trick' then her anger vanished and puzzlement set in.

'One thing you'll find about me...' she began, then trailed off.

From experience, Amy knew Headers was feeling hot and irritable, and wondering whence came the throb in her temples. She could look right at Nancy Dyall and not see her. And she wouldn't *want* to look at Poppet, since that was quease-making. Then, she'd forget where she was, as if her concentration were drifting during Double Geog… When the mists cleared, she'd be in a different classroom, a Latin textbook open on the desk, not knowing how many hours she'd been 'away'. Trying to think back to fill in the gap hurt like putting a finger into a candleflame.

Amy shuddered. It wasn't Dyall's fault she was born with a Talent. It was at least partially Amy's fault Dyall had learned to apply it.

'As you were, Poppet,' said Amy.

Dutifully, Dyall returned to her lonely bench. Amy gave back her comic.

Haldane recovered from befuddlement. Miss Gossage pointed to her mouth. Headers raised a knuckle, embarrassed, and wiped off a thread of foam.

'Sunset,' she said, not knowing the meaning of the word.

Amy shivered, but it was done now.

Poppet unfolded the corner of her page and read on.

'Amy should open the envelope, shouldn't she?' said Frecks to the charabanc in general.

'What envelope?' asked Haldane.

With a lash of mentacle, Amy whipped the seal off the packet.

III: Nine Hours Later: In the Fog

AMY ALIGHTED ON uneven ground. A sloping passage not a paved street. Just about wide enough for a bicycle – though cycling on these slippery cobblestones would be foolhardy. Buildings pressed in, leaning at each other. Yellowish water trickled in the gutter.

She had often heard of vile alleyways.

This would appear to be one of them.

She wasn't impressed.

A jangling sounded. Her eyebrows prickled again.

A fire alarm? Danger!

No… Just 'time, gentlemen, please' being called.

A sign hung from an arch spanning the alley. The Midnight Bell. A duck in pub cricket.

Drinkers barged out into the fog and had coughing fits.

Amy rubbed Frecks' scarf over her goggles, not improving her view much. Her nose stung from the fog.

How did city moths live with this?

She had spent most of her life in the country. Drearcliff Grange School was on the North Somerset coast, miles from the nearest town. Amy's family home was in Crossway Green, a Worcestershire village. Her only experience of London was passing through the railway stations – and a visit to Oxford Street when she was little, to see the Christmas illuminations. But, through books and magazines, she thought she knew the city.

Growing up, she'd devoured stories of adventure steeped in picturesque fogs. Holmes and Watson barrelling through stippled halftone in a hansom cab to thwart the schemes of Professor Moriarty. Chance encounters between strangers leading to excitement and drama. Princes and paupers switching places. Frightful fiends stalking innocent prey in Whitechapel or Limehouse. Cheerful cockneys and foolish swells. Sweeney Todd and Spring-Heel'd Jack. Chirrupy flower girls and irrepressible urchins.

The sea fog that sometimes shrouded Drearcliff was salty, but white as a cloud.

In films, London fog was thin and ghostly. Curtains of misty muslin. Of course, flickers were black and white, unless tinted blue for night or green for the jungle.

Films were never stained this uniquely disgusting green-yellow.

That was why London fogs were called 'pea-soupers', she realised.

Her mouth filled with spit. Too many deep breaths and she'd spew. That would not show the school in the best light. She kept licking her teeth to get rid of the acrid taste. This pea-soup was fouler even than the sludge they made in the Drearcliff Grange kitchens.

Should she add a gas mask to her Kentish Glory costume? To keep out the worst of the pollution.

It would be simplest to remain a country moth.

There was plenty of evil to be fought outside towns and cities. The shires were less well-served by established adventurers like the Splendid Six, Dr Shade or the Most Valued Members of the Diogenes Club. Even the dour gents of the Undertaking more often showed their top hats and dark spectacles in built-up areas.

But Kentish Glory would go where she was most needed.

Even if it was horrid and she wasn't dressed properly for it.

She tried to 'listen' out for Miss Gossage, but the teacher's Talent didn't work like that. She had to buzz you.

This was not going to plan.

Inside the envelope Light Fingers took from Haldane was a single sheet of paper, with a typewritten list. Clues leading to locations around London.

Helen's Hole WC1
Burnt Pudding EC3
Rache in Red SW2
Villa de Ville W1
Bad Luck Bertram E1

The team had the inside track on the first riddle. Helen's Hole was a code name for the Troy Club in Hanway Street, London WC1. Helen Lawless, the proprietress, was an Old Girl – Team Captain before the War when Drearcliff Grange racked a streak of wins in the Great Game. Dr Swan's former cygnet was now a notorious receiver of stolen information and paymaster of half the spies in the city and had a flirty, on-and-off enmity-or-alliance with Dennis Rattray, the hard-hitting paladin the papers called Blackfist. They were continually rowing, canoodling, bantering or sparring. Neither had definitively come out on top, so their game continued. According to Dr Swan, Miss Lawless was shamming shadiness, covering her true calling as a loyal agent of the crown. She polished her medals in secret, selflessly living as an outcast from polite society in order to protect it. The school was proud of her, though Amy thought Miss Lawless should give that overbearing cad the push – or chop off his granite hand with a scimitar and let him bleed out.

Frecks said that the Undertaking must be taking pity on the wooden-spoon holders to lob such an easy one. Amy bristled slightly at that thought. Drearcliff Grange didn't need or want special treatment.

Hjordis Bok was sent to Hanway Street. Haldane phoned

ahead, using codewords Knowles supplied from memory. Miss Lawless knew to expect a Drearcliff girl, and to put off the other teams.

Bok could safeguard the toby till it was tucked in Larry's pocket.

When the team put their heads together, they had *ideas* about most of the clues – though the only one they agreed on was 'Burnt Pudding EC3'. That must mean Pudding Lane in Eastcheap, where the Great Fire of 1666 started. History said a baker was careless with his oven, but the *Shadow Chronicle* told another tale – involving runes, a fire demon, and a bitter hatred the diabolist Maurice Wyvil nurtured for the architect Christopher Wren. Pages torn from Samuel Pepys' diary and pasted into the *Chronicle* gave the full story. The thief and fancy woman Moll Flanders was transported to Virginia rather than hanged on the condition she not reveal the real cause of the Great Fire (and the preceding Great Plague) in her memoirs. She wrote in plenty of scandal, gossip and amorous dalliance to fill gaps made by taking out terrifying truths.

As for the rest of the clues, the team was at sixes and sevens…

The application of guesswork and specialised knowledge was by no means sure, even with Knowles coughing up nuggets from maps and gazetteers. There was a Luck Street in the Old Jago in London E1. That rang a distant bell. Could Bad Luck Bertram be Burlington Bertie from the music hall song? No, said Miss Memory, that was a Bertie from Bow – EC3.

Light Fingers, a devotee of sensational literature, recalled Bert Stevens, tried in 1887 for the murders of a Salvation Army Major and her younger brothers. The *Police Gazette* called him 'the Ill-Omen of Luck Street'. Summoning court notices from the recesses of memory, Knowles recounted the story. The corpses were propped up at a dinner table with Stevens at the head. He claimed he'd sat there, paralysed with horror, while oriental hatchet men slaughtered Major Goodenough and the twins Freddy and Victor. Chinese laundrymen were attacked by mobs in the streets of the East End – one was killed – before the police, tipped off by a consultant, realised the bloodstains on Stevens' person were of a unique character. He could only have received arterial spray full in the face if he were none other than the murderer himself. A mild-mannered, pleasant-faced youth, Stevens was taken up as a cause by maiden ladies who sent him scented letters in prison and petitioned against his sentence. He went to the gallows all the same. 'And a good job too,' said Light Fingers, who had surprisingly little sympathy with miscreants in general and none at all for violent criminals.

The team agreed Stevens was 'Bad Luck Bertram'. The toby must be hidden at the scene of his crime. Understandably, no one wanted to live at 13 Luck Street after the murders. Knowles closed her eyes and remembered a particular page in the current street directory, then said the address was now a rag and bone man's storehouse.

Stretch ventured that 'Rache in Red' must be '*Rachel* in Red' but Frecks said the Undertaking didn't make typing mistakes. Thinking along the lines of the E1 clue, she prompted Light Fingers and Knowles to rack brains for murders in Brixton. Both, at once, hit on the 1881 killing of Enoch Drebber in an empty house in Lauriston Gardens.

'*Rache* – German for "revenge" – was written on the wall in letters of blood...' said Light Fingers. 'Which was strange,' continued Knowles, 'because Drebber was poisoned, so the murderer must have cut himself to write the word.' 'These days,' said Light Fingers, 'he'd have been caught in a trice because daubing his message would leave prints Scotland Yard would match.' 'Though, since he turned out to be a cab-man,' argued Knowles, 'he might have worn gloves. His name was Jefferson Hope, but he died before he came to trial so the case is listed as unsolved even if – thanks to that tattler Dr Watson – everyone knows he did it. The story's in *A Study in Scarlet*. It was to do with Morons.' 'Mormons,' corrected Light Fingers.

When Miss Memory relied on ordinary general knowledge

rather than cramming, she often got things slightly wrong. It was Light Fingers' habit to blurt out corrections. Knowles was getting a frown groove in her forehead from pretending not to mind. Accustomed to snubs from her Ordinary classmates for being 'too clever', Miss Memory was uncomfortably adjusting to the Remove, where girls who knew how her Talent worked thought she might really be something of a Dim.

Stretch, holding a flickering flame for the mistyped Rachel, wasn't convinced. She also thought the reasoning of the 'Bad Luck Bertram' clue was shaky... and, besides, what was 'Villa DeVille' all about?

'House of the House? How does that make sense?'

Light Fingers ended the debate with a canny suggestion. She admitted they couldn't be sure they'd puzzled out any of the clues properly, but they *could* trust Richard Cleaver – 'Clever Dick', the Most Brilliant Boy in Britain – and his Brain-Boxes to get the answers. All Drearcliff Grange had to do was tail the junior swots, then use their superior reach and height to force the infants to give up the tobies. 'Like taking sweeties from babies,' Light Fingers said, making quick passes which turned her hands invisible – a rather alarming effect. The suggestion wasn't entirely in the spirit of playing the Game, but certainly in the spirit of winning it.

Though Amy had private doubts, she hadn't spoken out.

For a start, she had no earthly idea what 'Villa DeVille' meant.

From Miss Gossage's buzzed report, she supposed the 'Burnt Pudding' and 'Bad Luck Bertram' tobies were in the bag, either by ingenuity or subterfuge. The plan was that the team would now divide. One group would head South of the River, at least starting with a poke around Lauriston Gardens. Another would feel their way about the West End, searching for the mysterious villa or dogging the tracks of the Brain-Boxes. Knowles and Light Fingers said too many murders were committed amid the glittering lights of the West End – more even than in the slums – for any particular one to stand out. Every nightclub, café and theatre had a horror story.

Standing orders were to stay on the alert against harrying from the House of Reform. Kali's point about not expecting a bacon tree was well taken. Queenie Quell's crew of she-pirates wouldn't sit idle while Drearcliff Grange collected their parcels. Sitting idly was indubitably what the Humblebumblers were doing though. Why the boys even bothered fielding a team was a mystery – they never took anything seriously.

Eyes now stinging as badly as her nose, Amy considered that the Humble College tactic of chucking in the Game and scoffing pork pies while chatting up waitresses might appeal to low, craven sorts of person. Such dereliction of duty was alien to the Spirit of Drearcliff Grange.

She was on the alert for rival teams. She was wary of Draycott's girls, but at least understood them. The Brain-Boxes bothered her more.

Would she even notice small swollen-headed figures creeping in the fog?

The oddest team in the field, they made her eyebrows itch. Clever Dick, youngest of the Splendid Six, was oldest of the Brain-Boxes. He was taken out of primary school for devising equations that opened portholes to other spheres while his classmates hadn't mastered the two-times table. His teammates were equally impressive. Some believed that, thirty years hence, these prodigies would be the guiding geniuses of Britain... Serene, unfathomable deep thinkers with huge eyes, egg-dome skulls and thinning hair. They would plan a perfect society, offer wise counsel to government, and wipe enemies off the map with thought alone. Amy didn't like the sound of it at all.

Unbeatable when it came to solving puzzles, the Brain-Boxes were still children. Spoiled children, at that. Amy pitied Miss Vernon, the haggard young governess who was their chaperone. Whatever holy hell the Remove put Miss Gossage through was pleasant balm beside the nightmare of daily dealing with the Brightest Sparks in the Nursery. The Boxes had invented their own language, using mirror-reversed Inca symbols, just to bedevil Miss Vernon. They once took her bicycle to pieces and put it back together as a giant fly trap.

New to the Great Game last year, the Brain-Boxes managed to come second – a poor second, admittedly – when Drearcliff Grange were derailed. Clever Dick & Co. fitted gears, cotton reels, rubber bands and bicycle-pump pistons into a suit of armour and despatched the automaton to snatch a toby. The clumsy contraption brought back pieces of china cupped in its gauntlets.

Cheated of a five-toby clean sweep, the House of Reform decided to see whether Sir Clankalot was up to swimming and heaved the clockwork knight into the Thames. The metal marvel took on water rapidly and went under. It pulled itself ashore on the Isle of Dogs and was torn apart by scavenging mudlarks.

Meanwhile, most of the Drearcliff Grange team was beyond reach of the Sausage's buzzes. When the Draycott's team owned up, the Undertaking sent a rescue party into Under-London. Moria Kratides and company returned in bad odour. An epic scrubbing with lye got the muck off, but their clothes had to be burned. They hadn't so much as sighted the bristles of a giant sow. Since then, any Draycott's girl who so much as glimpsed a Drearcliff Grange tie would grunt like a hog.

Even the Humble College boys did better, stirring from the pie house at dawn to claim an undistinguished Third Place.

They would throw it away again this year.

Humble College were famously big-heads and lackwits, featherbedded from the cradle. When they left school, they got on swimmingly. Cushy positions were held open in finance, the church and the law for the marginally intelligent. Commissions awaited in fashionable regiments for the totally dim. Debutantes lined up at balls, obliged to put up with being whirled off by a St Cuthbert's fellow in a dance that would zigzag towards a divan behind a potted palm. Old Boys were obliged to welcome nephews into secret government departments and exclusive gentlemen's clubs. It didn't matter if Humble College boys came a cropper in the Game or bungled their examinations. So long as they were 'good sorts' and from the right families, they were set up for life. Half the Splendid Six were Old Humblebumblers. Come to that, so were Frecks' brother Ralph and Uncle Lance, and – astonishingly – Kali's father Kabir Chattopadhyay, Bandit Rajah of Kafiristan.

If anything, the fog was getting worse.

She could have been given the answers to all the clues, along with a map showing how to get to the locations of the tobies… and still be lost.

Light Fingers' tactic was liable to be scotched by the fog too. Even the Brain-Boxes – *especially* the Brain-Boxes – would be impossible to follow. Anyone small could disappear in this without trying.

In theory, the Boxes were the cadet branch of the Splendid Six. Amy had read yarns in which Clever Dick saw through the schemes of diabolical nemeses like Stepan Volkoff or the Gaiety Ghoul and sent Lord Piltdown, the Palaeolithic toff, to fetch their (usually foreign) heads mighty cuffs with his long, hairy arms.

Everyone who worked with the Cleaver Boy said in interviews that he was, outside of his phenomenal mental capacity, 'as merry, decent a little fellow as you could hope to meet'. That they all used *exactly the same words* to describe him suggested someone had written the sentence down and requested it be said as often and as loudly as possible.

Frecks' Uncle Lance, formerly of Pendragon Squadron, knew Teddy Trimingham, the Blue Streak of the Splendid Six. He helped keep the Racing Swift – the Blue Streak's streamlined, land-speed-record-setting vehicle – on the road between daredevil chases and smash-ups. According to Frecks, Lance reported that when no one was writing down what he said for the papers, Trimingham declared Clever Dick, 'The worst pill I've met in all my puff… Everyone who's had the misfortune to spend more than five minutes with the blighter is itching for him to grow up. When he's tall enough to have his fat head punched, there'll be queues round the Hippodrome.'

Amy wasn't going to make assumptions on hearsay evidence.

But she was getting an impression that the stories in *Girls' Paper* and *British Pluck* weren't always 100 per cent truthful.

At the Off, she'd seen the Brain-Boxes. They had blue wool hats stretched over swollen heads and wore matching miniature duffle coats with clothes-peg fasteners. Miss Vernon kept counting heads, sure one of her charges was missing... and even more sure they were up to no good and she would come out the worst of it.

With his bulging eyes and fat cheeks, Clever Dick was more like a bipedal baby than a little boy. Dyall tried to get his autograph on his cigarette card, but he loudly informed the air that he didn't talk to 'twivial girls'. He must not get on with the youngest of the Boxes, six-year-old Trude Smarthe – the only English pataphysician Andre Breton accepted into the Dada movement. Her duffle coat was pink and she had cat-ears and whiskers on her knitted hat.

After the Off, they'd scattered.

It was hours past sunset.

Amy had lost track of everyone... on her team and on all the others.

She'd welcome a friendly, or even a familiar face.

A couple of fellows from the Midnight Bell stumbled through the alley towards her, harmonising on 'There is a Tavern in the Town'. They sang unfamiliar words that made her blush. In this version, it wasn't the singer's *harp* that got hung from a weeping willow tree.

She thought it best to stay out of their way.

Her brown-and-white markings made decent camouflage. She flattened against a cold, damp wall, covered her head with her cloak, and held her breath.

The singers – who really ought to be ashamed of themselves

to do such ruin to a harmless traditional ditty of infidelity and probable suicide – stumbled past. They were in a right state. Peeping through her wings, she saw the blurred outlines of fur-collared coats and silk hats. They might be drunk, but evidently weren't louts. She could have reached out and touched them.

She *did* reach out with a mentacle – imagining a padded mallet – and applied an on-your-way touch to their rears. Thus goosed, they yelped without breaking off the song and hustled onwards.

Leaning on each other, the two-man cats' choir got through the alley.

The practices they ascribed to the true love-stealing 'damsel dark' would have been anatomically demanding even for Stretch Devlin and medically inadvisable to boot.

She heard them for a while after they were gone from sight. The stink of beer lingered too, almost as pongy as the fog.

When they were gone, she missed them.

She let out a Drearcliff '*halloo cuckoo!*'

The team had agreed on the signal.

She called again…

…and thought she heard a faint answer.

'*Cuckooo hallooo…*'

She called, louder.

The response was definite. Not an echo of the alley.

Cautiously, but with determination, she walked through the fog. It eddied around her ankles. She tried to push it away with her mentacles. This made odd curlicue waves but didn't appreciably thin it out. Unlike solid objects, fog resisted being poltergeisted. She wasn't good with water either.

The alley kinked and got wider as if two teams of navvies working on completely different streets had met in the middle and decided to leave it at that.

The 'cuckoo halloo' came again.

Someone was huddled against a wrought-iron lamp post. The globe was smashed, so no circle of light fell.

Amy knelt. Prickles of glass under her knees made her stand again.

The lamp had been broken recently. Her brows itched.

'Thomson?' came a whisper from the huddle.

'Thomsett,' she corrected.

'The flying Unusual?'

'Floating.'

'Huh,' said the huddle, wearily.

Amy took a pack of Swan Vestas out of one of her pockets and struck a light.

The huddle shrank away, blinking.

Hjordis Bok sat under the lamp.

So far as Amy remembered, she'd never spoken with the Goneril Sixth.

She didn't really know what to say now.

The match burned out. She struck another.

Bok held her right knee, which was swollen and discoloured. She had dirt in her hair and on her face. She was pale and – despite the cold – sweaty.

'They've broken my leg,' said Bok.

Amy reached out and the Sixth drew back.

'Where's Larry?' she asked. 'The pocket Unusual,' she specified.

Bok tried to shrug, but that evidently hurt.

'Down the way,' she said, nodding further along the alley.

'Who did this?'

'Arrows on their coats and berets.'

'Draycott's girls?'

Bok nodded, and winced again.

The House of Reform uniform ran to dark-blue skirts and blazers with fine black prison arrows. It was dramatic, subtle and quite smart. Draycott's skirts were practically above the knee. Dosson, Chapell & Co. of Tite Street, who had the school-kit racket sewn up, seemed – annoyingly – more inspired when outfitting Lobelia Draycott's she-convicts than when inflicting drab, scratchy uniform on Drearcliff Grange girls.

Primrose Quell had a tiny arrow inked under her eye. A beauty mark for convicts. That showed a kind of School Spirit, Amy admitted.

'The toby?'

Bok breathed painfully. She was on the point of unconsciousness.

Amy wondered if the Sixth had other broken bones. Dropping her match, Amy dug out a tin of lozenges. She popped a Fisherman's Friend into Bok's mouth.

She should carry first-aid supplies – sticking plasters and such – in her Kentish Glory kit. She had needle and thread, but for repairing torn clothes not fixing open wounds.

Bok rolled the lozenge around her mouth and bit.

Her eyes opened wide and tears started.

'The Brain-Boxes beat me to Helen's Hole,' she said. 'The perishers were blubbing in the street because the bouncer shooed them from the door. When Laurence showed up, Miss Lawless handed over the toby... then Draycott's tried to take it. Quell was onto the trick from the start. They marked me the way Naisbitt said we should mark the brats. Came out of the fog like savages. This small girl – she wears one white glove – *touched* me... There was a *flash*, and my leg *twisted*. I heard the bone snap. Not even a punch, just a *touch*. Another Unusual. A *Wrong 'Un*! Laurence put the toby away... somewhere. What *is* she?'

Bok was dizzy from pain and puzzlement.

'Larry? An Ordinary soul... with a party piece.'

'Quell couldn't get her to give up the jug, not even when she had the Glove Girl threaten to *touch* her forehead... so the Draycott's girls just took Laurence with them.'

Amy was afraid for Larry. She was an Unusual, but still only an undersized Third. What would her captors do to get her to turn her pocket inside-out? They must know *three* parcels were posted in the Pillar Box. A winning score, if not a clean sweep.

Who was this Glove Girl? How did her Talent work?

What with the everyday enmity between tattletale Haldane and racketeer Quell setting the tone of the grudge match, Amy hadn't given much thought to Draycott's Hidden Talents. She'd heard the term Wrong 'Un before – meaning notorious Unusuals like the Slink or the Rat Rabbi, who put their Abilities to immoral or illegal ends. The House of Reform was a *whole school* of Wrong 'Uns. Lobelia Draycott probably gave out end of term prizes for the most inventive crimes.

Bok tried to focus. She was out of her depth.

An *Ordinary*, Light Fingers would call her – an Ordinary, in an extraordinary contest... Used to the light, but venturing among shadows. All that training to attain a physical peak... and Draycott's put her out of the Game with a *touch*.

'What are *you*?' Bok asked.

Amy gave the Sixth's shoulder a squeeze.

'Rest here,' she said. 'The Sausage will find you. I have to go after Larry.'

Bok looked blank but didn't make a move to stop her.

Amy left the tin of lozenges with the wounded girl.

The alleyway extended, widening. She was momentarily disoriented. Both sides of the road were obscured as the fog wrapped around her.

Up ahead, a light burned.

Another lamp post, with people gathered beneath it. Someone in a Drearcliff-grey coat had shinned up to the lantern cage. It was Larry, arms hooked over the crossbar, gripping the post with her knees. Her face was close to the glass – distorted by weird, hard shadows.

Three girls – arrows on their coats and berets – surrounded the post. One raised a glowing white fist. The Glove Girl. Electric arcs played and the post wobbled.

The Draycott's triad were jostling and stamping. Someone else was at the bottom of the scrum.

Metal boot caps sparked. Amy heard yelps of pain.

Who was this?

Something got under her feet – a four-foot stick. With a mentacle, she stood it on end and turned it round. It was forked and padded at the top. A crutch.

She supposed she shouldn't be surprised to find Draycott's girls kicking a cripple.

Still, it was Not a Done Thing.

She would not let it pass.

IV: Three Wrong 'Uns and a Right

AMY STOOD FIRM, arms crossed on her chest, concentrating. In her mentacle grasp, the crutch rose off the pavement. She got a sense of the heft of the thing and took crude aim by swivelling it to point at the lamp post.

She *propelled* the crutch, letting its own weight add to her fluence, and belaboured the Draycott's girls...

She remembered a grinning Doug Fairbanks showing off with a quarterstaff, bopping the bullet heads of the Sheriff of Nottingham's men-at-arms.

'Take that, Norman dog... Have at thee, knave...'

Owws, oofs and ouches were followed by language that would have earned an instant Major Infraction at Drearcliff Grange.

The Draycott's girls waved arms over their heads as if beset by wasps.

The Glove Girl tried to grab the crutch, but couldn't reach that high. Her teammates had to watch where she put her electric fingers.

The crutch was too light to do real damage. No blocks were knocked off and no coconuts cracked.

But Amy got their attention.

Everyone twisted around to look at her – Larry up the lamp post, the three brutes in berets, and the abused wretch on the pavement.

She spread moth wings and floated at them. As always when her boot toes lifted off the ground, she felt a pleasurable lurch in her tummy. Under her tingling feet was a rubbery delicious *nothing*. She trailed her wings through fog wisps, stirring dramatic eddies. Taking a breath, she ascended to roof level and surveyed the sorry scene.

She knew she was imposing.

If the foe were imposed upon, her own confidence swelled.

'Halt...' she said. Should she add 'in the name of the law' or 'in the name of the king'? Neither really applied, and 'in a just cause' sounded awfully priggish. Doug Fairbanks knew what to say – it was written on screen for him, with suitable exclamation marks.

'Stop kicking that lad,' she said. 'It's low, unladylike and wrong.'

The Draycott's girls goggled up at her.

Terrified? As if the cloak shadow of Dr Shade or the wingspread of the Aviatrix had fallen on them? Or just gob-smacked at the sight of a self-righteous Moth Girl?

She tried not to be nervous or hesitant.

Ideally, this could be settled without further violence.

The aspect of fighting for a just cause Amy was least sure of was the actual *fighting*.

Even with arrant injustice in view – three healthy harpies clog-dancing on one lame ragamuffin was almost a caricature of the wrong-doing Kentish Glory was against – she was in two minds about hitting people. Thwacking at a distance was one thing. Laying into loutesses with fists was another.

For a start, she wasn't terribly good at it.

At the school's last championship bout, Hjordis Bok held up through fifteen rounds with Pinborough, losing only on points. Bok and the Blonde Bruiser swapped blows that could smash bricks. Amy's punch could just about put a hole in crepe paper.

Her friends were better prepared for a ruck. Kali was trained from infancy in foot-boxing, a particularly spiritual form of kicking people where it hurt. She could break a bedpost with a whirling kick – though was on notice not to do it again since the House Mistress got suspicious about having to provide a replacement every time the Princess showed off. Frecks, a devoted Fairbanks fan, had seen *Robin Hood* seven times and could give a decent account of herself in fencing, archery and singlestick. She'd even tried to get the Pony Club to take up jousting, though Horsey Hailstone – the Viola Fifth who held the reins on all equestrienne endeavours – was horrified at the prospect.

Kali and Frecks weren't even *Unusuals*.

Light Fingers wasn't interested in fighting the Pinborough way, where the other girl has a chance to hit you back. She was quick enough to land fifty or sixty average jabs inside ten seconds. That would incapacitate an opponent before anything that could technically be called a fight got started. The one time she tried the tactic in the gym – even though pitted against the unpopular Lydia Inchfawn – she was booed for unsporting behaviour and slunk to the changing room muttering about 'slowcoaches'.

It *was* the tiniest bit like cheating.

What would the Lady of the Lake think?

Nevertheless, Amy supposed she should ponder martial applications of her own Talent. While you swallow the halfpennyweight of shame that comes with resorting to underhand methods in a just cause, a Wrong 'Un lying senseless on the mat can't hurt other people.

She knew this fight couldn't be avoided. The Draycott's girls were vandals and visigoths. The prospect of getting thumped was one thing. She was also squeamish about hurting anyone – even if they soundly deserved a walloping.

'What *are* you wearing?' said the tallest of the Draycott's girls. 'You look a Perfect Prawn.'

Amy fixed them all with a glare – which probably didn't come over that well through goggles.

The tall girl was dark-haired and thin-faced, with huge eyes, a deeply dimpled chin and a long neck. Her beret was fastened to the side of her head with a silver arrow pin. At Draycott's, that was the equivalent of a whip's braid. She must be a Sixth, and Top Girl in the Triad of Thuggee – but she wasn't Primrose Quell, the Team Captain.

She said 'one for luck' and gave the wretch a final savage boot to the bread basket then abandoned cripple-kicking to sneer up at Amy. If intimidated by a glare from on high, she covered it up well.

Her teammates also left off the aggravated assault to pay attention.

The Glove Girl – a Third or Fourth – was tubby, with tight blonde curls, short legs and fat knees. Her single glove drew the eye. Either it was padded like a clown's or her hand was grossly out of proportion with the rest of her. It was a man's dress glove. Three ridges on the back, black stitching around the wrist. Her raised fist radiated light – and, Amy could tell even from a distance, heat. An unimpressive, middling sort to look at, but she'd put Drearcliff Grange's second-best boxer out of the Game. So, one to be mindful of and stay away from.

While Amy was distracted by the glove, which infallibly drew the eye, something fast and heavy lashed out, disturbing tendrils of fog, cracking like a razor strop. She flinched, though the whip hadn't the reach to scrape her ankles.

The third girl's long brown hair was done up in a dozen ropy braids that spilled onto her shoulders like gorgon coils. The thickest, oiliest braid was wound into a fifteen-foot flail, with fish hooks woven into the business end. She wore arrow earrings – another frippery prohibited at Drearcliff but allowable at Draycott's. An old chin scar suggested early, clumsy experiments with her home-grown scorpion tail. No comfort in that. She'd obviously got more skilled since. It must have taken years to cultivate and fashion her weapon.

Amy noted the glove and the whip... and wondered whether the tall girl had anything as nasty about her person.

The fallen fellow groaned and hugged the base of the lamp post.

Amy made out ragged clothes and a battered, scabby face. It was a boy – perhaps a year or two older than her, but with ancient eyes. Rather beautiful eyes, in fact. Bright with martyr's tears. This was someone used to suffering. He tried to pull himself upright. A casual flick from the whip-braid ripped open his flimsy coat and bloodied his bony back. He lost his grip and fell badly.

He lay coughing in a bath of fog.

Whatever fight he had was knocked out of him.

Who was he?

Had he tried help Larry and been cruelly treated for it? She detected gallantry in him, a wounded dignity.

'Thomsett,' said Larry.

Amy was about to tell Laurence delivery was at hand, but saw the girl wasn't at all relieved. 'Where's Serafine?' she asked, disappointed and – unreasonably, in the circs – a little annoyed to see Kentish Glory floating to her rescue.

Amy would do her best to overlook the ingratitude.

Larry was distraught. She wasn't thinking it through.

The tall girl paid attention. She realised Larry knew Amy.

'Ah-ha,' she said, 'a Drearycliff girl! Though not the gallant our greedy lamplighter was expecting. And not in uniform. Doctor Swan wouldn't approve.'

Her friends grunted and made hog faces.

Amy deftly used the crutch to swipe the beret off the head of the Glove Girl.

'Oww, my crown!' she said.

Amy brought the crutch towards the Silver Arrow, getting mentacle weight behind it for a good old slosh.

The tall girl lifted her arm as if to parry the blow. Though there was no physical connection, the makeshift bludgeon swatted out of Amy's hold. It whooshed through fog and clattered against a wall. Once she couldn't see it, Amy couldn't grip it.

Bending over with an oof, the fat girl reached for her beret with her ungloved left hand. Amy could see – and fix on – the cap. She skipped it away from the girl's grasp.

'Stop that,' said the tall girl. 'It's rude.'

The Silver Arrow *knew* Amy was moving things with her mind.

Usually, Amy counted on people not realising that. They worried about a noisy ghost before they suspected her.

'I'm Kentish Glory,' Amy announced.

'The tick said you were Thomson…'

'Thomsett,' she corrected.

'Same diff. If it's aliases and alter egos we're using at the mo, Sparks and Sterlyng are the Glove and the Knout. You can guess which is which. Sparksie, show Thomkins some Glove Love…'

The fat girl grinned and thumped the wrought-iron lamp post, producing a crack of lightning and the stink of ozone.

Amy blinked away the light streaks burned into her eyes.

The lamp post tilted like the Tower of Pisa. Larry screeched and lost her knee grip. She dangled from the crossbar. One shoe fell off, and slapped Sparks' head.

'Oww, my crown… again! Is every blessed beetle going to take a whack at it this week?'

Sparks – the Glove – rubbed her bruised bonce with her left hand, which didn't properly reach where she wanted. She pulled a pettish face. Her Talent was formidable, but tricky to handle. If she made a mistake like her teammate had with her whip-braid, she'd have no chin left to show a scar.

Amy was glad she was floating out of the Glove's reach.

'Watch the dreg, Sterlyng,' said the tall girl.

The cripple was trying to crawl away again.

Sterlyng – the Knout – coiled her whip-braid around his throat and hauled him upright. He stood on one foot. His right leg seemed boneless. His clothes were mismatched. Frayed striped trousers from before the war, patched at the knees. A good, new-ish waistcoat. One shined brogue on his good foot and the string-bound remains of a curly-toed Persian slipper on the dead one. An overcoat three sizes too large, so badly stained it was impossible to tell what colour it was supposed to be.

The fellow grimaced as the rope tightened around his throat.

Amy winced in sympathy. Poor unfortunate puppy!

Was the Knout an Unusual – or just an Ordinary with unconventional grooming habits and nasty-minded ingenuity? Distinctions weren't always clear-cut.

Amy tried to get a mentacle to the flail. It was like scrabbling to pick up a needle with mittens. She couldn't take hold of other people – or *parts* of other people – as she could herself. So she couldn't free the Knout's captive or float Larry to safety. The most she could do was give a shove or a nudge. She couldn't hit a person with mentacle fists – which would have been useful at the moment.

'The Knout and the Glove,' said Amy, trying to sound confident – like Dr Shade exchanging pleasantries with Stepan Volkoff before they tried to kill each other with gas-guns and barbed-wire bolas. 'Sounds like a pub sign. A duck in pub cricket. I wish I could say it was a pleasure to make their acquaintance. Who might you be?'

The tall girl smiled.

'They call me Miss Steps. Can you guess why?'

'Is your name Stephanie?'

'Close. It's Stephen. Stephen Swift.'

Should Amy have heard of her?

'Did your parents want a boy?'

'They had two already. An heir and a spare. Stephen is a girls' name too. Like Jocelyn or Christopher.'

'Christopher isn't a girl's name.'

'It could be. In some circles. If your mind isn't closed. What's *your* name?'

'Amanda.'

'*That* could be a boy's name.'

'Doubtful. A lad named "Amy" would have a rough time of it at school.'

'"Amanda" has "man" in it. A-*man*-da.'

Amy didn't know what to make of Stephen Swift.

'You're joshing,' she said.

'I am not,' said Miss Steps. 'I am explaining names to you, Amanda. You have rather *provincial* attitudes, if you don't mind me saying.'

Amy had to admit Crossway Green was in a province, but *still…*

'I do mind, as it happens,' she said. 'Some provinces are advanced, socially. Daring, even.'

'You're on unsteady ground, there…'

'I'm not on *any ground at all*. Haven't you noticed?'

Hah! That would shut her up! Sophisticate Swift… with pavement under her heels, and a *boy's* name.

'Ah yes, we come round the houses again… and reach the front gate. My name *isn't* why they call me Miss Steps.'

Stephen Swift stepped off the pavement.

Up, off the pavement. Into the air.

She rose until she was on a level with Amy.

There was a flight of stairs only she could see. She ascended calmly, with no special effort. As if stepping on solid planes.

Steps.

She *made* steps.

'See,' she said.

Swift walked towards Amy. In the air.

Her teammates looked up. The Knout gave an absent-minded tug, and the cripple moaned. She dropped him and curled her whip round her arm. A high priestess petting a sacred snake.

Larry's hold on the crossbar was precarious. And slipping.

Amy bobbed up and down. Secure in the air, but not steady. Miss Steps might have been on a solid walkway feet above the street.

How did she *do* that?

'We have the same Talent, don't we?' said Miss Steps. 'Or similar. It's Abilities and Applications. Yes, we have those lessons too. Mater Draycott and Dr Swan got their heads together about how to teach Unusuals. They aren't so different. The way we aren't, though you've a long way to go to catch up... Amanda, are you trying to *fly?*'

Swift's one-sided smile opened and shut – letting out a seal-bark laugh.

Amy's face burned.

Miss Steps walked around her. Amy had to spin in the air – cloak twisting like an insomniac's sheet – to keep her eyes on the girl's face. Miss Steps walked around the other way. Amy's cloak unwound.

'You *are*, aren't you? The speckled shroud is supposed to be *wings.*'

Amy tried to spread them again, but the mentacle spines failed on one side. Half her cloak jutted like a railway signal.

Stephen Swift rattled her. If Amy didn't concentrate, she literally let herself down. Her Abilities became unreliable. Many Unusuals had the problem.

She sank a few feet and had to *focus* to rise again.

'What did you call yourself?' Miss Steps asked. 'Somethingish Whosamaflip?'

'Kentish Glory,' Amy repeated.

Not firm and resolute, like Dr Shade or the Aviatrix... but uncertain and embarrassed, as if she suddenly realised she'd worn the wrong dress and couldn't remember why.

'That's a... butterfly?'

'Moth,' she corrected insistently. 'Of course it's a moth! Everyone knows that. There are *important differences*.'

'Don't get so het up, child.'

Amy began to see important differences between her and Miss Steps.

Amy's Abilities manifested as mentacles – pseudo-arms, with floppy hands. What she could do was, by Ordinary standards, a wonder... but, compared with Miss Steps' *precision*, she was playing violin with a broom handle or shuffling cards with fireplace bellows.

Miss Steps didn't have mentacles. She used blocks – hard, physical objects, like bricks or flagstones. She could instantly make – *and maintain* – invisible stairs for her own use.

Stephen Swift didn't even seem to be concentrating. She had *confidence*.

No Drearcliff Grange Unusual was so *sure* of her Talent.

Swift could *rely* on her steps the way Pinborough could on her left hook or Bok on her long jump. It was something earned and learned, not an accident of birth. She must have had tutoring. The House of Reform must train Unusuals with a lack of ruth unknown to Sausage Gossage.

Amy wobbled in the air. Her wings dragged at her shoulders.

Miss Steps suddenly lunged – her huge-eyed, frizz-haired head loomed close to Amy's face – and let out a *yahhh*.

Amy's goggles misted from Swift's exhalation. There was spittle in there too.

Laughing her strange explosive laugh, Miss Steps leaped back.

Only Amy – maybe only Amy *in the world* – could appreciate that jump. Stephen Swift *imagined* a floor and pushed *against* it as she would any surface… then 'landed' again with perfect footing. Fifteen feet above the street.

'Gave you a spook-de-doo there!' said Miss Steps.

Was she showing off? Or had she such mastery of her Abilities she didn't even think of them any more? Like no one thinks about blinking or breathing… until they *can't*.

Swift walked around Amy again, this time climbing a spiral up above her head and down below her boots. She trotted, working her knees and elbows with slight exaggeration. It was clownish – but more absurd than amusing.

As if trying to shake off a sticky sweet wrapper, Miss Steps flicked her fingers towards Amy's face…

(with nine or ten feet of empty air between them)

And Amy was *slapped*.

Miss Steps *could* do that.

Apply her Talent to *hit* a person.

She did it again.

Amy waved mentacles between them, trying to interrupt Swift's fluence. A dozen more slaps came – playful, but stinging. Amy knew the Draycott's girl wasn't even hitting terribly hard. She didn't think Amy worth a real punch.

Miss Steps bark-laughed again. She was enjoying herself.

'Thomsett,' shouted Larry, now too worried about falling to be bothered that the wrong Moth had come to her rescue, '*Thomsett...!*'

'Hang on, Larry,' said Amy, not sure she didn't need rescuing herself.

She reached out with her mind. She couldn't make solid planes or strike blows, but she *could* slow falls.

She'd practised at forming a layer of nothing to serve as a fireman's life net. The invisible mattress was effective if she took the tumble herself, going limp and falling backwards off her bed. When her cellmates were prevailed upon to volunteer as guinea pigs, the process was iffier. Kali and Light Fingers didn't appreciate bumped bottoms sustained before Amy got the measure of her Application.

Now she really needed the break-fall to work.

Larry's was losing her grip on the lamp post. A violet seam of light across her stomach showed her pocket was acting up.

If she kept things inside too long, she got a tummy ache. Her pocket wanted to return what was stashed there.

Sometimes, *extras* came back. Purple duplicates.

Amy bit her cheeks and tried to support Larry.

'Four hundred and fifty-nine green bottles hanging on the wall,' she thought, teeth clenched, *concentrating*, 'four hundred and fifty-nine green bottles hanging on the wall...'

'Don't worry about the pilchard,' said Miss Steps...

The tilting lamp post righted itself. Swift had done that.

'And if one green bottle should accidentally fall...'

With a panicky little wail, Larry let go...

Whistle whistle whistle...

Then stopped dead in mid-air.

Kerr-*ASH!*

It wasn't Amy's mattress. It was one of Miss Steps' 'floors'.

Larry sat up in mid-air, surprised not to be on the pavement with a cracked head.

Miss Steps' plane tilted to become a slope and Larry rolled down to the Knout and the Glove. Sterlyng got her hair-encircled arm around the Third's neck. Sparks laid her spindly left hand on Larry's shoulder and raised her terrifying, shining right.

'Worry about *you*.'

Miss Steps thrust out her hand, palm first...

A flat plane of force hit Amy in the face, cracking her goggles. She smelled her own blood.

It was as if she'd been socked in the puss by Blackfist.

Miss Steps wasn't holding back now.

'Worry about you... *a lot*!'

Another beam-end struck her face...

Whistle whistle whistle kerr-*ASH!*

And Amy fell into the dark.

V: A Moment's Dream

TWO DAYS AFTER A. stood on Shark Shingles and watched her father's coffin pushed out onto flat grey sea, the Steward of the Purple House visited her mother... Coin was passed from purse to hand, and the question of what was to be done with the child settled.

A. was indentured in the kitchens... She was up before dawn to scrub the floor, carry brim-full pots of oven grease to the bottomless stock cauldron, cut crosses into the stumps of a barrelful of sprouts (with a wickedly curved little blade that scored a permanent mark into her thumb), and fetch haunches of meat taller than she was from the Ice Cellar.

She was not to speak out of turn and not to step off a line chalked on the floor for her... not that she had idle time for straying... her duties were set out on a page of a clothbound book... Every minute of every hour she was awake was accounted for... When she slept, arranged in a bed with five other girls like a set of spoons, she was too tired to dream.

And yet, once A. mastered her duties, she found moments in the day when she could draw breath... The chalk line got scuffed, especially down the stairs and along the passage to the Ice Cellar... She had a few seconds of tarrying time – more seconds every day – to consider the doors that led to other cellars... The Wrong Doors were all rust-red, with black locks.

She heard from older servants, who had been at the Purple House so long they came to look and sound alike, of girls who had walked her line before... and of what happened to those girls when – as they all did, inevitably and eventually – they opened one of the Wrong Doors.

A. kept the wickedly curved little blade in her pinafore pocket at all times... She completed her scrubbing, carrying and scoring more and more swiftly – and lingered longer each day in the passage to the Ice Cellar... She didn't want to pass through a Wrong Door, but was interested enough in them to wonder which cellars lay beyond each.

A. made friends – and enemies – among the other servants... When a looking-glass was passed to her, she saw she had come to resemble them, down to the twin feathery plumes of hair teased up over her mob cap and the glittery, slightly scaly patches on her cheeks... this was the look of the people of the Purple House.

On exciting occasions, she glimpsed a superior servant, an over-butler or a groom... and learned the names of the resident dependents of the Mistress of Purple House... Doktor Schatten, Mistress Wyngs, Count Dragon, Hugo Ape, Mr Night Hand, the Ghost Lantern Girl, Lord Leaves, Mr Whistle, Pandora Paule, Jennifer God... A. should never hope to see any of these persons, for they were set greatly above her station.

Millie, who sliced carrots while A. crossed sprouts, had a store of gossip about the House Above... Lying spoon-fashion before sleep, Millie's ankles next to A.'s pillow, A. asked her bedmate for stories of the resident dependents... Millie talked often of sickly, changeable Princess Violet, who was the Apple of All Eyes and a Great Cause for Concern.

Violet was cossetted and adored, and everyone who came to the Purple House brought her a present... The Princess received beautifully painted books with no words (even on the spines and covers) that she would foul with her food – the jellies and fondants prepared in dainty kitchens well away from A.'s grimy place of work... Fabulous toys would be loved for a week, a day, a moment, then cast aside with violence.

Millie spoke as if the Princess were a horror, but A. understood poor Violet suffered from an uncomfortable condition – something like a hot coal burned behind one of her eyes – and had to take it out on what came to hand, the more precious the better... One night, it was said, Princess Violet was so pained by the burning behind her eye she broke down the stout door of her apartment and tore off the nose of an unfortunate under-footman.

Behind one of the Wrong Doors, Millie said, were the presents the Princess had taken her pains out on... in a sorry state of repair, but kept because they were gifts from people too exalted to offend... Now, A. rushed through her duties in the morning and dawdled at each Wrong Door, fancying she knew which led to the cavern where the Princess's ruined books and damaged toys lay... three-legged rocking horses, music boxes that plunked half-tunes then sounded like an omnibus crashing into a penguin pool, regiments of invalid toy soldiers unfit for return to the front, a singed miniature theatre where mutilated cardboard players mounted tragical farces.

Suddenly, Millie was sent away... The new girl who walked her chalk line couldn't pass on gossip because she knew nothing of the Purple House... The Most Wrong of Wrong Doors had a peculiar fascination for A... She strained to hear the discords of the damaged music box, then hurried to the Ice Cellar and her duties... always, the steps of tantalised anticipation, the precious seconds of delicious wondering... then the getting-on-with-it of the Ice Cellar and the heft of the haunches of meat taller than she was.

On the day that the Wrongest of Wrong Doors was open, it still came as a surprise and shock – for it was open not when A. was on her way to the Ice Cellar, dragging her feet as was her secret custom... but open as she was hurrying back, bent double under cold meat... Her heart stopped for a long moment, then raced as she felt compelled to step off her chalk line and stand at the open door... There was only darkness in the Toy Cellar, but she smelled rotten foods smeared on lovely books and heard the cacophonies of smashed music boxes.

Then, it showed its great cracked face...

A.'s heart – and the whole world – stopped... for she had seen the Broken Doll!

VI: Awake and Fighting!

'THERE'D BE FOUR hundred and fifty-*eight* green bottles hanging on the wall!'

Amy's eyes watered.

Months had passed in the Purple House… but only a fraction of a fraction of a second in waking life.

She tried to hold on to the memory of her dream.

Rolls and rolls of tapestry, woven in an unconscious trice, minutely embroidered with a wealth of detail… came apart, rotted to muck, evaporated.

There was a house, wasn't there?

A house that now wasn't there. A house that *wasn't*.

A corridor, though. She fought to keep that.

A cold corridor. A nice room. No, an *ice* room.

A gory door. And who she saw when it was opened.

In an eye-blink, even the memory of the memory was gone.

All that remained – burned into her retinae like lightning ghosts – was a white mask. Living eyes in a china face. A cobweb of black cracks in translucent glaze. A blood-dab on cherub lips.

She blinked until the face was gone.

Her nose bled, her ears rang. She tasted sulphur.

She had been slammed in the face by an invisible block.

That had sent her… somewhere. Knocked her out of herself.

How could she be distracted by phantoms when beset by immediate peril? Others were depending on her. Before she could help them, she must help herself.

Newton got his own back. She persistently defied his Laws of Gravity. Now she felt the mighty pull of the Earth. She was heavy. A ton of plummeting bricks, alongside a ton of fluttering feathers. An elephant tossed off a cliff, umbrella clutched in her trunk.

She fell.

She'd been told to worry about herself.

Who said that?

Miss Steps. Stephen Swift.

She'd been told to worry about herself *a lot*.

Good advice.

So why was she more afraid of the ghost of a ghost than of Stephen Swift?

She fell faster. Flailing. Her cloak flapped.

While she was in dreamland – in the What-was-the-Colour House? – her Talent shut off.

Once upon a time, she floated in her sleep. She was cured of that. Thank you everso much, Miss Gossage, Mother *will* be pleased. You can tell her how wonderfully you curbed my bad habits at the funeral…

Whistle whistle whistle kerr-*ASH!*

She slammed onto a cold, solid surface.

The fall should have broken bones. She should be bleeding on the pavement.

She lay on nothing, well above the heads of the hog-grunting Draycott's girls. They held a sickly faced, struggling Larry Laurence.

Amy's Talent had failed but Miss Steps was in control of hers.

The reason Amy wasn't crumpled on the ground with many injuries was that Swift wasn't finished with her. She lay on one of Miss Steps' steps. She pressed her cheek to cold, dry nothing. Invisible ice veined with unmoving fog threads, pressed like flowers in an old book. Hard and smooth like polished marble. Not soft and yielding like her mentacle mattress.

Amy tried to get a grip on herself, to float of her own accord.

She must push back, hit back, fight back…

She made fists and tried to wrap mentacle gauntlets around them – copying Miss Steps' steps and the Glove's glove.

Stephen Swift laughed again and stepped down.

Amy's forehead bumped another layer of ice.

She was trapped between two of Miss Steps' planes. If they ground together, she'd be crushed.

'I call this the Duck Press,' said Swift.

She was glad of a chance to show off to a fellow Unusual who could appreciate her skill. Ordinaries never understood. Talent was never enough by itself. What impressed were the Applications.

'I also do the Cosy Coffin,' she continued, 'and the Iron Maiden, which is the Cosy Coffin *and* the Duck Press, but with *spikes*. I've only tried it on rabbits so far. Funny thing though, when the Iron Maiden's fully closed, it *leaks*. Can you hold liquids?'

Amy shook her head. With difficulty.

'Annoying, isn't it? I want to do a teapot that isn't there – raise the leaves in the air, surround them with boiling water from a kettle, swirl the big bubble so it brews, then pour cup shapes and pass them round. People could drink them. Wouldn't that be a stunner?'

More impressive than her own After Lights Out tea parties, Amy admitted.

'I wanted to be a magician when I was a little girl,' continued Swift. 'Top hat, white tie and tights… a dashing cloak, not unlike your silly wings… and a dancing wand I would never hold in my hand. Like your fling with the dreg's cripplestick.'

Amy understood.

She'd also thought of what she might do *for show*. Use her Talent not to help, but to amaze. She imagined gasps and applause. Considered fame and fortune. The thing missing was a just cause. Without one of those, it was all just magic tricks and party pieces.

'Then, Mater Draycott inspired me to set my ambitions higher.'

Amy's mentacles squashed against Swift's cold planes. She wrapped her mattress around her inside the Duck Press, straining to push the surfaces apart. Without apparent effort, Swift narrowed her torture trap. Amy gave her no more of a fight than one of her leaky rabbits.

'Have *you* played with animals, Amanda?'

Amy was disgusted by the gleam in Swift's big wet eyes.

Miss Steps licked her lips. She did that a lot, and sprayed when she laughed. She should keep a pocket hankie handy.

The girl was mad, Amy realised. Sick, almost.

Was that how tutors treated Unusuals at Draycott's? Drove them mad? Burned out any conscience, encouraged profligate cruelties, cultivated unspeakable instincts?

Made them into Wrong 'Uns?

'Is your Games Mistress still that silly Sausage person?' continued Swift. 'The daffy dilly who copped the wrong envelope last year? My, how we chortled. Guffawed, even. We never thought you Dreary Cliffettes would fall for the howler about the echo in the Quiet Room... or the Tall Tale of the Big Pig in the basement. Goes to show what they say. Fools beg to be fools. 'Tis only polite to oblige 'em.'

Miss Steps was vertical and Amy horizontal, but their heads were on the same level.

Amy felt Swift's breath on her face.

With her hands, Stephen Swift took off Amy's goggles. She stuck a thumb through the cracked lens.

'Clumsy, clumsy me,' she said insincerely, 'what a zany I be...'

Miss Steps had to press hard to pop the glass and cut her thumb doing it. She sucked her wound, frowning.

Amy saw it.

Swift's leaf.

The stabbable spot on Siegfried's back. Pinborough's fringe-flick.

Stephen Swift's leaf was that she was *weak*.

She relied on her Talent – her formidable, overpowering Talent – and neglected her Ordinary self. Physically, she was soft.

Miss Steps sneered at Miss Gossage, but she could do with a tutor who forced her to spend hours on a gym mat. It would do her good. Swift probably had a permanent sick note and spent every P.E. period murdering animals with her mind.

Amy crossed her arms on her chest as if in a real coffin.

She breathed steadily, trying not to taste fog. Her mentacles expanded.

'Amandakins,' Miss Steps said, 'are you *giving up*? Poor show.'

From below, the Glove and the Knout hog-grunted.

Amy *concentrated*.

'Bodkins, but you're a weed,' said Miss Steps. 'Couldn't you *try* to make it more of a challenge? I'm as bored as you are. This Game is No Fun At All.'

She reached across to slap Amy… not to slam her with invisible bricks, but to flap her soft little fingers across Amy's mouth.

Amy drew in breath and bit *hard* on the meat of Swift's hand.

Miss Steps opened her mouth in an O and *screamed*. Foam ropes dangled from her chops.

The Cosy Coffin popped like a soap bubble. Amy floated of her own accord. Gravity took hold of Stephen Swift. The distraction of pain switched off her Talent.

Amy spat out Miss Steps' hand. She blotted the salt taste of blood on Frecks' scarf.

She extended her cloak and lowered herself to the street.

Swift got there first, thumping at the feet of her teammates. She screamed and held her broken wing. Veiny whites were exposed around her pinprick pupils. In the back of her hand was a deep, bleeding crescent.

Amy knew she only had as long as it took Miss Steps to get hold of herself.

She could have used Pinborough's knock-out punch.

Or Poppet Dyall's mind-scrambling presence.

She got her hands under Miss Steps' arms and hauled her upright. She was, as expected, a thimbleweight. A dance partner who could be cakewalked backwards into a wall.

Amy thought of holding Swift up as a punchbag and prodding the Glove into laying out her own teammate…

Was that going too far? Would Miss Steps be injured or worse?

Some wouldn't care, but the Lady in the Lake would. A paladin couldn't be held to a lesser standard than a Pendragon.

Miss Steps would soon snap back. She had no scruples to overcome.

Sparks raised her shining fist. Larry's worried little face was lit by the Glove's glow.

Swift's tantrum didn't abate. She wriggled in Amy's arms, like a small angry child. She was blubbing, with howls and sobs. She hit out with tiny fists, thumping her own thighs as she tried to break Amy's grip.

''Old 'er up, luv,' said an unfamiliar voice.

The cripple.

Tottering on his good leg, he had his crutch drawn back like a golf club.

Swift wailed at the sight of the abused urchin hopping towards her.

Amy heaved Miss Steps up in her embrace and tucked in her own head. The cripple swung. The padded end of the crutch connected with Swift's dimpled chin.

Whistle whistle whistle… kerr-*SNAP!*

Stephen Swift went limp.

Now *she'd* be a skivvy in the Purple House and be there when the Wrongest Wrong Door opened…

Amy dropped the Draycott's girl.

She'd meet the Broken Doll.

'Luv, luv,' said the cripple, snapping his fingers in front of Amy's nose. 'Where'd you go?'

'I don't remember,' said Amy honestly.

She had lost something – again. She'd nearly had it, but it was gone.

It was a distraction.

Was this *her* leaf?

That dream she couldn't remember. Did it want her back?

She thought too much. That was more like her leaf.

A space in her mind was like Larry's pocket. Not always there, but ready to expand. It was behind a Wrong Door. An extra place, for storing and sorting... and wondering what to do with things that didn't fit.

'One dahhn, two ter go...'

The lad had his crutch in his armpit, hands free to make fists.

Miss Steps snoozed in the gutter. Drool poured from her mouth.

The Glove and the Knout had Larry.

Amy judged Sterlyng more dangerous than Sparks.

The Glove had a Talent, but was a stubby little thing. Shocked to see Miss Steps taken out of the Game, she was lost. She needed someone to look up to and tell her what to do. The Knout, a nastier piece of work, was just more determined to do someone an injury.

Sterlyng left Larry to Sparks and unwound her braid.

She scraped the fish hooks on the cobbles. That put Amy's teeth on edge.

The flail darted and Amy pushed herself up into the air, above the lash.

Oh for a giant pair of scissors!

'Sterlyng,' she said, floating above her, 'didn't you hear? This season, all the smart girls are wearing their hair bobbed?'

The Knout made an underarm whipcrack and Amy swum herself backwards, but let the hooks snag in her cloak.

She reached out with a mentacle and latched onto the lamp post.

It lurched – had all the hammering and blasting unmoored the post from the concrete? – but held.

Amy swung around the pole, drawing closer in a diminishing orbit.

The cripple jumped up and down and patter-sang the rude words of 'There is a Tavern in the Town' *vivacissimo*. The Knout was astonished and – *yes!* – distracted for vital seconds.

Amy unhooked the whip from her wings, gingerly so as not to get barbs in her fingers. She wound Sterlyng's hair around the lamp post above the crossbar, then tied it in a rolling hitch. Miss Borrodale, who taught yachting, would not award Amy's knot highest marks, for it was uneven – but couldn't deny it'd hold fast.

Sterlyng knew she was caught. If she ripped free, she'd lose her hair... and most of her scalp. She stood down and left it to Sparks.

Amy landed in front of the Glove. The littler girl was panicky. Which made her dangerous. Her fist was close to Larry's face.

'Amy,' said Laurence, alarmed.

'It'll be all right, Larry. This girl will let you go now.'

'Shows how much you know,' said Sparks.

'You're not going to be *made* to do anything,' said Amy, trying to sound soothing. 'You'll let her go of your own accord. It's your choice.'

'I choose... *not to!*'

The thumb knuckle of the glove brushed Larry's nubbin nose. The skin blistered. Larry yelped.

'You'll reconsider. Think it through. You don't want to hurt her.'

'Maybe I *do* want to hurt her. Maybe I want to hurt her *lots!*'

Amy nodded to Miss Steps, dreaming in the gutter, puffball of snot swelling from a nostril... and the Knout, stood against the lamp post, a sacrifice bound to a totem pole. She saw Sparks' glance follow her gaze.

'It's just you now, just you and your choice.'

The Glove might not even have been a Third.

Could she be a Second? Without her Talent, what would she have been? How was she treated at Draycott's? A little fat girl with a funny hand.

Drearcliff Grange whips were *horrors*. What were Draycott's Silver Arrows like? Did they hang hammocks from pillars made out of the skulls of Seconds?

Tears cut through the dust on Sparks' chubby cheeks. Her pudding chins wobbled.

'Choose, Sparks… choose…'

The cripple lurched lopsidedly, circling behind the Glove, readying his club for a second stroke. Another drive to the green. Sparks wasn't stupid though.

'You, horrid thing, stay still! No cracking my crown. Not any more.'

The cripple hopped back – deftly, Amy noticed – into Sparks' line of sight.

'I'm Amy,' she said. 'What's your first name?'

A long pause. 'Poll.'

'Nice to meet you, Poll Sparks.'

'No, it's not! It's not nice to meet me. It's never nice…'

With her left hand, Sparks – the Glove – pushed Laurence at Amy.

Larry tripped and turned halfway round. Amy caught her with mentacles and drew her into her arms for an embrace. Amy pushed her face to the top of Larry's head and kissed her hair.

The Glove stepped forward, snarling and shouting…

'It's never nice… to meet *the Glove*!'

She punched. Her glowing fist sunk into Larry's stomach.

Amy felt the *force* of the blow and there was an *explosion*.

VII: Tummy Trouble

VIOLET LIGHTNING STRUCK. Not from above, but from all around. Cold light flashed, dissonant bells sounded.

Amy was dazzled and deafened.

At the heart of the purple starburst was a white, cracked face.

Her again.

The Broken Doll.

The explosion was over and done in an instant. Instead of puffing out, flame folded away.

But it coloured *everything*.

Amy had a panic spasm. Would she see through purple specs for the rest of her days?

The bells were distant now… as if Amy were knocked out of herself, and far away from the street corner.

Noise rushed in again – shouts, clattering feet, smashing glass.

She rubbed her teary eyes to get rid of purple squiggles.

A high-pitched screech assailed her ears. Someone in agony. Someone *terrified*.

She was afraid it was her. Concentrating, she felt almost no pain. She wasn't even cold any more.

That was how you felt just before you died of cold, she remembered.

She'd been holding Larry Laurence. She wasn't now.

The crippled boy was on all fours, coughing and choking. He was within kicking distance of Sterlyng, but the tethered Knout – could she still claim the handle when her hair was tied away? – was not taking a chance. The hard-faced Draycott's girl was horror-struck. What had she seen in the moment of explosion? What did it take to chip through to her flint soul?

Did anyone else see the Broken Doll? Did *everyone*?

Amy lost the image again. She could only recall – from seconds ago – a white smudge. Eyes? No sex, no age.

A broken what? Something from the nursery.

The screeching hadn't stopped.

Fast footsteps told Amy people were running up the alley towards them. A distant police whistle shrilled.

All this commotion attracted attention.

A Great Game convention was that players dodge the constabulary – and civilian bystanders – as well as rival teams. The Undertaking did *not* have a quiet word with the Metropolitan and City police to get teams wriggle room with the law. Previous games led to players spending a night in the cells, on suspicion of offences from affray to impersonating a member of the clergy with intent to procure immoral services.

The proverbial quiet word was had the next morning and charges were dismissed, but being jugged meant being no use to the team… except that year when the tobies were hidden in police stations, black marias and courts. The final jug was tucked under the helmet of a bobby on the beat – ensuring an orgy of tossed bricks and cricket balls and swung hockey sticks and skipping ropes in the quest for the copper with the golden head. That naturally led to a deal of scarpering as bruised, bareheaded, non-prize peelers gave chase.

Amy tried to clamber to her feet.

Only she wasn't standing on the ground.

The explosion had tossed her into the air and she had *stuck*.

She stood as if on one of Miss Steps' steps – but one of her own making. Had she picked up the party piece from Stephen

Swift? Sometimes a demonstration was all the lesson she needed.

She looked down.

Smoke, fog and a swirl of crimson-purple vapour made it difficult to see what had happened. The lamp post flared. The electric bulb burst, the filament caught fire.

Stephen Swift remained conked out. A blessing.

The cripple and the Knout were in the flickering circle of illumination.

The screech must be Laurence.

Amy dreaded telling Frecks. If Larry were hurt, she'd feel *awful*.

No – it was Poll Sparks, keening like a mortally wounded animal.

Amy had seen – *was still seeing*, in her mind's eye – the white-hot, pulsing Glove punch into Larry's unresisting midriff... like a coal tossed at a wall of butter.

The Glove's arm went into Larry, up to the shoulder.

Tendrils of something slimy and alive streamed from the breach, splattering Sparks' contorted face.

Larry *must* be dead.

Amy despaired.

There hadn't been a fatality in the Game in more than fifty years. None of the current teams – except Humble College, smugly resting in last place for centuries – were in the lists then. A lad from Grimes' Aquatic Institute got his gills clogged with river filth while diving for a submarine jug and drowned. A finny cherub was set in the Thames wall in his memory. Tradition was that the winning team sacrifice one of their tobies – smashing it against the brickwork above the statue's alcove – to poor Walter Whep.

What memorial would Larry Laurence have?

Amy parted fog and smoke with her mentacles and kept people back.

She could do that now. With cold fury came precision.

Larry stood on her own two feet – alive! Sparks was on her knees in front of her, howling. Her shoulder was wrenched and pulled up at an uncomfortable angle. Her arm disappeared up to the elbow… not into Larry's stomach, but her *pocket*. If her punch had connected, her gloved hand would be stuck out of Laurence's back. Her glove was somewhere else. Waves of purple stuff radiated from the split seam in space, spilling onto the Draycott's girl's back and hair. Larry was *concentrating*. She was also learning more about her Talent. Amy had never seen Larry put a thing – or a person! – *partially* away before.

This was the point of the Great Game. Not the competition – though Amy wasn't prepared to give up on the school's honour just yet – but the education. Players had to work together, show initiative and imagination. They learned to be better… or, in more than a few cases, worse. Without a just cause, a player could become a Wrong 'Un. That was all too obvious.

In this situation, it was down to Amy to find a way out.

She lowered herself to the street.

People – men, smelling of cigarettes and beer – gathered, but stood back. Amy put a fence up around the girls. Not as unyielding as Swift's steps, but sturdy enough. She could maintain it without even concentrating. As if she'd nailed the planks together. The crowd didn't even realise there was a barrier. They just pressed only so far forward and were stopped.

Without understanding what they were seeing, the curiosity seekers knew not to interfere. People – she hated even to think the word, but *Ordinaries* – were like that. When they encountered the extramundane they didn't get mixed up in it but watched quietly. Not boys excited to see a shiny new locomotive steam by at top speed, but motorists waiting at a level crossing for the annoying train to be out of the way so they could drive on. Later the diamond-sharp images would go fuzzy. They'd convince themselves they'd had a couple of pints too many. Even if pals agreed they'd seen the same incredible things, it'd be dismissed as a will-o'-the-wisp or something funny in the pie.

All Unusuals seemed to emit a low-level version of Poppet Dyall's Talent.

It was also a mercy, and a convenience. The Undertaking, who cleaned up after goblins and fairies, relied on folk not taking wild tales too seriously – even folk who'd just seen a dragon burn down the town hall or an Egyptian mummy win the Charleston contest. Must be the drains. Or students playing silly beggars.

Without this effect, the world would be full of screaming, panicking people. Amy sometimes wondered why it wasn't anyway.

'Larry, are you all right?' she asked.

The girl nodded. She was smiling, calm but excited.

It was such a relief, Amy knew, when you stopped being frightened… when you realised you were *frightening*. She'd worry about Larry turning into a Wrong 'Un later.

Sparks' screech wore ragged. She made a high, cracked dog-whistle sound as if she'd torn something in her throat.

'Poll, can you hear me?'

The Glove was white with agony.

'Larry is to let go and you're to pull your hand out.'

Sparks was ashen, scared to imbecility.

'Nod if you understand.'

Sparks bobbed her head and winced.

'What hurts?' Amy asked. 'Your hand?'

A headshake.

'Your shoulder?'

Vigorous nod, which made the pain flare.

'Can you try to stand up? Larry, help her…'

Laurence put out a hand, which Sparks took. Awkwardly, she stood – arm anchored in the violet rift. With the back of her left hand, she wiped her face. She had finished crying.

Amy felt Sparks' injured shoulder and regretted nodding off in Nurse Humphreys' First Aid lessons. Was this a sprain or a dislocation? She seemed to remember the best way to tell the difference was the pitch of the screams that came when you prodded the problem area. Humph didn't reckon much to differing degrees of crybabiness. When a girl went to the Infirmary with a scratch or a sniffle, Nurse told her about a grievous injury she'd treated in the War. The treatment made patients feel guilty, if not noticeably better.

The purple traceries spilling out of Larry's pocket were impossible to look at straight on, so Amy didn't have to see the blurry cut-off point where Sparks' sleeve disappeared into nowhere. A dried-rose smell was all around.

In the Purple – another realm superimposed on the everyday world, which some Unusuals could reach – was a bodiless hand with a big fat white glove on it wagging? Would that attract some croc-mouthed creature to bite it off? Best not worry till it happened.

'Are we comfortable?' Amy asked.

That was something stupid Nurse said after her Vimy Ridge horror stories were out of the way.

Larry and Sparks both nodded. So maybe stupidity *was* soothing.

'I'm going to count to three... Larry, relax your pocket... if you can, let go of this girl's hand... maybe give a little *push*. Poll, don't *wrench*... draw your arm back normally, as you would if pulling it out of a sleeve. If possible, turn down the wick on your Glove. Can you do that?'

Sparks was doubtful.

How furious would Larry be if the scarf she'd lovingly knitted for Frecks got ruined when used as a tourniquet? Amy didn't have anything else at hand to treat a pulled-off limb.

'One...'

Sparks tensed and Larry breathed out.

'Two...'

Larry put her hands in her pockets – her blazer pockets. Sparks frowned and shook her fringe out of her eyes.

'Two and a half,' Amy said quickly... '*Three!*'

Sparks took her arm out of Larry's pocket.

Amy saw her sleeve appear, then her wrist, then her hand...

Larry gasped in relief – it had been an effort to hold Sparks – and stepped back.

'Where is it?' Sparks asked.

'What?' said Amy.

'It.'

Amy looked at the girl's big, pale hand. She had polished nails and very blue veins.

'*It*,' Sparks insisted, almost crying again.

Sparks wasn't wearing her glove.

Without thinking, Amy reached out and felt Sparks' hand... not with her own fingers, but with mentacles. It was as if she cast a net which attached to Sparks' nerves. Amy could feel what the other girl felt.

Nothing broken.

'Does it hurt?' Amy asked.

'No,' said Sparks, as if something were wrong.

'So... what's your problem?'

'It should hurt. It's *always* hurt.'

The Draycott's girl was confused, but not unhappy. Poll Sparks had been let go, set free. Amy pulled back her mentacles.

Sparks made a fist and patted it with the fingertips of her left hand – as if checking to see if a smoothing iron was hot – then grasped it fully. Weeping again, but not with pain, she touched her face with her right hand. Hesitantly, she reached up to her crown and rubbed her bruise – smiling in astonishment at the simple relief. She kissed her right hand. She looked from Larry to Amy and back again... at Sterlyng and the cripple... at Swift, knocked out on the pavement, and the circle of dazed witnesses. She gazed up into the fog.

'Are you... *cured*?' Amy asked.

Was that possible?

Admittedly, some Unusual Attributes – Dyall's mind-blotting haze, Gould's pelt, Lamarcroft's nightmares – were as much curse as blessing. Poppet might be useful to the team, but couldn't be friends with anyone without driving them mad.

Amy always felt sorry for her, for she was naturally a kind, helpful soul. Shrimp Harper was worse than Dyall. The Tamora Sixth *deliberately* sapped anyone she talked to, doing something she called 'breathing in'. Though it didn't excuse her leechery, Harper was a tragic case. Without meaning to, she'd nearly killed her own mother.

A dip in Larry's pocket might help these unfortunates, and even be a boon to not-much-use Unusuals who only wanted to fit in. Should Amy try to persuade her to refine the Application? What might seem a cure could be an injury. Laurence once put a mouse away, and decided her pocket wasn't for living things. The mouse came back not well. By Unusual standards, a gloveless Glove might be a sick, broken thing – no matter how happy Poll Sparks was to be able to scratch an itch or wash one hand with the other.

'It might not be permanent,' Amy told Sparks. 'Be careful.'

'If I'm not the Glove,' Sparks said, shyly but with a gleam of incipient joy, 'can I be *expelled*?'

She scratched her blazer, as if trying to get the arrows off.

Larry was quiet but shaking. She got like this if she held something in her pocket for too long. Drops of sweat flew off her forehead.

Normally, Amy would suggest someone fetch a bucket.

Larry bent backwards at the waist and threw her arms out.

A rip opened up in front of her stomach, and a shaft of violet light burst through. Oohs and ahhs came from the onlookers.

'Lumme, it must be *magic*,' said someone.

'Seen better at the Astoria,' said a cynic. 'The Great Edmondo. Now *there's* a conjurer and a half...'

Poll Sparks had just enough time, caught in the purple spotlight, to be jolted out of surprised happiness. Then, a purple toby jug belched out of the rip in space and smashed against her head.

'Ow, my crown,' she exclaimed, and fell down senseless.

VIII: H'Alfie 'Ampton

MORE DUPLICATE TOBIES shot out of Larry's pocket. The projectiles had gory, satyr-like faces with pointed Spanish beards and bulging dead eyes. Laurence wheeled around stiff-limbed, possessed by her Talent. China missiles shattered against walls. Shards rained onto the pavement.

Spectators hastily cleared the firing line. Some got tangled with each other.

The crowd broke and ran off in all directions, dwindling to indistinct shapes in the fog. Even their running footsteps were quickly swallowed. A few knocked-off hats remained.

Laurence calmed and her pocket closed.

She held her stomach as if she'd just eaten a whole cooking apple by mistake.

'All better?' Amy asked.

Larry nodded, but didn't say anything.

'How many jugs do you have in there?'

Larry held up three fingers.

'The originals?'

Larry nodded again.

Three out of five was a narrow win. But a win.

Headers Haldane would accept it. Sausage Gossage would be pleased...

But Amy knew it wasn't good enough. After the rout of last year, only a clean sweep would restore the school's honour. Victory must be complete. Preferably, the House of Reform should take the wooden spoon and be shamed out of hog-grunting.

She admitted this little skirmish was a Drearcliff gain.

Two Draycott's girls out cold, sleeping the sleep of the unjust. A third tied to a lamp post by her own hair. Amy glanced at Sterlyng. She was stoic, but alert. Even with her back against the post, she had to stand on tiptoes or suffer painful yanking.

The lame lad who'd presumably blundered into this skirmish with gallant intentions was up and about again, lurching in a circle around his crutch. He stamped his good foot and hitched his shoulders as if trying to wriggle his cuts and bruises away. Again, Amy wished she'd added first aid supplies to her kit. She wasn't getting much use out of her magnifying glass or compass.

She'd always thought of Kentish Glory as a knight, not a nurse. Given how she felt about fighting, maybe she should reconsider? Though, as non-fighters went, she'd given a fair account of herself in a scrap with a triad of terrors who were much more predisposed to settling things on the battlefield.

The chimes of Big Ben sounded.

The hour was tolled. Twelve green bottles hanging on the wall. Midnight.

The Great Game was played until dawn. In six hours, the teams would gather at the Finish, in the shadow of the clock tower – those that weren't lost in sewers or tied to lamp posts.

Just being up and about after midnight was exciting. Miss Gossage had tried to get the girls to nap on the charabanc so they would be alert later, but the benches were too uncomfortable for a snooze and everyone was overwound anyway.

Involuntarily, Amy yawned.

'Pardon me,' she said, not to anyone in particular.

Thinking about getting tired produced symptoms of tiredness the way looking down from a great height brought on vertigo.

Best to put those feelings away in a locked trunk, behind a crimson door...

With the worn-out toys...

And forge ahead. School Spirit.

She took stock. Two more tobies to collect for a clean sweep.

She was reasonably confident the girls sent to Lauriston Gardens were on the right track... but 'Villa DeVille W1' was still a mystery. Even Miss Memory hadn't got a clue about that puzzle.

A squeaking set her teeth on edge.

The cripple's crutch-end slid on the wet pavement. He tripped and began a nasty fall. Amy spread her life net and held him up. He was tilted at an impossible angle.

'Oo's got me?' he exclaimed. 'Some blighter 'as me 'eld, but I can't see 'im!'

'It's a her,' Amy said. 'Me.'

She walked up to the lad. He twisted unhappily in her mentacle hold. If he fought free, he'd smash his face against the street. She hooked her arms under him and carefully withdrew her invisible grip. His full weight pulled on her but she didn't crumple – thanks again to the gym mat – and was able to get him vertical.

When she got hands on him, she was shocked by his thin, filthy clothes and the bony scrawn beneath. Her imaginary arms could hold things, but mentacle tips had no feel for hot and cold, wet or dry, dead or alive.

The boy wasn't bleeding much, but she worried he'd got dirt in his wounds.

She pulled a flask out of the big side pocket of her waistcoat and unstoppered it.

The smell burned her nostrils but brought tears of delight to the patient.

'Ye're a life-saver, luv,' said the cripple, smiling through pain. 'A drop o' pick-me-up's just the ticket fer restorin' vitality ter the vitals.'

He reached out eagerly.

'You'll be disappointed,' she said. 'It's water and carbolic.'

He wasn't deterred.

'Any porter in a storm.'

She laughed.

He raised the flask to his lips – nothing she could say would put him off – and had sense enough to take an experimental sip rather than a full-throated swig.

He was aghast.

'Arggh, yer've pizened me!'

'I told you,' she said, smiling. 'It's for cleaning the outsides, not warming the insides.'

He handed back the flask and spat out more than he could have drunk.

Amy spilled the cleaning liquid onto a patch of scarf…

Did she imagine a scowling Larry aiming a purple duplicate jug at her then thinking better of it?

And raised a wad of wool to the lad's face.

'Back, away wiv yer, yer 'eathen 'arridan!'

'I'm going to wash your wounds. Don't be such a fusspot.'

'Ye're not tikin' me dirt, miss. 'Tis the thing what keeps spirit an' sinew together. An 'onest dirt layer is a comfort in this fog an' chill. More tonic fer abrasions an' abrusions than any o' yer fancy sticklin' plasters or badinages. If Ma learned me nuffin' else it's ter keep me dirt good an' even an' filthy all over. Blast the old besom an' the blokes she puts abaht wiv.'

She'd never heard such a thing. Dirt is good.

Nurse would be shocked. Amy didn't doubt the lad could gather a following if he preached Ma's gospel of filth to some Firsts and Seconds of her acquaintance. That tribe, however, were more likely to dye themselves blue as Boadicea with school ink than dirty up like a ragamuffin with soot and smuts.

Rather than force the issue, Amy took the scarf away.

'Who are you, boy?' she asked.

'H'Alfie 'Ampton, H'Esquire,' he said, managing a strange

curtsey by tapping his good knee with his bad leg and hunching over his crutch while lowering his head. 'Nimed fer H'Alfred the King and 'Ampton where 'e 'ad 'is court. H'At yer serveece, marm. Flotsam o' these streets. Jetsam o' this wicked 'ard life. Rescuer of middens fair, no matter 'ow much pizen they tries ter dose me wiv.'

'I'm... Kentish Glory.'

'Yer wot?'

'Kentish Glory. It's a... trade name? Call me Amy.'

H'Alfie 'Ampton shrank. 'Ooo, I can't call yer that. T'd be disrespectful, an' the 'Amptons is a most respectful breed. H'All the way back ter the Newman Cornquest and Mangy Carter.'

'You've earned the right to some familiarity with your gallant intervention.'

'You don't 'alf talk rum, Miss Glory.'

She wondered if he wasn't sneakily joshing her. His big eyes seemed too clear for deception. He wasn't like anyone she'd ever met. Truly, an original. And a Tragic Case.

Scrubbed and dressed properly, he might be presentable in a stick-thin, angular way. He had a noble nose and sharp cheekbones. His longish hair had a natural waviness where it wasn't thatched with dirt.

She would make him her Cause.

When the Game was won, she'd find him a position where he could at least learn about proper washing and sleep with a roof over his head. Despite his gammy leg, he was nimble and handy.

'This is...' Amy struggled to remember Larry Laurence's real name.

'Venetia,' Larry said, extending her hand.

'Delighted ter meet yer. Call me H'Alf.'

He tapped Larry's fingers and she giggled.

'You don't want to know who these other girls are,' said Amy. 'They're nasty pieces of work.'

H'Alfie rubbed his bloodied chin. 'I did get that impression, as it 'appens. Neversomatter, they booted me fair an' square from the front. None o' this roundabout pizenin' sneakery, nor no antigravitational owsyerfather neither.'

Amy was offended. 'I am *not* like them.'

'I don't know, beggin' yer parsnips,' he said. 'Yer seem to be like *'er* in particular.'

H'Alfie pointed at the unconscious Stephen Swift.

Amy hoped her dreams were plagued by…

…what was that crackface thing?

No matter. Try never to think of it.

…*the Broken Doll.*

'Was yer on wires? Like Pansy Peter in the show?'

'Were you?' Amy asked.

H'Alfie was frightened again. 'Ye're one o' *them*! A fl—'

Amy put her finger to H'Alfie's lips.

'Do *not* say that word. It's extremely rude. And gives offence.'

If H'Alfie 'Ampton said 'fluke' in Light Fingers' earshot, he'd find out what it was like to get punched sixty times inside ten seconds.

'—ying girl,' H'Alfie got out around her finger.

Once, when particularly aggrieved, Light Fingers admitted she wished there were an insult tossable at Ordinaries in the contemptuous way they called Unusuals 'flukes'. She jotted a list of likely expressions in her exercise book – 'dulls', 'plods', 'heavies'. None sneery enough for general use, though she underlined 'slowcoach' several times. Amy had qualms about the project, but her friend would not be reasoned with.

In the meantime, she had misjudged H'Alfie.

'More like floating,' she admitted. 'And I don't know what *she* calls it. Stepping, I think. She's better at it than me.'

H'Alfie prodded the senseless Swift with his crutch-end.

'Don't look better'n nobody now,' he said. 'You don't 'alf talk yerself down.'

Amy didn't like being told that, but he was right. She'd beaten Miss Steps – admittedly by going against the Code of Break, which forbade biting. She had earned the right to crow over the vanquished.

'Alfie tried to stop them when they chased me up the lamp post,' said Larry.

'Then they showed me what for. Me lumps 'as got lumps.'

The House of Reform had a different Code of Break, which let three girls kick one cripple. Amy suspected biting was allowable at Draycott's.

Larry knelt by Stephen Swift.

'Do you think she's pretty?' she asked. 'She has dramatic hair and eyes.'

Larry touched Miss Steps' chin dimple with her little finger. The Draycott's girl dribbled in her sleep. Unjustly, she seemed to be having pleasant dreams.

No purple drudgery and porcelain spectres for her.

'Best leave her be, Larry,' said Amy.

The last thing the team needed was Laurence developing a new crush. Especially on a Wrong 'Un.

Larry stood. She played with her own hair, sweeping it up like Swift's. It collapsed when she took her hands away.

'I climbed high, didn't I, Alfie?' she said

'Yes, yer did. Touched the moon. Leastways, touched the lamp.'

He put his hand in her hair and fondly scrunched.

She smiled at him.

That was better. If Larry needed a new idol, H'Alfie was a better bet than Stephen Swift. Though, with a little stab of shame, Amy cringed at the thought of his grubby fingers in the poor girl's hair. What if she got nits?

H'Alfie stood over Swift.

''Orrible lot,' he said. 'What 'ave they got against yer?'

Amy didn't know how much to explain. Outsiders were not to be involved in the Great Game. It wasn't strictly against the rules, though Humble College were disqualified for five years after the scandal of '87 when the boys stayed home and sent servants in their place.

'They was rabbitin' about some gime,' H'Alfie went on.

'When they was lampin' into me, they was goin' on about mugs an' somethin' ter do with the *Vanilla Devil*.'

Amy couldn't believe her luck.

'Villa DeVille?' she prompted.

H'Alfie nodded. 'Vanilla Devil.'

'W1?'

'Piccadilly,' he said. 'Number 347. Big 'ahse, boarded up. They was gonna snatch some mug called Toby from there. Poor blighter. Don't fancy 'is chances what with them loonytick females after 'im.'

Amy was astonished.

It couldn't have worked out better. Draycott's had let slip the final answer.

And H'Alfie 'Ampton – Alfred Hampton on his birth certificate, she presumed, if he possessed such a document – had paid enough attention to pass it on.

Life rewards those whose cause is just. That was the lesson.

If only Miss Gossage would buzz now.

She waited a moment, in the vain hope her wish would be granted.

No. Two enormously convenient turns were too much to hope for.

Stephen Swift moaned. Amy had a moment of concern. She'd put the Draycott's girl out of the Game once, but doubted she could again. Miss Steps wouldn't be surprised twice. She'd wake up angry and watermouthed at the prospect of trying out ideas nastier than the Iron Maiden and the Duck Press.

Had Kentish Glory acquired an arch-nemesis?

Amy reckoned such a figure was on the cards. Every paladin had a dark shadow. Captain Skylark had Hans von Hellhund, Dr Shade had Achmet the Almost Human, Captain Adonis had Duke D'Stard, Shiner Bright had the Slink. Even Clever Dick had a nasty-minded cousin called Wicked William. When Amy first donned her moth mantle, she knew she'd attract nemeses. Already, there were pictures in Kentish Glory's Rogues' Gallery.

Antoinette Rayne, Mrs Rinaldo, Rex Rowland, Uncle Ewald. But a true arch-nemesis was an equal, or more than an equal. A better in everything except what really matters – devotion to a just cause. Persistent enough to come back time and again. Never quite defeated – even if shoved over a waterfall. If an arch-nemesis went to jail for a long time or died, their grudges were inherited by disciples or children or strangers who picked up their names and masks.

If Stephen Swift were awake and she lying unconscious, Amy had no doubt Miss Steps would have the same thought but – being who she was – would tip over the board before the match was begun. She'd lower a twenty-ton step on Amy and blame a passing steamroller. Then pick another enemy to pester. Perhaps Grace Ki, the Ghost Lantern Girl. Or Captain Adonis's brawny sister Phoebe, who went by the showoff handle Golden Dawn.

A paladin couldn't kick a fallen foe.

Much less flatten her to pavement paste.

But Kentish Glory could arrange not to be here when Swift woke up.

Amy looked around, hoping to spot a street name. The fire in the lamp had died down and the fog was thickening at sign height.

'What's the matter, Miss Glory?'

'I am late for an, ah, appointment, Young Alfred…'

The lad was a year or two older than her, but she hoped the flying helmet made her seem grown-up and authoritative.

'You wouldn't happen to be able to give us directions to Piccadilly?'

A gleaming smile appeared on his grubby face.

'I'll do better than that, luv. I'll tike yer there meself.'

A sharp laugh sounded, prickling Amy's nerves.

It wasn't Stephen Swift, awake and dangerous… but Sterlyng, who'd been watching and listening all this time. Her face was stone again, but she found something hilarious.

'Don't mind me, Miss Glory,' she said flatly. 'I'm out of play.

You keep going as you are. School Spirit rah rah rah! We'll get you back next year.'

H'Alfie shot a glance over his shoulder at the tethered Draycott's girl and cringed.

'She can't hurt you any more,' Amy said.

The Knout laughed again.

'What is *so* funny?'

'It's just *you*,' she responded. 'You're *so*… Oh, nothing, what's the use? We're beaten and no use peesing and queusing about it.'

Amy *knew* she was being joshed…

But also remembered that Draycott's would use any tactics, including psychological warfare, to put rivals off their stroke. Even the hog-grunting was a tactic. The trick was to ignore the ragging.

So, not listening, and moving on…

She addressed H'Alfie. 'You can get us to Piccadilly, like a…'

She was going to say 'native guide', but thought better of it.

'Knows the 'ighways and byways of Old London Town I does,' said H'Alfie. 'The inns and ahts. The secret ways most passes by.'

'Just so long as you don't mean the sewers.'

H'Alfie was horrified again.

'Wouldn't catch me goin' down there!'

She was slightly surprised.

'Because of the filth?'

'Nah, 'cause of them *giant pigs*!'

IX: Eros and Venetia

DESPITE HIS INFIRMITY, H'Alfie set a pace Amy and Larry were hard put to match. When he got ahead in the fog, they caught up by following the squeaky clump of his crutch. Might he be exaggerating his limp for sympathy? She supposed he earned his living as a beggar. He probably picked pockets too.

By comparison, Amy dragged her feet. Her cloak was damp, heavy and caught on things. She couldn't stop yawning, which meant swallowing gulps of foul London air. One of her boots squelched. It had a permeable seam and she'd stepped in a puddle of something awful.

First, they had to cross Oxford Street – not free of traffic, even in the small hours and this weather. Fog churned along the thoroughfare like a river of melted ghosts. Amy took Larry's hand and plunged into the road, hoping they wouldn't be run over by a stray taxi. At the other side, Larry took her hand away and wrung it out as if she suspected she could catch an infectious disease from Amy.

They darted from one street lamp to the next, resting briefly in each thin cone of light. H'Alfie led them down the curve of Regent Street towards Piccadilly Circus. Neon signs shed sickly light on the statue of Eros. A cowboy flicker was announced at the Pavilion, *Wanderer of the Wasteland*. Amy wished she were in warm, dry desert, even with a dry-gulching owlhoot behind every cactus. Green-yellow tendrils veiled lit-up advertisements for Bovril, Gordon's Gin and Schweppes Ginger Ale. The Guinness Clock – above the dubious slogan 'Guinness is Good for You' – reminded her how late it was. Nearly ten to one.

Five hours till the Finish.

H'Alfie skittered across Piccadilly Circus like a giant stick insect.

If he noticed the girls lagging, he'd stop a moment and shift his crutch to his other armpit – left for moving, right for leaning, Amy had noticed – blowing on his hands for warmth while they huffed to catch up.

Amy had to keep watch on Larry. The Third frequently stopped for 'rests' where she made her pained stitch face and told Amy she was perfectly all right. Larry was no longer venting supernatural chinaware, but Amy was concerned about how long she could contain three important – if comparatively small – objects in her pocket.

Gravity worked on a different principle in the Purple. The weight of a thing came not from mass or density but intangible value. Larry told the Moth Club she'd worked this out experimenting with her mother's jewel box and a cast-iron basin left for the scrap-iron man. Putting the cracked basin away was a trial. She had to open her pocket wider than she was, stretching the seams with her fingertips, then she bent over the unwieldy item and *enveloped* it. Touched by the Purple, the basin lost shape as if turned to jelly and vanished with a *pop*! Larry kept the basin in so long and with so little discomfort she forgot it was there. A single emerald earring was easily posted, but couldn't be held for more than a minute without Larry doubling over in agony. She held the matching earring for half a day before the barest tickle prompted her to bring it back.

It wasn't monetary value – the 'hot' earring had a minute flaw that made it the lesser of the pair. When Larry asked her mother and father about that particular piece, they went pink in the face and wouldn't explain why but exchanged funny smiles and fond pinches she found irritating, though she was given candied almonds for being extra sweet that day. It wasn't strictly about value, but *meaning*. That earring meant something to Larry's parents.

The tobies wouldn't fetch ninepence in any knick-knack emporium, but their worth in the Great Game was incalculable.

Larry sat on the wet steps under Eros and pulled out the front of her pinafore. Violet light flashed and the three jugs rolled into her lap.

The Third let out a gasp of relief.

'Larry…' said Amy, impatient.

The House of Reform knew about the last prize. They might be at the Villa DeVille already.

'Just a mo,' Larry said.

H'Alfie capered back to them.

'What's the 'old-up?'

'She needs a breather,' explained Amy.

H'Alfie saw the tobies. He picked one up by the handle. His beaky profile rather resembled the jug's.

'Cor but that's an 'ideous fing. 'Is 'ead's been cut orff wiv a rusty rizer.'

The lower rim was uneven and splashed with red glaze. It wasn't one of the jolly, tubby jugs Uncle Bracegirdle – a brewer who made lethally potent ale, while insisting on strict temperance in his own household – collected and proudly displayed on his mantelpiece.

'I wouldn't fancy drinkin' aht o' this gruesome h'object. Not even if yer flask 'ad Neapolitan Brandy in it.'

Amy saw his point.

'Right now, if there was hot tea to be had, I'd drink it out of a rat-catcher's boot.'

H'Alfie laughed at that.

It was funny, but Amy did mean it.

'I'd not say no ter a cuppa neither,' he said.

All the tea stalls in the circus were closed.

'I've got peppermints,' said Larry, shyly producing a paper bag from the ordinary pinny pocket it was easy to forget she had. 'They have fluff on them. Sorry.'

She offered the bag to H'Alfie with a tiny hesitance.

Larry was tentative around Frecks too. Infinitesimal rebuffs pricked like the bite of an adder. A half-smile or offhand pat was like a kiss from a handsome officer or a medal from the King. Candied almonds were rarely bestowed on Venetia Laurence, Amy gathered. At home, she had to surrender a brutal tithe of any gifts to her coddled little bully of a brother Cecil. Amy felt sorry for the Third... but was ever so slightly irritated with her most of the time.

She still hadn't been thanked for saving Larry from that potentially fatal fall. Not to mention the triad of Draycott's girls. To Larry, Amy was as invisible as her mentacles. She didn't remember Larry calling her by name – by *any* of her names – even *once* before tonight. She'd only shouted 'Thomsett' when it seemed likely she would fall and break her bonce on the pavement. Even as she bounced in Amy's rescue net, she switched back to wishing Frecks were there with outstretched arms and braced legs to catch her.

H'Alfie took a peppermint ball and tossed it into his mouth.

He went wide-eyed and Larry laughed.

She sucked on a sweet too. She didn't offer Amy a mint and Amy was too tired of the pettiness to ask.

'Feelin' better, Veneetsier?'

Larry nodded, almost beaming now.

'Put these fings away, eh? In yer whatchamacallit oojamaflip?'

'Pocket,' she said.

H'Alfie gave the jug back, exaggeratedly shivering. She popped it into her pocket. The other two tumbled after it. Amy saw that jelly effect Larry mentioned. As they were put away, the jugs became less solid – infused with the violet light – and shimmered, then were gone. There was a tiny *pop*!, air rushing in to fill the vacuum where the tobies had been.

'Don't fink I'd ever get used ter that,' he said.

'You'd be surprised what you can get used to,' said Amy.

'That I don't dispute, Miss Glory.'

Larry tugged H'Alfie's sleeve.

'I'm ready to go on,' she said. 'I'm rested.'

'Good fer you, button,' he responded, taking her hand.

Larry fairly glowed with delight. Though, of the two of them, H'Alfie was more likely than Amy to give her an infectious disease.

The moon peeped through a gap in the fog. Eros' winged shadow fell on them.

Piccadilly stretched off to the West. And the last toby jug.

What else waited at Number 347?

X: Boldness and Mistrust

PAST THE GAUDY lights of Piccadilly Circus, they came to a parade of more dignified shops. Advertisements were smaller, price tags higher. Windows framed illuminated tableaux. Ripping at the Beach! Everyone for Tennis! Cocktails on an Airship! Slender mannequins modelled cloche hats, sack dresses and ropes of pearls. Amy had an urge to twist a faceless flapper's head as if she noticed friends walking by her window. H'Alfie and Larry would jump out of their skins. She stifled the impulse like a giggle in chapel. That might have been funny earlier. This side of midnight, it was no joke at all.

Beyond the fashion shops was Green Park, an ocean of fog lapping a seafront of big hotels. Even commissionaires who usually stood guard outside revolving doors retreated to warmer lobbies. Amy saw pale faces through glass, watching for guests returning from evenings in the West End. Most liveried staff were veterans of the Great War – the Great Game played across continents by boys who should have known better. The fog probably reminded them of watered-down mustard gas.

Like too many girls she knew, Amy had lost her father in the War.

Lost her father *to* the War.

The circumstance didn't earn much sympathy. Drearcliff

Grange tended, as Frecks put it, 'to orphans or semi-orphans'. Lord and Lady Walmergrave were spies, captured in Belgium. They refused to name the conscience-stricken German officer who passed them documents outlining a plan to spread terror and despair in England by launching air raids against boarding schools and children's hospitals. The firing squad was ironically supervised by that same honourable traitor. After the volley at dawn, the officer drew his revolver to administer the *coup de grâce* and blew his own brains out, rather defeating the point of the sacrifice. The Kaiser grumpily cancelled the raids, so Drearcliff Grange owed Frecks' parents for not being blown off the map by a long-range Gotha bomber.

Amy's father was killed – along with some thousands of other men – in the Second Battle of Ypres. 'Killed, with distinction,' Mother said bitterly, as she tore up the telegram from the War Office and tossed the pieces at the motorcycle messenger.

Nearly ten years on, she wasn't sure how well she really remembered Father. Mother only put the framed photographs on display when Amy was between uncles.

Many school staff wore tokens of dead or missing fiancés. Miss Tasker's lad Eric, who lived with her in a cosy cottage outside school grounds, was a poignant keepsake of the Classics teacher's lost lover, a pilot brought down by ungallant ground fire. A contemplative little boy, Eric had a portwine birthmark across half his face. A mask of blood.

Beyond the hotels were impressive residences – not all in good repair. They had walked off the map into limbo. Amy looked for house numbers. She couldn't think of a number without mentally adding 'green bottles hanging on the wall'. She hummed to herself. Fatigue and nerves made her light-headed, prone to lurches between whimsy and melancholy.

She tried humming something more serious: 'He Who Would Valiant Be'. Instead of ending each verse with 'to be a pilgrim', she thought 'to be a *paladin*'. It wasn't quite what she wanted for Kentish Glory's musical leitmotif. Light Fingers had suggested

'Flight of the Bumble Bee'. A good theme was essential. Dr Shade played Wagner selections through gramophone horns built into his autogiro to let crooks he was swooping down on know they were really in for it now.

H'Alfie strode ahead, putting his good foot forward, then confidently swinging the lame one after. He knew where they were going but not that they'd likely find trouble there. His bruises couldn't have healed, but he wasn't wary.

Amy didn't want to preach caution like a nervous nelly. Or, worse, a malingering minnie.

Miss Gossage coached the team in *boldness*.

Dr Swan, however, advised *mistrust*.

It was a conundrum. Amy was required to heed her tutor and the Headmistress, but how exactly did a person go about *boldly mistrusting*?

Something else niggled. She'd been exultant when the answer to the final puzzle fell into her lap. *Boldness*. Now she was thinking again. *Mistrust*. A saw about gift horses came to mind.

Miss Gossage set stock by such folk wisdom. A tweedy country sort, the Sausage was expert in making muckles of mickles. She swathed herself in clouts until well into June. A gift horse could have Ivor Novello's telephone number tattooed on its tonsils and Clemency Gossage would be none the wiser.

Dr Swan had a different policy.

If someone gave Headmistress a thoroughbred, she'd wrench its jaws open, shine a dark lantern down its throat, and take a long, lingering look. If someone left a magnificent wooden horse outside school gates, Dr Swan would light a bonfire under its tummy and tell the girls to listen carefully for stamping, jostling and Greek swear words.

H'Alfie had overheard Stephen Swift and her teammates discuss 'the Vanilla Devil' while they were kicking him to fish paste against a lamp post. They mentioned the address – Number 347, Piccadilly – clearly enough for him to remember it. They talked about a toby jug.

Who has such conversations while committing an assault?

Their priority should have been nabbing Larry. From her time at Drearcliff Grange, Queenie Quell had the gen on Miss Gossage's team. Draycott's must know about Larry's pocket and the tobies therein. If they brought her in, the Game was won.

So why were they rabbiting on about Number 347, Piccadilly?

Amy halted in her tracks.

'What's up, Miss Glory?' H'Alfie asked.

'You're sure you heard correctly,' she said. 'The girls who hurt you said the address out loud?'

He rubbed his side. 'Not likely ter ferget. Me kidneys is still ichin'. Most pertickuler they was. Piccadilly. Number 347. Big 'ahse, wiv big gites. Big trees in the front garden.'

That sounded more like an estate agent's brochure than a casual chat.

'It's a trap,' Amy said. 'They wanted you to hear and tell me. It's *all* a trap.'

H'Alfie was concerned.

'We *shouldn't* go there?'

'No,' said Amy. 'We must. The Drearcliff Grange motto is "*a fronte praecipitium a tergo lupi...*"'

'"A precipice in front...",' translated Larry, tapping her breast-pocket badge.

H'Alfie's eyes narrowed, annoyed at an assumption.

'"...an' wolves behind!" I ain't fick, yer knows!'

Actually, his Latin *was* a surprise. Sunday schools gave out hot dinners, Amy supposed.

'We are forewarned,' she said. 'So neither the precipice nor the wolves should deter us. Besides, it's not a trap for me. It's for Larry.'

The Third drew close to H'Alfie and gripped his hand.

'It's about being too clever by half,' Amy said. 'If I'd not come along, they might have got Larry down from the lamp post and made her give up the tobies – she had to bring them out under Eros, remember – but then they'd have to keep hold of them till dawn. None of them has a pocket, so far as I know. We'd have *hours* to rescue her and get the prizes back. So the sly dogs planted a seed – made us believe they'd been careless. We do their job for them, guarding Larry all night and bringing her straight to a stronghold. They'll be well set up at Villa DeVille. She-spiders waiting in their webby parlour for the unwary moth.'

'What a diabolical liberty!' exclaimed H'Alfie.

Amy shrugged. It was devious, but reasonably fair play in the Game. Letting rivals solve the riddles, then sneak in to snatch the tobies.

Had Draycott's even tried to get the jugs themselves? Only Clever Dick's team put up a showing at the Troy Club. Quell, the captain, wasn't with Stephen Swift's raiding triad.

They started walking again, cautiously.

H'Alfie kept twisting his head like an owl, expecting attack from all corners.

Amy counted the numbers.

They came to a street lamp. More rococo than the one in Fitzrovia. Its thin light fell on a brass plate fixed to high, spike-topped railings. Grime had recently been rubbed off so the address could be read.

No. 347, Piccadilly.

Scratched into the plate was a sentiment: 'Keep Out – Beware of the Bad Bat!'

'Bats is 'orrible,' said H'Alfie. 'Nasty great flappity fings. Gets in yer 'air... goes fer yer froat.'

Amy raised a hand to her neck.

Beyond the fence was an overgrown garden. Trees as tall as any in the park across the road spread to obscure the unlit house front. The gates were shut, but fresh marks in the gravel driveway showed they had been open recently. A coil of chain, shiny and new, lay on the pavement. Someone had picked the padlock.

Larry saw something peeping out from under the chain and tugged.

Amy was about to warn her about booby traps, but it was

a rolled-up magazine. Larry opened it to a page with a turned-down corner. Halfway through 'Sally the Stowaway'.

Poppet Dyall's *Girls' Paper*.

That meant Haldane was here, with Knowles and Devlin. They must have solved the riddle of the Villa DeVille.

It was a good thing Amy didn't have to show her workings-out, because she was here under false pretences. She had no idea how 'Villa DeVille' led anyone to this address.

Frecks, Kali and Light Fingers would be in SW2 – foraging in Lauriston Gardens.

Amy wished it were the other way round. Not so her friends were caught in Quell's trap, but because she knew she could rely on them in a tight spot. The Moth Club were better set up to deal with whatever Draycott's sprang on them than Haldane's crew.

She'd have had Devlin pick the padlock with flexible fingers – Stretch practised that – and waltzed up to the front door.

They'd have fallen through a trapdoor or been walloped by a bucket on a rope.

Being befuddling, stretchy or know-all wouldn't serve them against a Draycott's faction. Quell would have terrors in reserve. Bigger guns than Swift, Sterlyng and Sparks.

Amy remembered the Knout's keeping-mum expression.

A set mouth that was like a smirk. She'd nearly given the game away.

Just as Amy was supposed to give the Great Game away.

She *had* to go into the Villa DeVille. The last toby didn't really matter, but she was obliged to rescue teammates. Even ones she didn't like much.

She saw no reason to put Larry at risk. Or the prizes she held.

This was where she undid Quell's plan.

She bent down and talked to the Third.

'Venetia, this is important. I'm going to go into the dark house. If the jug's there, I'll snag it – but never mind if it isn't. Thanks to you, we're already *primus*. Three is a winning score. I want you to go with Mr Hampton and hide somewhere. Out of the fog. Keep the tobies safe. Have a nap if you can. Then he'll escort you to the Finish for sunrise. At six. If I'm not there – and I hope I will be – then Frecks will be waiting…'

Larry, dull-eyed as if in a lesson about the imports and exports of Peru, perked up at the mention of Frecks.

'Serafine,' she said.

She might be swayed by H'Alfie 'Ampton, but remained true to her first crush.

'Yes, *Frecks*. She'll be at the Finish – with the jug from Brixton, I expect – and will be ever so pleased when you present her with three more. You'll have come through for the school and saved the day. Miss Gossage will be cock-a-hoop. Dr Swan will be happy, if that's possible. Frecks, most of all, will be *over the moon*.'

Larry couldn't suppress an excited smile.

Again, Amy worried about leading Larry deeper into an emotional minefield. There'd be consequences. A mess to be cleared up another day. After Victory and – preferably – a three-day snooze.

'Are you clear on what you must do, Alfie?'

H'Alfie touched his greasy forelock.

'Clear as a clockfice, Miss Glory. See yer at Big Ben, rahnd abaht sun-up.'

'*Before* dawn. That's important. A second after and it's too late.'

'I'm an abbycuss, Miss.'

Amy was baffled.

'Yer can count on me,' he explained.

She held out her hand, palm flat against the air, and gave a *push*.

The gates swung open.

H'Alfie, not used to her Abilities, whistled in astonishment.

XI: Adventures of the Amphibaeopteryx

AMY STEPPED ONTO the driveway. Gravel crunched under her boots. Fresh tracks led into darkness.

The light from the street lamp didn't reach far into the garden. She looked back at the gates.

H'Alfie and Larry were gone. She'd asked them to leave, and was – *of course* – happy they'd not put up a fight about it and insisted on coming with her into danger. Plans must be stuck to. But she was on her own again.

Striking on, with *boldness…* but wary at all times, showing *mistrust*.

There *could* be a balance.

She had a battery torch clipped to her waistcoat but didn't want to use it yet. No need to present a target.

She'd been wrong. There *were* lights in the house. Not bright, and behind thick curtains – but enough to give an impression of the building. Like most houses seen front-on, Number 347 made a face. Doors for a mouth, windows for eyes – an array, like a spider's – and a sloping roof hat with decorative chimneys. Some houses had a bland, benign aspect. Some frowned, warding off hawkers and circulars.

Villa DeVille smiled, but not pleasantly.

It was the face of a cruel, confident tyrant.

The Devil, or a close relative.

Houses often look like their owners – or their tenants.

Her first thought was that no one was home. Judging from the state of the garden, no one had lived here in a long time. The only new-bought thing was the chain on the gates. Whoever had lived here could not be entirely got rid of. His sweat – she sensed it was a man, or at least male – had seeped into the bricks.

Thick, viscous stuff dripped on the grass in front of her.

She heard mewling overhead.

Were a family of cats stuck in a tree? Or the proverbial Bad Bat?

A bulky, unlikely shape was wedged into the branches of a gnarled oak. A very big roost for bad bats? A nest for giant wasps? Fresh, raw wounds – bark scraped away from wood flesh – showed the structure was a relatively recent addition. The noise was coming from inside.

Curiosity got the better of her. She unclipped her torch.

After pressing the switch several times and shaking the whole doodad, the lamp came on. The torch smelled funny. She needed to replace either the battery or the bulb or both. Or go back to lighting matches.

Her up-shone beam played across metal – burnished copper or brass – and flashed off portholes. A metal plate was studded with rivets. How had a diving bell or a tank got stuck in a tree?

Amy floated up to investigate.

The shrilling became more urgent. Small faces pressed against windows, mouths a-gape. Muffled thuds and yelps of frustration. Little fists hammered padded porthole rims.

It was a Heath Robinson contraption. Literally neither fish nor fowl, with bent fins and wonky wings. She saw bare struts and torn fabric, like a giant umbrella rendered useless by an unexpected gale. Spindly mechanical legs tipped with iron shoes. Two or three moved feebly, leaking oil from the joints. Others dangled, interior wires cut.

She swam around the tree, examining the marvel from all angles.

Clearly, it was a conveyance. A land-sea-air craft.

The work of several geniuses, but not a patch on Rattletrap. The charabanc had never landed them in a tree.

The metal gondola was fairly small. An enclosed capsule.

Not many sailors or airmen or whatever could fit in. The crew were cramped. Even if they were all titches.

She knew who was inside.

Richard Cleaver – Clever Dick – and his teammates. The Brain-Boxes.

This machine was more elaborate than their jug-gathering automaton. What did they call it? The Flying Spiderfish? The Underwater Locust?

The rapping and wailing grew even more insistent.

She saw why. A mess of tangled tubes – including gramophone horns copied from Dr Shade's nippier, less crash-prone autogiro – was squashed against the tree trunk. A buckled wing jammed the access hatch. The prodigies were trapped in their upside-down wondercraft, running out of air.

It was a shame Miss Vernon wasn't here to see this.

Amy couldn't let children suffocate, but it was best the Splendid Swots stay stuck for the moment. Out of harm's way. And out of the Game.

She picked a porthole even the tiniest titch couldn't wriggle through and reached out with a mentacle. Remembering Stephen Swift struggling to thumb-pop a goggle lens, Amy imagined a big thumb, exerting pressure. This wasn't something she'd tried before. She'd broken things with her Abilities, usually by dropping them – but never on purpose. She got a solid handhold on sturdy branches, then *concentrated*, pushing as she had with the gates but *focusing*, feeling for a flaw in the pane.

A crack sounded like a pistol shot.

The glass, thick enough to withstand water pressure five fathoms deep, splintered but wasn't smashed. Remembering Swift's hammer blows, Amy tried to *punch* with a mentacle. It felt wrong and made her wobble. The tree creaked and shook.

Faces crammed close to the cracked window.

'Get back,' she said. 'Beware of broken glass.'

There was scurrying. Someone got stepped on.

Amy whirled in the air and kicked the porthole. Chunks of glass fell out. She got a whiff of what it must pong like inside the capsule.

Someone very clever had wet himself.

High-pitched shouts issued forth.

'You, flying girl, open the hatch…'

'I want my mummy!'

'It's your wesponsibility, Wodgers. I instwucted you not to interfere with the contwols.'

'It's not my fault! It's you, Dick. You're not Clever, you're only *a* Dick.'

'Please, Miss, can I go home. I'm awfully sleepy.'

'Wahhhhhh.'

'You take that back, Wodgers you wotter… or… or…'

'Or what? You'll piddle yourself again, *Wichard*!'

'That wasn't me. That was Wude Twude!'

'Smarthe's not here, wetty-pants. You wouldn't let her in, remember! You said the Amphibaeopteryx was a "no girls allowed" invention!'

Amy thought The Flying Spiderfish was a better name.

'She… she… she…'

'She saw you'd got your sums wrong,' Rodgers continued, needling. 'The wings should have been fixed, not foldaway! Anyone could see they'd crumple.'

'Tweachewy and sabotage, I tell you!'

'Wichard Wetty-pants… Wichard Wetty-pants…'

'You're asking for a bunch of fives, Wodgers! A wight woyal walloping!'

Slapping sounds came from inside the Amphibaeopteryx, which rocked alarmingly. The Brain-Boxes were long on thinking power, short on team spirit.

'Now,' Amy said, lowering her voice, trying to sound like Miss

Borrodale, 'is anyone sensible in there? A fellow not fighting or crying or trying to blame someone else. A fellow interested in getting home safely.'

The rocking didn't stop. Or the yelling.

'No one?' said Amy. 'I don't believe that for a moment. I'll count to five, then leave. While you're in this tree, you may mull over the distinction between very very foolish and too too clever.'

A pause.

'Please, Miss,' said a high, firm voice. 'There's me, Miss.'

'Who might you be?'

'January, Miss. Jonathan January. They call me the All-Powerful Jupiter Girl...'

'He calls himself that, Miss,' said a new voice. 'No one else does.'

'Shush,' she said, 'I'm talking with... the All-Powerful Jupiter Girl.'

The handle showed ambition, if not practicality. However, if she'd come up with a trade name at six or seven she expected she'd have picked something sillier than Kentish Glory.

'Can you all breathe in there?'

'Yes, Miss.'

'Are any of your friends injured?'

'No, Miss.'

'Are *you* injured?'

'I bumped my head... but it's not hurting now.'

'Brave soul.'

'Thank you, Miss.'

'Thank you, Jon... All-Powerful Jupiter Girl.'

'Please, Miss... are you a Drearcliff Grange School girl?'

'Yes.'

'What house?'

'Desdemona. Fourth.'

'Viola is my favourite,' he said. 'I want to go to Drearcliff Grange when they'll let me.'

Groans from his teammates.

'Um,' said Amy.

'I'm awfully intelligent,' said January.

'Obviously.'

'And I can be a girl, if I want.'

Jeers from the other Brain-Boxes. And slapping and crying. Branches shook. Amy had to float back to avoid being whacked.

'Calm down in there,' she warned. 'Or you'll tumble out of the tree!'

'I *can* be a girl,' insisted January. 'You'll see. There are *ways*.'

'Maybe there are,' said Amy, hoping to settle the children. 'All-Powerful Jupiter Girl, I'm leaving you in charge…'

Wails and complaints.

'You others, listen to the sensible one.'

'*Sensible!*' squeaked Clever Dick, who then ouched.

'Thank you, Rodgers,' agreed January. 'Well thumped. Now pay attention. Show fortitude.'

'That's the spirit,' said Amy. 'Fortitude, Spirit, Boldness… You'll have to sit tight for a bit. I have to go into the house…'

'Miss… don't,' said January. 'There are dangerous girls in there. And other things.'

'I have to find my friends,' she said. 'I can't get you down by myself…'

She thought she probably could – but remembered Dr Swan's watchword… *mistrust*. The Brain-Boxes' wheedling gratitude would evaporate if they saw a chance to get back in the Game.

'I will come back. I promise.'

'Who are you, Miss?'

'You can call me Kentish Glory.'

'She's not a weal Miss,' said Richard Cleaver, 'she's one of them… from that twivial school, the one for *girls*.'

Another slap, another ouch.

Not all Brain-Boxes were contemptible squirts. That gave Amy hope for the future of mankind.

'Shall we sing a song,' piped the All-Powerful Jupiter Girl. 'I know one about green bottles that's super jolly.'

On the whole, Amy would prefer being caught in Miss Steps' Duck Press to spending a night in the Amphibaeopteryx with Clever Dick and Co, even with the All-Powerful Jupiter Girl in charge.

However, the Brain-Boxes were safe, tidied away in their fantastic pranging machine. After the Finish, she'd let Miss Vernon know what had happened. Hired men with ladders and hammers could fetch the children out of their tree.

XII: House of Dracula

AMY ROSE ABOVE the treetops. The roof of Villa DeVille was moonlit. She saw a tempting skylight. Quell knew she might make an aerial approach, knocking one of her advantages out of the game. Maybe the Draycott's team would be surprised if she walked up the garden path and knocked on the front door? If she kept pondering her next move, she'd be up here come the dawn – with frost in her eyelashes and an icicle on her nose.

'*Eeny meeny mackaracka,*' she said, pointing first at the front door, ticking off windows with each syllable, '*air eye dominacka, downhill davy, Drearcliff gravy, om pom push!*'

She was pointing at the front door again, which she didn't like the looks of, so she continued…

'*Penny for the ice cream, tuppence for the tea, thruppence for the hurdy-gurdy… out goes she!*'

A window on the second floor, on the far left.

Better.

Draycott's couldn't know she'd settle on that spot to break in. Quell didn't have enough teammates left – six at most, and some must be in Brixton skirmishing with the Moth Club – to post guard at every entrance.

'Over the top, ladies,' she said to herself.

She floated close to the house, pushing back at the last

moment so as not to smack into the wall.

The dusty window was fastened on the inside.

She twisted the latch with a mentacle – a simple use of her Abilities – then scrabbled at the edge of the window. For some fiddly tasks, fingers were best. Long-unopened, the stiff sash window eventually gave and she lifted it. Musty black material barred the way. A curtain pinned up to keep lamplight in or sunlight out. She punched through near the top and ripped the cloth from its pins down one side, then eased herself under the flap. Her boots set down on spongy carpet.

The room smelled of old clothes.

She got her torch working again.

Man-sized bats hung sleeping from a pole.

She held her breath, then aimed the beam at the creatures.

The bats were old black cloaks on a dressing rail. She touched one. Its mottled silk lining was a dull crimson, with a few scarlet streaks to show its original colour. It wasn't *entirely* a calumny when damage to stored clothes was blamed on moths… but mites and weevils foraged in neglected wardrobes too, and mucoid moulds were unconnected with insecta of any class.

In a hinged frame atop a Victorian dressing table was a dented wooden oval. On the tabletop were shards of silvered glass mixed with little dead bats that turned out to be pre-tied dicky bows and an untempting strew of dull green coins. Thick dust lay over everything. Whoever broke the vanity mirror had run through the seven years' bad luck a long time ago.

No one had been here recently.

She took one of the cloaks off the rail and flapped it, shaking off the dust. She whirled like a matador and settled the cape on her shoulders – a carapace for her own wings. Indoors, bat black was better protective colouring than rust brown. She fastened a tarnished clasp in the shape of a wolf's head.

The cloak was heavy. Weighted, like a Thuggee strangling scarf? Or simply made to be worn by a strong man. The hem trailed like a coronation gown, so he must have been tall.

Beneath the scent of rot was a doggy musk.

She didn't like it but wasn't compelled to shuck the cloak.

It felt like armour. If it had a charm, it wasn't predicated on the wearer pursuing a just cause. Quite the opposite.

Perhaps only those who would do ill could benefit from its aura of protection?

She should take the thing off – cut out the patch over the heart with silver scissors – and burn it in the cold grate.

But she didn't.

The unpleasant taste of blood had been in her mouth ever since she sank her teeth into Stephen Swift's hand. It was stronger now and different. Sweet, not salt. Cream, not copper. Delicious, even.

The door was not locked, but warped by damp.

She wrenched it open and stepped onto the second-floor landing.

Something fell off a nail driven into the door. With better reflexes than she thought she had, she caught it with her hand. Her fingers stung. It was an old crucifix – a ceramic figure of Jesus fixed to a wooden cross. She let go but kept it afloat with her mind. That stung too, so she let the trinket fall. Others like it were stuck to all the doors. Someone in the throes of religious revelation had bought a job lot. Nails were bent, hammered in haste. Crucifixes hung at different heights.

Her instinct was to raise the cloak to shield her eyes from the blessed presences.

A few steps along the landing, her torch died. No amount of shaking or thumping brought the light back.

But her eyes adjusted to the gloom. She could see tolerably well in this dark.

The flared collar of her borrowed cloak rubbed her ears.

She listened hard and heard animal scratching.

Evidently, she could hear better inside the house too. Not having fog in her head was a boon.

What she took for dusty gauze hung across her path turned

out to be ceiling-to-floor cobweb curtains. Among the husks of insects were the bones of rodents.

The spiders here were hungry.

She used her mentacles to sweep through the webs, which silently fell apart.

She came nose-to-snout with a snarling, rearing, stiff-haired white wolf. Big as a prize bull. Glass eyes the size of oranges. Breadknife fangs.

The landing was arranged around a staircase that was too grand for a town house. More like something for a theatre or a palace.

The floors above were dark. What artificial light there was came from below.

She heard murmuring downstairs too – and could pick out words.

'Cats... rats... bats... fats...'

She was several steps down before she noticed a thick chalk line on the carpet. Without thinking, she had been following it.

The line seemed new-made.

She was reminded of something... but didn't want to think of it.

Fetch the haunches for the kitchen, child... Don't dally in the passage to the Ice Cellar, and whatever you do never linger by the Wrongest of the Wrong Doors, for you don't want to see what's behind it... You don't want to see the face of the Broken Doll!

She stopped and shook her head.

A roost of bats took flight in her mind.

And she thought clearly at last. She looked again at the chalk line.

She'd known Villa DeVille was a trap, but did Primrose Quell really have the bare-faced cheek to give an intruding boob instructions on where to tread to be best positioned under a falling piano? Draycott's must take Amy for a specimen of genus *dimwittiae*.

In her bat-mantle, she felt intrepid.

Boldness, always *boldness*.

What was the other thing?

Miss Rust?

There was no teacher of that name.

She trod lightly and continued down the stairs.

The murmuring sounded louder. It was as much muttering.

'Cats… rats… bats… fats…'

The words pulsed in her head like the beating of her heart.

She still tasted blood. And was thirsty.

A girl lay on the first floor landing. The chalk line went round her, as if made after she'd fallen. Her eyes were rolled up to show only the whites. Blazer and skirt covered in arrows. Bobbed, dark hair. Overdone make-up. A slight upper-lip malformation gave her a permanent snarl.

Amy's toe-prod didn't rouse the sleeping blighter.

She had seen this girl at the Off. Tie knot loose, top buttons undone. An immodesty infraction at Drearcliff Grange. Practically a uniform requirement at the House of Reform. The Draycott's girl had lost – or snipped off – her top two shirt buttons. She couldn't cover up if she wanted to.

Fire, Amy remembered. Jennifer Fire.

Strictly, only the Captains had to be present at the Off, but the whole Drearcliff team lined up – to keep watch on Miss Gossage when pickpockets were about and mark Haldane lest she find some new way of losing the Great Game before it started. The diffident Humble College Captain – Geoffrey Jeperson, by name – put in an appearance. His striped blazer, straw boater and flimsy scarf were unsuitable for the weather. After wishing all the teams a jolly good innings, he beetled off.

Primrose Quell was there, in a black trench coat and Silver Arrow beret. This Fire doxy hung close by. Taking out a comb to fix her hair, she let everyone see the bone handle was whittled into a serrated blade. Kali pegged Jennifer Fire as the team 'trigger woman', ready to shiv any mug who got too close to her Captain.

Fire had her comb in her hand, gripped by the tines. No blood on the blade.

Someone had nobbled her. Swooped and knocked her out.

She thought of Light Fingers. But the Moth Club was in SW2.

Dyall? Amy couldn't remember Poppet putting anyone to sleep.

One more Draycott's girl out of the game. Good.

Dr Swan advised giving a sleeping dog a swift kick in the tail region. This time, Amy favoured Miss Gossage's more traditional approach.

Amy rearranged Fire's shirt and straightened her blazer. She would never be demure, but it seemed not cricket to leave her sprawled *en déshabillé*. The poor thing was most likely only badly brought up. As she fixed Fire's tie, Amy noticed the strong pulse in her throat.

She was thirsty again, but not for tea.

What was wrong with her this evening?

She went down the steps, treading the chalk line…

To the Ice Cellar.

She thought of Wrong Doors. And what waited beyond.

She smelled paraffin and saw light from the hallway.

The chalk line did not lead down the hall to the front door but round to a side passage.

Poppet Dyall sat on the bottom step, chin in her hand, elbow in her lap. Charlotte Knowles squatted on the floor, hugging her knees with one arm. She was the murmur-mutterer. The girls were handcuffed to each other, trapped by balusters.

Miss Memory turned to Amy. Her mouth worked strangely as she babbled, as if her jaw had been dislocated and set badly.

'The Count DeVille… he made girls ill… he drank his fill… was slow to kill…'

Amy cast a long shadow on the stairs. The collar gave her batwing ears.

She knew who'd worn this cloak before her.

Over forty years ago, he'd rented this house, and others

around London. He'd called himself Count DeVille, though he had other names.

Knowles should have remembered. Obviously, she'd been reminded.

Where someone like the Count rested, his shadow remains. Even when he's far away and long gone to dust, his stink can't be washed out. Not by bell, book and candle or silver arrows and penny-stall crucifixes.

Amy's flesh crept where the heavy cloak brushed her bare neck and wrists.

And she was *thirsty*.

Had *she* been fluenced?

With her new wings, she crawled from a cocoon.

It wasn't all *thirst*. She saw in the dark. She had sharp ears.

She was strong too. Stronger than when Stephen Swift had her in the Duck Press. How many Swifts were there in this house? She *needed* this strength.

She did not take off the cloak.

She tried to clear her head. She coughed.

Dyall turned and shrugged. Poppet was stuck and could do nothing about it.

Knowles knocked her head against the stair pillar.

'He cooked the cats to feed the rats... He killed the rats who served the bats... He bled the bats to make himself fats... for *this is the house where Drac bit*.'

This was fiendish.

How long had Knowles been shackled to Dyall?

Had their captors known what that would do?

Amy knelt by Miss Memory, who tried to shrink into an alcove under the stairs.

Amy had a headache. Dyall was getting to her too.

She couldn't afford to be got to. By Poppet, by the Sausage... even, she knew with cold certainty, by the cloak. And, most of all, not by what waited beyond the Wrongest Door in the Purple House. That person – if person she truly was – was a white absence in Amy's mind. If looked at directly, she wasn't there – but, like Count DeVille, she could not be got rid of. When Amy concentrated on other things, that person crawled out of shadows like a broken-legged lizard. She was the unwatched kettle, coming to a boil with a rattling hiss.

What Amy did – who she *was* – came from thinking. She wasn't as clever as a Brain-Box – though she wasn't enlisted in the Sisterhood of the Dims either. She was gifted with mental Abilities. She must find a way of shielding her mind. A magic balaclava for Kentish Glory. Or a super-scientific snood.

Knowles shook her cuffed wrist at Amy.

Addled as she was, she knew what would help her.

Amy tried to get a mentacle inside the handcuff lock and fiddled. Nothing clicked.

'The key is in a dish over there,' said Dyall. 'Out of reach. That Quell girl said we were to be *tantalised*.'

Relieved to have an excuse to get even a few steps away from Dyall, Amy found the dish on a sideboard. Cheap china in the shape of a smiling fish – stamped with 'A Gay Gift from Whitby, Yorks'. She reached in and an insect the size of her hand crawled onto her wrist.

In normal circs, she'd have been delighted.

A species new to London W1.

An armoured ground cricket. *Bradyporus montadoni* or *bradyporus macrogaster*. Native to south-eastern Europe or Turkey. Eggs brought to Britain in the Count's boxes of Transylvanian soil.

She set it down gently to be off about its business.

It sat ill to let such a tasty morsel go free.

Drat the cloak! Amy was *not* about to start eating bugs.

She found the key and undid the cuffs.

'Poppet,' she said, 'would you go and sit by the front door and read, please.'

'I haven't got my magazine. Devlin made me leave it outside.'

KIM NEWMAN

'That was an Indian sign for me,' Amy said. 'To let me know you were here.'

'Did you bring it with you?'

'Ah, no.'

'Pity. Sally the Stowaway was just about to be discovered by the pirates.'

She saw waves of dark light coming off Dyall – that was new, something to do with the cloak? – and started losing track of her thoughts.

She must get the meat for the kitchen. Cook would be angry if she dawdled.

Several tea chests were piled in the hallway, lids prised off. One was packed with books and pamphlets.

'You can find something in here,' Amy suggested.

Poppet walked to the chest, trailing light streamers... and Amy instantly felt better.

Haldane and Devlin were in the house somewhere.

Quell was here – Dyall had mentioned her! – with two or three other Draycott's girls. Wrong 'Uns. Worse than the Knout or the Glove.

There was a toby about somewhere too.

'Ugh,' said Poppet, throwing away a pamphlet, 'railway timetables! I'll bet half these trains don't run any more.'

She lifted a heavy book and opened it.

'*Necro-nommi-con des Mortis*,' she said, mouthing syllables she didn't understand. 'Printed in squiggle language. Not even French. No use trying to read *that*.'

She tossed the book – which Amy saw was old, and perhaps valuable – away. It landed with a thud like a fat man falling down and going oof. Poppet dug deeper into the chest.

Amy hadn't noticed how addicted Dyall was to reading. She supposed the girl was on her own so often she'd picked up the habit. Teachers made her sit in the far corner of the classroom and read by herself. If they didn't, they'd never get through lessons.

'*The Turquoise Book*,' said Poppet, riffling through a slim paper-bound volume. Amy thought its pages might be scented. 'This is in English... and has pictures. Ooh look, a *rude* lady... and two *very* rude gentlemen... and I think that's a chap with the hind parts of a goat...'

She wasn't sure Dyall should be exposed to such reading matter – even if it was fifty years old. She'd heard of *The Turquoise Book* from a short-lived uncle. A periodical much prized by sophisticated collectors, apparently. Mother gave Uncle Bainbridge the yo-heave-ho when she found out he'd invited Amy to browse in his Library of Sauce.

But, at present, Amy was relieved the nuisance Unusual was distracted. Poppet sat cross-legged on the doormat and turned pages. The illustrations were covered by membrane sheets that had to be peeled off.

Knowles' muttering slowed and stopped.

Amy snapped her fingers in front of Miss Memory's face.

Knowles rolled her eyes – showing whites, like Jennifer Fire – and lolled, asleep.

Amy thought of putting the cloak over her, but worried she'd come back from the Ice Cellar to find Knowles biting Dyall's neck.

Besides, she didn't *want* to take it off yet... If she fell as a paladin, could she rise in a darker mantle? Not Kentish Glory, but *acherontia atropos* – Death's-head hawkmoth.

With rotters like Blackfist – who was perfectly foul to Light Fingers' parents while putting them in prison – and spoiled brats like Clever Dick entered in the lists as paladins, what was the difference?

Could a person be a Wrong 'Un in a just cause?

She left Miss Memory and Poppet and followed the chalk line.

The side passage led to a small open door. A large crucifix was nailed above the lintel. Sad china Jesus, crowned with scratchy thorns, drops of red nail polish on his glazed face. The sight of the Christ stabbed her eyes.

She hid behind the cloak as she stepped under the cross.

Wooden stairs led down to the cellar. The chalk line was thick.

She was about to set foot on the next step when she saw something glistening at knee-height. A thin wire stretched where it would trip her. The kind of low tactic she expected from Draycott's.

She knelt and breathed on the wire. Nothing.

She extended a mentacle and twanged it.

A stone cherub fell off a perch. It put a dent in the stairs and would have done the same to her head if she'd been under it.

Amy looked into the dark stairwell. Ropes were slung on the walls for handholds. Convenient for anyone of a mind to set more booby traps. Steps could be rigged to give way. She could tumble headlong and break her neck.

Something occurred to her. She was amazed she hadn't thought of it before.

A girl who can float shouldn't be afraid of getting hurt in a fall.

XIII: What Amy Found in the Cellar

THE LINE LED down the stairs. Whoever chalked it must have used more than one stick.

According to Miss Borrodale, authoress of *A Girls' Guide to Booby Traps*, the point of the wire-strung-across-the-path trick was sometimes to be noticed. The proverbial booby, thinking herself clever, would carefully lift her foot over the wire then step heavily on a concealed detonator.

Unlike the average paladin, Amy had the option of not putting her weight anywhere iffy. Doing her best to copy Stephen Swift's aerial stride, she rose over the tripwire and walked down to the basement without touching stairs, walls or the guide ropes. 'I like to think none of my pupils will have to be buried in a bucket,' Fossil told the Remove at the beginning of her course on navigating life's little traps.

In an end-of-course test, deadly devices were placed around the Conservatory, with custard pies instead of high explosive. Amy and her classmates got thoroughly splattered – but did learn their lesson. Next year, Miss Borrodale promised to teach them to set traps for other boobies. A few classmates – Light Fingers and Kali, especially – were worryingly enthusiastic about opening that chapter.

The weight of the cloak inclined her to stay vertical rather than assume her diving pose. It also lent her a propellant push when descending. Was this why many paladins wore cloaks, capes or long-skirted coats? Amy worried her Kentish Glory wings were too easy to trip over or get caught in doors. But many a screen swashbuckler sported a swishable cloak. She and Frecks had swooned through *Blood and Sand*, in which Rudolph Valentino twirled a half-length cape to distract bulls as he crept up on them with a long thin knitting needle. He hardly ever got gored. A cloak could be disguise, shield, diversion, concealment or weapon.

The stairs led to a low vaulted space with an earth floor. The cellar was divided into many chambers. Was this the feature the Count DeVille noticed in the estate agent's brochure? A private crypt would be handy for him.

Long boxes were piled all around, with their lids off. Someone very untidy or very determined had poked into all the packing cases. Expensive coffins – once shiny black with red-silk lining, like the cloak – were in poor condition. Layers of dirt had been carelessly shovelled in. One overflowed with bulbous, sickly white mushrooms. Others were littered with crumbled vegetable matter and scraps of dried old biscuit, garlic flowers and Roman Catholic wafers.

She understood another use for her borrowed finery – resting on a bed of native soil without ruining your nightie.

The cloak was inside her head like Miss Gossage's buzzes, wheedling and whispering.

Reasons not to take me off…

She wove a way between boxes.

She almost didn't notice one of the caskets was occupied. It was leaned against a pillar. A girl in a Draycott's uniform lay inside, beret over her face, arms crossed as if to protect her heart from a stake.

Cautiously, Amy lifted the hat.

A girl she didn't know was conked out. Her eyes were open and blank, like Jennifer Fire's. She had the biggest mouth Amy had ever seen on a person. Bloated and engorged, like two leeches stuck together. Was that supposed to be attractive? She'd heard of 'bee-stung lips', of course. It was part of the flapper look, along with beauty spots and kohl eyes. The Draycott's girl might actually have injected venom into her face. Spooning with her must be like kissing someone's weeping bruises. Yuck.

She heard the sleeping girl's steady heartbeat.

Something was off. Dyall and Knowles were caught and cuffed by Quell – Poppet said as much – but Floozy Fire and Miss Lush Lips had also been put out of the Game. By whom? Surely not their own Captain.

There were others in this.

Trude Smarthe of the Brain-Boxes wasn't trapped in the Amphibaeopteryx with her teammates. The little pataphysician might know a magic slogan that put people into comas. It was even possible the Humblebumblers had joined the fray – though this was too subtle for them. If they played, the lads preferred straight bat and raised dukes. Amy couldn't imagine the Sons of the Humble and Pious clamping chloroform pads over girls' faces.

Who was to say that this was even to do with the Game?

The Count DeVille might be gone, but he'd still resent violation of his abandoned domain in the cause of what was, after all, just a schools sporting event? Things left behind could act on his resentment.

The cats, rats and bats Knowles muttered of... and the persuasive black thing on her back.

Amy floated from vault to vault like a diver exploring a sunken temple.

More boxes. More dirt. Broken furniture. Chairs smashed so sharpened legs could be put to use. The remnants of generation after generation of Transylvanian ground cricket. A shell Amy could have sworn used to be an armadillo. Money chests, empty but for one or two old coins. From the antiquarian ghost stories Frecks read aloud by candlelight after Lights Out, Amy knew not to take souvenirs from a place like this. Each and every token would be cursed. She had worries enough without ticking off wraiths and spectres.

The chalk line, broken and scratchy, led her into a larger chamber.

A square of trestle tables was set up here, arranged so a person could duck under and stand in the middle. A miniature train set linked several realms. A toy castle was defended by lead knights in armour. On a papier-mâché hillside, ragged skeletons were impaled on sharp lolly sticks. Someone had gone overboard spotting red paint around the bases of the stakes. In contrast, an English country halt from the last century was populated by a half-inch stationmaster and plump little painted passengers. Tiny trunks were unloaded by wooden porters. At the end of the line was an H.G. Wells city of the future where bullet-nosed, tube-shaped scarlet trams ran on a single gleaming rail. Panther-eyed, long-limbed, hairless utopian humans wore togas made from cellophane sweet wrappers and had little dried squid creatures for pets instead of cats and dogs.

A long coat bearing the insignia of the North Eastern Railway Company hung on a hatstand in the centre hole. A peaked hat and a guard's whistle completed the uniform.

It was said the Count DeVille had a 'child-brain'. His library bore that out: occult tomes, saucy pictures and railway timetables. Still, Amy generally pictured him crawling head-first down a crumbling wall, cloak spread like bat wings. Or as a mist pouring over a windowsill into a maiden's boudoir, coalescing as a red-eyed, sharp-toothed lothario. Had the Demon King really spent his happiest hours with a railway cap perched on his oversized head, solemnly toot-tooting as toy trains chuffed through Bufflers Halt?

Even monsters were not simply one thing.

A 'child-brain' wasn't necessarily sweet-natured. The Brain-Boxes proved that. The Count might play with trains, but that didn't make him a charming eccentric like Uncle Cedric with his battalion of painted Hussars. Perhaps Count DeVille saw no difference between people and toys. He had no qualms about sticking either on sharpened poles. Little boys and girls could be cruel. Children with Abilities – and, though she was loath to admit it, the Count had been as much an Unusual as she – could be *monsters*.

She floated close to the train set.

One length of line passed a square-fronted doll's house which was out of proportion with the rest of the set. Its nine-inch mistress would be an ogress among titchy model folk. The mansion seemed abandoned – doors broken from the inside, fist-sized dents in its walls. A ship-shaped weathervane was wonky, as if a storm had blown down its masts. The windows were ovals with white crossbars.

Amy couldn't see why such a thing was tolerated in this pretend empire. So far as she knew, the Count didn't have a younger sister. This arrangement smacked of a governess trying to make peace between warring siblings. She imagined a small princess beaming smugly as a place was found on the table for her doll's house, while her brother insisted it made no sense to have stupid big dollies mixed with sensible consistent-to-scale puff-puffs.

The chalk line curved around the other side of the train set. Amy set down on the floor and followed it.

She looked down on the ruin of Contention City, Arizona. Nestled in the remains of the station house, a rat gnawed on a matchwood cowboy. When Amy's cloaked shadow fell, the rat scarpered with a panicked squeak. A gouge in the prairie showed the bare wood tabletop. Earth spilled into the central well of the trestle square.

Amy had an idea what had been dug out of the Wild West Lilliput. She scouted about for a toby jug.

In one corner of the chamber, a tarpaulin lay over something that writhed feebly.

A hand – or something like a hand – crawled out from under

the tarp. Elongated inchworm fingers pulled across the floor, trailing a boneless pink python.

Amy hooked the tarpaulin with a mentacle and tore it away.

Honor Devlin was tied in knots. Her arms and legs were ropes of putty. A yard of drum-tight skin showed between shirttails and skirt waist. She raised her head on a cobra-neck column, face a yard long from crown to chin. Mouth, nose and eye sockets pulled as if by hooks. Only her panicked eyes were their proper size, peas a-swim in raw oysters.

Amy was about to say 'pull yourself together' but realised how that would come out.

Stretch opened her vertical mouth. Someone had yanked her tongue and made a messy bow of it. Yes, she was tongue-tied. Amy was tiring of the pawky, mocking humour which seemed to be the dominant trait of whoever was felling her teammates.

She didn't know where to start untangling Devlin.

Headers Haldane was still unaccounted for.

Even by a charitable estimation, the Captain was the least formidable girl in the Game. Snitching, toadying and observing each and every rule was no protection in the crypts of Villa DeVille.

Stretch tried to draw in one of her arms. She usually snapped back into normal shape like a rubber band. Now her elastic had perished. She was sweating – though it was ice cold in the cellar – and sickly. Amy didn't want to touch her unstrung teammate, but tentatively extended mentacles. Perhaps moulding her like clay would help? Devlin uncoiled her legs enough to stand. She had to bend her neck in a place where it wasn't supposed to bend so as not to scrape her head on the ceiling.

'Good work, Stretch,' Amy said.

Devlin smiled at the encouragement. Her mouth made a man-in-the-moon crescent, sticking out either side of her thin face. She looked like the Longity-Leggity Raggedy Man's Daughter.

Someone kicked the lid off a coffin and jumped up.

A Draycott's girl with stiff braids.

A First or a Second. Just a child.

Agile as a monkey, she hurled herself into the air.

Amy raised her cloak, cushioning the impact as the girl landed on her.

Amy's ribs hurt as her chest was gripped by bony knees. The impertinent snip tried to clap her palms over Amy's ears.

With a mentacular shrug, Amy repelled boarders. The little hands slammed to a halt inches away from her head and her assailant was frustrated not to be able to squeeze. Then, Amy expanded her mentacles and shrugged the pest off her. As she was tossed onto the train set, the girl's face was a picture of shock and resentment.

She was young enough for it not to have sunk in yet.

She wasn't the *only* Unusual.

Clockwork mechanisms were triggered and trains began running. Clicketyclick clicketyclack. The wheel of an Arizona gold mine turned. Buried Indians burst from sands on mousetrap springs and fired teeny arrows. Flags emblazoned with a D-shaped dragon winched up over the mine, the castle, Bufflers Halt and Utopiopolis.

The Draycott's girl saw the batwing-shaped cowcatcher of the Count's Special aimed straight at her. The smoke-belching engine was black, with red trim, its carriages coffins, its funnel a crenellated tower, its lamps lit-up skulls and wolf heads. The girl jumped off the table and grabbed Stretch's lapels, shinning up her thin body. She took hold of Devlin's neck – which bent like hanging bread dough – and clamped with her knee-pincer hold. Stretch's torso squeezed like a tube of toothpaste clutched in the middle.

Both girls panicked.

Devlin's spine gave out and she flopped heavily on the train set. One of the trestles gave way, and a fourth of the Count's railway company was suddenly on a sharp incline. Sand, buildings, cowboys, Indians, a miniature hanging tree, and yards of narrow-gauge track poured onto the struggling girls.

Devlin, irked, wrapped an arm around the other girl and began constricting. The younger girl *didn't* have a flexible ribcage.

'Not fair,' she squealed.

With an effort, the Draycott's girl twisted in Stretch's hold until she was looking her in the face.

Smiling nastily, she clapped her hands over Devlin's long-lobed ears.

Amy heard a *pop*.

Devlin's eyes rolled up and showed whites. She slithered in a jumble on the floor. A model train barrelled off the edge of its world and soared in an arc, dragging five full carriages and a baggage car into an abyss. The train slapped down on Stretch's head in a crooked tangle. Devlin didn't react to the battering.

She was out of it like Jennifer Fire and Miss Lush Lips.

The Draycott's girl peeped out from under the unconscious human jelly and wriggled free as if out of a collapsed tent. She stood and shook earth out of her sleeves. She flicked a frontiersman off her shoulder.

Amy knew to keep her distance from the menace.

Her cloak collar grew stiff as an Elizabethan ruff, protecting her ears. She didn't know if that was her doing it or the cloak.

The Draycott's girl hopped up onto the hatstand, winding legs about the column, leaving her hands free.

Her party piece was the ear-clap trick. She was a living Knock-Out Drop. The Niece of Mickey Finn. The bouncing around was a learned skill. She needed to be an acrobat to get close enough to her enemies to clap them to sleep.

'Who are you?' Amy asked.

'Aurelia Avalon,' she said. 'They call me "Nightcap".'

She clapped her hands and made a loud noise.

Apart from setting off an echo, it didn't do anything.

'Not "Nightclap"?' said Amy. 'That's clever. You don't want to give too much away in a handle. Retain the element of surprise.'

'When I'm older and stronger, it'll be "*Deadly* Nightcap".' She clapped again and showed sharp little teeth. 'Then I won't just send people to Bedfordshire. I'll send them to Gravesend.'

'What a horrid thought,' said Amy.

'I like to be horrid. I won't be told not to be horrid. *I won't, I won't, I won't...*'

Amy had an idea Nightcap was off her team. She'd clapped out at least two of her own side.

'Did your friends tell you not to be horrid?'

'My *friends*?'

Nightcap said the word as if it had come up in a Latin vocab test she'd not crammed for. She had no idea what it might mean.

'The girl on the stairs and the other girl in the box.'

'Oh, them! Fire and Purdie. They're not friends. They're pills. As much as any of you Drearycliff sows. Upper Schoolies think they're so clever. And *rough*! Fire notches her comb handle every time she draws blood. Purdie kisses boys and makes them *scream*. But I dropped on their necks, from behind. When they weren't expecting it. And clap! *Pop!*'

She clapped again.

Did the walls shake a tiny bit?

'They got sent to Bedfordshire,' she said, smugly. 'Like your *friend*, the India-rubber girl.'

'Why did you put them to sleep? Aren't you on their team?'

Nightcap poked her tongue out. 'They wanted to play their horrid game. They wanted me to do things for them. Send people to Bedfordshire. But when *they* wanted. I can't stick being bossed about. I have a Talent, so I *shouldn't* be bossed about. It should be me, bossing Upper Schoolies about. Stands to reason.'

This was a lesson. Picking only wilful, selfish Unusuals for your side was a bad idea. Wrong 'Uns might be formidable in ones and twos, but a whole team will turn on each other. That was the Draycott's leaf. At Drearcliff Grange, things were otherwise. School Spirit. Boldness, over mistrust – no matter what Dr Swan said. It worked. After all, whatever happened in this cellar, the Great Game was won.

Amy folded her arms. The cloak settled like armour.

She extended mentacles throughout the chamber, feeling for something thrown away.

She halted trains in their tracks. She felt around the doll's house, but drew back as if stung. That wasn't what she wanted.

Looking at Nightcap, she thought of Violet – the sickly little girl in the Purple House who broke all her toys.

But she didn't *know* any Violet or any Purple House… even as she stood on a chalk line.

'I'm Amy,' she said. She held up her hands as if they were the only things she could wrap round a person's throat.

She found what she wanted and lifted it from the floor. Steadily, silently.

Nightcap's eyes narrowed.

'Now you're being reasonable,' she said, 'but you don't mean it. You're pretending.'

'How can you say that? You've only just met me.'

'When pills are being reasonable, they never mean it. I know. They're just trying to put me off my guard. They have tricks up their sleeve.'

'Funny you should say that…'

'Why?'

'Look up, look down… look *all the way to town*!'

Nightcap looked up and saw what Amy had done.

The tarpaulin that had been over Devlin was unrolled on the ceiling above Nightcap's head. Amy saw it had old writing stencilled on it. S.S. *Demeter*. Goddess of the Harvest.

She *let go*.

The tarp fell on Nightcap and flopped round her. The hatstand fell over and the Draycott's girl crawled between trestles, wrapped in thick, slick material. Amy took hold of the struggling bundle and gathered the trailing edges in her fists. She twisted them into a knot.

Nightcap could probably breathe… but it would do her good to be *sent to Bedfordshire* for a change.

Amy shoved the bundle into a corner and checked on Devlin.

In her sleep, Stretch was slowly shrinking into her proper shape.

Nightcap squealed. She kicked and screamed.

'Any more nonsense and the sack goes in the river,' said Amy.

Through the muffling of the cloak collar and with the echo of the cellar, she didn't recognise her own voice.

It was lower than normal, and curiously cadenced.

There was little light down here, but she could see clearly.

She heard heartbeats – Devlin's and, inside the oilcloth, Nightcap's.

And someone else's. Two more someone elses.

'Come out, you,' she said, in the direction of two rapidly beating hearts. 'You can't hide there.'

A section of the wall wrinkled at the touch of a mentacle and was drawn aside. A curtain, painted like brickwork, hid a recess. A fixed ladder led up to basement windows. A way out into the garden.

Prima Haldane was in the alcove, bent over uncomfortably, fingers scratching at a thin wire noosed around her bulging neck. She'd lost her boater. Her blazer pocket was torn. Serious uniform infractions.

Standing with the tugging end of the garrotte in one hand and a toby jug in the other was Primrose Quell.

The names were close together. Prima and Primrose. Martine, the humorous whip, mentioned that long ago, 'sometime between the Peloponnesian War and the execution of Perkin Warbeck', when today's crop of jaded, seen-it-all Sixths were blinking new bugs, Haldane and Quell used to be sat together. They were known as 'Prim and Proper'. Martine didn't recall which was Prim and which Proper. No wonder they hated each other later on.

Quell's Silver Arrow shone.

As Draycott's Captain, she ranked a silver pin that was actual silver – not paint.

The shine made Amy's flesh creep. The cloak hated silver.

Quell tipped the toby. Arizona sand poured through the china

Spaniard's gouged eyeholes and over his stuck-out tongue.

'Looking for this, dimmie?'

Quell let the jug go. It fell *slowly…*

Amy reached with a mentacle, but just knocked the prize off course. It landed on the platform at Bufflers Halt and cracked into three pieces.

'Oops,' said Quell. 'Butterfingers.'

She gave a cruel twist of the garrotte. Headers winced as the wire cinched.

'No one gets the point then,' said Amy.

Quell snickered.

'You're not still playing that Gormless Game? Deuced dogs, but your clock'll be red at the Finish. Not 'alf it won't.'

After a term at the House of Reform, Quell had changed her manners to match her modus operandi. Her father was an archdeacon in Haslemere, but she spoke like a tough scruff from the mean streets.

'It doesn't matter what you do,' said Amy. 'We've already won.'

Quell pushed Headers away, with a knee in the back. The wire uncoiled with a slicing *snick*, leaving a nasty red weal… and cutting through skin. Drops of blood welled.

The taste in Amy's mouth was overpowering, like a swallow of raw curry powder or boiling water.

She saw red… as…

Quell made her way up through the basement window like a coalman, with Nightcap in the makeshift sack slung over her shoulder.

Amy could have stopped them, but was distracted.

She saw the *smear* on Haldane's neck and fingers.

Her teeth were sharp. Headers' pulses quickened.

'Thomsett, what's wrong with you?' croaked the Head Girl. 'Your eyes are awful.'

Amy raised her hands and reached out for Haldane.

But with her mentacles, she unsnapped the cloak fastening

and shucked it, spreading her true-coloured wings.

Kentish Glory, not Death's-head.

The taste and the craze went away.

But everything was dark. Then she saw again – in gloom. Quell had left a lantern behind.

The cloak fell onto the train set with a slither, a giant bat knocked out of the sky by ground guns.

She even fancied the thing gave out a rat screech at being separated from her.

Had it been impaled on the weathervane of the doll's house?

No, the material wasn't pierced.

'That's better,' she said, suddenly feeling the cold, grateful she could feel *anything*.

What had the cloak done to her?

'I'm still marking you down, Thomsett. What were you thinking? Who's side are you on?'

Amy's shoulders itched, and she felt a rash on her neck and cheeks, as if the cloak collar were lined with a thousand tiny mosquito probosces that had stuck into her skin and suckled on her blood.

The cloak lay black-side down, showing its lining.

While wrapped around Amy, the silk had *healed*. The mould was gone except for a few small spots and the once-mottled lining was rich scarlet. Even the wolfshead clasp was shining gold.

Amy wished the cloak *had* been torn.

She also wished it had flattened the doll's house.

Villa DeVille was unoccupied, but the Count – and, she thought, other tenants not on anyone's books – left evil things behind.

Devlin sat up, rubbing her more-or-less normal head.

So Nightcap didn't send people to Bedfordshire for long. The Draycott's girls she'd clapped out might be awake too – and liable to be annoyed and dangerous.

'It doesn't matter,' Amy said. 'Hang as many stains on me as you want. I sent Larry ahead. She's got three tobies.'

Devlin saw the pieces of the broken prize on the train table. Experimentally, she put them together. If she stretched her fingers to press certain spots, the toby looked whole.

'And that jug either counts as a point or can't be claimed by any other team,' said Amy.

Headers was doubtful. Her red weal made an ugly necklet.

'We've won,' said Amy. 'Drearcliff Spirit!'

XIV: The Last Leg

THE FOG WAS finally thinning. Pre-dawn light stained half the sky, outlining the Palace of Westminster. The government lived in a gothic fortress like the castle home Count DeVille abandoned for addresses in Purfleet and Piccadilly. Close to sunrise, the Houses of Parliament had a purple tinge. Amy had a flash of terror. Did chalk lines on the flagstones lead to the basements Guy Fawkes filled with gunpowder barrels? What broken things lay forgotten down there? Promises or puppets?

The clock faces were illuminated. She could tell the time.

Ten minutes to six.

Close to the Finish.

She was bone-weary, uncomfortably damp and horribly sure she'd never cough the taste of London out of her mouth. Her cloak-scratched neck itched angrily. Yet she was exhilarated.

Soon, Big Ben would toll the hour in celebration.

The Great Game was won. Hurrah for Drearcliff Grange! Victory at dawn!

Her party – Haldane, Devlin and Knowles, with Dyall trailing at a safe distance – managed a last spurt of pep, speeding up to a trot along Great George Street.

She had a twinge about Bok. Should they have made the effort to collect their fallen teammate? The poor girl was presumably

137

huddled in a Fitzrovian alley, nursing a knackered knee. Amy could have led an expedition to retrieve her. Larry must already be home free with the tobies safe, so Amy didn't actually *need* to be in at the kill... but she didn't want to miss the Finish. A measure of crowing was merited, to pay Draycott's back for a year of hog-grunting. She hoped Quell was there to have her nose rubbed in it a bit. Also, she wanted to see Sausage's face as her 'gels' came through for the school.

When they were back at Drearcliff Grange, hailed as heroines of the term, she'd make it up to Bok. If medals were awarded for wounds sustained in the line of duty, Bok should be honoured. She wasn't the only casualty. Knowles was discombobulated. Devlin was out of shape. Even Haldane had a red weal around her throat. Headers would have to wear a scarf unless she planned to infract herself for Impertinent Scarification.

Leaving Villa DeVille, Amy had checked on the Amphibaeopteryx. Floating to the treetop and listening at the gondola, she was relieved to hear the soft sounds of sleeping children not murdering each other. Well past Lights Out for the Brain-Boxes. From her vantage point, she scanned the garden for Draycott's stragglers. Purdie was out of her box and Fire gone from the stairs. Either scarpered or in hiding. Like Clever Dick's prodigies, Draycott's were handicapped by lack of discipline. Let off the leash, they were as likely to bolt for the hills as play the Game.

That didn't make sense to Amy.

Indeed, things about the whole night troubled her.

'You're not still playing that Gormless Game?' Quell had exclaimed. 'Deuced dogs, but your clock'll be red at the Finish. Not 'alf it won't.'

Amy supposed the Draycott's Captain was trying to throw her off.

She also remembered Sterlyng's I-know-summat-you-don't expression.

'Don't mind me, Miss Glory. I'm out of play. You just keep

going as you are. School Spirit rah rah rah! We'll get you back next year.'

Loose threads, all around – harder to follow than chalk lines.

Another game was being played inside the Great Game. An Invisible Game. She was on the field without knowing the rules, the sides and how to win or lose. Just that the result would be a Significant Notch – White or Black.

Walking from Piccadilly to Parliament, she'd gone over the events of the night several times. She scoured her fresh memories the way Miss Borrodale advised regarding a room that might be booby-trapped. Amy tested every moment, as if it were deceptive… awaiting explosive realisation.

No, she couldn't see it.

'You're floating again,' said Stretch.

Amy had to concentrate to keep her feet on the ground and not zoom ahead of the pack. As Captain, Headers should take the lead. She'd said little since her rescue from the wire noose. She hadn't mentioned a single thing they would find about her for hours.

Amy suspected Haldane was mentally drafting her report, with an annotated list of infractions and suggested punishments. Lucretia Lamarcroft's brother Casimir had written a book that made politicians, newspapers and bigwigs apoplectic. In *Caught Between the Kaiser and the Cuckoos*, he said the only realistic way of fighting a war was to ignore idiots whose orders would get their men killed. Then – after a battle was won by improvisation, daring and sheer bloody-mindedness – the 'cuckoos' had to be convinced their shining inspiration rather than their mutton-headed tactics had saved the day.

It was touch-and-go with Haldane. She wasn't happy with the team's showing, even if they had won. At least Headers couldn't send girls who knew the whole story on suicide missions to stop their mouths. Cuckoos had tried that wheeze on Casimir Lamarcroft several times. He'd come back with medals, which he wore every time he had to share a platform with armchair

Alexanders who'd got no closer to the front than the officers' club in Aldershot. Amy had cut a picture of Casimir out of *The Illustrated London News* and stuck it up by her cot, along with pictures of her father, Dr Shade and the Aviatrix. He was an Old Humblebumbler, proving *some* good could come out of the place.

Amy wasn't sure about her own conduct. She'd earned any infractions Haldane stuck in her timetable book. She'd made too many mistakes. Putting on that cloak, for one – though she'd an inkling it helped for a while, even as it whispered in her mind and scratched her neck. With the bat-thing settled on her shoulders, she'd seen better in the dark. That was odd, since bats were famously poor-sighted and got about by echolocation. More worryingly, she'd not always conducted herself according to School Spirit. She'd left Bok to be captured or worse. That would tell against her if the secret lesson of the Game turned out to be to value living comrades over tokens like toby jugs.

It was *boldness* of a sort to bite Stephen Swift's hand, but using teeth in a scrap went against the Code of Break. A paladin should be better than a Wrong 'Un, even in desperate struggle. Amy hadn't been wearing the cloak while fighting Miss Steps, so couldn't blame its wicked influence.

'Where was that crooked man who whipped his crooked dog?' sing-songed Knowles. 'He stole a crooked ha'penny, left on a crooked log… misled a crooked girl, who gorged on crooked cream… and they all drowned together in a little crooked stream.'

Miss Memory had been babbling for hours.

Devlin saw her cellmate didn't go astray. She had a grip on Knowles' shoulder, and her arm stretched like a dog lead. One wrist – a knobbly, muscular stick – showed nine inches of skin between sleeve and hand.

Amy fixed her attention on the Clock Tower. They were nearly in its shadow.

Rumour had it that Dr Shade maintained an autogiro hangar behind the clockface. Was he inside the mechanism, spying on the Finish?

The Splendid Six sponsored the Brain-Boxes, but Dr Shade seemed above the Great Game. A lone wolf among paladins. Romantic, but not Drearcliff Spirit. Was the man behind the black surgeon's mask lonely? He had those loved ones to protect, but Amy didn't imagine a Mrs Shade waiting at home with shadow children, serving up bacon and eggs when the Doctor flapped home after a long night's battle with Spring-Heel'd Jackanapes. If he had close family, they were most likely dead, murdered long ago. His grim demeanour suggested he took evil personally. He'd not drop a girl from the team for justifiable biting of a she-rat like Miss Steps. His cloak was as black as any on the DeVille wardrobe rail.

'Hulloo, Drearcliff!' came a cheery shout. 'Wait for us.'

It was Frecks.

The party stopped in their tracks – except Knowles, who skipped on for a few paces, extending Devlin's arm. Stretch brought Miss Memory to heel.

Wading through fog, coming from the direction of Westminster Abbey, was a familiar trio. Frecks wore a deerstalker hat two sizes too big for her, sloshed over her silver coif. Kali had acquired an old-fashioned policeman's helmet and truncheon. Light Fingers clutched a Gladstone bag.

'We have wild tales to tell thee, miladies bold,' announced Frecks. 'Of mystery and mayhem in a mansion flat of murder... of writing on the wall and bloodstains on the carpet... clues all over the shop... and a merciless, cunning coven of Draycott's dozies who got the walloping they deserved.'

A ripe shiner nearly closed her left eye.

Amy couldn't conceal her concern.

'Thou shouldst see the other fellah,' she said, making fists and smiling. 'A perfect fright, by the name of Deidre "the Strangler" Simons. Beneficiary of a sock to the choppers. She'll have a gap in her grin unless they fit her with porcelain fangs. That'll learn her to try it on with the Moth Club. A like fate befell her fellow horror-hens Rebecca Kensington, known as "Kensington Gore", and Alicia "Vandal" Vickers.'

Kali drew her thumb across her throat and stuck her tongue out.

'A punch-up for the ages,' Frecks said. 'Shame you missed it.'

'Frecks'll give you blow-by-blow,' said Kali, 'till you think you was there. Boot to the brisket... bop on the button... elbow in the ear. Rat-tat-tat. It was a murderalisin', ma'am. Them eggs reckon they're hard-boiled, but we cracked shells till the yolks ran. They can serve it up, but they sure can't swallow it down.'

Amy's friends had enjoyed fighting more than she had. If she'd 'murderalised' Miss Steps, she didn't want to talk about it yet. Frecks and Kali were elated by their showing in battle, and eager to share gory details. Amy didn't know if she should be ashamed or not.

Was it possible a paladin should have a want of feeling?

A Lionheart was not the same as a kind heart.

Light Fingers wasn't bragging. She preferred to get fights over quickly and shut up about them, for fear of being tagged a fluke and a cheat. She opened the bag and produced a bright red toby.

'It was in the study,' said Light Fingers. 'And it's scarlet.'

'Along with five others,' said Frecks, 'superficially identical, of shoddy plaster manufacture. Balanced precariously on a loose shelf, so that if one was removed, the others would fall and be smashed. In theory, a girl had to pick right first time... only—'

Light Fingers motioned with her hands so fast they seemed to vanish.

'Only one among us was quick enough to catch six falling jugs before they came a calamitous cropper,' said Frecks. 'After Large Dark Prominent's clean sweep, close examination through a magnifying glass weeded out the true toby from the ha'penny imposters.'

'There's a watermark,' said Light Fingers, pointing it out.

A little top hat on a coffin. The sign of the Undertaking.

'The spares came in handy as missiles, for the purpose of pelting the competition,' said Frecks. 'And panicking 'em simultaneous. The felonious fillies misperceived and were frit by potential points a-breaking on their berets.'

Light Fingers was less pleased than Frecks with the night's work.

'We should have seen the watermark,' she said. 'Afterwards, it was obvious. We were *supposed* to solve the mystery.'

'All's well that ends with us up and Draycott's down,' said Frecks.

'It's not cheating to use Abilities,' Amy told Light Fingers.

'I know,' she said, bristling. 'I didn't say it was. Only – we should have seen the clue.'

'Always looking for a cloud,' said Frecks. 'Must be jolly being you.'

Light Fingers managed a smile. Of sorts.

'Where's your haul?' Frecks asked Amy. 'The Sausage buzzed to say you'd swept the board. Good show and well done that girl.'

Haldane had charge of the broken jug from Villa DeVille. She took out the handle, which had a jagged piece attached. A blank eye stared out from the china.

Frecks whistled. 'That must count for something – providing you have the rest of it, of course.'

'We do,' said Amy. 'And Larry's got the other three. I sent her ahead.'

'Young Laurence? On her own?'

'She's being taken care of. I... ah... recruited someone.'

'Good oh, that's the spirit. *Boldness...*'

'And mistrust,' said Light Fingers.

'We can trust this fellow. I saved him from a battering. He'd barged in to help Larry. His name's Alfred Hampton.'

'Capital,' said Frecks. 'Old English King's name... and the house of a newer Welsh one. The cake-burner of Wessex and the much-married Tudor. If this fellow's middle names are O'Brian and McStuart, he'll be Britain in miniature.'

Seeing Frecks bright as a new penny made Amy realise how tired she was.

Her friend had been in the wars, but all her bruises were on the outside. She just refused to bother about them. Her blessed chainmail probably helped. She'd fought the good fight – without biting – and hadn't left a girl behind.

'What happened to your neck?' asked Light Fingers.

Amy realised she was scratching herself.

'Nothing fatal,' she said.

'Where's Bok?' asked Light Fingers.

'Safe, I hope. She got hurt and couldn't walk. Some tyke from Draycott's hobbled her.'

'I trust she got hobbled back double for her pains,' said Frecks.

Amy remembered what happened to the Glove.

'More than double,' she said.

'Good show, Amy,' said Frecks.

'That was Larry, not me.'

'Good show, young Larry, then. She'll win her wings in no time, that one.'

What Laurence had done to Poll Sparks would take some explaining.

Luckily, there was much more news to share. Frecks and Light Fingers – who always knew which questions to ask – didn't press her on the matter of Larry's pocket. Amy wasn't sure it was her place to tell that story.

The clock hands were nearly a vertical bar.

Six o'clock and all's... well?

'Come on, Drearcliff,' said Frecks. 'One last push...'

XV: At the Finish

AS SOON AS the girls stepped into Parliament Square, Miss Gossage *buzzed* in all their heads at once – with excitement, not an actual message. Amy felt the *buzz* in her temples and teeth.

Rattletrap was parked in front of the House of Commons, along with Draycott's Black Mariah, Miss Vernon's blue Bentley (and the cerebellum-grey caravan hitched to it), various roadsters driven (recklessly) by the show-offs of Humble College, and three hearses from the Undertaking. Miss Gossage and Miss Vernon sat on the pavement in out-of-season deck-chairs, wrapped in blankets and scarves.

The gruesome attendant from the House of Reform – a stout, hawk-eyed matron with a bludgeon on her belt – stood with several Undertakers. The funereal fellows sported top hats and dark glasses. Chief referee of the Great Game was Mr Jay, a scissor-legged sage with grey side-whiskers and saucer-sized black spectacles. Amy didn't like to imagine his eyes. Knowles said the special glasses meant agents of the Undertaking could see through clothes and skin to the skeleton beneath – then had to make out she'd made it up when Haldane refused to step out of the charabanc in full view of Mr Jay and Co.

Many players were already at the Finish. Humblebumblers were in a worse state after a night's indoor roistering than folk who'd chased around fogbound streets trying to win the Game. Primrose Quell and Miss Steps had limped home, with some of their surly gang. Draycott's would already be plotting next year's revenge.

Amy couldn't immediately see Larry. She was easy to miss, of course.

The Finish was an exciting prospect, but much of the chatter in the Drearcliff party was of tea and toast. Especially tea. Just now, it seemed a miracle elixir. The least the Undertaking could do was lay on a slap-up breakfast.

'Show 'em the scarlet,' said Frecks.

Light Fingers produced the toby and held it high.

'Headers,' said Frecks, 'give us marching orders. Let's romp to the Finish chins up and chests puffed.'

Haldane was jollied out of her introspection.

'Yes, indeed,' she said. 'Drearcliff Spirit. At the right, *off*!'

It wasn't a parade. Their close order wouldn't pass inspection, but this wasn't that prideful sort of march. This was a return from the wars, with trophies and honours. And wounds.

Headers – General Haldane of the Queen Mary's Women's Auxiliary Army Cadet Corps – marched like an automaton built for stamping cobblestones to powder. Frecks fell in with her and the rest of the girls got in step… except Knowles, who tried to keep time while skipping. Even Dyall, bringing up the rear, swung her arms like a wind-up toy soldier.

Miss Gossage *buzzed* again.

Amy saw another bundle between the Misses Gossage and Vernon. Small, and wound thickly with blankets – with a woolly bobble hat on top.

Trude Smarthe of the Brain-Boxes?

No, it was their own Larry Laurence.

Hooray!

Was H'Alfie 'Ampton lingering for thanks or reward, or had he vanished into the fog? Amy should track the street lad down and see him set on a better course in life. Or at least get a decent meal in his tummy and a newer, warmer coat on his back.

Someone grunted, but Amy didn't care.

Mr Jay sat behind a baize-topped folding table. A junior undertaker stood by him, holding a large black umbrella. Another watched the Drearcliff column march home, a spyglass held up to one lens of his spectacles.

Various parties crowded around. Even a few Humblebumblers deigned to take notice. Amy assumed they had bets down on the outcome.

Haldane marched the team past Miss Gossage and up to the referee.

She produced the bits of the Piccadilly toby from her reticule and laid them on the table.

The attendant with the spyglass aimed it at the shards. Mr Jay held up a hand, thumb down.

'Discounted,' said the attendant with the umbrella. 'And voided.'

Haldane stepped back. Light Fingers stepped forward and put the scarlet jug in front of Mr Jay.

Thumb up.

'Counted. Valid. One point to Drearcliff Grange School for Girls.'

Frecks and Devlin launched a premature 'hurrah'.

The swaddled Laurence hadn't stirred. The goose was asleep. Understandable. The Sausage would put salt on her tail, wouldn't she?

Miss Gossage *buzzed*...

The message came through, but scrambled.

Everyone looked at Amy in expectation.

'Show us your hand, *Amy*,' said Stephen Swift. 'You've three trumps hidden, haven't you?'

A quease sprouted in the pit of Amy's stomach.

She saw two of herself, reflected darkly in Mr Jay's circular mirrors. Her mouths were open. She was shocked and surprised.

The referee waited. The spyglass was aimed at her.

Someone hog-grunted. Nasty chuckles rippled among the Draycott's faction.

'Pardon me for one moment,' said Amy, holding up a finger.

She turned and trotted-flew across the square, mothwings a-flap. Toes off the ground, paddling against pavement and grass.

As she neared the cocooned Laurence, the Third's eyes popped open.

The girl was yawning when Amy laid a hand on her.

'I was having a lovely dream,' she said.

'You can tell us about it later, Larry,' said Amy. 'Where are the tobies?'

Laurence was confused. Amy's quease became a pang.

Frecks ambled over. She would sort this all out.

'Ho, young Larry... we have ranged far and wide through shot and fire to meet at this brave dawn.'

'Serafine,' said Laurence, smiling, eyes wide.

'Amy gave you three jugs, my girl,' said Frecks. 'Now's the time to cough 'em up. The sun's nearly 'bove the horizon.'

'Oh, *those*,' said Larry. 'They aren't in my pocket any more. I got an awful ache from keeping them in so long.'

The pang became a stabbing. Amy was a foot or more off the ground, angled so her shadow fell on Laurence.

'Where are the tobies?' Amy asked.

Laurence smiled and said, 'Safe.'

The stabbing went away and Amy set her feet on the ground. Miss Gossage was unaccountably not congratulating the team.

After a pause, Frecks asked, 'Safe *where*, Larry?'

Larry's hand poked out of her blankets and she pointed...

'Mr Alfred is taking care of them,' she said.

Amy and Frecks turned round. Larry was pointing at the knot of fellows no one paid much attention to. Their faces were all unfinished – handsome, but uninteresting. Cheeks raw or downy, depending on whether they'd mastered shaving. Amy hadn't thought even to tell one Humblebumbler from another.

What earthly use was knowing which was Jolyon Goodfellowe and which Pericles Pfister? They were all of the same stripe. Even Geoffrey Jeperson, the Captain, only stood out because his cricket cap had an extra stripe.

The lads cheerily waved at the girls. Someone whistled. Merriment rolled across the square.

Amy looked from face to face and didn't find the sneak she expected.

She was too shocked to feel anything. Not so her best friend.

All Frecks' face turned the colour of her bruise.

'Oh, *Larry*,' she said, expressing a century of sorrow and disappointment in the simple name. 'What *have* you done?'

Laurence was fully awake now – and stricken to the heart.

Frecks turned away as tears started from the younger girl's eyes. Larry's chin wobbled. She turned urgently to Amy, imploring her to prevent an abandonment... hurt, confused, angry, desperate.

Amy didn't have time for the little twit just now.

The Humble College lads bellied up to Mr Jay's table as if it were a saloon bar.

Thump... a cheer...

Amy and Frecks raced back towards the table.

Another thump... a louder cheer...

Amy and Frecks barged through the boys, just in time to see a final toby jug plonked beside two others.

A great tumult of back-clapping and good fellowship erupted.

It died – or, at least, paused – after a withering flash of black specs.

'Counted, counted, counted,' said the attendant. 'Valid, valid, valid. Three points – and a *match victory* – to St Cuthbert's School for the Sons of the Humble and Pious.'

'*Primus*,' said Mr Jay. He had a broad, bitter Northern accent.

The back-clapping resumed in earnest. Throats opened to regale the Houses of Parliament with an ancient, lascivious song in Latin. The ditty celebrated the exploits of a St Cuthbert who did not much resemble the renowned Northumbrian hermit. This fellow was more interested in chasing shepherdesses than attaining the grace of God.

The chimes of Big Ben rang out and the song matched the metre.

Amy found her own back being clapped by bluff fellows. The clapping felt like being thumped.

Frecks had to slap exultant Team Captain Geoffrey Jeperson when he tried to kiss her on the lips and dance her round in a jig. No shepherdess she.

A victory for... Humble College?

How?

The hour tolled. Six resounding bongs.

Suddenly, Amy was flanked – Quell held one of her arms and Swift the other. Their matched smiles were serpent-like, not the apish grins of the Humblebumblers.

'See the buckos enjoying this, dimmie,' whispered Quell. 'They think they've won something worth winning. It's their right, you see. Always has been, always will be. They barely have to stir themselves. They don't understand why you'll hate them for it. They think it's funny you take the Game seriously. These past few years, they've sat it out and let Drearcliff and Draycott's pass prizes back and forth between us. When we win, it doesn't count really – but they think they're encouraging us, letting us take part, put up a good showing. They know they'll take the prizes in the end... for they *own* everything. It's been handed down to them from their fathers and their fathers' fathers, all the way back to 1066.'

'You didn't think you could really beat me,' whispered Miss Steps.

Even in her cold rage, Amy thought she could and that she had – no matter what Swift said now. She hoped the harpy's hand still bled. She should have bitten clean through to bone.

'We gave you to them, Amy Thomsett,' said Quell. 'They picked you as easiest to gull.'

The St Cuthbert's team elevated one of their number onto

their shoulders and bounced him around the square. Amy didn't recognise his face, but knew the crutch he was carrying and the rags he wore.

'Alfred Henry Wax,' said Swift. 'Never shows the same face twice. That's not the real him, no more than the crippled beggar. You know, I don't even think he's a *good* actor. The disguise is excellent – you have to give him that. What he does with paint and crepe is a wonder. Lon Chaney couldn't touch him. But the accent was all over the place. No one talks like that, Thomsett. And, really, didn't shuffling urchins die out when they transported the Artful Dodger?'

A.H. Wax didn't look like H'Alfie 'Ampton.

He was taller, longer-faced, redder-lipped.

He saw Amy and waved, shrugging something that might have been apology… not that he really cared or expected her to. She wasn't worth gloating over.

Amy wished she were still wearing Count DeVille's cloak.

'You went darker than we reckoned, though,' said Quell. 'If you're expelled for this, there'll be a place for you at Draycott's. With a little work unstiffening your stays, you could be a proper discredit to the Disapproved School. Think about it.'

Not Kentish Glory. Death's-head Hawk.

Amy reckoned Draycott's would drop the gloveless Poll Sparks from their team and had learned something about loose cannons from Aurelia Avalon. The irony was that the House of Reform needed girls with a glimmer of the Drearcliff Spirit. Quell wouldn't want to admit it but she was Team Captain at her new school because her old school prepared her for it.

The St Cuthbert's song had more verses than any non-Humblebumbler could be bothered to memorise or bear to hear. The pious rake pursued the lasses of Lindisfarne in unsaintly fashion through at least a dozen more. Amy's Latin wasn't up to the bawdier couplets, which she suspected was a mercy.

'Why?' Amy asked, hearing a bleat in her own voice.

'Why d'you think, dimmie,' said Quell. 'They're rich and

we're... unscrupulous. The Humblebumblers did what they always do. They *paid* us.'

'What about...'

'The brats? Easy. We bribed the works foreman at Trimingham's to loosen a nut and puncture a tank. The best Ability of all – cold cash. Takes no special training. No hidden Talent.'

Frecks had seen off Geoffrey Jeperson and pushed in to extract Amy from the grip of the enemy.

Swift's mouth pursed – one of her Siegfried's leaf tells – and she blinked – *another!* – as she nodded at Frecks, expecting to land an invisible blow to her already-bruised face.

'It's no go, Stevie,' said Quell. 'That bloody silver protects her.'

'How'd she get the eye?'

Amy wondered that too.

'Your Strangler deserved a thorough thumping. I doffed the coif so I was free to administer the sort of thorough punishment a parfait gentil knight would refrain from. I hope she appreciates the effort.'

Frecks got Amy away from the Draycott's girls.

'Well played, ladies,' said Geoffrey Jeperson, draping arms around both of them. He stuck his mucky lips on Frecks' cheek again and Amy's for the first time... that did *not* count as a *kiss*.

Certainly not as a *first kiss*. Though it was April, Amy would start a diary for this year – she hadn't kept one in yonks – and fill in pages and pages with what dull stuff she could remember of since Christmas, just to be certain to write an entry in capital letters stating plainly that on this morning Geoffrey Jeperson's lips did not touch hers and barely brushed her cheek... which, somehow, was wet. Ugh!

He had beer on his breath. His blue eyes sparkled with a moral imbecility worse than malice. If you stuck a Christmas pudding sixpence in his chin cleft, it'd stay put.

The Humblebumbler let them go and rejoined the elevation of Alfred Henry Wax.

Amy was fagged out.

On Mr Jay's table were three tobies in one group and one-and-a-smashed-muddle in the other.

'*Secundus*,' said Mr Jay.

'A match placing to Drearcliff Grange School for Girls,' said the official.

'Well done,' said Miss Gossage, as if she'd just watched her cats thrown into a furnace one by one. 'I understand all gels in the team will get book tokens.'

The Humblebumblers piled into an open-topped sports car and drove the wrong way around the square. Alfred Henry Wax posed on the bonnet like the Spirit of Ecstasy.

Amy thought everyone was looking at her.

But they weren't.

No, no one was. They were looking away from her.

She was a foot off the ground. Her insides empty. Her neck itching.

Silence in her head – no buzzes from the Sausage, not the cloak's whispers… if this last green bottle should accidentally fall, no one would give a fig. You could get change from a fig and it still wouldn't be what anyone would give.

Frecks put an arm around Amy and settled her on the ground. She gave her arm an understanding squeeze.

The Great Game had been played and won… by the rules.

'Mistrust,' said Light Fingers, to no one in particular and not very helpfully.

Miss Gossage swallowed a sob and jammed her hand into her mouth.

She remembered *boldness*, but always forgot mistrust.

This hit the Sausage worse than anyone else, Amy realised. Worse even than Amy, who was gripped by a calm acceptance that would give way to tears and screams if she didn't keep hold of herself. For the girls, the worst had happened… and they were too exhausted and wrung-out to make a fuss. Miss Gossage had to go back to Drearcliff Grange and report to Dr Swan. After last year's fiasco, a movement rose to depose the Sausage. The team might have been Miss Borrodale's. Headmistress in her wisdom gave the teacher – an Unusual, the only one on the staff – a chance at redemption. Which had not turned out well.

By Miss Gossage and Laurence – who was grimly wiping away tears that would not stop flowing – was Hjordis Bok, her knee bandaged.

'A Humble College harry – a blister called Pfister – brought me here in his car,' she explained. 'Said they couldn't leave baggages lying about in the fog. They wanted to be perfectly decent about it.'

'What utter curs!' exclaimed Frecks.

'Yes,' agreed Bok. 'Pfister asked for the telephone number of the Goneril dorm. He talked up the prospect of driving me down to Valmouth next Bank Holiday, for high tea and champers at the Hurstpierpoint Hotel. Said he didn't mind the limp. I gave him a wrong number.'

'Good for you,' said Frecks.

'Then he tried exactly the same line on some sulk from Draycott's he had to untangle from a lamp post. I think she gave him a wrong number too.'

'Good for her, I suppose,' said Frecks.

'I was as much a chump as any of us,' said Bok. 'Worse.'

'I blame myself,' said Amy.

'Don't,' said Frecks.

'Plenty of others will,' warned Bok.

Amy looked about for Larry. She knew how hard Frecks' brief, instantly regretted glance of disappointment would go with the girl. She would feel that worse than the rest of the team felt the loss of the Game.

The Humblebumblers were tooting their horn and singing their horrible song. Quell, Swift and Miss Vernon were press-ganged to join the crew, and crammed onto the laps of victorious chaps, persuaded to come along on what promised to be a rag to end all rags. Swift blew a nasty kiss at Amy.

A traffic policeman – bright white gauntlets shining –

stepped out of a hut where the road around the square divided in a scissors point. He tooted his whistle at the rotary rebels and Alfred Henry Wax knocked off his helmet with a swipe of his crutch. He lost his grip on the prop, which went sailing out of his hands and whooshed towards Amy, Bok, Frecks and Miss Gossage.

Amy saw the fellow's face – the face he was wearing – freeze and express concern... he hadn't meant to hurt anyone and was mortified.

The crutch came, whirling like a boomerang... and stopped in mid-air, clutched in Amy's mentacle.

She *squeezed* and snapped it in two.

'Good save,' said Frecks.

With sportsmanlike admiration, the carload of revellers cheered for Amy.

They'd add a verse to the song, celebrating her good heart in Latin.

Amy turned away and almost ran into Mr Jay, who was being helped back into his hearse by his attendants.

She saw her white distorted oval face in his glasses.

She looked like a doll. She looked broken.

No, that wasn't her face. That was someone standing behind her.

She turned... and the Broken Doll wasn't there.

Though Amy was sure she had been.

Secundus

Moria Kratides

1: Goodbye, Miss Gossage

FOR ONCE, AMY felt heavier than air. Hauling herself aboard Rattletrap was a labour, as if her pockets were stuffed with lead shot. Jouncing on her bench in the back of the charabanc, she unpicked the Great Game in her mind. The more she thought about it, the worse it seemed.

Around Micheldever, she fell into a doze against Frecks' shoulder.

Her purplish dreams were peopled by nimble marionettes and leg-dragging dolls. Men with red toby jug heads and handles for ears sat in judgement. Amy was in the dock, but no one would explain the charges. The presiding magistrate wore a thick veil over her cracked white face. A Humblebumbler in a straw hat jumped up to speak in her defence, but spieled nonsense Latin verses. He concluded his address to the court by trying to plant a wet smacker on Amy's face. His tongue was a two-foot worm. The judge banged a giant gavel... and she started awake with a crick in her neck. Stirred from her own dreams by Amy's convulsion, Frecks groaned. Others joined in. Even before Amy opened her gummy eyes, she knew where she was. With the roof retracted, she tasted the salt air of North Somerset. The smells of school rolled in, unmistakable as London fog. A melange of chem-lab stink, carbolic soap, chalk and custard.

'Burned f-f-feathers,' said Miss Gossage with feeling.

In the dead of night, assured the team had secured three tobies, the Sausage spoke to Dr Swan from a public telephone box. She must have been overwhelmed by delight to fritter away shillings on an after-hours trunk call.

As Rattletrap rolled through Girls' Gate and settled into the ruts of the driveway, it must have fallen on Miss Gossage that she had been rash in declaring premature victory.

In the aftermath, the Sausage swallowed her own disappointment, determined the team not feel demoralised and take an honest pride in their *secundus*. She made sure girls showed proper gratitude as Miss Oh of the Undertaking handed each a ninepenny book token. She told them to pay no mind to the Humble College showoffs, who took advantage of being temporarily proof against whatever their school's equivalent of being infracted was. Bottles of contraband champagne popped and they played conkers with their gold medals.

What with this distraction, Miss Gossage forgot to ring up and tell Dr Swan the final result. Amy sympathised. If it were her duty to report failure to Headmistress, she might 'forget' too. Flickers of expression seldom registered on Dr Swan's mask of a face, but she made her displeasure felt throughout school. Staff who did not come up to snuff were known to disappear. When Smudge Oxenford reported an absentee was suffering far from home – digging ditches in a Sumatran leper colony or cultivating snowdrops in the Antarctic – the notorious exaggerator was disbelieved less than usual.

As Rattletrap crawled up the drive, the stricken face of the Sausage was tragic to behold.

Amy's teammates were roused from uncomfortable, uneasy sleeps by the blare of the Viola Fifth brass band launching into Miss Dryden's setting of A.E. Housman's 'Soldier from the Wars Returning'. The piercing contralto Paço sang 'Soldier from the wars returning, spoiler of the taken town, here is ease that asks not earning... turn you in and sit you down.' The soloist

Tallentyre puffed red-cheeked into a euphonium bigger than she was, furiously fingering stiff keys.

The sparsely leaved trees were hung with bunting and streamers.

The whole school – pulled out of lessons and assembled on the playing fields – raised glorious, raucous exhilaration as the charabanc hoved into view. Their cheers drowned Housman's later, more problematic verses. Joxer had added hours to the journey by taking one of his celebrated short cuts, so the marshalled ranks had been standing about for most of a chilly afternoon. Stamping life back into their frozen feet, girls flung boaters to the skies and flapped scarves like banners.

Not for the first time, Amy wished her Talent was turning invisible.

'Put a mute in it,' shouted Frecks at the hooting throng, 'some of us are trying to get some kip.'

Joxer braked in front of the Crush Hall, and dozing girls rolled off Rattletrap's benches. The driver wrenched the door open and unbent his old bones to get free of the hated conveyance and sloped off sharpish. A supply of scrumpy was kept in the shed behind his cottage, under lock and key and mystic sigil. Joxer obviously intended to turn him in and sit him down and get him sloshed.

Byrne of the Sixth, whose jolliness was welcome at most times, eagerly boarded the bus with a party of smiling whips. 'Hurrah for the heroines of the age,' she shouted. 'Let jubilation rip! Slaughter the goats and oil the pageboys!' The welcoming party handed out garlands of paper flowers. Amy knew that when the truth came out, the team would be wearing sackcloth and barbed wire. Byrne set a cardboard laurel – sticky with fresh paint – over Haldane's boater… then gathered something was awry. Her twinkling eyes frosted as she correctly interpreted the team's downcast, gloomy, sullen, exhausted expressions. The bubble of joy deflated like a punctured bicycle tyre.

'Oh, not again,' said Dungate bitterly.

'Defeat snatched from the jaws of victory,' commented some wag.

Unkind, but not inaccurate.

The whips weren't sure whether to take back the garlands. After huffing, they decided – with exquisite cruelty, in Amy's opinion – not to. Groups of Seconds had cut out flowers and gilded laurels all morning. The band must have been rehearsing ever since the team set off yesterday. Glorious welcome was planned and would jolly well be executed, even if it was now hideously inappropriate.

Amy bet Haldane regretted rooking Byrne out of the double braid now. Head Girl and Team Captain wasn't going to be a comfortable office for the next few hours. This wasn't the Army, where Cuckoos could shovel blame onto lower ranks. If anyone faced a firing squad for this humiliation, Headers was elected piggy on the rifle range… though Miss Gossage would be offered a blindfold and a last gasper beside her.

The team disembarked with the enthusiasm of a coffle of political prisoners clanking off a train at the end of a long, long ride to Siberia.

Miss Tasker, a particular chum of Miss Gossage's, was on the steps of the Crush Hall. Her little boy was dressed in velvet, with an Eton collar and floppy bow. Eric's portwine face stain was powdered white – an effort made only on the most special occasions. At the sight of the Sausage, Miss Tasker's smile convulsed and died. Catching the mood change, her son scraped crimson stripes down his cheek.

Shrouded in shame, Amy walked past flag-waving Firsts and Seconds. Her feet dragged as if she were wearing diving boots. Eager hands shoved her onwards and upwards. Her knees gave out, and Kali supported her. She felt like an invalid. Wherever the stricken team passed, the reception stilled.

From the Crush Hall, they were hustled into the Refec.

At the far end of the vaulted chamber, Dr Myrna Swan sat. An Empress in full academic robes. Her gown was a riot of stripes, tassels, orders, badges and decorations from the many institutions which had awarded her degrees. Her mortarboard was as simple and unadorned as the black-silk caps judges wore when issuing death sentences. Laid before her on the High Table were bowls of trifle and jelly, bottles of pop and pots of tea, crumpets and cream, jams and biscuits, candied almonds and Turkish delight. Drearcliff Grange Refectory hadn't seen so voluptuous a feast since Founding Day. On any other occasion, just dreaming of such tuck would be a Minor Infraction. For the victors of the Great Game, no treat was out of bounds. By decree of Headmistress, they must stuff themselves.

Amy would rather have gone to the guillotine.

Nellie Pugh, chief cook, stood by with her kitchen staff – two severely underfed girls from town with whom Amy now had a strange sympathy she didn't have time to think about – in newly cleaned and starched aprons. They had excelled themselves in preparing this highest of high teas.

Nellie was the only person who'd benefit from the catastrophe. As school bookie, she'd dutifully taken many, many bets. Pennies and thruppences, sixpences and shillings, postal orders for even greater sums. All on Drearcliff Grange to win. Even at the shortest odds, she must have worried her capital would be wiped out – but couldn't afford to turn anyone away and lose future custom. Her book was full of bets now irretrievably lost. She'd get scant pleasure from her windfall profit. Last year, after the rout, she'd bought a smart new bonnet with her takings. The hat mysteriously disappeared, then turned up – with holes cut out of the brim – on the head of Joxer's nag Dauntless.

Miss Gossage was in tears – presumed by many to be tears of joy – and trying to tell Miss Tasker what had happened. When the news got across, it spread through the throng like the Red Death. Whispers passed and shouts rose. Calamity! Failure! *Secundus*! Worse than the wooden spoon! Those book tokens would be wisely spent on *How to Change Your Identity and Disappear From the Face of the Earth* or *Thirteen Appetising*

Recipes Involving Bitter Ashes and Sour Lemons.

The brass band outside coughed to a merciful halt as Tallentyre ran out of puff and signed off with a raspberry. Hallelujahs and hosannas subsided to stunned silence. A few small sobs were heard and some cynical laughs. Girls safe in the anonymity of a crowd made unkind remarks. It was little comfort that the sneering brigade would have done no better themselves.

So far as Amy was concerned, this was all her fault.

She had trusted… and been gulled.

Was Alfred Henry Wax now her arch-nemesis? A boy whose face she wouldn't know if she ever saw it.

An ache for revenge ran deeper than her abstract desire for justice. It was not the spur of a paladin. It was personal and intimate. An impetus to emerge from a cocoon as a darker moth with skull markings on her back.

Wax was not alone. Stephen Swift. Primrose Quell.

Eventually, word reached Dr Swan… who decreed that the team must still have their feast. Ostensibly in reward for the not inconsiderable achievement of *secundus*.

Amy faltered. Frecks and Light Fingers steadied her.

Only Dyall was unshaken. She scrambled up to High Table like a monkey.

Amy sat next to Poppet as penance, inadequate though it might be. At this awful juncture, losing concentration – and her memory – would be a blessing.

Haldane had no option but to sit on Dr Swan's left-hand side, just as Miss Gossage must take an honoured place on Headmistress's right. The rest of the team shuffled to whatever chairs they could find. Kali, Frecks and Light Fingers – who had, after all, brought home an unbroken toby from Lauriston Gardens – made a show of holding heads high and sneering back. Bok was colourless with pain and Devlin alarmingly rubbery. Knowles muttered crooked rhymes. Laurence's face was knotted tight with resentment.

The view from High Table was usually the privilege of staff

only. From here, a beak could survey all the girls' tables. Amy scanned the Refec. She saw many faces and few smiles. Here and there were smirks from girls with particular reasons to see one or all of the team done down – likely prospects who hadn't been picked for the side, mostly in Goneril... old foes or false friends, including the persistent sneak Inchfawn... and many trampled or infracted during Prima Haldane's rise to Head Girl. Even these contrarians were just finding scraps of comfort in a cloud of despair. Amy saw her own numbed misery reflected back a thousandfold. There were glints of sympathy even – which was no comfort. She understood why the Regiment of the Damned was never short of volunteers.

Orders were given that the team should eat.

It seemed the whole school watched in sullen silence as Amy forced spoonful after spoonful of trifle into her mouth. Only Dyall tucked in gratefully.

'Smashing tuck, what?' she said to Amy, with jam on her nose.

Devlin crammed her portion down in one go, like a small python swallowing a wriggling piglet. She excused herself and rushed out to be sick.

Amy ate on.

She felt the beginnings of what she recognised as a Poppet headache but didn't forget anything.

Larry offered Frecks her bowl of candied almonds, her own favourite treat. Frecks half-heartedly tousled her admirer's hair – a supreme effort, considering Laurence was The Girl Who Gave Away the Game – but spurned the tribute. Larry tipped the almonds on the floor behind the table. She looked at Amy with bright, hard eyes. A voodoo stare.

Someone else would agree that it was all Amy's fault.

Larry coughed up the tobies because Amy told her to trust a lad who wasn't even real. She should not be blamed for what she had done.

And nobody did blame her. Not out loud.

Dr Swan said nothing. She dissected a small glazed roast

pigeon with a skewer and a scalpel and consumed every scrap of flesh.

No one else at the table was given a bird.

At last, the meal ended. Nellie and her girls took away the plates.

Here, Dr Swan would have made a speech... and Miss Gossage would modestly have hemmed through her own remarks. The medals would be shown. The tobies would be cooed over, then reverentially placed in the trophy cabinet.

The team's one jug was left back on Rattletrap, Amy realised.

The moment stretched.

There was a scraping sound as Miss Gossage pushed her chair back. She stood up, at first defiant, then bewildered, finally terrified.

Dr Swan flicked a glance up at her.

If the Sausage wanted to explain, Headmistress would not stop her.

Amy didn't know what Miss Gossage could say.

And neither did she.

Someone with a soul blacker than Count DeVille's cloak started clapping. Slowly, rhythmically, with a mocking beat.

Clap... clap... clap... clap.

Others joined in, till each shared clap was a thunderstrike.

It was the toll of a death bell... The drum of a slave galley... The stones tossed at an accused heretic... The hammer blows on the end of the stake...

The Sausage was blubbing. Not silent tears, but actual sobs.

Then she *buzzed*.

Amy felt a shock to the brain. Her teammates were similarly stricken.

Sorry, that's all.

Sorry.

The *buzzing* became a *howl*.

The slow clap continued.

Miss Gossage left High Table and ran from the Refec.

As she kicked up her skirts, the pace of the clapping sped. When she made it to the Crush Hall, the applause became voluminous and rhythm broke.

The noise drove the Sausage away.

'Resignation accepted,' said Dr Swan quietly.

Everyone somehow heard what she said.

Even Amy, mind still buzzing, caught the words.

The whole school was silent now. Even the echoes shut off.

'I have thought, for some time, we were not bringing out the best in our Talents,' said Headmistress. 'A new attitude is required. A new approach will be taken. New staff will be engaged. This assembly is concluded. Disperse.'

II: Ghost Moth

THE NEXT MORNING, awake early, Amy hid under her blankets. Light Fingers was already up and half-dressed.

'Remember those dolts who said things wouldn't seem so bad after a good night's sleep? They lied.'

Frecks sat up in her cot and swore to corner any utterer of platitudes and prevail upon her to eat her own hat.

'Put pepper on it from me,' said Kali.

Light Fingers whipped off Amy's top blanket, exposing her to air and the new day. She wanted to shrink and scream when sunlight fell on her and had a flash image of herself shrivelling to dust and maggots. She hoped that was the last scratch of the cloak's influence, being burned out of her.

'Show a leg,' said Light Fingers. 'Whips will be out to infract us for anything they can think of. Tucking into that ghastly mess in front of the whole school won us no friends.'

'I feel sick,' said Frecks. 'I'll never touch trifle again.'

Aching and unrefreshed, Amy got up.

The worst part was that nothing had changed.

It was a normal school day. She had to get dressed, wash and be presentable, then turn up for everything listed in her Time-Table Book. Rise, Breakfast (Refec), Assembly (Chapel), Double Geography (V4), French (D4), Dinner (Refec), Calisthenics

(Gym), Break (the Quad), English Composition (K4), Tea (Refec), Prep (Library), Supper (Refec), Activities (Common Room D), Lights Out.

Sleep, when it came, was troubled – again. Then the next day would be the same. And the day after that. And so on, until the last syllable of recorded time or the end of Summer Term – whichever merciful release came first.

The boxes in the grid were filled. Amy's presence was always required. In body and – strictly – spirit too. She had to pay attention. She was more liable than ever to be infracted for misbuttoning her blouse or tying an asymmetric knot in her shoelace. Light Fingers was right about predatory whips. The whole team were dogged by witches eager to mark a Black Notch in their Time-Table Books on the flimsiest of pretexts.

Being a ghost was no excuse.

And she *was* a ghost – a ghost among ghosts.

There were reminders.

At dinner, taking her pew at the Desdemona Fourth table, Amy reached for her glass tumbler and found a miniature toby jug in its place. Glancing around the Refec, she saw her teammates were similarly mocked. Instead of the usual lunchtime libations – thick milk or thin apple juice – the tobies were brim-full of cold custard.

Amy pushed the gunge away, until a whip – Bewe-Bude of Tamora – came round on inspection.

'Drink up, Desdemoaners,' she drawled. 'No one rises from the trough till you've emptied your jugs.'

Frecks gargled the custard down in a single quaff.

She gave a theatrical belch and wiped her mouth with the back of her hand.

'*All of you*,' insisted Bewe-Bude.

Light Fingers raised the toby in a mock toast and did something fast – then angled the jug to show the whip it was empty.

Amy got through her portion of shame in a few gulps.

She couldn't really taste it, but the oily sludge was horrible. She bit into pellets of dry chalky matter.

Other whips at other tables forced other team members to take the same medicine.

'Special treats for special girls,' said Bewe-Bude.

At the Desdemona Third table, Poppet Dyall – who had free places either side of and across from her – had already emptied her jug. She looked up at Ziss, the worst whip, and politely asked if she could have seconds.

Ziss went frost-eyed at that and wandered on. The rest of Dyall's table could breathe again, but the terror lasted for days. Each girl feared that when she was alone, Ziss might come back... and *whisper*. The whole school knew about – and dreaded – the whispers of tall, quiet, meticulous Heike Ziss.

A chalice of custard stood in Haldane's setting at the Whips' Table. Headers was absent. Her first ever infraction. Whisper was she'd done a bunk in the night. Hjordis Bok wasn't at table either. Her punishment would have to be taken on a tray to the Infirmary, where she was laid up with her wonky knee. Being *hors de combat* would not get her out of the custard.

At the Ariel Third table, Laurence made her portion disappear, jug and all – and not into her mouth. Dungate, standing over her, didn't know what to make of that. A voodoo stare dissuaded Dunners from forcing the issue.

If this continued, someone would toss custard in a whip's face. Or worse.

At Break, milling about on the Quad, the Moth Club were joined by Knowles and Devlin, who weren't among their regular intimates... but not by Larry, who was. After the famous wash-out, the team were in bad odour. Devlin and Knowles were brought to a midnight trial before Kyd, the Desdemona Fifth Form Captain. She ruled that no one on their corridor was to speak to them for a week. Then the situation would be reviewed. The banishment to Coventry might be renewed indefinitely. Kyd had no use for Unusuals before the Great Game and seized on the opportunity to give the flukes in her dorm an excessive pasting.

One floor below Kyd's domain, the regime was more enlightened. Alice Wright, the Desdemona Fourth Captain, had Inchfawn and Hoare-Stevens apple-pie the Moth Club's cots and let it stand at that. She said the team deserved sympathy rather than scorn. Wright had been in the Game last year and lost in the sewers. So far as she was concerned, *secundus* was a step up from the wooden spoon.

Amy would have preferred harsher treatment.

Occasionally, she spotted Laurence out of the corner of her eye.

Amy had an impulse to join the younger girl. To exorcise herself.

She didn't deserve her friends. She had let them all down.

Larry's voodoo stare was always directed at Amy. She was the only girl in school who blamed her as much as she blamed herself.

It was precious little comfort for either of them.

The Third was in exile. When Frecks blurted out 'Oh, *Larry*, what *have* you done?' she was devastated. To her, that not-really-meant remark was a banishment to a region far more remote than Coventry. Nothing could have hurt her more. Larry's appearance was in decline – her uniform less smart and neat, almost to the point of infraction. The odd neglected scrape or bruise suggested she was crawling – or being dragged – through bushes in her free time. She was as unhappy at school as at home.

Amy *ached* about that.

It was a mistake to think of Laurence as a pet or harmless encumbrance.

Amy hadn't told anyone about Sparks and what happened when her hand got caught in Larry's pocket. Was the change in the Draycott's girl permanent? Amy's guess (fear) was that it was. Sparks wasn't the Glove any more. She was no longer an Unusual. Hjordis Bok, for one, wouldn't be unhappy to hear that news. What with everything else, Amy didn't have enough free worrying time to fret over Larry's Application. She needed to talk about it with Light Fingers. Her friend thought deeply about the ins and outs of Unusuality. She'd have definite views on Venetia Laurence's new party piece.

That evening, at supper, Dr Swan announced the new Head Girl. Alicia Wybrew.

The Goneril tables erupted in spontaneous cheering. The Ariel tables were silent in shock. For the first time, Head Girl came from another house. If Dr Swan had swallowed a cat whole, it would have excited less comment. One fifth of the school saw a dangerous step towards Bolshevism.

The choice was popular with the other houses.

'If Good Egg Alicia'd been Team Captain, we'd have bagged *primus* for sure,' brayed Sieveright, the Goneril sharpshooter. 'She'd have picked a pukka side, not a load of flukes and foolies.'

At the word 'flukes', Light Fingers seemed to judder in her place… and Sieveright had a pocket full of custard.

She started up, yellow seeping from the trailing edge of her blazer, and froze – eyes on Kali, who'd casually adopted a fighting stance.

With her foot-boxing displays, Kali won a few grudging plaudits from the battlers of Goneril – who looked down on the misfits of Desdemona almost as much as they did the weeds of Viola.

'You and me in the ring, trigger-gal?' suggested Kali.

Sieveright ignored the custard seeping into her skirt.

'No dice,' she said, making a finger-pistol. 'Now, you and *Pinborough*. I'd lay half a crown on that with Nellie.'

Kali side-eyed the Blonde Bruiser, who was forking down a second helping of bangers and mash. A clique of fight followers always donated to her plate. Sieveright backed off.

The excitement of the Wybrew elevation trumped all.

Kali sat.

Light Fingers pointed to her eye, held up ten fingers, then made a Q shape with thumb and forefinger. Eye. Ten. Que. I Thank You.

'Nertz,' said Kali.

Amy sensed a shift in the mood of the school.

Wybrew as Head Girl was Something Else.

It wouldn't have happened without the Great Game and Haldane's decampment – expulsion? liquidation? – but it was *new* news. There were implications. The order of the school, as it had been since Founding Day, was changed. In the Ariel Common Room, this would be taken seriously. Privileges were under threat. Could Byrne, passed over again for a position that once seemed hers by birthright, maintain her jollity? If she stopped laughing, would she start screaming?

With Something Else to editorialise about, the Great Game slipped below the fold of the *Drearcliff Trumpet*... then off the Front Page... and shrank to the Other Notes.

Days passed.

Once or twice, Amy had a conversation of five minutes or more that was not wrapped up in the humiliation of *secundus*. Life Under Goneril was a big topic. Other situations and circumstances demanded attention. Frecks received a letter with a Humble College return address and was uncharacteristically shy about sharing its contents with her cellmates. She let slip that the signatory was the odious Geoffrey Jeperson. Amy worried her friend hadn't been properly alerted to the perfidy of the race of Humblebumblers and noticed Frecks didn't pay full attention when she retold the terrible tale of duplicitous Alfred Henry Wax. Light Fingers attempted a beauty mark to match Frecks' moveable spot, using soot and fixative from the chem lab. The formula was a recommendation from Sally Nikola of the Fifth... but the result was a little blemish that wouldn't be shifted by soap and water.

Amy applied herself to gerunds again, but got distracted when Gawky Gifford popped into her cell to claim the bounty of a farthing on a moth cocoon she talked up as a fabulous rare species. As usual, it was really a dried leaf rolled into a tube. The Gawk, always on the scrounge, had tried this several times before – and at least wasn't offended to be booted out unrewarded. She left behind the leaf, which unrolled to show a mould stain in the shape of a death's head.

Chatter often shut off when Amy rounded a corner. Some girls got up and moved away whenever she sat down. It was the same for the rest of the team – though Dyall had always been treated like this and didn't notice any difference. When Bok limped out of the Infirmary, she got into a habit of knocking glumly around at Break with her teammates. The all-rounder might have expected preferment in the rise of Goneril, but excuses were found to deny her a whip's braid. Bok hadn't been part of the Moth Club's extended circle – unlike the Unusuals Knowles and Devlin – before the Great Game. But there were things only the team understood.

Not just the loss. The girls of the House of Reform. The lads of Humble College. The Amphibaeopteryx. London fog. Lauriston Gardens and Villa DeVille.

All sorts of stories were in circulation. Knowles collected them.

The most persistent, pernicious rumour was that Amy had kissed a boy and thrown the Game. In the *Trumpet*, the parasitical editrix Shrimp Harper ran a cartoon depicting this mythical moment. Drawn by the talented Acreman of Viola, it was entitled 'The Big Smacker, or Kiss Those Tobies Goodbye'. The image made Amy's cheeks burn. She was even offended when girls said they didn't believe it because no boy would ever kiss Amanda Thomsett... though no boy *had*, because Geoffrey Jeperson's cheek spittle didn't count.

Not at all.

She must get that diary and start work on that verification. This was not a point she could let stick.

Other stories went around.

The Humblebumblers had bribed the Drearcliff Grange girls to stand back and give them a clear field. Primrose Quell and Prima Haldane were in it together all along, sworn in blood as sisters of a secret society that extended beyond houses and schools. They'd fixed the whole thing between them and were luxuriating together in Leamington Spa, gloating over the havoc they'd caused.

Some said Kali had kicked a policeman in the back of the head.

When Smudge Oxenford trotted that one out, Kali sneered, 'When I boot a bluebottle, I do it to his *face*!'

An elaborate theory was that Haldane was still on school grounds. She had been boiled down to replace the skeleton in the biology laboratory – though Lucy Lankybones had hung there since Founding Day, in a sorry state thanks to generations of infractors snaffling the odd tooth or knucklebone on dares. In another version, Headers was chained in caves under the cliff, waiting for the monthly high tide to drown her. Dr Swan visited regularly to gloat. The rumours persisted, even after a chauffeur – quite a dishy one, actually – showed up to collect the de-braided Head Girl's trunk. Helfrich and Saxby, competing flirts of the Fifth, tried to worm information from the liveried fellow, more as an excuse to have a go at fluttering about near an interesting man than out of any concern. The driver said Prima was being packed off to a Finishing School in Dusseldorf.

The other Absence was less noticed.

Miss Gossage was well and truly gone.

The Remove, which was her purview, only met for lessons two afternoons a week and every other Saturday morning. The outbuilding which was their study hall had been spruced up last summer. Once Temporary Classroom Two, it was now marked on the school map as the Conservatory. Amy and her fellow Unusuals were the core of the invisible class, which cut across year and house lines. A few fringe Talents – including Frecks and Kali – were also on the register.

Turning up at the Conservatory two days after the loss, the Remove found Miss Tasker in the Sausage's place.

She told them to sit quietly at their desks and get on with other work.

Amy looked around – there was Larry, still *staring* – and saw girls opening books and pencil cases. Unusuals who hadn't been on the team were lumped in with the pariahs. Fleur Paquignet, who had more sympathy with plants than people, stroked the flower-bearing vines that wound around the Conservatory's support poles. Picking up on the mood of the class, the plants were downcast and off colour. The Girl With Green Thumbs whispered soothingly in their ear-like buds, but they hadn't rallied. Polly Palgraive smiled as ever, a dead girl piloted by a worm in her brain.

Harriet Speke, a Viola Second, had hard-shelled hands, with eight dextrous pincer-tipped digits apiece. She could write four separate lines in different-coloured inks at the same time and was a whizz at picking locks. Next to her sat Gillian Little, a Goneril First who was six-foot four from stockings to crown and a yard across from shoulder to shoulder. Her yellow hair curled in stiff corkscrews like wood shavings and her pinafore was sturdy canvas so she wouldn't rip it too often.

And the others... Aconita Gould and Janice Marsh, the Scottish Wolf Girl and the American Aquatic Prodigy. Susannah Thorn and Dilys Frost, who ran hot and cold – one could make fire, the other ice. Jacqueline Harper and Poppet Dyall, the school leeches. Amy owed Harper a ragging for that Big Smacker cartoon, and floated her pencil case beyond her reach whenever she was distracted. Bizou De'Ath, an Ariel Fourth, drank vinegar to increase her pallor and dyed her hair raven-wing black. Of a macabre bent, she augmented her uniform with black-lace cobwebs and hairpins in the form of spiders and bats. Unorna Light, a Viola Fifth, claimed to be a white witch – she could cast all manner of terrible spells but was too much of a prig to do so.

Amy could relax slightly in the Remove. Most of these girls were already beyond the pale. If they'd hoped a victory in the Great Game would elevate the status of flukes, they didn't make a fuss about the way it had turned out.

However, Gould and Marsh – veterans of the year of the false trails – weren't notably more sympathetic to their successors. Amy didn't remember them being treated so shabbily, but they hadn't been given a bunfest in front of the whole school.

The next lesson of the Remove was the same.

Miss Tasker. Getting on with other work.

Amy sketched Death's-head Hawk wing designs. She'd see about getting Light Fingers to make a domino mask with the colouring. If she couldn't hack it as a true paladin, she should at least consider other options.

Even Smudge didn't dare speculate on the fate of the Sausage.

Miss Gossage was simply gone. No chauffeur came for her trunk.

Amy drifted, a ghost to herself. Her neck rash cleared up. Sometimes she thought she saw chalk lines on the floor. She occasionally floated objects, but became shy about using her Abilities. They'd been little help at the Finish. For the moment, it was best she stay curled up in her cocoon. She'd assessed her performance in the field and grounded herself. Rather than fly, she trudged.

Head down. Other work. Getting on with.

Saturday morning came.

III: Look to Windward

T HE CONSERVATORY WAS locked. Through grimy glass, Amy saw Paquignet's vines were dry and yellow, shrivelled without her healing touch.

A typewritten card was fixed to the door.

Lessons for the Remove will now be held in Windward Cottage – Dr Myrna Swan, Headmistress.

'Windward Where?' quizzed Frecks.

They all looked to Knowles.

Miss Memory frowned. She usually had the school map off by heart. After a dose of Dyall, Knowles' sense of place was topsy-turvy. Not yet fully undiscombobulated, she was frustrated to find her Abilities unreliable. Amy sympathised. Since the Great Game, she'd been leery of extending her mentacles. A massive part of any Talent was confidence. Theirs had taken a hard knock.

'The only cottage on school grounds I know of is Joxer's,' said Light Fingers. 'Even Headmistress wouldn't dare turn that into a classroom.'

The Remove had mostly turned up on time. Girls crowded around the Conservatory. Everyone wanted to read the notice for themselves – perhaps expecting to find secret writing in spaces between the words.

No one came away any the wiser.

'Is this some bally guessing game?' said Thorn hotly.

'More likely another rag,' said Marsh, gills rippling.

Regular outdoor Saturday morning activities continued. Goneril dragooned scratch cricket sides from other houses. The duffers would be bowled out double quick, then have to field for an age while sportists amassed tedious centuries. The Viola band practised a brass arrangement of ballet music that provoked riots in Paris before the Last War. The Queen Mary's Women's Auxiliary Army Cadet Corps practised rifle drill so as to be prepared for the next one. On the whole, lessons were preferable to all this brouhaha. Few in the Remove complained of the additional block in their Time-Table Books.

No staff were in view, so answers couldn't be sought from higher authority. Amy was surprised Miss Tasker hadn't showed up. She supposed the teacher was already snug in this mysterious new site, surveying an empty classroom and a register of twenty soon-to-be-infracted-for-tardiness names.

'I say we bunk off to the beach and make a driftwood fire,' said De'Ath. 'As an offering to the spirits of wind and water.'

'That would be begging for a blistering,' said Unorna Light. 'Fire is a primal, elemental force and should not be summoned lightly.'

De'Ath and Light did not get on.

Thorn clicked her fingers and made tiny flames dance behind Light's head. De'Ath giggled. Her high-pitched titter didn't go with her vamp look. She affected a low, breathy voice and put drops in her eyes to make them glow wickedly like Theda Bara's. But, when surprised, she laughed like a pickled hen.

Feeling a waft of heat, Light was cross but kept mum. She knew she'd missed a joke, but wasn't going to make herself more ridiculous going on about it.

'I could probably pick that lock,' said Amy.

'I *definitely* could,' said Speke, clacking her strange fingers.

Amy re-read the note from Dr Swan and decided breaking

and entering would be a bad idea. The Conservatory was out of bounds.

'There *was* a Windward Cottage,' piped up Devlin, extending her forefinger three inches. 'Only it's not been called that for ages and it's not really a cottage. You know the fair-sized old house up on the cliff, with the "Keep Out" signs and the twisted weathervane. *That* was Windward Cottage. No one's ever lived there.'

'You mean no one's lived there for years,' said Knowles.

'No... *never*. Sir Wilfrid Teazle started to build it for Jo Pike, the girl he named his ship after. It was to be their love nest. When she jilted him for that Welsh bard, he had the house finished then shut it up. He swore no one but Johanna would ever live under its roof. He put that in his will, with a clause entailing future masters of Drearcliff to abide by it... or else.'

'Or else what?' asked Kali.

'Something nasty and legalistic. And Cap'n Belzybub's curse.'

Logbooks found in the *Johanna Pike*, a full-rigged frigate discovered last year in the caverns under Drearcliff Grange, proved that the outwardly respectable Sir Wilfrid, Squire of Drearcliff Grange in the 1750s, was secretly the notorious pirate Belzybub. When raiding up and down the Severn Estuary, he dressed as a red devil and wore two twisted burning tallow horns on his sea-captain's hat. His crimson tunic and cloak were supposedly stitched from the tanned skins of murdered Welshmen – which suggested how well he took the news that he'd been chucked for Taffy the Poet.

Now Devlin mentioned it, Amy knew the house. So did everyone else.

It was just a short hike across the grounds. It was odd that the place was so seldom visited. A Keep Out sign would normally be taken as an invitation – luring girls to prohibited premises for secret feasts or ceremonies. Daring clots were always accepting dares to spend nights in forbidden caves, copses or attics. Invariably, they got pestered by woo-woo-wooing chums in sheets. It was strange that the Keep Out signs of Windward Cottage were taken seriously. In Amy's experience, girls got *everywhere*... especially where they were told not to be. Trespass might entail a Black Notch, but some bold pioneer always took up the challenge to plant a house flag where none had flown before.

However, no one wanted to be first to set foot in the home Johanna Pike never called her own.

'Is that even on school grounds?' asked Frecks.

Stretch shrugged. 'Drearcliff Grange used to be the Teazle Estate, when Sir Wilf was Squire of These Parts. Windward must be part of that. You'd have to go over the deeds to be sure.'

Devlin had a passion for tall stories of the sea. She'd retrieved the logbooks and other items of historic interest – but no treasure, sadly – from the wreck of the *Johanna Pike*, and was putting together a history of the Life and Crimes of Cap'n Belzybub. Knowles said there would be a market for such a book. She knew about publishing. Her father, Carleton Knowles, wrote complicated detective stories about impossible crimes – with scrupulously fair logical explanations in the last chapters that still felt like cheating.

'Shouldn't we hike to this Windswept Cottage before we get infracted for not being there,' suggested Frost.

'Windward,' corrected Devlin.

'Windward, Windswept, Wind-Up,' shrugged Frost.

Stretch wagged her long finger. Frost flicked droplets of ice at her.

It should have been the duty of the Captain of the Remove to lead the way, but that had ended up being undersized, unpopular Jacqueline Harper. Everyone knew to keep shy of Shrimp. Her Talent was draining the pep from anyone she latched onto. Dyall scrambled wits without meaning to, but Shrimp was a deliberate, calculating leech. She would find Count DeVille's cloak a perfect fit.

The other Sixths – Bok, Marsh and Frost – weren't inclined

to take command. Bok, knee thickly bandaged, had been turfed out of the Infirmary and sent to the Remove. The All-Rounder smarted at her exile, but gained a helpful familiar as Laurence experimented with a fresh crush. When stiff-legged Bok needed support to negotiate a door or stile, Larry was always handy. Frecks professed not to notice her former worshipper's new devotion.

As so often, it was down to the Moth Club to go over the top.

'You're the expert, Stretch,' said Frecks. 'Lead the way. The rest of us will fall in. Kali, watch for snakes in the grass. Come on, Amy. Give the sour face a rest...'

Amy didn't even know she was pulling a face.

She tried not to, which made it worse.

Devlin set off and the full register of the Remove – twenty girls – followed in a scattered crocodile. The Viola band interrupted 'Rites of Spring' to deliver a mocking, ragged 'Funeral March of a Marionette' as the Remove trooped past. *Te-tum-te-tum-titty-tum-titty-tum... Te-tum-te-tum-titty-tum-titty-tum... PARP!... Te-tum-te-tum-tum... Tum-te-tum-tum... Tum-te-tum-tum... Tum-titty-tum-titty...*

Gillian Little's tread shook the ground. Green bottles hanging on any wall near her would fall all at once, making for a short song and a lake of broken glass. The ogre-sized First was sweet-natured if babyish, but could damage property or people by sitting down thoughtlessly or flinging her arms out. What would she be like as a Sixth? Amy thought the Little Girl hadn't finished growing.

The Remove skirted the Dorms and marched between cricket pitches. Play stopped so girls of all houses could make unkind comments. After the Great Game, a licence to pick on the Remove was accepted. Amy suspected it would soon expire. Not a few of her classmates were the sort it was unwise to irritate. Nuisances were liable to be singed, frozen or foot-boxed. A lass brave enough to jeer at 'flukes' from fifty feet away in broad daylight might be more respectful if she found a snarling Aconita Gould at the end of her bed in the middle of a night of the full moon.

Early last year, during a school-wide crisis, the Remove had shown what they were capable of if they worked together. A year was an age in school life. So much had happened since the Reign of the Ant-Queen and the Dance of the Runnel and the Flute that even Amy sometimes recalled that winter term as a purplish dream. Other worries plagued her now.

North of the playing fields, beyond a thicket of uncoppiced trees, grassland gently sloped to the crumbling cliff edge. An outcrop once called Suicide Rock had been renamed Lamarcroft's Leap when the former Captain of the Remove executed a high dive from it to erase the spot's bad reputation. A notice prohibiting imitative feats stood in Lungs' honour.

Long grass was dotted here and there with blue and red wild flowers. Good moth country, though Amy had rarely explored this part of the grounds. Crossing the meadow, she wondered whether the shadow of Windward Cottage had put her off. She certainly didn't like the look of Sir Wilf's folly.

'Come on, leadfoot,' said Light Fingers. 'Race you there.'

Amy knew better than to take that bet.

Devlin strode through the grass. She literally stretched her legs – and her spine – till she was a head and a half taller than most of the girls wading after her. Paquignet stopped to coo at particular flowers, but Speke clacked crustacean fingers by her ears to remind her to keep walking. Little left crushed footprints wherever she trod.

Harper trailed along with Palgraive, the only girl she couldn't feed off. Palgraive's pep was long since spent and her puppeteer worm beyond Shrimp's draining. Even among Unusuals, they were flukes.

Here was Windward Cottage, the cage Cap'n Belzybub made for his faithless songbird.

When Sir Wilfrid, an ancient crock of thirty-seven, pitched unwelcome woo at her, Johanna Pike was barely older than Amy was now. No wonder she preferred her harp-plucking beardless bard. In those days, unmarried girls the age of Fifths or Sixths were written off as old maids.

Windward Cottage was what a grown-up would imagine a child would like. A life-and-a-quarter-sized wendy house. Big oval windows looked to sea, so the Cap'n's pining bride could scan the horizon for sight of his sails. The pretend home was spruced up – by Joxer, presumably – in anticipation of the Remove's arrival. The Keep Out signs were taken down. A path mown into the grass led to the front steps. The oversized door was freshly painted bright, inevitable purple.

The house was familiar. Part of the scenery.

But the last time Amy had seen the cottage wasn't at Drearcliff.

The ship-silhouette weathervane was fixed to the tallest chimney. Amy recognised it. The doll's house in the cellar of Villa DeVille was a miniature Windward Cottage. Exact in every detail.

Frecks, bringing up the rear, pushed past Amy and caught her hand, then dragged her towards the Remove's new classroom.

'Feet on the ground, old thing,' she said.

Without meaning to, Amy had floated off the grass. Frecks now tugged her like an errant balloon.

Stepping down to the ground, she let herself be drawn along the path towards the purple door.

'It doesn't look so bad,' said Frecks.

'Death traps never do,' said Amy. 'That's the point.'

Frecks gave her a cheer-up-you-clot squeeze. Over her friend's shoulder, Amy saw Larry – waist-deep in grass – giving her the voodoo stare, hands clamped over her middle as if she had a tummy ache.

'It can't be haunted,' said Frecks. 'No one has ever lived here.'

Amy would need to see a thorough report from the Hypatia Hall Psychical Investigation Soc before accepting that. Even then, with the Remove in the house – even if not overnight – several candidates for resident ghost would come forward. De'Ath might already have picked out the corners where she'd hang crochet cobwebs. If there was a cellar, there'd be a nice niche for Harper's dirt-filled casket.

Amy went with Frecks, towards the now-open door.

Five neat wooden steps led up from the path.

Most of the others were already inside.

Little had to scrunch and sidle to get into the house, and even then needed some help. Little often pulled off doorknobs and got stuck inside rooms – which set her off on crying fits, since she had an understandable funk about close spaces. Speke, sanguine about her own oddity, looked out for the huge First, deftly negotiating fiddly tasks for her. Speke was one of the Remove's better eggs.

Once Little was inside, Amy set foot on the steps.

Light Fingers poked her head out of the cottage, quivering. Standing still, she shook with excitement and flickered. If she vibrated fast enough, you could see wallpaper through her blur.

'Hurry up, slowcoaches,' said Light Fingers. 'Kali's defending our square!'

IV: Old Girl, New Miss

INSIDE, WINDWARD COTTAGE was mostly one big, airy room. Those porthole windows let in a lot of light. Chairs stacked against the back wall were the right size for Gillian Little, but too tall and thick for other girls. Doll's house furniture, Amy realised. The kitchen probably had a wooden play stove and a bin full of plaster loaves. Was there even a privy? Squire Teazle seemed to think women were indistinguishable from porcelain milkmaids.

Devlin was disposed to picture pirates as dashing Doug Fairbanks types, but Amy suspected Cap'n Belzybub was more like the gruesome boobies Mother brought home and introduced as uncles. A portrait of Sir Wilfrid posed in his red devil costume covered most of a wall. He stood on a foredeck, candles burning on his hat, cutlass in one hand, pistol in the other. By his side, Johanna was dressed as a curvy cabin boy. Their huge heads topped tiny bodies – reminding Amy nastily of toby jugs. No doubt Jo's saucy costume was the Cap'n's idea. The wench wasn't happy *en travestie*.

Ordinary school desks were set out in four rows of five. Amy knew the torture devices all too well. A lidded oak escritoire (with blackened hole for inkwell) bolted to an iron frame. A plank polished by generations of restless bottoms served as seat.

Their chief virtue was indestructibility. Manufactured in the era of the Great Exhibition and Wackford Squeers, the desks would still be in use when lessons were taught by tickertape and pupils came to school by monorail.

Drearcliff Grange tradition was to sit in houses, with alphabetical order within that grouping. The system was suspended in the Remove, which instead operated the principle of gold rush. Girls scrambled to stake favoured spots. Shunned spaces were left for those inclined – or encouraged – to keep their own company. Disputes were settled by whoever sat down first gripping her preferred desk with both hands and hissing.

Kali had bagsied a back corner for the Moth Club, fending off claim-jumpers with designs on this desirable region. Beyond the beak's sight line, it was perfect note-passing country. Opportunities for huddling and giggling were unlimited. Amy slid behind her desk. She had Frecks to the right, Light Fingers behind, and Kali over her right shoulder. A Moth Club square. In the Conservatory, Laurence positioned herself in front, semi-permanently turned in her seat, paying more attention to Frecks than Miss Gossage. Larry ostentatiously took a desk on the other side of the room – in front of Bok, of course.

Dyall – at Larry's prompting, Amy suspected – made a slow beeline for the desk on Amy's left-hand side. Mercifully, Bizou De'Ath got there first, not to be beside Amy but to secure an unimpeded view over Knowles' shoulder, an ideal position for a girl more inclined to copy another's work than do her own. To be polite, Amy nodded at her new neighbour, who ignored the gesture and concentrated on scratching a pentagram into her desk lid with a nail file. Amy's Talent troubled the would-be weird sister. De'Ath felt Abilities should be bestowed upon those who performed the proper arcane rituals, not allotted randomly at birth like hair colour or complexion. As it happened, she was unhappy with her lot in those departments too.

Speke and Little sat together at the front, eager for a teacher's benison. In a droller moment, the Sausage observed 'Little says little, but Speke speaks for 'em both.' When a question was asked, Speke's hand went up – all eight fingers wiggling and chittering. If she didn't know the answer, she'd take a hopeful stab. She once ventured that Keats' 'La Belle Dame Sans Merci' was 'probably a beautiful woman who never says "thank you"'. Asked a direct question, Little would blush crimson and whisper in her friend's ear. Miss Gossage set the chestnut about the single question which will identify the twin who always tells the truth and the twin who always lies. After Little whispered to her, Speke reported, 'Little would thump them both and ask "Who wants another poke in the nose?" The lying twin will be the one who says "me, please!" The truth-teller will be the one who says "no, thank you".' The Remove agreed the Alexandrine solution made as much sense as the one in the back of the book. That put such a smile on the Little Girl's face the Sausage hadn't the heart to overrule the consensus.

Paquignet, Palgraive and Dyall occupied the other front row desks. Dyall couldn't confuse Palgraive's worm. Amy had a moment of concern for Laurence, sat directly behind Poppet. A glance across the room – greeted by the voodoo stare – quashed her worry. Larry seemed to have invisible armour plating. If immune to Dyall, she might be proof against every Unusual in the room. After all, she could strip a girl of her Talent. Did she wonder whether Amy had shared her secret? She hadn't – yet.

Along with Kali and Light Fingers, the back row – popularly known as 'the Animal Kingdom' – was home to Gould and Marsh. Harper was at a far corner, urged with menaces to shuffle her desk out of formation.

'I think you're all horrid,' said Shrimp as her desk scraped floorboards.

'Further back, Remora Girl,' said Marsh.

Shrimp's desk bumped against the wall.

Marsh and Gould exchanged looks and shrugged.

'That'll have to do,' said Gould, drawing four sharp fingernails across her varnished desk lid. 'But if you so much as sniff, I'll take it out in patches of your hide.'

'Lovely, I don't think,' said Shrimp.

'And don't go battening on Bok,' said Marsh. 'She's Goneril, like us.'

Bok, hearing her name, paid attention. Gould made a potato-fist sign that Amy recognised as a secret Goneril salute. Bok reluctantly returned the favour.

'You'll all be sorry,' said Harper. She was Tamora, but couldn't expect support from Thorn, the Remove's only other specimen of that fierce house.

Gould growled at the Shrimp, and she stopped whining.

Thorn and Frost sat together in the second row, evening the temperature between them. Equally inevitably, the desks next to them were taken by Devlin and Knowles. All the pals acts sat together, in twos and fours. Light took in the only remaining spot – next to De'Ath. Amy suspected this was what the sorceress and the vamp preferred. Their enmity was as clubbish as the exclusive friendships of Thorn and Frost or Marsh and Gould. Hot and cold, fish and game, light and dark. Some opposites couldn't be kept apart.

The clatter and screech ended. The Remove had arranged themselves.

All eyes looked to the front. Where there should be a teacher.

Miss Tasker was tardy. Which was out of character. Her habit was to be early at her desk to watch girls file in sheepishly.

Other teachers let their audience settle, waited for the rustle of programmes to die down... then made a dramatic entrance. Miss Borrodale once began a lesson on propulsion by shooting an arrow through an open window into a target chalked on the blackboard. The nick in the slate was still there.

The Remove sat quietly for all of a minute.

Devlin stuck her neck out. Her head revolved like a lamp in a lighthouse. That put painful creases in her throat.

'Nope, no beak on the horizon,' she said. 'Though a new shipmate hoves into view.'

One of Stretch's more alarming party pieces was pointing by semi-popping her eyes, which swelled like eggs on the point of hatching. She aimed her egg-eye glance at the wall, between two big portholes, and everyone swivelled in their seats.

A girl stood there. Slight, slim, dark-haired. Her face was in shadow.

If she'd been there all along, no one had noticed. If she'd come into the room after the girls, no one had noticed that either. Which was a party piece in itself. Though *titchy* – as short as Shrimp Harper or Larry Laurence – she shouldn't have been able to slip past the huntress eyes (and nose) of Aconita Gould. Was her Ability fading into the woodwork?

Amy thought the undersized newcomer might be a Third. She wore skirt and blazer, but instead of the mandatory tie and house pin, she sported a gauzy red foulard and a white-gold cameo. The brooch showed a Victorian woman in profile, with piled-up hair.

'Egads, *multiple* uniform infractions,' said Speke, clacking. 'Better get a neck-rag on, chum-ess… before Miss shows up.'

The girl pushed away from the wall. Light fell on her face. She smiled, with only one side of her mouth.

Scarlet lipstick. White powder.

A blatant cosmetics rebel! No wonder she'd been Removed.

'Thanks for the warning, ah' – she glanced down at a maroon-bound register – '*Speke*, but I'm not afraid of Black Notches. I *am* Miss.'

That took a moment to sink in.

The young teacher walked to her chair, with a shimmy Amy suspected she couldn't help. Something was awry where her hip bone connected to her leg bone. She didn't limp like Bok or lope like Gould, but her gait was irregular. A crimson band held back her curly hair – as black as De'Ath wished hers was – giving her a Shakespearean expanse of brow. One side of her face was unmoving, but her half-smile put a crinkle in her left cheek.

No one would ever call her pretty, but she was *striking*.

Amy now recognised her. As did others.

'*Moria Kratides*,' blurted Gould. 'Good gravy…'

'Is *that* an infraction, Miss?' sniped Harper.

Girls were not permitted to use teachers' first names. To do so was to invite anarchy.

'Gould, Goneril, Sixth,' smirked Harper, prompting.

Miss Kratides' half-smile widened, showing a flash of teeth.

'No snitching in the Remove, *Shrimp*,' said the teacher.

A beak using a girl's handle – particularly a nickname meant unkindly – was so unheard of Amy wasn't even sure it was an infraction. Rules were for girls, not staff. Yet beaks, on the whole, abided by conventions as rigid as the Code of Break – the Charter of Chalk and Gown.

Frecks cheerfully introduced herself as such, though this last few months she'd let slip that her brother and a few other non-school intimates knew her as Seraph. Light Fingers was happy with her handle, and even proud of its larcenous implications. But Harper wasn't tagged Shrimp with affection. She *hated* the name. Whenever it was spat at her, she inked a black skull beside the spitter's name. At some point, the tally would be consulted and she'd exact her terrible vengeance.

Now Shrimp sat back, terrified.

Amy had often seen Harper cringing, sly or sulking – but not *afraid*.

She started remembering things about their new teacher.

Kratides had been a Tamora Sixth when Amy came to Drearcliff. Unusually, she wasn't a whip. Infractions held over from her earlier career disqualified her. She wasn't one of those soul-twisted creatures who delight in tormenting younger girls. That sort weren't barred from becoming whips. Indeed, predisposition to cruelty was often *qualification* for the tassel. Kratides earned her numberless Black Notches through acts of rebellion. She disregarded School Rules, damaged School property, disrupted School routine, departed School premises, and defied School staff. She famously picked a fight with the towering Stheno Stonecastle and kept getting up after being knocked down. At the end of Break, Miss Dryden had to dash water into Kratides' bloodied face to rouse her for a caning she can hardly have felt.

What was Dr Swan thinking – assigning the Remove to a teacher barely out of her teens? This Miss needed to pile her chair with cushions to see over her own desk. This class would test the patience of several saints and Moria Kratides was scarcely staff material. If Headmistress *had* to bring in an Old Girl to replace the Sausage, why not buy Lucretia Lamarcroft out of the Regiment of the Damned? The Remove would sit up and pay attention to the Amazonian Lungs. Tossing an outlaw pygmy into the classroom was an admission that they were beyond redemption.

Miss Kratides put her register on her desk and stretched like a cat.

Her chair wasn't a wood plank bolted to a desk, but on castors. As she stretched, it rolled back a little.

Why had Miss Kratides returned to a place she must have *hated*? She hadn't been away long enough to start lying to herself about jolly old girlhood days. She was, after all, still limping.

Prefects at Drearcliff Grange were called whips by tradition – their use of actual whips having been abandoned before the Boer War. For Moria Kratides, the lash was revived. After the Stonecastle fight, Sidonie Gryce – last year's most despised Sixth – took an antique riding crop from the Tamora trophy case and used it on the arch-Infractor. Half-smiling as she was flogged, Kratides drove Gryce into a frenzy. Her coven had to drag the witch away and calm her with lemonade. Was that how Miss Kratides' hip got injured? Afterwards, Gryce – whom Amy couldn't think of without tasting sick – left the insolent girl alone. Beaten, not broken.

By virtue of her *perfect* bad record, Kratides showed steel enough to be picked by Lamarcroft for the Great Game. Because she could fit easily through a manhole, she was packed off to the sewers to hunt mythical pigs. Everyone knew that ended badly. Kratides was not destined to be one of those *Girls' Paper* delinquents – 'Tessa the Terrible' or 'Contrary Jane' – who show true mettle after a teacher or an older girl has dished out a sound talking-to on the subject of School Spirit. Those prodigal heroines inevitably mend their ways in time to save the school goat from drowning in Wrackfall Weir or score a match-winning century after the Captain sprains her wrist. Given a chance to change her spots, Kratides turned out to be as almighty a dud as teachers said she was.

So she passed unhappily through Drearcliff Grange.

She might have been a more fitting prospect for Lobelia Draycott's House of Reform, though Lord knew the fate of persistent Infractors at Draycott's. Thumbscrews, at least. She wasn't an Unusual either.

The new beak kept her register open on the desk, but didn't call it.

If Miss Kratides knew Harper's nickname, she certainly knew who everyone was. She was prepared. Or thought she was.

A low *hum* started. Amy didn't know for certain, but Gould and Marsh, the eldest and most arrogant of the Remove, usually began this lark. The hum spread like fire in dry bracken, taken up by De'Ath and Light, then Thorn and Frost. Kali, Light Fingers and Frecks hummed. Amy joined in.

It was a ritual. Laid down in the Code of Break.

If a teacher can be broken, she should be. It was the duty of the class to give her the Treatment. Some – Miss Downs and Miss Borrodale – were too wily and iron-willed to fluster. Others – Miss Gossage – were too well-liked to merit more than token ragging. Ninnies who flew into tizzies were more entertaining. Making Miss Dryden go red and say 'oh really really really *really*' or shrill her whistle was practically on the curriculum. The drolly sinister Wilding triplets once swapped her whistle for one without a pea so her puff was wasted on futile silent tooting. The blonde trio didn't own up, and the whole year was infracted for the prank. Some didn't reckon the jape worth the hour of extra pull-ups, and the Wilding Girls were ostracised at Break for months.

The hum continued. Amy felt it in her cheeks and nostrils.

This could go too far. Last year, Dr Swan hired Mrs Flora McMichaels to teach mathematics. She'd survived as a message-runner in the trenches, but a clique of Tamora Fifths, led by the callous Crowninshield II, made a blubbing wreck of her. Whenever she turned her back, Crowninshield's cronies banged their desk lids. When she turned around, they left off and were attentive, smiling angels. Mrs McMike didn't last a term. Lessons reminded her too much of Hun bombardments. For her, the Treatment was a Test to Destruction. Amy hadn't been in the rowdy lessons but felt sickly shame about the woman's fate. Only a few Fifths were actively guilty, but Amy thought the remainder of the class – who'd sat silent while a decent beak got a barracking she didn't deserve – were almost as currish.

As a girl, Miss Kratides had been a hummer, a desk-banger and worse.

As a beak, she was on the other side of the Treatment.

This ought to be interesting.

A tipping point with the mass hum was reached. Girls who didn't join in immediately – because they were out of sorts with the rest of the Remove, predisposed to good conduct, or fearful of getting stuck with Black Notches – had to make a snap choice. Be a sheik or be a sneak. Everyone except Palgrave – too weird to count – took the side of the Mess against the Miss. Who *wouldn't* want to be a sheik? Even Shrimp Harper, who hated everybody, contributed a nasal, vicious vibration. When good-natured Little added her comb-and-paper honk, the Kratides cause was wholly lost.

This form of the Treatment could be dished out by girls who appeared to be sitting obediently. At least the mass hum was done to a teacher's face. Ragging a junior beak only when her back was turned was cowardly.

An epic hum, sustained properly, could rattle windows as well as nerves.

Amy felt the thrill in her sinuses.

Miss Kratides half-smiled at the class.

She had dark eyes. Greek eyes.

Assassin's eyes, Amy thought.

The teacher stood and walked around her desk. She drew in breath and began to hum herself – louder and at a higher pitch than the combined chorus of the Remove. She placed her hands on the desk in the middle of the front row and looked over Paquignet's centre parting, directly into the guilty Susannah Thorn's face... and hummed all the more. Her face seemed to expand.

Little sputtered into a giggle, gulped the wrong way and stopped humming.

Amy's hum died in her mouth. As one, the Moth Club shut up.

The tipping point came again, and tipped the other way.

Uncommitted hummers quit and pretended they'd not been part of it. Most of the second row, where Miss Kratides directed her attention, kept it up on principle. Gould and Marsh pulled out of what they'd begun. Harper, stung by teacher calling her Shrimp, kept going, louder and whinier than ever, gripping her desktop. Her range of draining expanded. Bok turned to swat the nuisance with a rolled-up exercise book. Harper's leech-tipped mentacles must have brushed her hackles. That took them both out of the hum.

A stubborn square persisted – Thorn and Frost, De'Ath and Light.

And Miss Kratides.

Who could breathe and hum at the same time.

That took practise.

De'Ath and Light shut up.

Miss Kratides gave her full Counter Treatment to Thorn and Frost.

The Unusuals weren't just humming. Smoke curled from Miss Kratides' shoulders and ice formed on her brooch. She was warmed and cooled at the same time. Thorn and Frost could break glass with their combined party pieces.

Still Miss Kratides *hummed*.

She let go of Paquignet's desk and twirled – lithe enough to make Amy wonder whether she was shamming her semi-limp – to face the class again, raising her hands as if she held conductor's batons.

She nodded – and her eyes opened wide, showing whites all around the pupils. Huge, dark, magnificent eyes! Theda Bara eyes! Medusa eyes!

Now she was *insisting* on the hum.

Black Notches for those who didn't join in!

Speke and Little, seeing it as a game, gave full throat. Devlin, reconfiguring her tonsils, positively hooted. Amy and the Moth Club harmonised. That prompted Gould and Marsh to start up.

Miss Kratides stopped humming now she was in control. She walked up and down in front of the class, spotting those who weren't contributing and pointing lightly, bringing them in like reserves. She even prevailed upon Palgraive to emit a keening whine almost too high for the human ear. Somewhere near, dogs would be driven mad.

Miss Kratides could breathe freely.

And the whole class had to keep humming.

Amy felt strain in her diaphragm. She had the beginnings of headache. She glanced at Frecks, whose eyes were shut as tears coursed over her cheeks. The class grimly hummed on, through clenched teeth, out of nostrils and ears.

Thorn and Frost weren't using their Talents any more. It was all they could do to keep up the hum. Miss Kratides flicked flecks of rime off her brooch.

The teacher posed, waving like a bandleader.

Her eyes were warm. To her, this was hilarious.

It struck Amy that Miss Kratides might have *invented* the

Humming Treatment. It was certainly in use in her day. Trying to use it against her was as stupid as challenging Robin Hood to an archery contest or entering a Viola Firsts' Tug-o'-War side against long-armed Lord Piltdown.

Amy thought her eardrums might burst.

De'Ath pressed her cheek onto her desk and gripped tufts of her own hair. She was purple in the face. Not the complexion she aspired to.

'*You*,' said Miss Kratides, pointing to Dyall – taking in Larry, Bok and Harper behind her – '"Glorious Things of Thee Are Spoken"!'

The row began humming the hymn. It was returning to services after being out of favour for sharing a tune with the German National Anthem. The higher notes were a challenge.

'*You*,' said Miss Kratides, pointing to Speke – and Devlin, Frecks and Kali – '"On Yonder Hill There Stands a Maiden"!'

That side of the class took up the old song.

'*You, you* and *you*,' she said to Little, Paquignet and Palgraive, '"The British Grenadiers"… "I Wish I Could Shimmy Like My Sister Kate"… "D'Ye Ken John Peel"!'

Everyone followed orders.

Amy tried her best, humming along with '*Some talk of Alexander, and some of Hercules…*' in her head.

Cacophony ensued.

If anyone flagged, Miss Kratides pointed at them and they had to make a greater effort.

Little stopped humming and made hunting noises. '*T'was the sound of his horn, that would waken the dead…*'

Palgraive's worm can't have paid attention to human songs, and screeched as the row behind her did their best.

Girls coughed, croaked, screamed and fell silent, too exhausted to rejoin the choir.

In the mass hum, Amy heard a jumble…

Saviour, if of Zion's City I through grace a member am… Ranter and Royal and Bellman and True… of Hector and

Lysander and such great names as these... she wobbles like a jelly on a plate... I will court her for her beauty... fading is the worldling's pleasure... who know no doubts and fears... all the boys are going wild... from the drag to the chase... she must answer yes or no... from the chase to the view... oh no John... from a view to the death... no John no... in the mo-o-o-o-rn-ing!

One by one, or in whole rows, girls gave out.

Amy wasn't the last in the game.

Devlin, with her pliable throat, and Bok, with grim determination, hummed longest.

Then even they could hum no more.

Amy looked about the Remove. Girls were bedraggled, smear-faced, wild-haired... tie knots pulled loose or drawn tight, shirt tails out of skirts. All infractions. Frost was blue in the face. Thorn was steaming. Frecks' beauty mark had come unglued.

Only one hum resonated. Amy turned.

Light Fingers sat comfortably, at her ease, still holding the tune.

She was used to the vibration – if she could breathe while moving quickly, she could keep up her hum while all about her fell.

Having outlasted the rest of the class, she reached the end of the song... '*May they and their commanders live happy all their years, with a* tow, row, row, row, row, row *for the British Grenadiers!*'... and stopped.

Miss Kratides applauded politely.

'Remove, we have had our first lesson together,' she said. 'You have learned something about me... and about yourselves.'

She gave them a moment to tuck in shirts, adjust ties and smooth hair.

'If you will open your desks, we come to the *second* lesson...'

Amy gingerly lifted the lid, half thinking Miss Kratides might have hidden a snake-in-the-box toy inside.

Written in red, red ink on the underside of the lid was...

Thomsett, Amanda.

Gasps and other expressions of amazement from all around.

The Remove were sat in a different configuration in Windward Cottage than in the Conservatory. Larry's migration across the room had thrown the pattern out. Girls took places as they pleased. No one told them where to go.

But Miss Kratides had known where they would sit.

Almost perfectly.

She had Thorn and Frost in each other's places. Both were too sheepish after the humming ordeal to crow over the understandable error. She didn't force the issue by having them change desks.

'There are envelopes for each of you,' said Miss Kratides. 'In your desks.'

Amy found hers. Thorn and Frost exchanged theirs.

'Inside your envelopes are two secrets. One is yours, one belongs to another girl in the class. I expect you to find out who holds your second secret. To this end, you are free to use any means at your disposal. Espionage, deduction, intuition, intimidation. We will discuss your progress next week, when each of you will report to me for an individual tutorial. Please, and taking care *not* to let your neighbours peek, open the envelopes... *now!*'

Amy opened the ungummed envelope and slid out a card.

It had been written on in red ink, too. The copperplate suggested the most infracted girl in the history of school at least deserved high marks for penwomanship.

You are right to be afraid of the Broken Doll.

She will blame you for not telling what you know about Laurence.

Exclamations rose from around the classroom. Several girls looked as if they'd been slapped. Knowles said 'that's not true' in exactly the tone of someone admitting that it was. De'Ath squeaked – a suppressed sob only the girls either side of her could hear – and then glared ferociously at Light, clutching her card to her chest. Little tried to show Speke her card, perhaps because she needed help understanding – or even reading – what was written on it. Speke warded her off with a wave of crab-leg fingers. No one else wanted to share… and no wonder.

Of course every girl in the Remove had a secret. More than one, probably. Everyone had secrets. The girl who went around telling everyone what they should know about herself was Prima Haldane, and she had fled. Shared confidences were precious tokens of friendship, but keeping mum about some things was good sense and, furthermore, good manners. Amy realised Miss Kratides had infected the class with a deadly suspicion, at least for the next few days. Miss Gossage never set prep like this. Even innocent secrets could do a lot of damage if they came out.

Several of Amy's uncles had slunk off after Mother told them, 'It's not that you did *that thing*… it's that *you didn't tell me*.' In every case, the issue absolutely was that the rotters had done that thing. Uncle Simon borrowed the Wedgewood dinner service on the pretence of finding a match for a chipped plate then pawned it to buy a banjo. Uncle Peasegood was seen boarding the Brighton train with a barmaid from The Hand and Racquet when he was supposed to be spending Bank Holiday weekend in Troon attending an ailing Archbishop.

Amy pressed her card face down on the desktop.

Miss Kratides showed no concern.

Thorn's card burned in a flare. She stuffed the black ashy bits into the inkwell.

'Get out your Time-Table Books and pens,' said Miss Kratides. 'From Monday, the Remove will meet every afternoon, here in Windward Cottage. I advise you to cut Break short and be here at half past three sharp. Tardiness on the part of any girl will mean Black Notches for the whole class…'

Hisses of disbelief.

'Absence, for any reason other than death or dismemberment, will result in *expulsion* – without refund of fees. Those of you who have mummies or daddies will have an idea how such news would be received at home.'

Hands went up. Miss Kratides ignored them.

'These aren't my rules, so don't try to debate them with me. If you have complaints, Dr Swan will receive you. I can assure you, from unhappy personal experience, that there will be little profit in visiting the Swanage with a moan. Headmistress is perfect. The school is perfect. Any complaint, therefore, is an indication that the complainant is in error… which, when you are facing Myrna Swan, is not a comfortable situation.'

Hands went down.

'Score through whatever lessons you used to have in that slot,' continued the teacher. 'From now on, in that period, you'll be mine. I have posted a schedule for personal tutorials. These will be a great part of your future education. Dr Swan has faith in the potential of the Remove – in each of you. She also has concerns that a drift to slackness has put that potential at risk. We are all going to see a lot of each other and we are all going to *learn our lessons*.'

Amy realised everything had just changed. Again.

V: Secrets

AFTER SUPPER THE Moth Club convened an extraordinary meeting. Only one item was on the agenda: Miss Kratides' Game of Secrets. Amy's envelope was snug in her inside front blazer pocket. Light Fingers was last to sit at the baize-topped folding table that barely fit into the square between their cots. She'd nipped around the dorms double-fast, to see how others in the Remove were faring.

Knowles, ash-faced, peeped into the cell and asked casually if anyone had seen Devlin. No one had. Desdemona Fifths seldom had reason to visit the Fourth corridor. The visitor lingered on their threshold a moment longer than necessary, but didn't volunteer any secrets or boldly ask after theirs. The Moth Club didn't ask Knowles in or shoo her off, just waited. Unsatisfied, she drifted away, muttering as she did when crammed facts poured out of her mind like flour through a sieve.

Kali got up and firmly shut the door, then returned to her place.

'Devlin's on the sick list, by the way,' said Frecks. 'She's had a relapse and come over all floppy again.'

'I'm surprised Knowles doesn't know that,' said Amy.

'She does,' said Frecks. 'That was a fishing expedition.'

'So was my night patrol,' said Light Fingers. 'Miss Kratides said espionage was allowed. We live in a glass house now.'

In only one lesson, their new teacher had turned all the Remove into twitching snoops.

Light Fingers reported that Frost and Thorn were on the outs. Amy supposed they'd been given each other's secrets and whatever was written on their cards was shocking enough to blot their friendship. Conversely, De'Ath and Light were in a huddle, negotiating on terms of new intimacy. If they'd exchanged secrets, the swap brought them closer together rather than drove them apart.

'Psychological warfare,' said Light Fingers. 'To set us against each another. Miss Kratides' secrets don't even have to be the truth to hurt.'

'Though they sting more if they are,' said Frecks.

'Yes,' said Light Fingers. 'In my case, it is and it does.'

'It could be that telling the truth in the first secret is a way of getting you to believe the second,' suggested Amy.

'That's too clever by half,' said Kali.

'Which wouldn't be half as clever as Moria Kratides thinks she is,' said Frecks. 'The woman can hum, I'll give her that. But who's to say about the rest of it? Wasn't she a duffer as a girl?'

Frecks, for once, didn't sound convincing.

'She didn't knuckle under,' said Light Fingers, 'but that doesn't mean she was a Dim.'

'I'm not sure I even understand my secret,' said Amy.

'But is it true?' Frecks asked.

Amy thought about it. 'The wording is odd. It's not something concrete, like water is wet or lollipops are sweet…'

'You don't say,' put in Kali, pantomiming astonishment.

'I'm told I'm right about something… No, I'm told I'm right to *feel* something about something. It's not a clear-cut true-or-false secret like "the diamonds are hidden in the chandelier" or "Uncle Frewin already has a wife in Canada".'

'*For example*,' prompted Frecks.

'Yes, for example,' said Amy. 'On top of that, my second

secret is a double conundrum. Oh, I think it's about you, Emma.'

Light Fingers wasn't shocked.

'My second secret definitely *isn't* about you,' she said. 'I mean, I don't think it possibly could be. No offence.'

'None taken.'

'So they're not all straight swaps,' said Frecks. 'Miss Kratides has mixed things up to make it more amusing. How delightful. I can see this game catching on at weekend parties... like the country house dos in Carleton Knowles books, where the host turns up dead under the compost heap and everyone has a motive but nobody could have done it.'

Amy kept touching her envelope, then pretending she had an itch under her arm which needed scratching.

'Ah, this is Nicholas Ridicholas,' said Kali, slapping her card down. 'Come on, kittens, follow suit. We won't get any shuteye unless we put all our cards on the table.'

Frecks put her card down too – white side up, like Kali's.

Light Fingers matched them.

They all looked at Amy. Going last in this game made her friends think she was hiding something terrible.

Which she didn't think she was.

'Fess up, Amy,' said Frecks.

'Yeah, full house or no house,' said Kali, hand over her card.

Amy opened her blazer and fished her secrets out of her pocket with a mentacle.

'Show-off,' said Frecks.

She was too clumsy to open the envelope without using her fingers. Two weeks ago, that would have been a simple party piece. Since the Great Game, the trick was beyond her.

She slipped her card out and laid it down carefully.

They all took deep breaths.

'Ready,' said Kali.

'Steady,' said Frecks.

'Aim,' said Amy.

'*Fire!*' said Light Fingers.

A moment's hesitation, then a turning-over of cards. The Moth Club sat back with arms crossed, waiting for the ceiling to fall.

Amy knew her own secrets.

You are right to be afraid of the Broken Doll.

She will blame you for not telling what you know about Laurence.

Now she read the others – as they read hers.

Light Fingers had:

You refuse to visit your father in prison.

She could use her Talent to heal the sick – but won't.

Kali had:

Your mother is alive.

Her father makes plans to murder her.

Frecks had:

You hate your blessing.

She has cause to hurt you all.

They all looked at each other.

'It's true,' said Light Fingers, with relief. 'I stopped visiting Dad last term. I know I shouldn't, but I blame him for being where he is. Not Mum so much... but Dad... He was a headliner. He performed before the King and Queen in the Royal Variety Show. He didn't have to be a crook. You don't hear of Nervo and Knox or the Tiller Girls making off with the silverware or shoving heirlooms under their shirts. With all his Talent, the best Application Dad could think of was burglary. Not Robin Hood, but a sneak thief. Smiling as he lifted jewels. Stealing from awful people, sometimes. But also from folk who were nice to him, invited him to their homes. He didn't steal for the money, even... but for the thrill, to puff himself up, to show up the slowcoaches. Dad never makes or gives or adds anything... just takes trinkets and sells them cheap. Meeting his fence made me see that. Runcorn Fowley, of Fowley, Fowley and Wisk, Antiques and Estate Clearances. He was at the trial every day. He gave me his card and asked if I planned on taking over "the family business".

Then he smiled, showing his real face for a fragment of a second. Another thing I've not told you is that I've a new Application. My eyes are fast. I see people's real faces, expressions that just show in a flash. People give themselves away. Then they cover up, and put on a sham. Fowley's real smile was a leer. Remember the old man on the beach that time when we were in our bathing costumes and wet and shivering? Fowley's real smile was like his. You were right to kick the old man where you did, Kali. Fowley's smile made me knot up inside. I knew then I wasn't like Dad and didn't want to be. I've been thinking of joining the Women's Auxiliary Police when we leave school. Dad'll disown me, but I'll feel better. I think I have to make up for him.'

Amy, Frecks and Kali were stunned. They'd had no idea how their friend felt.

'Sorry,' said Light Fingers. 'I'll pipe down now.'

Frecks hugged her and kissed the top of her head.

'Do you hate your handle now?' asked Frecks. 'Because of criminous connotations?'

'Not at all,' said Light Fingers. 'Too late to change anyway.'

'I hope that's not true,' said Frecks.

Amy wondered whether Frecks would prefer to be called Seraph.

'Kratides is right about the coif, if you doubted it,' said Frecks. 'Snaky as she be, our new Miss ain't been caught in a lie... yet.'

'But your blessing protects you,' protested Amy.

'On its own terms, which ain't mine. The Lady in the Lake is a colossal prig and her gifts are more nuisance than not. Paladins lumbered with her patent dripping wet swords, shields or magic drinking horns all totter off to bad ends, you'll have noticed. That went for the original Round Table Mob as much as for the prawns of Pendragon Squadron. The wire-wool is ruination on the hair and has scabbed up my lugholes. See...'

She lifted her locks to show slight reddening of the ears.

'I wouldn't notice,' said Light Fingers.

'You would. Honest. The blessed thing protects me from all

harm… except when it decides to teach me a lesson and harm me itself.'

Frecks turned to Kali and said, 'So… Ma alive, then?'

Kali shrugged. 'Hold the front page… I've had a letter smuggled out of a lamasery in the Himalayas. The Ma'am says she's lying low there. When Dear Old Dad sent her to the chopping block, she sweet-talked the family *fakir* into spiriting her out from under the scimitar and spiriting in some other disposable dame. No one looks too close at the face on a lopped-off noodle, it transpires. I'd have spilled sooner, but the tea smelled too sweet to drink straight off. I suspected a long con and had ideas about the grifter who might be working it – an individual who has the same last name as me. Word from Miss Kratides that the Ma'am's still got a hatstand on her shoulders is credible corroboration. If I didn't half believe before, I do now. All the way.'

Amy realised her friends were looking at her.

Not only were their cards on the table – they'd explained their first secrets.

'So what's this Broken Doll?' asked Frecks.

'I don't really know,' said Amy.

The rest of the Moth Club had speeches – almost prepared. She had a bad dream she only vaguely remembered.

'You had a doll when you came to school,' said Light Fingers. 'A doll that got… if not broken, then ripped a bit.'

Amy remembered all too well. Roly Pontoons. A keepsake of her father. Cruelly treated by – ugh – Sidonie Gryce and her Murdering Heathens.

'Not him,' said Amy. 'You sewed his arm and leg back on. He's safe in my trunk.'

She had a guilt pang. Once, she couldn't sleep without Roly Pontoons on her pillow. Her private superstition was that he anchored her to her bed. Without the stuffed clown, she might turn insubstantial and float through coverlet, ceiling and attic – then rise into the night sky until the air became too cold and thin to breathe. If Mother tidied Roly away on a shelf, she'd throw a fit. On her first night at Drearcliff Grange, Amy watched in horror as the elder Crowninshield ripped off Roly's limbs. He was invisibly mended, but not the same. The doll was thrown in with books she didn't need any more and shoes she'd grown out of. She'd not thought of him in months.

'This doll is china, not cloth,' she told the Moth Club. 'Old-fashioned, like something from when Mother was a girl. I don't know where I heard of her. Or anything else about her, really.'

'But you're *afraid* of her?' asked Frecks.

Amy thought of her friend as fearless. Which made her think of herself as timid.

'I don't know,' she said. 'I might be. I suppose it's a silly secret.'

'That's not what's on the card,' said Light Fingers. 'As you said, "the wording is odd". The secret isn't that you're afraid of the Broken Doll, it's that you're *right* to be afraid of the Broken Doll.'

The lights went out and Amy jumped.

At Lights Out, Kaveney – the Desdemona House Captain – yanked a master switch and turned off the electricity throughout the dorms. Then she patrolled the corridors with a battery torch, ensuring all were properly a-bed.

'Get your feets under them sheets,' shouted Kaveney. 'Up early for Chapel.'

Loud groans from Peebles Arbuthnot's cell next door.

Amy shivered, glad she couldn't be seen.

Ghost squiggles – in the shape of electric-light filaments – danced across her vision. She got used to the dark and blinked. Across the table, where she knew Frecks was sitting, a white oval appeared. Across it – a forked crack. Around it – long, dark hair. No, shadows in the *shape* of hair. Velvet black against matt black. In the oval, live eyes opened. Deep, liquid, cunning. Amy was looked over. Unkindly.

The Broken Doll knew her. Knew her for what she was.

A fraud and afraid... No paladin, no exemplar of School Spirit.

A curse. A pest. No Glory. A Death's Head.

She couldn't move a muscle. She couldn't move a mentacle.

A lighter flared. Kali lit an emergency candle.

Frecks – with uncracked face and red hair – sat across from Amy. No one else – nothing else – had taken her seat. Amy saw concern spark in her friend's eyes.

'Are you with us?' she said, snapping fingers under her nose. 'Or wandering off in the wild woods?'

Amy turned to Light Fingers and asked, 'Did you see *my* real face?'

'You don't have a false one. Your face always tells the truth. Even when you wear a mask.'

'I've been meaning to talk about that. I've had a thought...'

Frecks rapped the table.

'Matters in hand, Moth Clubbers,' she said. 'Our secrets are shared and need no further discussion. That's not the whole story. We could do with hours and hours of further discussion, and I don't doubt we'll get to that – but for the moment we've only addressed the first secrets. The easy ones. The set prep is the *second* secrets. The tricky dickies. Unless I mistake myself, which I think not to be the case, we're no wiser as to any of them.'

'Amy, you thought your second secret was about me,' prompted Light Fingers.

Amy was uncomfortable.

'I saw *that* face,' said Light Fingers. 'I said you were no good at hiding your thoughts.'

'I spotted the tell too,' said Frecks. 'An almighty Siegfried leaf. Come on, cough up...'

'What do you know about Laurence you think I'll blame you for?' said Light Fingers.

Kali moved the candle nearer her. Now Amy felt like a culprit, hauled in for the third degree. Light Fingers leaned forward.

'You'll make a good policewoman,' Amy told her.

Light Fingers nodded. 'Nice, but no answer.'

Amy sighed and talked. 'Something happened in the Game. To

a girl from Draycott's. Poll Sparks. Alias the Glove. An Unusual. A Wrong 'Un. She did for Bok's knee.'

'I've heard of her,' said Light Fingers. 'Packs a punch.'

'*Not any more*,' said Amy. 'She stuck her glove where she shouldn't have… Into Larry's pocket. When she pulled her fist out again, she wasn't a Wrong 'Un any more. She wasn't hurt. Not immediately. But her Talent was gone.'

'For good?' asked Frecks.

Amy shrugged. 'I think so. She lost her glove in the Purple. Her hand was electric when it went in and ordinary when it came out.'

Light Fingers sat back, thinking. Her expression went blank. Since discovering what flashes of feeling could give away, she must have worked hard on showing a wooden face.

'And I'll blame you for not telling me?'

'I know how you feel about Unusuals and Ordinaries, Emma. You've gone on and on and on about it. Larry can turn one into the other.'

'I'd like to see her fit Gillian Little in her pinny pocket,' said Kali.

'If she tried, I think she could,' said Amy.

'And, what? Little would come out *little*?'

'Ordinary size for her age. Yes, I think so.'

'It might be a kindness,' said Frecks.

'Says the paladin who wants to pawn her magic hat,' said Light Fingers.

'I wasn't getting at you,' said Frecks. 'I mean no harm.'

'Of course you mean no harm. You never mean harm, Seraph, but sometimes – just sometimes, not often and with no ill intent – you *do* harm. Just pinpricks. But done all the same. I'll bet that's why your ears chafe. Your blessing *knows*, and pays you back.'

'Is this what Miss Kratides wants?' asked Amy. 'Us tearing each other to shreds?'

'Quite likely,' said Light Fingers. 'But cards are on the table, and we have to finish the hand. Amy, yes, I *am* annoyed you kept this to yourself...'

Amy felt a clutch of shame.

'But I can't blame you. Your second secret isn't mine. Think about it. *"She will blame you for not telling what you know about Laurence."* You *have* told me. You've told all of us. *Now*, in the present. I *might* have blamed you if you'd kept it under your hat and I found out about it another way... but now I won't. I will not blame you in the future. The secret means *someone else* will. That girl has a card with "You will blame her for not telling you what she knows about Laurence" written on it and is wondering what the jenkins it means.'

'If I tell the whole Remove next week – get up and make an announcement – can I get out of it?'

'Is that fair on young Larry?' said Frecks.

'Who cares,' said Kali. 'There's more than one limpet's tender feelings at stake. I like how Amy's thinking. Go all out on the offensive.'

'It's a secret, not a prophecy,' said Light Fingers, shaking her head.

'It feels like foretelling,' said Amy. 'Not a mystic one, but a clever one. Remember Miss Kratides knew where we'd all sit in Windward Cottage. She worked that out. Probably on a board, with chess pieces. That's the kind of thinker she is. Headmistress hired her despite her Black Notches. I reckon she's a top brain. A mastermind, even. She's got a high forehead behind that crimson band. She observes and makes calculated guesses. She's not always right – she got Frost and Thorn mixed up, remember – but she's thought all this through. We're chewing over our secrets. Maybe that's her way of stopping us trying to get at hers.'

'If you made your announcement, how do you think Larry would feel about you?' said Frecks.

'No worse than she does now, in case you haven't noticed.'

It was Frecks' turn to flash a real face for a moment.

She double-knocked the table. Crushes were not spoken of. No teasing on the subject was permitted within the Moth Club. The double-knock – a recognised signal for expanding the agenda – accepted Laurence as a topic for discussion.

'Since it's been raised… yes, I have noticed Larry is no longer our Moth Mascot, and that's my fault. I know exactly what I said and when I said it. My *blessing* gave me grief for it, like a hot coal down the back of the neck. We were none of us at our best at the Finish, but – still – I was thoughtless, and – thank you *so much* for pointing it out, Emma – I can hurt people without meaning to.'

Kali waved the sincere confession away. 'Ahh, balloon juice. Pinny Pocket got off easy. She blew the Game for us all, handing over three tobies to some rubberface any smart mug would peg as a rat a mile off. She shoulda got a slapping for it.'

'That's not fair,' said Amy. 'What she did was because of me. A.H. Wax fooled me first. I told Larry to trust him. I've tried to make amends, but she doesn't want to know. Can't say I blame her.'

'My second secret,' said Frecks. '*She has cause to hurt you all.* Is that Larry?'

'Or Shrimp,' said Light Fingers. 'Or Palgraive, or Palgraive's worm, or whatever combination of the two sits on the front row posing as a living person?'

'Could *she* be your Broken Doll?' suggested Frecks.

Amy didn't think so. Palgraive was flesh not china. Surely one girl couldn't be the answer to two secrets? Unless the game was more fiendish even than it appeared.

'*Her father plans to murder her*?' mused Kali. 'If that was on any of *your* cards, I'd reckon the daughter set up for the knock-off was me.'

'I thought it was you planning to murder him,' said Light Fingers.

'True, but not contradictory.'

'The phrasing isn't consistent with it being you,' said Light

Fingers. 'Besides, that'd mean you have two secrets.'

'Youse dames only has one apiece?'

They looked at each other.

'*She could use her Talent to heal the sick – but won't,*' said Light Fingers. 'Could that be Laurence? Maybe a dip in her pocket's a cure-all. Aches, agues, palsies and pustules banished to the Purple.'

'Possible,' said Amy, doubting. 'Sparks was relieved to lose her glove, I think. She didn't love her Talent. But I'd hate to be "healed" like that and so would you.'

Light Fingers nodded.

'Besides, Larry *did* use her Talent to do whatever she did.'

'She hasn't done it again,' said Frecks. 'But I can't see her sitting in the Infirmary at the bedside of some girl with mumps or measles, chortling about not lifting a finger to help. She's not like that.'

'She *used* not to be like that,' Amy nearly said – but bit down on it.

She couldn't forget the voodoo stare.

Now their secrets were out, Amy did breathe easier – the thing with Light Fingers hadn't been as bad as she'd expected – and the others almost shrugged off their secrets. As if they didn't matter. They were glad to share things that gnawed inside them. They could talk about these things with their best friends.

Talking about the Broken Doll wouldn't help.

'One thing else,' said Light Fingers.

'Uh oh...' said Kali.

'Our secrets... Our first secrets... There are four girls out there trying to match their second secrets to us. So far as I know, De'Ath and I are the only ones with fathers in prison, so that's an easy-ish win for someone.'

Blake De'Ath, father of the De'Ath girls, was a jobbing henchman. He'd been in the Ghoul Mob, the Slaughter Boys and the Knightsbridge Knobblers. Nabbed by Scotland Yard after a sorry career, he was now in Princetown Jail. Bizou's sister

Angela, who passed out of Drearcliff Grange last year, was more ambitious. She would have her own gang. 'Mine applies only to those with *supposedly* dead mothers,' said Kali.

'A club few want to join, which I happen to be in too,' said Frecks.

'Knowles' father's a widower,' said Light Fingers. 'There was suspicion about how she died. Carleton Knowles invents murders for his books, after all. Gould's mother was sick for a long time and died last summer. I don't know about anyone else. It's never come up. Crumpets, do you suppose Polly Palgraive has *parents*? How must they feel about the worm plastering that simper on their dead girl's face?'

'Mine's so general it could be anyone,' said Frecks. 'I doubt Dyall loves her blessing... or Speke. Those hands of hers make my skin crawl.'

'I think Speke's genuinely cheerful,' said Amy. 'She doesn't mind her fingers being strange. Have you heard her play the piano? Her hands scuttle across the keys.'

Frecks let her fingers dangle and twitch.

'I reckon the girl's just putting a good face on bad hands.'

'Speke's face is real,' added Light Fingers.

'We're getting a teensy weensy bit weary of this new Application,' said Frecks.

'I can't *not* see...'

'Couldn't you *try*?' suggested Frecks.

Light Fingers shook her head. 'I can slow down running, but I can't slow down *thinking*.'

'My Ma might know a lama who could help with that,' said Kali.

'I'll consider it... There, did that, thought it through... No ta muchly. Benefits outweigh drawbacks.'

'For *you*,' said Frecks.

'My secret is so specific it'll take serious digging to uncover,' said Amy.

'True, but don't underestimate the other girls,' said Light

Fingers. 'We're not the only clever clogs in the Remove. Knowles has never met a mystery she couldn't solve. If she reads up and asks around, she'll put it together. And Marsh can read minds if she soaks her head in saltwater. Under the sea, speaking out loud doesn't work so her people have more refined telepathic Ability than poor old Miss Gossage's One-Way Telegraph.'

'I bet Marsh hates her blessing sometimes,' said Kali. 'What with everyone who claps peepers on her thinking she's got a fizz like a fish.'

That struck them all as humorous, and the chortles got too loud.

The dread knock of Kaveney returned.

'Walmergrave's cell, second warning, Minor Infractions for all four. Snuff the candle, stopper the gobs and get some bloomin' kip!'

VI: A Further Moment's Dream

WITH GROWING PANIC, A. realised she was alone in the Purple House.

No, not *alone*.

But alone with it... Her... The Broken Doll.

She ran up from the cellar.

She went from room to room, straying far from her scuffed chalk lines, dashing to regions of the house far from the kitchen and the servants' quarters... Strictly, these were regions where she was not permitted to be, but no over-butler remained to chide her for her missteps... no masters or dependents were surprised that a mouse of a maid should trespass in their velvet-hung chambers... should set unworthy eyes on their painted ceilings.

These parts of the house smelled of dried roses... All the clocks had wound down, and some had cracks across their faces that made her look away lest the numerals X and II clicked aside and eyes peeped through slits...The wonderful automata that provided eases and comforts for the masters – a lazy susan that was also a music box, a marionette with a stiff brush that swept ashes from fireplaces – were long since stilled.

If A. stood on tiptoes in the Windward Room, she could see a dramatic seascape through big round windows... The gentle rustling she had mistaken all the while for the sound of her own thoughts was really the noise of waves shushing against rocks on the beach below the Purple House.

So what *did* her thoughts sound like?

And where was everyone?

Between heartbeats, as she was transfixed by terror, years had passed in the house above... Everyone went away or died... or went away and died... even the ghosts, and the servants... Princess Violet, rages burned out in old age, was the last of household... Free to smash anything she liked, yet too feeble even to break fine glassware with her shrivelled little fists... she finally faded, leaving a strew of hair, teeth, nails and bones in her bed and drippings of candlewax on her counterpane.

The Wrongest of the Wrong Doors had been open... A. could have hurried past, but lingered – for only a moment, she intended – and was caught by the basilisk stare...

...For an age, A. looked into living eyes set in cracked white china...

Then the Broken Doll lurched up from her rocking chair, and limped towards A., kinked over and unsteady... her toby jug head too big for her ballerina body... her black hair hanging to her knees.

In four or five irregular steps, the Broken Doll reached the open door... A stiff little hand shot out, and the jagged stubs of porcelain fingers scratched A.'s cheek.

The touch broke the long moment, setting A. free.

Now she realised everything in the Purple House was too big for her... The seats of chairs were level with her chin, tabletops beyond her reach, doors two or three times her height... Rooms took minutes to cross.

Perhaps she was a different size in this part of the house than when she kept to her chalk line.

She could not find a door to the outside... Even doors beside picture windows through which she could see grounds opened into other rooms... Maybe the only way out was onto the roof, and down the walls... She went upstairs in search of skylights and found only more stairs.

Along with the wave rustle, she heard tiny, irregular footsteps... The Broken Doll had followed her up from the cellar, or was merely wandering according to her own whim... A prisoner once, but now – if anyone had the title – she was Mistress of the Purple House... By the terms of the indenture agreement, A. was hers to boss about or pinch or reward or treat howsoever she saw fit.

A. went up so many flights of stairs she worried the house had grown into a tower.

She passed through a room where a dozen old paintings, deformed by mould and mildew, were piled against the wall... All the pictures showed the Devil, identifiable by horns and curly tail, and his Darling, identifiable by décolletage and sour expression, in fancy dress... Pirate Captain and Cabin Wench, masked cowboy and bloody-wigged squaw, Crimson Knight and Harlot Squire, a skull-faced man-sized bat with red-lined black wings and a pale blonde lady in a wet white shroud... Their big painted heads were wrong for their bodies, though the more pictures A. looked at the more she wondered whether she was the one made out of proportion... She felt her head, worrying that it was too small for her shoulders.

Folding back slatted wooden shutters she saw glass doors and a balcony... Moonlight spilled into the room, and A. stepped into it, hoping to feel a ghost of warmth... The doors were rusted shut by salt-spray, so she couldn't get out that way... She lingered, to take in the view.

Out at sea, a great lantern was moving fast under the water... a sea serpent cyclops with an eye of fire... The creature made waves like the wake of a fast-moving ship... A funnel stuck out of its head broke the surface first, and belched smoke... An iron face pushed out of the sea – scowling, moustached, slat-fanged – the red-black prow of a locomotive.

Above the water, the cyclops engine roared, louder than thunder... Pistons pumped and screamed as razor-rim wheels ground on rails... The train rolled along on what A. now saw were tracks mounted on thin poles, pulling coffin-shaped carriages... The poles swayed under the weight but the structure did not collapse... The train rushed onward, water pouring from gargoyle-like fixtures that wet the wheels... The great beast whistled as it passed the Purple House, a pirate lover hailing a mistress on the shore... Then the railway curved back under the water... Making a huge splash, the train crashed into the waves, its shrill toot turning to submarine burble.

Clouds drifted across the pitted face of the moon... With darkness outside, the window became a mirror... A. saw herself.

Instinctively, she had raised an arm to wave at the train... Her short fingers touched her long hair... Her mob-cap was absurdly small... Her face was much too big, and there was a crack across it...

She was not, in fact, A.

She was the Broken Doll!

Amy was startled out of a bad dream.

She was cold, wet and *floating*.

She was not in her cell.

Above was the night sky. Beneath was rippling blackness.

Somewhere below, and a way off, waves crashed against shingles.

She was over the sea!

Her Kentish Glory costume was insulated against the cold, her flannel nightie wasn't. She couldn't feel her fingers or toes. She rolled in mid-air, trying to get sensation back in her extremities.

She thought she was drifting out over the estuary, but had no way of telling.

This hadn't happened before, not in the worst days of her nocturnal floats. At home, she'd never blown out of a window... and woke in the wind.

Only fliers knew how bitingly cold it was up here. Pilots

didn't wear fleece jackets, padded boots, goggles, scarves and leather helmets because the ensemble cut a dashing figure. They pulled on all the kit, then wound blankets around their legs – twenty-two-year-olds mummified like ancient relatives in bath chairs – because even ten or twenty feet off the ground, air temperature dropped sharply, and the wind made it worse. Soaring to higher altitudes was an invitation to frostbite. Frecks' Uncle Lance lost two fingers – frozen, then snapped off – while night-raiding. Airshipmen watched what they ate because they risked the contents of their bellies turning to ice and rupturing their bowels. After landing, they had to thaw carefully before going to the lavatory.

Amy was too cold to worry about what might happen *after landing*.

Her wet hair sloshed across her face. She scraped it away and rubbed her eyes.

She tumbled – not flying, but floundering in the air – trying to tell up from down. She got control of herself and let her hair hang like a plum bob, so she could tell where the ground – no, the sea! – was. She turned over, as if floating in a pool with only her face poked out of the water.

The sky was huge. She scanned it for the moon.

Waxing gibbous. A good size. Enough light to get her bearings. And a million diamond glints of starlight to steer by.

She took hold of herself, ignoring the shivers wracking her whole body, and became vertical. Her nightie hung on her. How had she got sodden? Dipping in the sea or passing through rain?

Above the dark swell of a cliff she saw the weathervane of Windward Cottage.

With that reference point, she could find the dorm.

She set a course and flew home, struggling against thick air and myriad pinpricks like ice darts.

She arrived bedraggled and aching, and had to halt herself before she slammed into the wall.

The cell window was unlatched and ajar. Had she done

that, with her fingers or her mentacles? She pulled it open and fit herself through, trying not to get wrapped in the curtains. She did not want to make a racket. She fastened the window behind her.

Her cellmates were asleep. Light Fingers' feet poked out at the end of her cot. In other circs, that would be an invitation to a tickling.

Amy's bedclothes were on the floor in a heap. She picked up a blanket and towelled herself with it. Then she peeled off her nightie and towelled again. It took an age to get the wet out of her hair. Rather than fetch a fresh nightie from her trunk, she took her dressing gown off the hook and put that on. She arranged her sheets and blankets on the cot and crawled under the covers. She concentrated on getting back control of herself. Within minutes, she'd stopped shivering and could feel her fingers and toes again.

Frecks, who sometimes murmured Latin phrases in her sleep, said something Amy couldn't catch and turned over, pulling a pillow over her head.

Amy lay on her cot, arms across her chest.

It must be near dawn. Light seeped in through the curtains.

Would she be able to sleep? If she dropped off, would she be able to wake in however many hours' time it was? Missing Chapel was an infraction she couldn't afford. How had she floated out of the cell and not woken anyone up?

She had night eyes. She looked at the ceiling, which she must have scraped... the pictures above Kali's cot – film stars with hats and guns... the stained patch of wallpaper above the door that sometimes took the shape of a disapproving owl and sometimes of car headlamps. Just now the stain was a big-eyed face with a crack across. Amy shut her eyes and wished for sleep.

Something about the picture of the cell was askew.

She opened her eyes again. The stained patch was definitely an owl now. A relief, but neither here nor there.

The askew thing was that the door was open a crack.

Amy didn't think she'd done that. It had been shut firmly when they went to sleep. Kaveney would have made sure of it.

Someone had looked in on them. Who? And to what purpose?

Amy breathed slowly and stretched out a mentacle.

Gently, she pushed the door. With a click of the latch, it shut.

VII: Chapel and After

WITH THE POST of chaplain vacant, Sunday Chapel was given over to inspirational readings and devotional music. Dull after Reverend Rinaldo's fiery, swoon-inducing sermons – but, on the whole, safer. No girls were smitten with the vapours or suffered hysterical palpitations. A briefly popular theory had it that the Reverend was Harper's real father. What she did to girls on their own, he could do to a whole congregation. Unlike Harper's victims, many girls said the swooning was worth the draining. It turned out that Rinaldo was not the leech, but only the lure for his hungry wife.

The Ariel Sixths Teller and Terrell stood up and intoned yards of Old Testament tedium. Auditors were lulled into such a stupor no one cried foul when they impudently made bits up... 'And so the sons of Ara were Uz, and Hul, and Turpentine, and Meshech, and Aphaxad begat Shillaleigh, which himself engendered Eber... and to Eber were born two sons – the name of one was Brontosaurus Maximus, for the land was parted in his days; and the name of his brother *was* Joktan... and Joktan begat Almodad, and Heffalump, and Parp, and Hadoram, and Bovril, and Diklah, and Havabanana, and Sheba, and Fido, and Jelleebaibee.' Joktan, evidently, was a busy begatter.

Fagged from her poor night's rest, Amy kept nodding off.

Frecks saw to it she didn't slide off the pew, nudging her to wakefulness with elbow jabs.

Whenever her head snapped up sharply and she opened her eyes wide, Amy saw Miss Kratides. She sat in the raised staff pew, in an apparent yogic trance. Her colleagues must remember the mischief she'd wrought until recently, but accepted her without obvious rancour. Unlike most beaks, she wore no academic gown or mortar board. She hadn't had time to earn a university degree in the two and a half terms she'd been away from Drearcliff Grange. Staffroom opinion last year would have Moria Kratides more likely to end up with numbers after her name than letters.

How must Miss Borrodale – who had famously got bloodied putting an end to the Kratides-Stonecastle fight – feel sharing a pew with the former terror of her classroom? Dr Swan, architect of the extraordinary appointment, sat in her elevated throne – plumped on the only cushion allowed in Chapel – as blankly imperturbable as ever. Yet again Headmistress had set a scheme in motion to teach the school a lesson it wouldn't enjoy one speck. The Swan method made Machiavelli seem like Squirrel Nutkin.

Teller and Terrell were hooked off the lectern. Miss Dryden sat at the wheezy organ to play 'Gladly the Cross I'd Bear', 'Holy, Holy, Holy' and 'Rescue the Perishing'. Girls opened fifty-year-old copies of *Hymns Ancient and Antediluvian* and raised voices – like generations of pew-sufferers before them – to risk mass infraction by singing 'Gladly the Cross-Eyed Bear', 'Roly Poly Goalie' and 'Rats Chew the Paraffin'. Beauty Rose silently opened and closed her mouth like a goldfish. Ten or twenty caterwaulettes scattered throughout the flock would have done well to follow her example.

During the hymns, Amy scanned the pews for her fellows in the Remove. She hadn't cracked her second secret. *Who* would blame her for not telling what she knew about Laurence? Whenever she met a classmate's gaze, she suspected the girl trying to pin their own second secret on her. Someone must be wondering who was right to be afraid of the Broken Doll.

Every few minutes, after her glance had roamed around Chapel, she couldn't help meeting Larry's voodoo stare. Amy couldn't imagine what was churning in the girl's mind, and worried about what was boiling in her pocket. Telling – warning? – the Moth Club about Laurence's new Application had been a relief, but nothing had really changed... except Light Fingers would now be cautious about sticking her swift hands into Larry's pocket.

Light Fingers was saved from being turned into a slowcoach. Her personal private sneer had expanded from being a less polite way of saying Ordinary. Now she meant anyone who couldn't keep up with her, which was everyone... Unless she was due for a shock like Amy had when she ran into Stephen Swift. There must be other fast folk. Lesson of the day for paladins and Wrong 'Uns alike: there's always someone quicker, stronger, cleverer, purer – find a way to best them!

Where had that come from? Amy looked at Miss Kratides.

Somehow she was being *taught* – all the time, unconventionally, by methods she didn't understand. Even her dreams were lessons.

After the hymns, Miss Dryden was allowed to indulge an enthusiasm for the baroque school. Wringing something close to spiritual beauty from her ill-maintained instrument, she played selections from Telemann's 'Twenty Little Fugues for Organ'.

Amy drifted again and Frecks' fingers stuck her in the ribs.

Smarting, she opened her eyes wide and was bedazzled. Larry's voodoo stare filled her vision as if the small girl's face were inches from her own, mouth a thin line, brows knit, eyes glinting like dagger points. Laurence's head seemed inflated to fluke size. Pressing fingernails into the heels of her hands, Amy dispelled the illusion. She closed and opened her watering eyes, and all was normal.

But Larry was still giving her the evil eye from across the Chapel.

She has cause to hurt you all.

Frecks' second secret was about Laurence.

Amy was certain she was right, but not sure she should tell Frecks. Not yet.

The Moth Club had put cards on the table. But, despite her qualms, Amy was already accumulating fresh secrets. She'd not told her friends about her involuntary night flight. Doubt and guilt inclined her not to share her insight about Laurence's secret – though keeping quiet didn't help Frecks get her prep done. Whatever Amy decided, she would be blamed by someone. For not telling what she knew about Laurence. And now for not telling what she only suspected.

The real culprit was their new teacher.

Moria Kratides used to make mischief by passing notes. Her copperplate red-ink couplets could turn an obedient class into a tank full of sharks in a feeding frenzy. While the beak struggled to regain control, Kratides sat back, half-smiling. As a teacher herself, she had refined the tactic. The mischief was now the lesson. At the end of this exercise, the Remove would know a lot more – but the knowledge would make few of them happier.

Her turn finished, Miss Dryden invited Harriet Speke to play.

Hissing rose from some pews. Disarmed by her unassuming manner, girls in Speke's year liked her. Others couldn't see past the crusty hands. The whips called her Spook Speke – pronounced with sinister sibilance *Sssspook Sssspeke*. She bore the handle with good humour, infuriating fluke-haters all the more. If monsters roamed the Quad, they should have the decency to act the part – growling like Gould under a full moon or slinking like Marsh at high tide.

Speke nodded pleasantly as if hearing polite applause rather than mocking susurrus and sat at a dainty harpsichord. She held up her hands, for inspection. The hissing turned to groans of revulsion. From a distance, Speke's hands resembled crabs: each with rows of pointy-tipped spiny 'fingers' at the sides and thicker, slightly bifurcated 'thumbs' where the pincers would be. Amy admired arthropods of any description, but even she found Speke's Attributes unattractive. The Second took a deep breath as her hands hovered over the keyboard. With considerable front, she tore into 'Funeral March of a Marionette', the piece some girls whistled when an Unusual passed. The anthem of flukes. As a rule, Gounod composed for musicians with the normal complement of fingers, but – using all sixteen digits – Speke added extra notes.

Intent on her virtuosity, and not a little pleased with herself, Speke had the sense to play something short. The funeral march was over inside a minute.

She finished with a flourish.

Tuttlety-tittlety-tootly-tum-titty-tum-tum! CRASH CRASH TWANG!

On the front row, Gillian Little thumped her hands together and hooted 'bravo'.

The Moth Club clapped. So, Amy suspected, did the rest of the Remove.

All flukes together…

Viola were happy to claim the virtuoso as one of their own. Others were won over in every corner of Chapel. Miss Dryden was proud. Even whips applauded. Girls enjoyed a good show and admired a good sport. That was School Spirit too. General opinion was a see-saw. The reversal of the Great Game devalued the stock of the Remove and the Unusuals. Speke's performance didn't restore them to glory – what could? – but it was a start.

Amy saw who wasn't joining in the applause.

Laurence. She kept up her voodoo stare.

Frecks clapped loudly and shouted, 'Encore!'

'You were right about Sssspook's ivory-tinkling,' Frecks said to Amy. 'I'll never doubt you henceforth. You are a spotter of hidden Talents and a generous soul who should be rewarded with bon-bons and balloons.'

'She really is very good,' said Light Fingers.

'And smart,' said Kali. 'They slung that tune at us like mud, and she's caught it and made it ours. It's the "Battle Hymn of the Remove" now.'

Speke resisted calls for an encore.

She held up her hands again, for all to see. Her cuffs, sizes bigger than her sleeves, fell away to show her wrists, where carapace turned into regular skin. She finger-wiggled, making octopoid shadow puppets. She touched her boater with a cheery salute and trotted back to her pew.

Mrs Wyke took the lectern and made the regular announcements: who was in the Infirmary and uninfectious enough to visit; what flickers were to be projected in the afternoon (something soppy with Mary Pickford, something funny with Charlie Chaplin); who could collect freshly censored letters from the outside world; and what lost property was held by Keys, the custodian.

Chapel was over for another Sunday.

Dr Swan descended from her throne and left, followed by a crocodile of staff.

Miss Kratides said something to Fossil Borrodale, who stifled a laugh. They were like Captain Skylark and Hans von Hellhund joking together. After all the dogfights, they had more in common with each other than with folk who only read about the War in the papers. Moria Kratides' conduct as a girl no longer told against her. Judging from what she was like now, Violet Borrodale must have been a perfect savage as a pupil. When a girl passed out of Drearcliff Grange, her Time-Table Book was torn to confetti. Black Notches were expunged. An Old Girl who came back as a new Miss started afresh in the enemy camp.

A Kratides-Borrodale collaboration was an alarming notion. What tribulations would they visit on girls under them? Would Dr Swan's next bright idea be giving Crowninshield II a whistle and putting her in charge of calisthenics?

Once the staff were gone, girls filed out pew by pew, house by house. Whips eagerly watched for sooners or dawdlers and slapped infractions on them. One or two always fell into the net. Amy left with her cell-fellows, not too soon, not too late.

Outside, it was a bright, crisp day. After a single night of London fog, she had become grateful for Drearcliff weather. The air only tasted of sea salt. And she could see across the Quad.

Two hours stretched until Sunday Dinner.

Smells of slow roasting fowl emerged from the kitchen. The birds were at their best, fresh and crisp and delicious – but would stay in the ovens till they were tough as infantry boot leather. Only Aconita Gould's teeth were sharp enough to bite through Drearcliff chicken, and she'd prefer her dinner raw – bones and feathers and all. Spuds and gravy took some of the taste away. No one minded if you scraped the swede into the slop bin.

Girls milled about, forming activities clubs or prep groups, or beetling off on solitary pursuits.

Tamora Seconds played marbles on the fives court. Goneril Firsts got competitive at leap frog. On the steps of the Playhouse, Violas with sheets tied over uniforms rehearsed the assassination of Caesar. Gallaudet made such a meal of dying that conspirators Pulsipher and Hailstone deemed throttling the tyrant – with the side effect of stopping her soliloquy – preferable to further stabbing.

The Remove were no different, though Amy noticed her classmates stood out because they tended not to mill. They stood in ones and twos. De'Ath and Light plotted together. Larry talked to an unengaged Bok, all the while shooting her stare at Amy and Frecks. Speke was with a proud Little and a small circle of new fans, signing autographs four at a time. She let Firsts touch the backs of her hands then shocked them into giggles by wriggling her crusty fingers. Frost and Thorn, on opposite sides of the Quad, experimented with unsatisfactory new best friends – Dyall and Paquignet. Knowles and Devlin were absent from Chapel – and only Devlin mentioned on the sick list.

Shrimp Harper sidled over to the Moth Club.

At first Amy thought Harper was bleeding, then she realised she'd got splashed with cold tomato soup by Gallaudet's death throes.

'Here,' said Shrimp, giving Frecks her card. 'Read the beastly thing. I don't care.'

Amy, Light Fingers and Kali crowded around.

You have done many good and kind things people don't kno about.

Her mother is alive.

Ah-ha! Harper's second secret was *Kali's*.

Her first didn't match any of theirs, though.

Kali was on the point of owning up, when Light Fingers plucked the card from Frecks' fingers.

'The writing is different,' she said, 'and the ink's still tacky. It's not the same red either. Oh, and there's an egregious spelling error.'

Harper cringed.

Amy felt the leeching touch.

Kali spun and put her shoe sole an inch away from Harper's soup-dripping nose. The draining stopped.

'It's not even a *convincing* false secret,' said Light Fingers. 'Who'd believe you'd ever done good and kind things?'

'That people don't know about... because they're secret.'

Amy almost felt sorry for the Sixth, but the icy tickle of her Talent brought her up sharply. Pathetic as she might be, she was a Wrong 'Un in the making.

'Push off, Shrimp,' said Frecks.

Light Fingers tore the card – which wasn't the same size as the real ones – in half and gave the pieces back to Harper.

'Don't try that again,' said Frecks. 'We'll warn the others.'

'You wouldn't snitch! What about the Code of Break?'

'Warning isn't snitching,' said Amy.

Harper sloped off. As always, she made everyone feel better by leaving.

'She only faked her *first* secret,' said Light Fingers. 'Her second's Kali's.'

'Which she ain't hearin' from me,' said Kali.

Amy had pondered the practicalities of getting the Remove

together like the Moth Club and prevailing on everyone to share secrets. It would mean dealing with some difficult, even frightening girls – but the prep would get done. Maybe that was what Miss Kratides wanted them to do. She foresaw embarrassment and uncomfortable explanations, but assumed a balance of shame would emerge when everything was out in the open. Thanks to Shrimp, she saw that wasn't going to work.

Passing the Playhouse, Harper got another dollop of soup on her blazer.

Gallaudet was splattering pedestrians on purpose. Cowper-Kent, a pedantic whip, swooped on the troupe and infracted them for historical inaccuracy. She infracted them again for cheek when they argued for artistic truth over mundane reality. At this rate, Joan Hone – waiting at the foot of the steps in her toga – would never deliver 'Friends, Romans, countrymen...'

Leaving the Quad, the Moth Club were accosted by Gawky Gifford.

'Another pest,' said Frecks. 'Quite the day for gnats and leeches.'

'I was told you'd pay a penny for this,' she said, holding up an envelope.

'Who's it from?' asked Frecks.

'Such information costs,' said the Second.

'Ach, it's a racket,' said Kali, raising her hand to cuff the carrier.

'No, no, pax, pax,' said the Gawk. 'This is the God's Honest. Cross my heart and hope to marry a policeman.'

Amy was sceptical, but Light Fingers produced a halfpenny from her purse and held it between thumb and forefinger.

'Half price bargain offer,' she said. 'Take it or leave it.'

She and Gifford did a back and forth dance, then exchanged. Gifford looked at her empty palm and pouted, then tasted something bad. She spat out the halfpenny Light Fingers had pushed into her mouth.

Light Fingers held the envelope. The junior cadger scarpered before a refund could be solicited.

'You shouldn't encourage her,' said Frecks.

Light Fingers held up the envelope. 'Recognise it?' she asked.

'It's… one of *those*,' said Amy. 'A real one.'

Light Fingers turned it over. 'Knowles, Charlotte,' she read aloud.

The card was still inside.

Again, the Moth Club craned to read.

Your father makes plans to murder you.

She can't feel anything.

'Knowles' first secret is my second,' said Kali. 'Unless this is snide too.'

Light Fingers held the card under her nose as if sniffing a cigar.

'It's authentic. Right card, right handwriting, right ink.'

Amy wondered who couldn't feel anything. Palgraive, possibly?

'How come the Gawk gave it over?' said Kali.

'She'll have been paid at both ends,' said Light Fingers. 'In for a halfpenny, in for another halfpenny.'

'Something's written on the other side,' said Frecks.

Light Fingers turned the card over.

'Come to the Library Annexe – Miss Memory.'

'We've been summoned,' said Frecks.

VIII: The Archivist in the Annexe

THE LIBRARY ANNEXE was behind the Library Proper. The stout-walled building used to be the estate's ice house. Cap'n Belzybub used the gothic shed to stash contraband rum, gunpowder and abducted barmaids. According to Devlin, his rakehell notion of a weekend lark involved a combustive mix of strong drink, high explosives and a village spitfire. The escape attempts of many a prize baggage must have been thwarted by the arrow-slit windows, especially if the tavern wenches of the 1760s at all resembled the barmaids of today.

The path to the Annexe was overgrown. Joxer didn't roll his grass-mower this way often.

'This could be a trap,' said Amy, hating herself – and, because her waveriness was his fault, A.H. Wax – for being over cautious.

'Don't see how,' said Frecks. 'Unless Miss Memory's going to drop a hundredweight of old sermons on us – and you could toss them aside with your mentawhatchumacallits...'

'...*cles*,' said Light Fingers. '...*cles*.'

'Yes, them fellers,' said Frecks.

Amy sensed vague, formless menace.

Kali stretched and yawned. Not from fatigue, but to look around without being obvious. Least Unusual of the Moth Club, she had the best instincts and reflexes.

'I spot her too,' said Kali, not whispering obviously but low enough for only Amy to hear. 'We've got a tail. Lonesome Larry.'

Amy hadn't seen Laurence before and didn't now.

'*Young Larry*,' piped up Frecks, loud enough to be heard back on the Quad. 'Isn't she off mooning around Bok, poor thing?'

Now Amy spied a small figure withdrawing hastily behind a bush.

It was possible to feel a voodoo stare through shrubbery. Amy's hackles rose, she was sure Larry's peepers were fixed on a point between her shoulder blades where a dagger would do the most damage.

'She shadows us off and on,' said Light Fingers. 'I reckon she hopes to overhear our secrets. I wonder what hers is.'

'"She has cause to hurt you all"?' said Kali, quoting Frecks' second secret.

'That's not fair,' said Amy, bristling – though more shocked that Kali agreed with her unspoken suspicion. 'It's only me she has anything against.'

'And me,' said Frecks. 'My own foolish fault, as you kindly pointed out, Emma.'

Light Fingers shrugged. She'd always been impatient with Larry.

'This is a distraction,' she said. 'And the limpet's pushed off now.'

Amy wasn't sure of that. She still had a *frisson*. There were plenty of bushes and shadows in this part of the grounds. Dr Swan put things here she wanted buried.

The Annexe held books relegated from the Library Proper for the sin of being 'pre-war'. Dr Ailsa Auchmuty, the librarian, was a modernising fiend. Some beaks got het up when prep-dodgers reported half the reading list was no longer available to girls without an Annexe pass. Mark Robarts' *A Counterblast to Agnosticism* and Dr Graeme Ruxton's *Fairy Sprinkles and Monthly Matters: Hygiene for Young Ladies* had been taught at Drearcliff Grange since Founding Day. To Doc Och's way of thinking, that was reason enough to drop them from the curriculum and into a ditch.

The Annexe collection also purportedly included material too racy for delicate sensibilities. Bizou De'Ath talked of eldritch grimoires and tomes of wicked summoning. Everyone else imagined stacks of confiscated smut.

Charlotte Knowles was custodian of this literary abyss. Dr Auchmuty trusted Miss Memory to oversee the Annexe while she patrolled her airy, neat, modern library, where all information was bang up to date and every book had numbers neatly stamped on its spine. It was in Knowles' gift to admit girls to the Annexe, though she kept a meticulous log of whose twitching nose poked into which forbidden books.

Amy had visited before, hoping to turn up moth-related rarities. However, the Annexe's entomology section consisted of a row of slim, yellow-backed copies of *Formis* by Professor R.R. Rayne. A year after the sudden end of its vogue, that tract – not pre-war, but pre-posterous – had few remaining admirers at Drearcliff Grange.

The Moth Club approached the squat, grim building.

Kali boldly strode up and rapped on the heavy door.

Instinctively, Amy started fiddling with the tumblers of the lock. She had neglected to practise this since the Great Game.

The door was wrenched open before she could work her party piece.

Knowles stood there – hair awry, eyes pink, temples scratched. Her face suffered from bulginess, as if her brain were swollen to twice normal size, warping her skull plates.

Miss Memory was still suffering from her overdose of Poppet Dyall.

'Come in, come in,' she said, fussing like a bowed old woman, hauling the door open. It scraped the stone floor and stuck halfway, but the Moth Club sidled round it.

Amy was last in. She looked back at the shrub and didn't see Larry.

The girl's persistent, determined presence was perturbing. Her resentment went beyond thwarted crush. Amy realised, with regret, she had made a stubborn enemy of Venetia Laurence. Another potential arch-nemesis. She was collecting them. Did all great enmities begin with a small wound – 'Oh, *Larry*, what *have* you done?' – which could never heal? It was hard to imagine Achmet the Almost Human first vowing to devastate European civilisation because he was snubbed at a May Ball or refused service in a newsagent's – but maybe something in his past festered, something as unintentionally devastating as the casual comment that twisted Larry's insides. Sidonie Gryce was a witch from the cradle, though. Amy had no doubts about that.

The Annexe was a cramped labyrinth of bookcases – volumes stacked two deep, with items of inconvenient size shoved in to fill horizontal gaps. Anyone who wanted to take a particular book from the jammed shelves would need a chisel and some tongs. Spongy bundles of periodicals barricaded fields of obsolete learning. This was a repository for things fallen into disuse but too old or expensive to put out for the dust cart. An ornate globe with *terra incognita* blanks representing unexplored continental interiors. Trays of photographic slides that wouldn't slot into modern projectors.

Knowles ushered the Moth Club into an octagonal room where she was set up with a good-sized desk – balanced on three of its original legs and seventeen volumes of Billson's *A History of the Low Countries*. Amy sat down on nothing – a trick adapted from Stephen Swift – but the Annexe was so gloomy nobody noticed. Miss Memory had electric lamps to read by. They were on a generator not the mains, so light wavered unnervingly. There was a persistent smell of burning dust.

'What fun,' said Knowles. 'It's like being in an air raid. I enjoyed air raids. Mama sang *lieder* and gave me cherries *glacées* for being brave. Papa fulminated against the Hun. He's highly patriotic, you know, Papa. Foreigners in his mysteries are always baddies, even if they aren't the murderer. During the

War, he wrote leaflets which Mama translated into German. The RFC dropped them over enemy lines. He made up far-fetched fancies that silly fritzes bought book, lie and stinker. One was a genealogy pamphlet by Prof Sigismund von Doppelganger, proving the Kaiser was actually a Dutchwoman with a false moustache. Another was a set of "secret" instructions to Hussar officers about how to impress High Command and win lots of medals by sustaining the most casualties among their men. That wasn't distributed because the British and French generals in charge of propaganda thought Papa was getting at them. How foolish! Papa was ever so cross. Ever so ever so.'

Knowles was in a dizzy tizzy. That was what Poppet had done to her.

'Now what was it I wanted to talk with you about?' she said.

Frecks gave her back her card.

'Ah, yes,' she said. 'Secrets.'

'Your father plans to murder you?' asked Amy, concerned.

'Your first is my second secret,' said Kali. 'But I'm not the frail who can't feel anything.'

'No, that's Stretch,' said Knowles. 'Ever since – well, that house, you know the one, Thomsett, in Piccadilly, where the – um, *the thing* – happened, she's been numb. Pliable as ever, but losing sensation in her skin. Can't feel hot or cold. Doesn't notice pins.'

Kali whistled. 'She can't be *hurt*? That's some handy Ability!'

Knowles shook her head, whipping her cheeks with her bangs.

'Uh, ah, no... there are drawbacks. She can't feel the pins going in, but she bleeds all the same. Just because she can't feel pain doesn't mean she can't be *harmed*. She could break an ankle or something – like poor, angry Bok – and do herself more of an injury by walking around on the break. Pain is the body's way of sending messages to the brain. Keep your fingers out of the fire. Don't put those scissors there. Not all feelings hurt, of course. There are nice feelings too. Feelings you'd miss if you couldn't have them. I'm worried about her. Very worried. I'm worried about me, too. I expect you've noticed. I lose my train sometimes. The choo-choo chuffs off out of the station and – whoops, *silly me*! – I'm not on it. For instance… what did you ask me, Thomsett?'

Amy had lost track too.

Then remembered. 'Your father—'

'—plans to murder me? Yes. Often. All the time. In ingenious ways. He'd never get caught. There aren't any really clever detectives any more.'

Light Fingers solved it. '*In his books*,' she said. 'Your father thinks up murders for his books. *The Body in the Belfry, The Head in the Hat-Box, The Corpse in the Coal Hole…*'

Knowles nodded vigorously.

Carleton Knowles, a university lecturer, wrote murder mysteries as a hobby – though Amy suspected the sideline raked it in, topping up the stipend that came with the chair in classics at Brichester. Improbably for the father of Miss Memory, Professor Knowles pooh-poohed the notion of Talents and Abilities. Murderers in his books were never Unusuals.

In *The Novice in the Niche*, the anchorite strangled inside a walled-in cell was not throttled by someone with mentacles. The author abided by strict rules. Hocus-pocus was as unfair to the reader as having a victim turn out to have killed themselves or died by accident. It needed three chapters on Catholic doctrine for eccentric detective Guilbert Phatt to rule out suicide. In the last chapter, Phatt proved the bricked-up Sister Carlotta was killed by rosary beads strung on a wet leather thong that shrank round her neck on a hot day. Amy was sure that wouldn't work, just as she *was* sure a murderously inclined person with Abilities like hers – Stephen Swift for instance – could nix the nun in a trice. It was obvious from the first page that the most helpful, learned, handsome monk did it. Several nasty, dried-up, sniping elder brethren were obvious red herrings. In Carleton Knowles' books, the most helpful, learned, handsome suspect always did it… just as it was always a woman who had it done to her.

Professor Knowles – whose books she and Light Fingers scorned and picked holes in, but read avidly – had changed his spots. In Guilbert Phatt's early outings, the victims were mature, attractive, amusing women. In *The Body in the Belfry*, the helpful, learned, handsome dentist/campanologist killed his mature, attractive, amusing wife by ringing a bell at a particular frequency that cracked the cyanide-filled false molar he'd glued in her gob.

Five books ago, with *The Corpse in the Coal Hole*, the murderee was suddenly a fresh type. A clever, pretty, infuriating schoolgirl. The murderer was the same old helpful, learned, handsome fellow. Subsequent victims all fit the clever, pretty, infuriating girl model.

'He used to murder Mama,' admitted Knowles. 'She was like us – at least, like you and me, Thomsett, and Naisbitt too – an Unusual. Not with Attributes, but Abilities. If she heard a language, she understood it. All it took was "*Ou se trouve le plume de ma tante?*" and she could read Diderot in the original. Like my cramming, it didn't last. She'd be fluent for a week, then it'd fade.'

That sounded like a Talent with Applications.

'Mama wasn't a dunce like me. Even when not dosed up with Japanese or Swahili, she was bright and clever. Papa's friends said she was too interesting to be married to a stick like him, though they are to a man stickier sticks than he ever was. Classicists take his boring book about the Comedies of Eubulus seriously but sneer at him for sullying his first-class mind with "shilling shockers". Papa disapproved of Mama's Talent. No matter how often it was proved, he claimed it was a parlour trick. If real, it was cheating. It rankled that he had to spend years struggling to translate fragments of cuneiform, while she overheard a Neapolitan fishwife cursing her Giuseppi and could suddenly talk nineteen to the dozen in a whole new language. I expect that's why he murdered her—'

'*I knew it,*' said Frecks.

'—in his books. Over and over. She thought it funny, at first. After six or seven murders, she brought it up in conversation. He had a queer turn and got offended, then said his characters were imaginary and not important anyway. Readers only pay attention to the puzzles. That's the artistry. He kept murdering her and she stopped reading the books. Sometimes, when people were chuckling about the new Guilbert Phatt, she'd ask me about the latest victim, then not listen when I told her. After she died – a brain aneurysm, which is something we have to worry about, Unusuals with mental Talents, because it's a common complaint among us – Papa stopped murdering her... and started murdering me. I've been chopped up in a coal bin... drowned in a desert... stabbed in the arras... fed to beetles.'

'Do you mind?' asked Frecks.

'Well... *yes*. Wouldn't you? Like Mama, I tried bringing it up and...'

'Let me guess,' said Light Fingers. 'The characters are imaginary and not important anyway.'

'Exactly.'

'You don't think he'd ever... you know, try any of his plots in real life?' asked Amy.

'Why ever would he do that? What an odd thing to say!'

'It must mean *something*,' said Light Fingers. 'Even if he doesn't know he's doing it.'

'It's just Papa being Papa. Mama used to say that all the time. In languages he didn't understand. One thing he was terribly good at was catching her. Amusing, but sly. Teasing dry old sticks with such cunning they had to smile and put up with it. I re-read those books up to the chapters where Mama is murdered, to remind myself of her. When she said something funny to you that only you understood, it was flattering. She turned heads. Especially the heads of dry old sticks, I can tell you. The meaner a classicist is about Papa's "shilling shockers", the harder you knew he'd been knocked back by Mama. Papa's not nearly as good at catching me.'

Amy didn't think that was true. Sister Carlotta was Knowles to the life – well, to the rosary-throttled corpse. Talking knowledgeably about everything under the sun, with interjections, digressions and footnotes. The novice chose being bricked up over a vow of silence she knew she'd break inside two minutes. It struck Amy that Carleton Knowles murdering his wife over and over – and now his daughter – might honestly be an expression of tender feeling.

She didn't understand how the Professor ticked, but there was something sweet and sad about him – at least, about the part of him he showed in his mysteries. Maybe that was why Amy stuck with Guilbert Phatt after nineteen disappointing last chapter explanations. Light Fingers was more interested in the guessing game. While they were reading the latest, passing a copy back and forth between chapters, Light Fingers was always trying to out-think Phatt and see how the murder was managed before he tumbled to the trick. Amy preferred the odd, funny, sort of pompous/sort of melancholy bits and bobs between the grinding plot gears. Often, they made her titter in a way she couldn't explain to her friend.

So Knowles' secret was out and explained.

Amy wondered if Miss Kratides wanted each girl just to identify the classmate who matched up to her second secret – or would she quiz more deeply? Was this just a guessing game? Or were the other things important. Carleton Knowles didn't care about motive – he was as evasive about why his murderers murdered as he was about whether his characters were drawn from life – but Miss Kratides might.

On Knowles' desk were bound volumes of the *Police Gazette*, the *Strand Magazine* and the *Newgate Calendar*. And other sensational literature: *Famous Edinburgh Trials. The Life and Actions of Jonathan Wild. The Memoirs of Vidocq. The Many Faces of Colonel Clay.* She was always more interested in true stories than made-up crimes.

'My mother's name was Frances Hall,' Knowles said. 'When I

write books, I shall call myself "Charlotte Knowes-Hall". It was Halle, originally, but her family changed it in the War, just like the King.'

The post-Poppet Knowles was a different creature. She retained more of what she crammed into her head, and coughed up titbits once wiped off her blackboard which now popped up again. All the facts, learned and unearned, were shoving Knowles' essential self into a smaller and smaller space.

Knowles' eyes looked about to burst.

It had never occurred to Amy that her Abilities might have ill-effects. She'd never even had a nosebleed. What Knowles said about her mother was troubling. You couldn't fend off brain aneurysm with extra helpings of carrots or long walks in the fresh air. In less trying times, she might have suffered a spasm of hypochondriac worry. Now she had too much on her mind to get worked up about the ill-effects of getting worked up about things. Nevertheless, she would ask Kali to explain the calming practices of Eastern religion. After a busy week's banditry, Mr Chattopadhyay sat cross-legged on a mat and hummed for hours – then sprang up refreshed, feeling not at all sorry about the villages he'd plundered.

'Why did you send for us?' said Frecks, getting to the point.

'I sent for you?' said Knowles, brows knit. 'Yes, I did. Paid Gifford a ha'penny to deliver the message. That girl knows the value of every service. She'll go far…'

'Unless someone catches her,' said Light Fingers.

'Anyway…' prompted Frecks.

'Anyway, yes, *anyway*… Moria Kratides. Who knows – and *shares* – our secrets. Our new Form Mistress. An interesting sort – unusual, but not strictly an Unusual. Though the definition is blurry. Her antecedents, known and unknown, are remarkable. Her presence as a beak is a mystery—'

'You're telling us,' said Kali.

'Yes, I am. It's what I asked you here for. To tell you… Now, where was I? Steeped in crime. That's her background. Miss

Kratides' records are sealed in Dr Swan's files, but she has a drawer to herself. Stuffed with infractions, I'll be bound. From her first day at Drearcliff Grange to the last. I hear she stole a copy of the School Rules and marked off each as she broke it. Her placings were never poor, though. Fourth or fifth in most subjects. Top in Cookery one term, when the rest of her year got food poisoning and didn't complete the exam. Lost down the sewer in the Great Game. Rotten at cricket and netball too. No one trusted her and she wouldn't trust others. Fatal drawback in team games. Better at pursuits like archery and orienteering. Rock-climbing, javelin, fencing. Not stupid, obviously, but *wilful*. No school loves a wilful girl. She didn't make it easy for herself, or anyone else in her lessons – including the teachers. Know who her mother was? No reason you should, though the name comes up a lot in these...'

Knowles indicated her pile of crime books.

She turned over pages until she found a photographic plate. A woman, in profile. Amy recognised the original of Miss Kratides' brooch. A strong family resemblance – though the mother had even more masses of black hair and a longer nose. The caption on the plate was 'Fig 7: Sophy Kratides, Graustark, 1895'.

'Same last name as the daughter,' said Light Fingers. 'No husband?'

'Having a baby on the, ah, wrong side of the blanket is the least of Kratides' mother's... I was going to say "indiscretions", but in point of fact she's been extremely discreet most of her life.'

'*She* looks wilful,' said Frecks. 'A woman with decided *views*.'

'That's sharp, Walmergrave. Views, yes. Decidedly decided. A woman of her times, but in advance of them also. You've heard Wicked Wyke or Miss Dryden harp on about being Suffragettes and the inroads women have made in this young century. The Vote is just the start of it. The Law, Parliament, the police forces, business and trade... even the Army and Navy and the Church. Petticoat pioneers have secured positions in all these fields where once men were unchallenged. Inevitably, some equally determined women have made careers in *crime*.'

Kali whistled. 'Miss Kratides' Ma was... what, a purse-snatcher? She roll drunks or cosh cabbies?'

'Nothing so, ah, street-level. Before the turn of the century, Sophy Kratides was the first European woman to earn a living as an assassin for hire. Not as a domestic poisoner or cheesewire-under-the-pillow seductress, either. She's a long-range rifle shot and up-close knife woman. In one of these *Strands*, there a story about how she started as a naïve heiress, who fell prey to a pair of English rogues. These nancy boys talked her out of her boodle and gassed her brother to death. Which she did not take well. The villains got gutted in a hotel room. Either Sophy did it herself or got them to do it to each other. After taking personal revenge, she got the taste for blood. She usually did away with folk nobody much missed. Arch-Dukes, snitches and swindlers she killed for high fees. Brutal husbands, fathers and slavers she went after *gratis*. She liked to leave men who hurt women alive, but not whole. It's a surprise she let a fellow near enough to get in the family way.'

'So who is Miss Kratides' *father*?' asked Amy.

Knowles smiled and shrugged. 'Sophy's never said... and she's not a person anyone presses for answers. She knocked around with tantalising possibles, though. In America, she learned gunfighting from a cove with either too many or too few names and hunted outlaws for bounty. In London, she was a member of the Moriarty Mob. After the Prof got shoved over that waterfall, she knocked about with his Number Two, Sebastian Moran. They got into all sorts of scrapes. Remember Johnny Barlowe, who broke the bank at Monte Carlo? Sophy and Moran robbed him. Then lost all the winnings to a confidence man who never showed the same face twice. Colonel Clay. You have to watch those types closely...'

As Amy knew all too well. Incidentally, Clay... Wax... a connection, perhaps? Malleable materials. Fitting for a face changer.

'In Paris,' Knowles went on, 'Sophy was with the Opera Ghost Agency, working under Erik de Boscherville. Also known as the Phantom. I wondered whether he might be Miss Kratides' father. That half-frozen face of hers could be inherited. Erik was supposed to be *hideous*. My favourite candidate, though, is Basher Moran. Getting on in years when Sophy got up the duff, but a notorious skirt-chaser... and dishy in his prison photographs. Women loved a man with moustaches like jug handles back then.'

'Such a remarkable woman's daughter must have better prospects than drumming times tables into the skulls of we sorry Dims,' said Frecks. 'With her pedigree, shouldn't she be tunnelling into the Bank of England or impersonating a Russian princess?'

'She's not set us Maths prep,' said Amy.

'I'm not certain what sort of prep these secrets are,' said Light Fingers. 'We're learning, I'm sure – but not things which come up in examinations.'

'But she is teaching us lessons,' said Amy.

'Yeah – and how,' said Kali. 'Maybe we're not seeing her square. Maybe there's a point to this.'

'If she's at all like her mother, a sharp point – aimed precisely,' said Knowles.

Amy's back itched again.

'What was it you said about the rogues who took Sophy for a fool?' said Amy. 'She might have got them to kill each other? Moria used to make trouble in lessons by setting off fights. She'd pass notes and girls found they had bones to pick. They were too angry to think about who dug up the bones. Is this prep just that on a bigger scale? Does Miss Kratides expect us all to murder each other over whispers? Devlin going numb all over... or your father thinking up ways to murder you... or me being afraid of the Broken Doll.'

Knowles was brought up short.

'Who said anything about a Broken Doll?'

IX: The Real Spook-Spotters

AFTER SUNDAY DINNER, most of the school pursued activities that involved sitting or lying down. The leather chicken was followed by the heaviest plum duff known to science. Charlie Chaplin would play to pained groans. Laughing at the Little Tramp on a stomach full of Drearcliff din-din was not recommended. Even the sport maniacs of Goneril weren't up to a cross-country run.

Some Ariels volunteered for extra helpings because the more they ate, the easier it was to sick up. They aspired to flapper fashions wearable only by pinch-waisted, hipless, breastless sylphs. Amy thought there was something wrong with competitive purging, but Banks, Lowen and Vigo – prime advocates of the craze – swore they attained a higher state of consciousness while bent over a lavatory puking. Chastity Banks claimed that at her emptiest she saw violet skies and mauve mountains. Vomiting was not an enviable Ability, though – even if a girl could, say, spew acid or retch gold coins.

Knowles didn't trot along to the Refec with the Moth Club. Whips would infract her for dodging Chapel. They'd agreed to reconvene at the invalid Devlin's bedside. More was to be said of the Broken Doll. Amy anticipated that with a mixture of eagerness and dread. Deaf to the jollities whizzing around the Desdemona table, she imagined a cracked china face in her helping of duff. Mean currant eyes stared out from a mask of stodge. Frecks and Kali put mysteries out of mind while stuffing their faces, and bantered with un-Removed girls. Light Fingers was quieter, more thoughtful – but, then again, she always was. She spirited bread rolls and an apple from the table and wrapped them in a handkerchief – provisions for Miss Memory. Amy deliberately squashed evil currants with a spoon.

After Dinner, the Moth Club split up and made their separate ways to the meet.

Kali suggested they shake off tails. Their classmates were out and about, trying to unearth each other's secrets. Outside the Refec, Light Fingers zig-zagged away on a rapid tour of the grounds. Amy spotted Frost and Harper dogging her, but knew they'd soon give up. Larry, as ever, was peeping round a wall, eyes like neon fog-lamps. Amy turned to nudge Frecks, but she'd slipped away. Kali began bending, stretching and kicking the air, drawing a small crowd. With most eager eyes on Kali, Amy pantomimed a 'drat I've forgotten something' finger snap and doubled back into the Refec, thinking hard about an imaginary book left on her table. She nipped through the kitchen-side door, which led to an alley that happened to come out just next to the Infirmary.

She ran smack into Susannah Thorn, loitering by the swill bins, puffing on a cigarette. The Fifth only smoked so she could show off by lighting up without a match. Amy hadn't had much to do with Thorn this year. She was usually in a huddle with Frost. Thanks to the estrangement of firelighter and icemaker, Thorn was making do with Fleur Paquignet as a fill-in bosom companion. More comfortable with plants than people, Paquignet held an unlit ciggy as if no one had ever shown her which end to stick in her mouth.

'Hello, Amy,' said Paquignet.

Amy couldn't remember the Ariel Unusual ever using her first name. She was a Fifth, and Fifths didn't address Fourths familiarly. Even in the Remove.

Everyone had changed. Was it down to Miss Kratides?

Would *Paquignet* blame her for not telling what she knew about Laurence?

It was hard to imagine Green Thumbs blaming anyone for anything. Plants don't blame. They accept. They live with seasons and weather.

'Hello, Fleur,' said Amy.

'Have you noticed she's shot up,' said Thorn. 'Someone's been *watering her*.'

Paquignet smiled. The expression struck Amy as artificial. Not an obvious sham, like Palgrave's impersonation of a living girl. But wrong.

Now it was mentioned, Paquignet *was* taller this term.

Flowers liked moths. Bees get all the credit, but night pollination is almost entirely down to moths.

Paquignet's smile reminded her that some flowers *ate* moths.

Thorn stubbed her smoke out on the wall and flicked the dog-end into a bin.

'Come on, Goosegog,' she said. 'Let's go to the picture show. Maybe Mary Pickford will get thrown in a lake by orphans. She's been simpering for an age and could do with a dunking.'

Thorn beetled off and Paquignet followed. As she left, she gave Amy a wave – *to be continued…*

Thorn and Paquignet out of sight, Amy walked past the bins to the Infirmary. She was the last of the Moth Club to arrive. Knowles had been with Devlin for a while.

Nurse Humphreys briskly welcomed the visitors. Leaving them to cheer up her patient, she retreated to her office to spend an hour with a racing form and her spirit guides. Humph was Nellie Pugh's most loyal customer, and always either flush or skint – depending on how her nags were running at Taunton. A devout believer in her Abilities as a spirit medium, she got tips by communing with champions long since departed (after a brief, unpleasant stop-off at the knackers' yard) for the Elysian paddock. Silver Blaze, the Wessex Cup winner, rapped race and jockey numbers with spectral hoofs.

'I've solved that mystery,' said Stretch. 'The kitchen is next door and a ventilation grille means someone with a crafty ear can listen in to the Infirmary Office. Nellie knocks on the pipes with a horseshoe. She gives Nurse wrong steers two-thirds of the time, with enough solid gen to give the ninny a win whenever she gets depressed and thinks of packing in the gambling lark. One for the Hoax File.'

When dedicated investigators Knowles and Devlin ran the Hypatia Hall Psychical Investigation Soc, they kept two files – Hoax and Haunting. One much fatter than the other. Both neglected now. Gwendolyn Nobbs, new President of the Spook-Spotters, was a mean-spirited japestress who stocked the Soc with sheet-wearing cronies. Their chief activity was devising cruel frauds to perpetuate on the gullible.

The Moth Club and Knowles sat on chairs around Devlin's bed. Knowles did her best to eat her smuggled lunch quietly. Stretch's foot-long feet poked out from the blankets at the end of her bed. She was pulled long and thin like a prisoner on the rack in a *Punch* cartoon. Without thinking, she tugged her chin into a potato shape. Another casualty of Villa DeVille who was not yet her old self.

When she thought Devlin wouldn't notice, Light Fingers stuck a pencil in her arm.

No reaction.

So the numbness was confirmed.

'I'll be up and about again in no time,' said Stretch.

'Of course you will,' said Knowles.

Only two other beds in the Infirmary were occupied. Millie Trundleclough, a Goneril Second, was laid up with her latest sporting injury. With more pluck than sense, she was forever barging into rucks and getting something sprained, bruised or skinned. At the far end of the room, Kathleen Vaughn wheezed in a curtained bed, felled by a mystery illness. Devlin said Vaughn had eaten soap, with an eye on being cast as Malingering

Marguerite when the Viola Players put on *Camille*. She was a devotee of the Stanislavski Method.

Two more visitors arrived. Little and Speke. With a clacking of finger-things, Speke pulled a card out of her sleeve and gave it to Knowles.

If she closed her eyes, Amy could hear Speke's playing.

Te-tum-te-tum-titty-tum-titty-tum…

If she opened them, she could see the girl's crab-hands.

Amy was disturbed by Speke's Attributes and ashamed of her reaction. She couldn't suppress her instinctive revulsion. Speke wasn't Harper or Palgraive – who gave everybody the creeps. So far as Amy could tell, the Second was a kind, bright, decent girl… It was just her hands…

She tried to concentrate on the girl's bland, shiny face.

Little was happy to be invited anywhere. She sat on an empty bed, which bowed and strained. Speke was curious.

'You know this mob,' said Knowles. 'They sit at the back, in a square.'

'The Butterfly Brigade,' said Little, flapping her huge arms.

'Generally, we go by the Moth Club,' admitted Frecks.

'I'm Harriet and this is Gillian,' said Speke.

'This is about the Broken Doll,' said Knowles.

Little stopped flapping and sat quietly, frightened.

Speke's hands writhed and clattered in her lap.

'My second secret is… *She is right to be afraid of the Broken Doll*,' said Speke.

'That's my first,' admitted Amy.

'I don't want to tell mine,' said the Second. 'If that's all right.'

Amy and Frecks exchanged looks. They had wondered about the kind of secrets no one would want to share.

You could use your Talent to heal the sick – but won't.

Was that Speke's first secret? Could her crab-hands take away pain and suffering?

'Some girl *shaves*,' said Little, fright forgot, giggling.

'That's her second secret,' said Speke. 'An easy one. What's her name – the Scots doggie girl?'

'Gould,' said Amy. 'Aconita Gould.'

Little growled and giggled at the same time.

'She *shaves…* like a man. She has stubble.'

'I doubt she just shaves her face,' said Light Fingers.

'My first secret is nothingish… *You don't think your name is half as funny as others do.*'

Speke shrugged sadly.

'I'm used to it,' said Little. 'Sometimes when girls make fun, I don't see the joke. It gets boring after a while. Besides, names don't mean anything. They're just names. You don't pick them.'

'Little has a big heart,' said Speke kindly.

'And everything else,' said Devlin, slightly spoiling it though Little didn't seem to notice.

'May I ask a question?' said Speke.

'Of course,' said Knowles. 'We're not beaks and this isn't class.'

Speke asked, '*Are* you afraid of the Broken Doll?'

'I don't even know who or what the Broken Doll is,' said Amy.

'But are you afraid of her? Like the secret says.'

'The secret doesn't say that, though.'

'No, it doesn't,' said Speke, one hand climbing over the other, fingertips scrittering on carapace. 'It says you are *right* to be afraid of the Broken Doll. Which means we all should be, doesn't it? The Broken Doll isn't just frightening, but dangerous.'

Amy realised something. She was not a fearless paladin. Unmitigated courage was foolish. Trundleclough was fearless, and look where that got her. Amy was afraid of being hurt or being responsible for others getting hurt. She was afraid of Stephen Swift and Nightcap, and Wrong 'Uns in general. She was afraid of Count DeVille's cloak, and the things inside her it had woken. She was afraid of Larry's pocket, and what it had done to Poll Sparks. She was afraid of floating off in her sleep and freezing or gasping her last in the upper atmosphere.

But – despite seeing a face in a dream or in pudding – she

wasn't afraid of the Broken Doll. Not really. Not yet.

Though, if Miss Kratides was on the money, she should be.

'Since Speke came to me, I've investigated the Broken Doll,' said Knowles. 'I have collected reports.' Knowles tapped her swollen head. 'The first mention is one of the earliest ghost stories of Drearcliff Grange. Older than the Bloody Bosun or Mauve Mary. Not even a proper story. Just a description. Of an Apparition. Two apparitions. A figure in a long dress. A grown woman with a doll's face – cracked across. Sometimes, she's limping. Sometimes, she's missing an arm. She carries a doll herself, but a doll with a living child's face. The child's mouth is open as if screaming. But these are silent spectres. Visitors to the Grange saw them if they opened a wrong door. Always, behind the door was an abandoned playroom...'

That detail chilled Amy.

'But it wasn't always the same door. It could be a cupboard or a stable door as easily as a bedroom or a cellar door. From descriptions, it was always the same playroom. Full of broken toys for the Broken Doll. The woman with the dead doll's face and the doll with the living child's face. Folk who saw that didn't forget it easily. The local versions of the story you hear from old wives in cottages or rambling gents on the beach often end with the ghost-seeing visitor dying before the month is out... or, worse, their children dying and becoming playthings for the Broken Doll. I've gone over the records and that part's not true. Three diarists and one vicar left accounts of the haunting, over a period of 150 years. All lived to ripe old ages afterwards, and none had any problems with their children. Except the vicar, whose daughter dressed up as a boy and joined the army. She came home in the end. With a medal. Ghosts get blamed even for things that didn't happen. It's human nature to make sense of a manifestation by making up a story to go around it. Even an unhappy ending is an ending.'

'Our folder on the Broken Doll is in the Haunting File,' said Devlin. 'No Hoax detected. Since she'd not showed her face in over a hundred years, she wasn't exactly a pressing concern. Not like Mauve Mary or Eyeless Egbert.'

'Some ghosts have lifespans after life,' said Knowles. 'They linger a while, then fade. Like an echo dying. There are theories… but you don't need to know all that. We'll put it in the footnotes. That Broken Doll – for the want of more evidence, let's call her the original – retired even before Squire Teazle's day. Others have claimed the name. In the 1860s, Bath and Bristol were plagued by a Broken Doll Gang. Little girls waved sad, smashed-face dolls under the noses of decent folk as a distraction while other children lifted wallets and watches. These weren't urchins, but well-dressed, well-spoken, well-off brats. A few got arrested but juries let them off for being polite little rotters. Speculation was that a dismissed governess was behind the racket. Adults didn't want to admit that the kids might have come up with the game on their own. They should have asked children what children were like. As we know, the dullest Dims can sparkle with ingenuity when devising larceny or torment. The Broken Doll Gang may have startled the burghers of Bath, but I'd bet they'd not last two days at this school. The whips would have them.'

'There's a song called "A Broken Doll",' said Kali. 'Jolson sang it.'

Knowles nodded. 'Yes, and Stretch found a storybook by Uncle Satt, *The Beeswax of the Broken Doll*.'

Devlin nodded. 'My Auntie Ruth was given it when she was a little girl – as a prize for eating all her greens during the Golden Jubilee. The verses are piffle but the illustrations are lovely.'

'The artist might have heard the Drearcliff Grange Broken Doll story,' said Knowles. 'One of his pictures shows a big doll and a small child.'

'Auntie was so frightened by that picture she gummed two pages together so she wouldn't have to look at it. The glue got old and I used a breadknife to uncover the dread sight.'

Devlin pulled a face – big eyes, stiff cheeks – for a moment.

Little jumped and was upset. Speke calmed her down with a smoothing pat on the back. Little wasn't disturbed by her friend's hands. That made Amy determined not to be either.

'Other broken dolls might be Chinese whispers versions of ours, or might be fresh manifestations of a many-faced entity,' said Knowles. 'Thomas Carnacki, the Ghost-Finder, dealt with an entity in the shape of a Broken *Russian* Doll. You know, those *babushkas* with smaller and smaller wooden dolls inside. Each smaller doll was more deformed. In the centre was a writhing centipede with the head of a miniature human baby. That's supposed to be in the Mausoleum now, where they keep all the cursed objects, captured entities and convicted Wrong 'Uns.'

The Undertaking was in charge of the Mausoleum. They served as a combination of prison warders and museum guards. Their involvement in the Great Game was one of their minor functions.

'Oh,' put in Stretch, 'there are lots and *lots* of yarns about mud dolls made by witch doctors. When broken or burned, the people they are supposed to represent snap their necks or melt like waxworks left near the fire.'

Devlin couldn't mention a snapped neck without unconsciously kinking her own at a terrible angle and poking out her tongue. It was a funny habit, but not at all amusing. The face she pulled when she mentioned melted wax figures was so disturbing Speke clapped her hands over Little's eyes.

Amy didn't know if any of these stories related to *her* Broken Doll.

'Why have you dug this up?' Amy asked.

'Not because of your secret,' Knowles admitted. 'Because of what happened to Speke and Little. Which is why I've roped them in. Amy, I think you'll need to hear this. The rest of you too. Harriet, if you'll do the honours…'

X: What Happened to Jimmy Wood

'I DON'T KNOW IF you've noticed,' said Harriet Speke, 'but my hands are funny. Peculiar, not ha ha. Here, look at 'em. I've more fingers than you and in different places. The skin is hard and rough, like seashell or painted muslin. You could strike a match on it. Hold the flame to my palm and I feel only a tickle. People say my hands look a bit like crabs.'

'You can touch them,' said Little. 'She doesn't mind.'

'I really don't. They're not special. Just different. When I was Removed, Miss Gossage told me about Unusuals and Talents and Abilities and what not. It took me ages to twig she wasn't talking about the rest of the class. She meant me. It still doesn't feel right. On one hand – ahem! – I'm different and a tidge strange, but we *all* are, aren't we? Like Gillian being bigger than most other Firsts—'

'Than *any* other Firsts.'

'Or you lot, with your floating and stretching and whooshing and so forth. When you think about it, all girls are different and a tidge strange. We wear the same boaters and skirts but that doesn't make us all the same. I have crabby hands. Williams has that white patch in her black hair. If a beak chalks a complicated sum on the blackboard, Toulmin can write down the answer without jottings or crossings-out before the rest of the class have sharpened their pencils. If my hands are *weird*, so's her face. Being in the Remove is a wheeze. The lessons are livelier than the babyish subjects I have as a Viola Second. But I don't see I'm *that* unusual. Patch Williams hasn't been Removed. See my point? You've got Abilities. I've only got Attributes. Gillian's not the same, because she's big *and* strong. As soon as my hands changed, I was booted from my old class and sent to Miss Gossage.

'I wasn't crabby until last year. I was born with "doll's hands". There's a Latin name for it. Dad got splashed with chemicals before he was married. Which might have something to do with it. He does secret work for the Department of Supplies. To do with germs and gases. Anyway, they were unbendy lumps. My baby hands. I know that's an odd expression – I mean it like baby teeth. I had the usual number of fingers, but stuck together like mittens. I could wiggle my thumbs a tiny bit. Generally, not much use.

'Last summer hols, my hands swelled as if I'd been bitten by wasps. My fingers fell off, one by one. I have them in a cigar box. There's no Finger Fairy to reward little girls like me. I'd ask half a crown for a finger. Gum leaked from the stumps and wrapped my hands in a jelly that set hard. The colour of Pears soap. For a week, my hands were like toffee apples. They itched but I couldn't scratch. No fingers, no finger*nails*. Then the crust turned brittle and flaked away from these lovelies.'

Speke held up her hands, and clacked all her fingers.

'After years of holding a beaker between my paws and dipping my head just to have a sip of milk, it's a relief to do things everyone else can. Fasten buttons, use a pencil, tie a shoelace. I don't care how it looks. When I pitched up for Autumn Term, Mademoiselle 'Obbs took one glim at my hands and had me Removed. I was pulled out of my cell and sent to the Green Room—'

'Where she met me!'

'Yes, where I met Gillian. Goneril didn't even try to find her a cell. First Year cots aren't her size. Sixth Year cots aren't either. Do you know the Green Room? It's off the Music Room in the Main Building. Third floor. Low ceiling this one keeps bumping her head on. Before me and Gillian moved in, it was a storeroom for old instruments and sheet music. It was the only place the school could spare for us. A normal cot for me and a reinforced bed for Gert Gertie.

'I know what you're thinking. It wasn't my cellmates who chucked me out. Williams, Wheele and Ring are stout fellows all. They were kind to me when I couldn't twist a doorknob. They are almost as kind now I can open anything, even if it's locked. *Almost.* Dad wrote School a letter about what my hands get up to at night and Dr Swan decided to put me in the Green Room. I wish he hadn't made a fuss but see why he did. I'm happy to muck in with Gillian.'

'We have many larks.'

'Yes, Gillian. We do.'

'When my new hands appeared, the doctors came back and prodded me a bit. Does *anyone* like doctors? I'd rather have a once-over and some salts from Nurse Humph than be prodded and have a syndrome named after me in Latin. It wasn't just the outsides of my hands that changed. I got the impression doctors wanted to peel the shells and poke about inside to see what's what. Dad sent them packing. Miss Borrodale says a cove called Othniel Marsh put about the funny idea that dinosaurs had extra brains in their bottoms and knees. Fancy that! Bums with minds of their own! There's a theory that I have brain tissue – not brains, but brain tissue – in my hands. It doesn't go to sleep when I do. You've heard of wandering hands? Well, I have two of the beasts. At home, I woke up a few times to find my hands had decided to crawl out of my bedroom. I was being dragged over the landing carpet. Once, I was bumped downstairs. I don't know what they want – what the brain tissue wants, rather – and I don't think they do either. They aren't clever, just alive. They're like cats or dogs… They want to wander, get the lie of the land, leave scratch marks.

'I read a big book about crustaceans, but it wasn't much use. I've not woken up in a rock pool yet. My hands *aren't* crabs. They're hands that look *a bit* like crabs. What they get up to when I'm asleep is another thing. Dad tried tying bags over my hands at night – but they got shredded. Then tied me to the bedposts but – guess what? – one thing my hands do perfectly well on their own is untie knots. My littlest fingers have sharp, knify sorts of nails. I have to be careful not to cut myself. Locking the bedroom door was a joke. My fingers can pick locks just like snap! I've learned to do that when I'm awake. The way I've learned to play the harpsichord. No sense in letting these clutchers have all the fun while I'm asleep and can't join in. Eleven years of doll's hands was enough for me.

'Dad was worried I'd hurt myself… or my hands would break something dangerous. He keeps a laboratory at home and worried about me getting splashed with chemicals. He said I might end up with lobsters for feet or a winkle for a nose. That's hardly likely but he's a fusspot. He started sitting up to watch me fall asleep. He said he was fascinated by the way my hands crept over the counterpane and scuttled around on the end of my arms. If he didn't put a stop to it, they'd drag me out of bed and into mischief. Once, he dozed off and woke up with my hands on his face, pulling his beard. I stayed asleep through it all and don't remember anything about it.

'Can you guess how Dad solved the problem with my wandering hands?'

Shaken heads all round. Gillian Little grinned.

'Simple,' continued Speke. 'He gave them something to play with. First, it was a knitted ragdoll – but my hands saw that as a lot of knots done up in a doll shape and undid them, letting the stuffing out. Then he took an old soldier toy out of a trunk of his own dad's things. Carved from a single piece of wood. Sat on a little horse. With a musket and busby. Most of the paint gone. Dad says Jimmy Wood was in the Light Brigade when they charged. He looks like he's been in the wars – ha ha, that's funny. Grandad must have had big battles in his nursery. I'm sure Jimmy was once one of a set, but all his comrades were casualties. He's a sole survivor. When Dad inherited his dad's toys, he sent Jimmy on punitive expeditions against hostile tribes—

'Sorry, Chattopadhyay – I didn't think. I'm sure hostile tribes are very brave by their own lights.

'Jimmy Wood got speared and burned a lot. Dad was interested in chemicals even as a lad and dripped acid on Jimmy's tunic. Grandad was in the Royal North Surrey Regiment. Dad remembers him saying Jimmy was typical British Army. You could do all sorts of horrid things to him, but he'd report smartly for duty the next morning. It turned out that my hands couldn't unpick him or shred him or pull him apart. The most they could do was scratch – and not very deeply. Old wood is like baked iron. With Jimmy on my pillow, my hands were busy – and I wasn't dragged out of bed any more. So, a happy solution.

'At School, this wouldn't work. Besides all the rules about dollies and such – which that horrible Gryce explained when confiscating Cecily Wheele's Sir Boris de Bruin last year – there's the question of the scratching. No one could be expected to sleep with that to-do in the room.'

'Except me.'

'Yes. Except Gillian. She's a sound sleeper.'

'I'll say.'

'So it's been the Green Room for us. A Remove of our own. Not as cosy as a dorm cell and we keep tripping over musical instruments.'

'She means *I* keep tripping over musical instruments.'

'The Green Room isn't warm either. We have to pile on extra blankets and it's a long walk to the washroom but it's a quiet place to do prep and I can nip next door and practise the harpsichord all I want. Even late in the evening. Because – whisper it! – we have no Lights Out. Flyte and Kite, the Viola Sixth whips, can't be bothered to hike over to the Main Building to scold us. At night, we've the run of the place. Gillian, me, my hands... and Jimmy Wood. He's been granted special dispensation. No dollies allowed at Drearcliff Grange, *except veterans of the Crimean War*. He's been in the Green Room all year. One of his eyes got clawed away before Christmas, but it was only a paint blob and I fixed it with pencil. For two terms, things settled. Then, in the last two weeks, things unsettled. Someone new has come to school. She doesn't like Jimmy Wood at all.'

'The Broken Doll,' said Little.

'That's what Gillian calls it.'

'Her. I've seen her.'

'So have I, but I'm getting ahead of the story.

'At first, I thought my hands were wearing Jimmy down. His musket broke. I couldn't find the barrel anywhere. If my hands had snapped it off, the bit'd be there, wouldn't it? But it was gone. Spirited away. My hands don't have mouths, so they couldn't have eaten the thing. They couldn't shove it in my mouth and make me swallow it without me noticing. We didn't give it much thought. It must have rolled away somewhere, I said. Gillian agreed. Jimmy Wood looks wrong without half his musket, though. The stock is still there. Just the barrel and bayonet gone.'

'His face changed. He's angry and scared.'

'I didn't see that. He looks the same to me. But Gillian may be right. She notices things. The next night, Jimmy's horse's head was off. Like it was chopped with an axe. The wood inside was white. The head was just gone. I blamed my hands.'

'Bad hands.'

'I thought they'd gone too far. I put Jimmy in my trunk and gave my hands something else to play with – an old violin case, with a face painted on it. They scratched at that, but I wasn't dragged out of bed. Gillian said she missed Jimmy and wanted to know he was all right—'

'In the trunk. Nobody should be locked in a trunk. Or the

wedge-shaped cupboard under the stairs that smells of tennis balls. That happened to me once a few times and I didn't like it much at all.'

'I unlocked the trunk and found Jimmy Wood. He had a cleft in his head. Through his busby and forehead. As if someone had hit him with an axe.'

Little started sniffling.

'It's all right, Gillian. He's stout-hearted. He doesn't feel it. A British soldier.'

'Are you sure, Harry?'

'Yes, I'm sure. You could chop him to bits and he wouldn't feel it. He'd still be him and he'd still be on duty.'

'But the Broken Doll…'

'The name didn't mean a dickybird when Gillian first said it. I didn't know all those stories, Knowles. The doll-faced grown-up and the living-faced doll. The pack of pickpockets. They don't sound like *our* Broken Doll. She isn't a life-size dress-shop dummy or a wax murderer in Tussaud's. She's only big for a doll. Bigger than any child who'd own her. A doll for babyish princesses or millionaires' daughters. Her frilly dress must have cost as much as a ballgown. It's old and crinkly stuff, scummy with lace mould. She scurries like a monkey, but her face doesn't move. It's china, cracked across. Her hands are like mine used to be. *Doll's hands.* Stiff, but if she presses them together she can hold a chopper.'

'Harry said I was dreaming when I saw the Broken Doll… but she *chopped* things.'

'Not just Jimmy. She dented a bassoon. We got infracted for that, because we were the only girls in the Green Room so we must have done it. We didn't tell Flyte and Kite about the Broken Doll, because we knew they'd say we were fibbing. We told Knowles because I read one of her father's books and wondered if she'd ask him if Mr Phatt could solve the mystery. She was so nice and didn't say Gillian was dreaming or my hands must have done it. See these marks – like healed cuts. I didn't have them last week. The Broken Doll did them. I don't know why she didn't chop me where it would hurt. I'm not hard-shelled all over.

'You said the Broken Doll was a ghost. I don't think she is. Ghosts are mist or water. Not solids. They can scare you but not hurt you. Not all people see them. The Department of Supplies asked Dad to make a chemical solution to wash ghosts out of places. The Navy has a haunted submarine they'd like back. In the end, the chemicals didn't work. It's easier to recruit a crew who don't see drowned sailors and get on with their duties. This Broken Doll isn't a drowned sailor. She's more like a goblin in a dress and wig and mask. Drowned sailors are sad. The Broken Doll is spiteful. She's a thing. A girl. An Unusual. She's not a practical joker in a phosphorus-soaked sheet, going *woo-woo-wooo*. Nobbs of the Fifth tried to throw a fright into Gillian and me the first week we were in the Green Room—'

'I thumped her. She stopped wailing and started crying.'

'As if anyone wouldn't recognise the stink of phosphorus. Or tell a sheet from a shroud. This Broken Doll is no practical joke. I knew she was real even when only Gillian saw her. Then I started seeing her too. Not in dreams… but while lying in bed, not awake or asleep. She pokes about early in the morning, well before getting out of bed time but after it's light. I don't think she likes real darkness. No ghost would be afraid of the dark, would they? When she's around, I don't move… it's not that I can't, it's that I forget to… I lie stiff as a board, eyes shut but for a sliver so I can peep out. I don't know what's worse – seeing her full on or not seeing her at all but knowing she's there. She crawls up onto my cot and plays with my hands. Then I *do* shut my eyes all the way, because I don't want to see her cracked white face too close. I hear her, though – scratching and breathing.'

'She *tuts* like a Governess,' said Little. 'Mrs Fessel always has a hatpin ready for when Mama looks away.'

'I don't know where she hides most of the time or how she gets into the Green Room,' said Speke. 'She doesn't glow. No phosphorus. Her dress is old, not a costume. You can't *make* mould. She's not pretending. She is what she is. She doesn't carry a chopper that I can see. She's not interested in hurting Jimmy Wood any more. That was to get our attention. Now she wants to hurt people who *aren't* wood. Or she will soon. She's playing with us.

'I wondered if she was a girl on the register, booted from the Remove. Too unusual even for our mob. Weirder than that Desdemona Third who smiles all the time with her mouth but has screaming eyes. Weirder than the Scots doggie girl or the Yank carp girl. Knowles says no one like the Broken Doll was ever in the Remove, all the way back to Founding Day. This Broken Doll has only been at Drearcliff Grange for two weeks. She's a new bug.

'She started after you came back from the Great Game. I think she came back with you.'

XI: Yorick of Basingstoke
Viewed Rosie in Garters

*S*O THE *SECUNDUS* prize Amy had won for Drearcliff Grange was a spiteful ghost. Perhaps not a ghost, but something worse.

The Broken Doll.

After a procedural chinwag, the combined forces of the Moth Club and the Real Spook-Spotters determined to put a night watch on the Green Room. While Speke and Little slept as soundly as possible under the circs, a two-girl team would mount a vigil in shifts. Speke said the Broken Doll most often manifested in the hour before dawn. So, for the final shift of the night, the girls would wake each other properly with slaps and water and both be fully alert. In theory.

Knowles drew a rota and everyone tossed coins. Light Fingers and Kali were up for the first night. After Kaveney finished corridor patrol, they slipped out of the dorms. Light Fingers' speed and Kali's stealth fit them for night work.

Amy and Frecks stayed behind.

In case of a bed-check, all the cots in their cell were occupied.

The Moth Club rented wickerwork frames and papier-mâché heads from Lucinda Leigh of the Fifth. Though not listed on the Desdemona register, Sleeping Betty and Dinah Snore were among the most popular girls in the house. Dissatisfied with the hoary device of plumped-up pillows, Morrigan McHugh and Adrienne Penny had fashioned the twins to lie in for them while they jaunted on nocturnal adventures that were – all things considered – fairly mild. They mostly sat on the roof in their nighties and giggled while drinking ginger beer. Their handiwork was more inspired than their misbehaviour. Sleeping Betty's clockwork mechanism raised and lowered blankets to simulate breathing. A balloon inside Dinah Snore gradually let air escape in a gentle murmur. McHugh and Penny passed out last year, leaving their creations to the enterprising Leigh, who made them available for a fee to those in-the-know... which was practically every girl in the house except Kaveney.

With the cell to themselves, Amy could talk with Frecks about Laurence. Something should be done about her. Something should be done *for* her. Amy needed to make it up to the girl, but Larry wasn't interested in reparations from her. She sought only Frecks' grace.

Before Amy could initiate that thorny conversation, Frecks fell asleep.

Amy didn't. She lay on her cot, listening to the breathing clockwork and the sighing balloon.

How did all these Broken Dolls – the ones Knowles dug up stories about, the one Speke and Little had seen – fit with her Broken Doll? It couldn't all be a lot of coincidences.

Other worries nagged.

Her personal tutorial was tomorrow morning. Miss Kratides was seeing each of the Remove in alphabetical order by first name. The system was unthinkable anywhere else in school. Not calling a register by surname was like reordering the colours of the rainbow.

Amy still hadn't matched her second secret to a name.

She will blame you for not telling what you know about Laurence.

Could it *be* Larry? No – the girl blamed Amy for a wealth of wrongs, but surely not for keeping quiet about her new Ability.

It wasn't as if Larry proudly announced her pocket could make Unusuals Ordinary.

Amy turned over in her narrow cot. Her pillow got on top of her face. Her sheets and blankets were loose and her bottom stuck out into the cold. She turned over again, wrestling the pillow under her head. She tried to settle comfortably and wasn't satisfied. Now she was too hot under all the swaddling. Expanding a mentacle, she lifted the bedclothes and let cool air into her cocoon. Then, she withdrew and the blankets settled.

Her thoughts drifted back to her first secret.

You are right to be afraid of the Broken Doll.

Whoever or whatever the Broken Doll was, Miss Kratides *knew about her*. They all took their teacher's wide-ranging knowledge for granted... but *how* did she know these things? How *much* did she know about the Broken Doll?

More than just the name, obviously.

Tomorrow, should she ask Miss Kratides about the Broken Doll?

Could she trust any answer from the teacher? The most infracted girl ever to pass out of Drearcliff Grange. Daughter of a professional murderess.

Amy lay flat, trying not to fidget. She shut her eyes but didn't sleep. She opened them but saw only gloom.

She needed a good night's sleep tonight. Apart from wanting to be alert for her tutorial, she mustn't be too tired to stay awake tomorrow when she was on vigil.

She thought of green bottles, accidentally falling...

She lost count but did not lose consciousness.

The clockwork and the balloon sounded like a hammer on an anvil and a blacksmith's bellows. Amy was tempted to silence the dummies by getting mentacles into their chests and pulling out wires. Turning an automaton off wasn't murder. Even the small, contented, happy-sleep sounds Frecks made were a cats' chorus. Amy could stifle the noise with a pillow, without even getting off her cot. She shrank from that thought, as if she'd touched her tongue to a battery.

She wished she'd won the coin toss. If she had to be awake all night, at least she'd have been some use on watch in the Green Room.

How much more broken could the Broken Doll get?

Would she be such a horror as the Smashed-to-Bits Doll?

At length, exhaustion and numbness quieted her thoughts. Her bedclothes felt not too heavy and not too light. She was on the point of dropping off... when Sleeping Betty made a loud noise – wicker struts creaking and internal gears screaming – and sat up in Kali's cot, papier-mâché head kinked sharply to one side, a rip across its smiling face... and live eyes staring venom at Amy!

'Stir yourself, or you'll miss breakfast.'

Dark turned to daylight in a snap.

Betty's terrifying new face... dissolved into Frecks' first-thing-in-the-morning bleary jollity.

Amy had been asleep and now was jolted awake.

Her heart was racing. Her eyes were gummy.

Frecks shook her again.

'You were far gone,' said Frecks. 'Dismal Drearcliff day awaits...'

Kali and Light Fingers were back in the cell. Kali was lively and awake. Light Fingers was alternating lassitude with bursts of speed. Kali had found perfect poise and balance cross-legged on a flat mat. Light Fingers had cricked her back and neck trying to get comfortable in a hairy chair.

They were folding the twins' wicker frames. The disembodied heads – unbroken and smiling – went back in a pillowcase. Betty and Dinah could be dismantled and concealed between napping appearances.

'It was a no-show,' said Kali. 'We were ready to give 'em the works, but no one turned up.'

'Speke's hands *are* weird though,' said Light Fingers. 'When she's asleep, they get frisky as kittens.'

'Light Fingers tried to talk with 'em.'

'Morse code,' said Light Fingers. 'I tapped on the knuckles and gave them a pencil case to tap back on.'

'No dice?'

'None whatsoever. I had to pull back sharpish not to get nipped.'

Amy got out of her cot and unstuck her nightie from her back. She had sweated it through – all in a spasm, at the sight of that *face*.

She was calming, soothed by the chatter of her pals – but where had the night gone?

Had she only dreamed of lying awake for hours?

In the Refec at breakfast, Knowles slid down from the Fifth table to get a report from the Moth Club. She talked too fast and got sidetracked often. She bombarded the night watch with Psychical Investigation questions about cold spots – Kali thought she meant cold sores – and other phenomena. Light Fingers admitted they'd heard a slight twang of string instruments in the Music Room next door. Miss Memory said it was probably differential cooling.

'First seek a natural explanation,' said Knowles.

She was misquoting Guilbert Phatt, whose dictum was 'First *and last* seek a natural explanation.'

Amy didn't mention Sleeping Betty sitting up wearing the face of the Broken Doll.

Dawn had come and gone uneventfully in the Green Room.

Had the Broken Doll come to the Moth Club's cell instead?

XII: Notes from Miss Kratides

AFTER BREAKFAST, AMY had an hour of Mademoiselle 'Obbs on *passé simple*, *passé composé* and *passé antérieur*. It was dawning on brighter sparks – who had scored high marks when the subject was taught by the lively, departed Miss Bedale – that Mademoiselle 'Obbs only knew French *in theory*. Her lessons were stuffed with tenses, cases, rules and exceptions but devoid of speaking, reading or writing. Her practical skills were limited to talking in English with an *ooh-la-la* accent like a maid in a variety turn. As a consequence, Monday Morning French supplanted Thursday Double Deportment as Dullest Lesson of the Week.

Amy heard 'Madame-Weasel' droning but could not concentrate.

At ten o'clock, according to her Time-Table Book, she should have Sciences with Miss Borrodale – who was often alarming, but never boring. Today, she was required to report to Windward Cottage for her tutorial with Miss Kratides. A note of passage shielded her from prowling whips who would otherwise infract her for being out of class.

Walking on her own to Windward Cottage wasn't like trooping there with the whole Remove. That had been almost the start of an adventure. This was following a chalk line to doom:

beside the playing fields, through the trees, past Lamarcroft's Leap, across Clifftop Meadow.

To avoid thinking of what was to come next...

She will blame you for not telling what you know about Laurence.

She thought about what would come later.

An all-night vigil in the Green Room, with Frecks. Would their quarry show her cracked face? Itching for a scrap, Frecks went about loudly defying 'the Damaged Dolly' as if the frightful thing could hear her.

You are right to be afraid of the Broken Doll.

Everything came back to secrets.

Amy walked into the copse. Shoes hung in front of her face. A girl sat on the lowest branch of a tree. Amy tensed, thinking Laurence might be perched in wait, purple stones in her pocket like bullets in a gun. Her mentacles went up, to bat away missiles.

It was Fleur Paquignet.

'I should be before Amy,' the girl told the tree.

The whole class was flummoxed by Miss Kratides' informality.

'F isn't before A,' Amy said, trying to sound cheerful. 'P is before T, but only everywhere else. In the Remove, things are different.'

Paquignet didn't seem to hear. Her ear was pressed to a knothole.

'Talk to trees all you want,' said Uncle Freddie, who thought he was a card. 'Get worried when they start talking back. Ha Ha.'

Uncle Freddie had no idea about Unusuals.

Amy couldn't talk to moths, but Marsh could communicate after a fashion with fish. Amy wouldn't be surprised to learn Paquignet got sounder tips from oak and ash than Nurse Humph got from dead horses.

Leaving the peculiar Fifth to commune with nature, Amy stepped onto Clifftop Meadow.

Windward Cottage seemed picturesque and inviting. It was a

pleasant morning. Someone nimbler than Joxer had straightened the weathervane. With fresh paint on tin sails, the ship proudly indicated a north-east breeze.

Amy remembered the gingerbread house was a booby trap set by a witch.

The front door opened. Gould loped out on all fours – face pushed forward like a snout, teeth bigger and yellower than ever, a crop of bristles on cheeks and forehead. The moon was down and not full, but the Sixth was at her wolfiest.

Aconita came before Amanda. She had first tutorial.

Gould spied Amy on the path and reared. Not sitting up to beg, but establishing dominance with fangs and scowl. Gould's body was rearranged. Not stretched like Devlin, but corded with animal muscle. Her shoulders strained her blazer seams. The stub of a tail pricked up her skirt.

Rather than have her throat bitten, Amy doffed her boater.

Satisfied, Gould stalked off on two legs.

Amy pitied the whip who tried to infract her for improper tail display.

She went up the front steps and into the cottage.

The classroom was empty, but a door – previously unnoticed because it stood flush with the wall – stood open.

'Come in,' called Miss Kratides.

Amy sidled into a room decked out as a Captain's cabin. A grilled porthole cast a wavery sea reflection on the low ceiling. Fitted shelves had ropes to keep books from spilling in rough seas. A figurehead thrust over a low roll-top desk, spongy face worn off by salt spray.

Miss Kratides was beside the desk, cosy in her chair-on-wheels. Her feet didn't touch the carpet. She wore polished black Sunday pumps, strangely speckled with scarlet. Amy had forgotten how *small* the teacher was. Germs were small too – and more died of influenza than in the War.

An armchair was set out for the victim. Miss Kratides indicated it. Amy sat. Gripping the arms, she noticed new scratches.

'Don't mind the wear and tear,' said Miss Kratides. 'Last customer had claws.'

Amy put her hands in her lap.

'I've twelve of these tête-a-têtes today,' said Miss Kratides. 'I'll be here till ten o'clock at night. What fun. The other eight of you on Wednesday. Imagine – an hour with Polly Palgraive. I'm supposed to talk to the worm in her brain. Dr Swan insists no girl is written off in the Remove. Even the smiling dead. We all must answer to Dr Swan. Girls and staff.'

Amy wondered what Miss Kratides had planned for tomorrow – maybe she had Tuesdays off.

'Amanda,' said Miss Kratides. 'Are you an Amy or a Mandy?'

'Amy,' she admitted.

'You have other names.'

'Uh… Thomsett.'

'Not that one,' said Miss Kratides, half grinning. 'The night-time name.'

How did she know about *that*?

'The same way I know everything else,' Miss Kratides said.

She was a—

'Mind-reader? Overrated Talent. People don't think clearly enough to give telepathists much advantage. No… I pay attention and make notes. I'm naturally nosy. A bit of it's a parlour trick. I look at your shoes and tell you that you squandered your inheritance on worthless opal mines in New South Wales, are foreman in a bicycle factory, and are about to leave your wife for a left-handed acrobat. You're amazed. I imply I've *deduced* all this from mud on your trouser cuffs. But really I've combed newspaper archives and listened to gossip in your local. I know all there is to know about you before you even come through the door. A man my mother worked for said deduction was much less reliable than simply *finding out*.'

When she talked, Miss Kratides was animated. Her curls bobbed. The smile-side of her face dimpled.

'So, your other name?'

'Kentish Glory,' said Amy shyly.

Few outside the Moth Club had even heard the handle. No one who'd seen her in her costume immediately identified the markings.

'That's the one. A Kentish Glory is a kind of moth. I looked it up. That's your theme, isn't it? Moths. Territorial. Colourful display. The name has *glory* in it. You don't merely flutter, you *soar*. You are the flying girl. Aspirational and inspirational. Amy, do you see yourself as – what do they say in the *Girls' Paper* – a *paladin*?'

Amy didn't answer.

'You don't immediately say yes. Good. Don't be too quick to take up a heavy shield. Or accept definitions foisted on you by others. That can get you into hot water. Do you remember me as a girl? When I was on your side of the desk.'

Amy wasn't sure whether to answer.

'You won't get in trouble for speaking up,' said Miss Kratides. 'In this cabin, there are no infractions. So, me as a Drearcliff girl? You could hardly forget. It only seems five minutes ago. I've had *adventures* in the months since I passed out. Perils, exploits and misdemeanours. As predicted, I've been up to no good. Possibly, as was *not* predicted, I've learned my lesson. Dr Swan thinks so and even at my worst I knew not to argue with Headmistress. The whole school knew me as Arch-Infractor. I cultivated the reputation. If I had to be bad, I'd be the worst. The most terrible. It did me little good. Oh, I had a few victories... but there was usually a whipping at the end of it.'

Her hand slipped to her wonky hip.

'Do you enjoy my Game of Secrets?' asked Miss Kratides. 'Here's a secret of *mine*. I'm *not* intractable, though I made the school think I was. I'm flexible. Slippery, even. Any other impression I give is a distraction. From what I'm playing at.'

Amy couldn't help looking at Miss Kratides rubbing her – aching? – hip. She didn't see her other hand coming.

Deft as Light Fingers, Miss Kratides brushed Amy's lapel.

She opened her fist and Amy saw her own house pin.

'See,' said Miss Kratides.

Amy took her pin and put it back.

'I don't limp, by the way,' Miss Kratides said. 'The lollop is for Hjordis Bok's benefit. She needs someone she can talk to about being surrounded by flukes she thinks have a head start on her. Me being hobbled too is a hook into her heart. I can use that. Gryce's whippings hurt, but she knew better than to do permanent damage. I told her I'd take one of her eyes if she lamed me. I still might. Dr Swan talked me into being a beak, so I can't hate Drearcliff Grange as much as I thought I did… but I hate Sidonie Gryce more than you do. I'm not just saying that to use a hook in *your* heart. You're not like Bok. You merit plain talking-to, not nudges and winks. Even in the Remove, you shine. Don't puff up. I'm not flattering. I'm telling you what you already know but don't want to admit you know. Like Miss Call of the Wild. She had to be let off her lead. Aconita needs to run true to her bloodlines, not see-saw between Lady of the Laird and She-Wolf of the Glens.'

On cue, a howling sounded. The frozen side of Miss Kratides' mouth twitched – trying hard for a full smile.

'Drearcliff Grange has its Apostle Spoons, Amy,' she continued. 'Head Girl. Captain of the First Eleven. And other notables – School Clown, School Saint, School Slut. Stock figures, like Chaucer's Pilgrims or commedia dell'arte characters. In slots in a display case. All schools have a full set. Imagine the Draycott's Bully! Or the Humble College Dunce. I was School Wrong 'Un. You're School Paladin. You showed that during the businesses with the Ant Queen and Mrs Rinaldo… and the cad who tried to elope with Isabella Fortune…'

Amy's mouth opened.

'Hobart Gunt, alias Rex Rowland, Hiram Q. Hollardollar, or the Belted Earl of Buckfastleigh,' said Miss Kratides. 'You're surprised I know the story, but remember what I said. I snoop. I listen. I find out. Gunt was a wretched excuse for a man. You served him right. If with too much restraint for some tastes. After you dropped the bounder into the sea – not too far from shore for even a weak swimmer – he got over Fortune and pitched woo at the dumpy daughter of a manganese magnate. Called himself Roger Manley then. Got to Gretna Green with the nitwit before someone with a *heavier* touch caught up. So, Mrs Manley is a widow at seventeen.'

Amy was shocked.

'No, I wasn't the kindly soul who stuffed stones in Gunt's sporran before his midnight dip in the Esk. It wasn't my mother either. Miss Memory's told you about her. *Mitéra* would happily take a shy at a bad egg, but in these enlightened days she has competition. A Drearcliff Old Girl to boot. Sister of my next appointment. Since she passed out, Angela De'Ath has collected five purses on the likes of Barty Gunt. The widow's family paid up with some grumpiness. The girl won't thank them, but it's the principle, isn't it? If a forty-two-year-old roué in a wig dupes their porky princess into marriage, any decent family would hire the Angel of Death before paying him off.'

Amy remembered De'Ath's sister as a serious girl – top in languages, merciless bowler. Now, mercenary assassin. Dr Swan was probably proud.

'Didn't think to send a bill to *Bella Fortuna's* old man?' Miss Kratides went on. 'Remiss of you. Then again, you're not in it for the spondulicks. What are you in it for? Not the larks. Those are the worst of 'em. You should hear the Blue Streak laugh. It'd give you the chills. You've not been knocked about enough – not even in the Great Game – to be in it for dark vengeance, like that Shade fellow. No, you're in it for the… what, the *goodness*? Because it's the thing to do? Know what terrors like the Slink or Sally Nikola's dad call treasures like you? Right 'Uns. You don't tend to hear it properly. It's Right Ones, as in "she looks a *right one* in that get-up with the feathers and sparkles". Which, though it pains me to bring it up, you certainly do.'

Amy was brought up short, as if slapped.

'Your second secret…'

'Ah...'

'Yes, I know. You've no clue.'

'I thought maybe...'

'As I said, no clue. Amy, Amy... you have advantages. With your Abilities, all sorts of underhand ways and means of finding things out at are your disposal. Light and De'Ath use the occult to pry and peep. Staring into bowls of water and chanting. They read your card yesterday. They didn't even need to. Their cards have each other's secrets. Acting on their own initiative, they're learning what they can accomplish if they set aside their mutual dislike, which for them was the point of the exercise. Your fast friend could have picked pockets and read everybody's cards on the way to supper. You can float silently outside windows and open locked boxes with your mindfingers. Yet you and Naisbitt have failed to solve your second secrets. Why is that?'

'Mine *isn't* a secret – it's a guess.'

'Do I strike you as someone who *guesses*?'

'You strike me as someone who'll try anything.'

Miss Kratides sat back a moment. Then she laughed.

'See, you could do it if you just piped up more often. Didn't *think* so much. You think *a lot*. You all do, bless you. But you especially, Amy. Knowles *knows*, but you think.'

Amy remembered wondering if thinking too much was her leaf.

But it was hard to think your way out of thinking.

Maybe more than hard. Maybe impossible.

She could lift a stove by thinking. Her whole Talent was *thinking*. Kali's lamas might witter on about chi energy or soul, but her mentacles *were* her mind – not a nebulous ectoplasm shroud she had to not think of to let loose... If she thought, she could fly... if she let her mind go blank, she fell.

'You'll have gone through the whole register, ticking off the girls whose secrets you know... wondering about all the rest. Too distracted by your first secret – your own secret which is no secret at all – to get the answer.'

'So, what? Do I fail? Am I booted from the Remove?'

'Not so fast, not so easy. The Remove is like Devil's Island. Once here, it's for life. Not even passing out of school will get you out of the Remove. I was Removed for a term. Here I am, back again. All these months later. If I can pick up the chalk, then you can peel off the mask. Why haven't you found out who will *blame you for not telling what you know about Laurence*?'

Miss Kratides leaned forward. Her face was close to Amy's.

The dead side of her mouth twitched tinily. If she could fake a limp for a few days, could she fake her half-fixed smile for a whole lifetime?

'It's not a secret anyone has *yet*,' Amy replied. 'She *will* blame, not *does* blame… that's not like guessing *who shaves* – which obviously isn't the girl with gills.'

'Little's second secret.'

'The easy one!'

'And why not? You look at Little and see a grown-up woman with the mind of an eleven-year-old girl. You know that's a mistake.'

'She's an eleven-year-old girl the size of a grown-up woman.'

'Remember that. Don't think of her as simple. Think of her as young. Her friend with the hands sees that and she's only a Second. You can do better.'

Amy realised she looked at Miss Kratides and saw a girl. Not a beak. When she *listened*, she heard someone else.

'You know you're one of Dr Swan's cygnets?'

Amy nodded.

'So was I. School Wrong 'Un. Did everything I could to get booted. I half expected to go the way of Primmy Quell and get sentenced to the House of Reform. Or skip that entirely and wind up in the Mausoleum. But Dr Swan wanted me at Drearcliff and kept me at Drearcliff. She won't be missing a spoon from the set. Dr Swan keeps track of us all. Wrong 'Uns. Right 'Uns. Not just at this school. If you think you hate these lessons now, wait till the *exchange students* join in. One's already here and others are on their way. I'd say more, but don't want to spoil the surprise. There will be controversy. There will be excitement. There will be upset.'

Amy's stomach turned over.

'Do you know what being School Wrong 'Un was? A distraction. Think back to last year when I spent all that time scrubbing the heel or getting slippered. Remember what I did to deserve it. All the rules I broke. All the infractions. They issued me a new Time-Table Book when my old one ran out of room for Black Notches. A Wrong 'Un I was. But what does that mean? Amy, what's the worst you can do? Not specifically... in general. What's bad?'

Amy thought. 'Hurting people?'

Miss Kratides snapped her fingers. 'Hurting people! Good answer. Yes, that's the bad thing. I was School Wrong 'Un. Worst record since Founding Day. But can you think of a single time when I hurt someone?'

'You picked a fight with Stheno Stonecastle.'

'Which I lost.'

'Deliberately. Stoney was a foot and a half taller, but Duchess of the Dims. You're small, but you're not weak. I'll bet your mother taught you how to trounce a bigger opponent.'

Miss Kratides nodded.

Amy thought of Stephen Swift – and the taste of her blood when Amy bit her hand.

She'd not told anybody how she won that fight. After losing the Game, no one was interested in the preliminary bouts anyway.

'Well observed, Amy. Yes, I could have put Stonecastle down. I got hurt more than I hurt her. That wasn't the only ruck I had at Drearcliff Grange. The others started when girls picked on me. I won those, but no one noticed. I got infracted for the barney. Why?'

'Because fighting is against School Rules?'

'Nonsense. Fighting is a *school sport*. Dr Swan likes us to fight each other. We learn from that. It distracts us from fighting her. No, fighting *in certain circumstances* – on the Quad at Break, with a circle of braying girls and Nellie taking bets – is against School Rules. I needed to tick that one off.'

So it was true. Miss Kratides had set out to break *all* the rules. In public, flagrantly. Not interested in getting away with it. Making a point.

'A good thing there's no School Rule against murder,' said Amy.

'I think that's assumed. Dr Swan is a famous assumer.'

'Did you really go through the whole book?'

Miss Kratides laughed again. 'I gave up. There are so *many* rules. It's such a bother to break them all. One Saturday, I walked around the whole school making sure to wear my boater where I shouldn't and not wear it where I should. It took ages to get noticed. I knew the rules better than any whip. At the height of my campaign I was as ruled by the rules as the goody-goodiest of goody-goodies. How clever was that?'

'Not very.'

'I spoke when I should be quiet and shut up when I should talk. I smoked cigarettes and drank cider. I ventured out of bounds and was always out of uniform. I spooned with Shoshone Brown's brother at a dance. I stole things I didn't want – chalk from classrooms, sweets from the tuck shop. I got caught and infracted, over and over. I didn't enjoy the sins – except Brown's brother, a teensy bit – but I burned with *righteous delight* when I got my Black Notches. I loved hating it all. I was a perfect idiot. I more than earned my bad reputation. I hurt people. People who tried to hurt me or who I saw hurting other people... but, still, not a paladin thing to do. Dr Shade would understand though. The worst thing you can do is hurt people who don't deserve it – smaller, weaker, more innocent. But is hurting wicked people so wrong? I doubt Barty Gunt enjoyed his swim to shore. It was February. You did that to him. If a whip knew you were out of your cell – wearing a non-uniform cape, to boot – and flying a gigolo out to sea for a dunking, you'd get infracted for it. If you get caught on any of your After Lights Out jaunts in the name of a just cause, you'll be Black Notched for the rest of your days at Drearcliff.'

That was true.

'Here's a strange thing – something you might want to think on. I read the rule book cover to cover. There's a rule against fighting... but no rule against *hurting*. If a whip slaps your face, it's not an infraction. If you slap back, it is. All punishments the School dishes out are for things done against the School – and I've had the lot of 'em. Break a window and it's penal servitude with lashes. Break a smaller girl and it's best settled between the two of you while staff look the other way. You know what – that's fair enough. Life outside School is like that. School prepares you for it. You're here with terrible girls, the *worst*. They're not punished, but you are. Never forget that, Amy. Dr Swan watches and lets it happen. No preferential treatment for her cygnets. If they *can* be broken they're no use, so the Remove takes all the lumps going and then some.'

Amy was jaded about School Rules, but Miss Kratides – a *teacher* – sounded more revolutionary than Absalom of Ariel, whose slot in the spoon case was School Anarchist.

'Did you enjoy the Great Game?' Miss Kratides asked. 'I didn't. I was surprised to be picked for the team. After not being in *anyone's* club for so long – I kept throwing away my house pin but it always got handed in and given back – the invitation to participate was so shocking I paid attention. I had to be a fool and rally to Lamarcroft's standard. She said I'd showed grit and determination. I couldn't argue with that. I told her Draycott's would cheat so we should cheat first. She regarded me with pity, but kindness. She said we'd play the game. Our cause was just and we would prevail. She convinced me. I was wrong and *Mitéra* was wrong. School Spirit. Then I waded through muck in the dark and made it back to the light to have buckets of more filth emptied on me. Gossage was a pitiable booby and Lungs a tragic martyr, but I'd run true to my form. A Wrong 'Un.'

Amy understood Miss Kratides' still-burning indignation.

She knew some girls muttered about the team not trying hard enough or deliberately slacking off. Larry Laurence suffered the most from those rumours. After all, she'd handed the winning tobies to Humble College.

'I was obviously in cahoots with Draycott's and threw the game,' Miss Kratides went on. 'My last term at Drearcliff was more an ordeal than all the others rolled together. No girl got infracted for doing anything to me. Ever been beaten with a cake of soap in the foot of a gym sock? Doreen Stockwell did that. She used to sing with that clear contralto. She sang as she thumped, too. "Nymphs and Shepherds". Lovely. After we passed out, I found the nice clean church Stockwell goes to in York. Sat at the back several Sundays running. Wearing a veil, just to be on the safe side. Our Doreen's engaged to a curate. Nice chap. Surprisingly chinny for a clergyman. An idealist. Some slyboots told him his zeal was wasted on endless tea calls on the comfortable wives of Yorkshire burghers and standing weekly in a pulpit to tell his fat flock that Jesus didn't really mean them when he was talking about the camel and the eye of the needle. No, he's fit for a more exalted calling. Missionary work overseas. Somewhere *challenging*, with Lassa fever and leprosy or warlords and witch doctors. I hope he doesn't tell Doreen her tropical honeymoon will be more exciting – and extended – than she expects until they're two days out of Southampton.'

Now Miss Kratides did sound frightening. A Wrong 'Un.

'You don't approve, Amy? I'm not surprised. When you heard Stockwell sing in Chapel you weren't being beaten. I've kept track of all my chums who've passed out. I send postcards as reminders. Sidonie Gryce can't hold on to a fellow for more than a month or two. She's on the gin too. Glugs down a bottle a night, at least. Reversals in her family's fortunes. Bad investments. She might – whisper it – have to go into trade. A tragic case. Something is sad about girls who do jolly well in school but founder when cast adrift in civvy street. Ah, you're seeing it now.'

Amy shivered. 'What do you mean?'

'The face behind the mask. The skeleton grin behind the sinister smile. The real Moria Kratides. The Wrong 'Un they all say I am. Well, you've had a Right 'Un teaching the Remove. Poor old Sausage. I won't hear a word against her but she did not serve you well. She strove to bring out the best in you when you needed to be at your useful worst. After our Great Game, Gossage went about apologising. Said she'd do better. You know how that turned out. She was no help to me when Stockwell – enacting the will of the whole school – was shoving soap into a sock. Four girls held me down. When you heard Gunt splash into the sea, did you have a little thrill? A private, shameful pleasure. It was nothing beside the *glow* Stockwell and her pals had when they were feeding me my just desserts. I heard that in their voices. "Nymphs and shepherds, come away, come away..." They called themselves the Good Sports, can you credit it?'

Amy could. Laurence had sustained bruises in the last week – as if she'd suddenly grown clumsy. She'd reckoned the sulking girl was getting careless about her appearance. Now she wondered whether Ariel had its own Good Sports? What with her second secret – which Miss Kratides was clearly *not* going to explain – Amy had chewed over the Larry question so much it hadn't occurred to her that the girl might have problems with her own dorm-mates. That made Amy feel even guiltier.

'The Worst Girls in School,' said Miss Kratides suddenly. 'Name them. Don't think about it. Just say the names.'

'Gryce is passed out. No one after that is as bad, but... Crowninshield II, Harper, Ziss, Nobbs, Inchfawn...'

'Pfui. *Inchfawn*. She annoyed you *once* and you won't let it go.'

Amy was struck. That was true. Four Eyes had steered clear of the Moth Club this year. So far as Amy knew, she'd not done anything wrong in ages.

'Your other picks are shrewd though. You've not noticed Esther Stuckey, but there's no reason you should. She hides her dark under a bushel. Ziss is well spotted though. She's a cold creature. Even Gryce had friends, of a sort. Ziss is always by herself – unless she spots a stray. Then she sits down next to them and *whispers*. She walks off, leaving her victims to tears and nightmares. Not just Firsts and Seconds either. She used to do it to older girls. Now she has braid and tassel, it's an infraction to run from her. She *loves* being a whip.'

Ziss, a Tamora Sixth, had never spoken to Amy. She sat next to Light Fingers once and whispered things Light Fingers wouldn't repeat even to the Moth Club. Amy's friend was upset and shaken at the time and – no matter what she said – not really over it now, *whatever it was*.

'The Ziss family own hotels in Germany, Holland and Belgium,' said Miss Kratides. 'I'll never stay in a Zisshof. They'll find bodies in basements one day. Anyone who's seen Ziss dissect a dead frog knows she'd prefer a live one… and she'd not stop at frogs. In the staffroom, they shudder at her name. She's an acceptable eighth or ninth in most subjects and has the bare minimum of infractions. Yet she's a prodigy of awfulness. If you, as School Paladin, want to pick an arch-nemesis, I recommend her. She's not your Broken Doll though. That's another lesson altogether. I was up to my frillies in hot water from the time I arrived at Drearcliff to the time I passed out, but Ziss has technically done no wrong. Dr Swan has never thought of Removing her. We swam in the same pond. I a minnow, she a pike. Yet I was the Wrong 'Un. Think about that.'

After telling her not to think so much, Miss Kratides gave Amy a lot to think about. Being confusing wasn't unique to her. Beaks contradicted themselves all the time. With Miss Kratides, Amy suspected it was deliberate.

Were Heike Ziss's whispers that different from Moria Kratides' red-ink couplets?

'If you're in it for the *goodness*, Amy, be sure you know what *goodness* and *badness* are. Moreover, be ready for the time when those terms aren't useful any more. If you go by the files of the Diogenes Club, my mother is a dangerous criminal... though they've hired her twice. Ask women whose husbands and fathers and employers can't or won't hurt them any more. Ask the parents of dead girls who've been avenged. They won't call Sophy Kratides a paladin. They might call her an Angel. If *Mitéra* had noticed Barty Gunt early in his career, several foolish women would be wealthier *and* happier. If I didn't do that much bad as School Wrong 'Un, ask yourself if you've done that much good as School Paladin.'

Tertius

Night of the
Broken Doll

1: Night Watch and New Clothes

AFTER LIGHTS OUT, Amy floated across the Quad on her new, dark wings.

She had a fine aerial view of the Heel, a huge foot dug out of a rubbish dump in Thessaly. Moonlight gave its marble toes a heroic ghostliness. Its job was to get dirty in the week. Every Sunday a party of infracted girls cleaned it with toothbrushes. Moria Kratides must have spent more hours scrubbing the Heel than the unknown sculptor did fashioning the original colossus. From sorry experience, Amy knew the point of the punishment was its Sisyphean pointlessness.

It was only Monday. Absalom hadn't yet adorned the Heel with her weekly graffiti. The dedicated anarchist always waited till later in the week to daub the slogan she would have to scrape off at the weekend. A wag had sloshed red paint over the ankle stump. The foot looked freshly severed.

What girl would dare such a gruesome prank?

Recalling scarlet specks on a certain pair of shoes, Amy laughed in admiration. Whips couldn't make a beak scrub the Heel. Had Miss Kratides indulged in satirical vandalism?

The Main Building was dark but Amy saw where the Music Room was. Speke had marked its window by making a death's head with sticking plaster. Amy floated close to the ivy-covered wall and gripped a web of well-anchored branches. Relaxing, she felt the drag of her weight return. She hung among bitter-smelling leaves. Her new cloak settled on her shoulders, heavier than her old wings. She climbed up to the window and peeped over the sill.

Torchlight flashed. The death's head leaped out at her.

Startled, she let go of the ivy but did not fall. Someone gasped in fright. Little. The big girl had seen a dark figure looming at the skull-marked window.

Amy was sorry but also gratified.

She *wanted* to be frightening. Though she needed to *aim* the effect, so only the right people were afraid. The wrong people, rather. Not big softies like Little, but guilty parties. Culprits, crooks, boors and bullies. She needed to reassure and inspire the innocent. Though she wasn't altogether sure there was such thing as a comforting death's head.

The torch beam waved all around the room – was that a white face in the corner? – then shone at the floor, lighting only the carpet and several sets of feet.

Amy heard whispered, annoyed debate. Frecks was telling someone off for showing a light that could get them all infracted. While kerfuffle continued, Speke came to the window. She impishly put her face to the skull design, staring through eye sockets. Her peculiar hands fussed with latches and sash cords. The window lifted.

'Come in, come in,' said Frecks. 'Every other bod has.'

Amy rose, cloak folded back from her shoulders to present a slimmer shape. She slid through the open window without touching the frame. She hovered for a few moments and stepped down to the floor without pranging her ankles.

If she expected applause, she was disappointed. She'd floated into an argument.

'Amy, back me up,' said Frecks. 'We agreed on a rota.'

The torch-wielder was Knowles, whose glance kept skittering away from the telling-off. According to the coin toss, Miss

Memory wasn't supposed to be here until tomorrow night. Knowles was in a state, and intermittently distracted by something fascinating in the region of the skirting board.

'There must be scientific method,' she said. 'Equipment, measurement, verified record. Or else it's just superstition... airy-fairy ghost stories.'

Frecks confiscated her torch and aimed the beam at the floor. 'We *agreed*,' she insisted.

Knowles ignored her. Amy had a chill as she realised what was wrong.

Miss Memory *couldn't remember*. She hadn't recovered from discombobulation by Dyall. What she put into her head by cramming had always faded. Now her other memories were in the same sinking boat. What they'd discussed yesterday was partially blotted out. If this went on, Knowles would become a human goldfish – constantly surprised at bumping her nose against the bowl.

Speke closed the window and let down rattly Venetian blinds.

Little turned up an oil lamp. The Music Room was warmly illuminated.

It smelled of rosin and brass polish. The white face Amy had seen was a man-in-the-moon painted on the head of a banjo. Instruments were everywhere, hung on stands or stored in cases. Instead of a desk, Miss Dryden had an upright piano shoved against a wall. From her revolving stool, she could conduct, critique and chastise a whole class with flicks of a baton. Portraits of composers frowned down on the classroom. Wagner scowled as if every duff note tooted, plunked or sawed here gave him earache. Liszt's nasty smile suggested to Amy that he was winding piano wire around his hands below the frame, intent on throttling Allegra Bidewell next time she murdered his *Hungarian Rhapsody No. 2*.

A dais reserved for star performers was kitted out with a truncated Grecian column, a waxy aspidistra, and a backcloth representing an overcast Arcadia. The fauns had itchy hoof rot.

The nymphs were cheesed off about their last shampoo and set. Ladymeade's double bass was propped against the plaster column. Risking infraction, she hadn't properly stowed it in its big black case after her last performance.

Little and Speke, in nighties and dressing gowns, stood together.

Knowles wore a white coat, pockets deformed by scientific instruments. She dangled a whirring little gyroscope on a watch chain. Black waterproof gloves stretched half way up her arms. Her hair was a mess.

'She doesn't know what night it is,' said Frecks.

'The night has a thousand eyes, and the day but one,' said Knowles, 'yet the light of the bright world dies with the dying of the sun.'

'She's digging up Second Year poetry. Francis Bouillabaise...'

'Bourdillon,' corrected Speke.

'My point is proved,' said Frecks. 'By a Second.'

'The mind has a thousand eyes and the heart but one,' Knowles went on, 'yet the light of a whole life dies when love is done.'

'Very cheery I don't think,' said Frecks. 'But popular. Half the class bicker about who gets to be the one to recite it from memory.'

'It's the shortest poem in the book,' said Speke. 'So it's a doddle to get off by heart.'

'I don't like it,' said Little. 'Those night eyes. I know what they are. Peeping through chinks into the cupboard that smells of tennis balls. Cat's eyes, rat's eyes and bat's eyes.'

'Pfui,' said Frecks. 'The fathead poet means stars. *Those* are the night's eyes. Twinkling. It's cheery. The day's one big eye is the sun. It's an astronomy lesson.'

'And all the eyes a mind has,' said Little, not calmed, 'I don't like that either. A big, pulsing brain with eyes all over it, thinking wicked thoughts.'

'That's not what the poem's about,' said Speke fondly.

At last Frecks really looked at Amy.

'Sherry trifle,' she exclaimed. 'What *are* you wearing?'

Amy put her hands on her hips and stuck her chest out.

'I had Light Fingers make a few changes to my costume,' she said. 'For night-work. I needed a warmer cloak... and black, to blend with the shadows.'

Something like Count DeVille's cape but less debilitating.

Frecks walked around Amy, considering the new outfit.

'It'll take getting used to,' she said. 'Are you sure about the mask?'

Amy's domino covered her forehead, nose and most of her cheeks. Moulded to her face. Black, with a white death's head where a third eye would be. She'd wondered about painting it with phosphorus to show a frightening skull to her enemies. Light Fingers said that was 'a bit too Gwendolyn Nobbs, if you know what I mean', and Amy had to admit she did.

'We might have to conceal our true identities,' she said.

Frecks laughed. 'Amy, you are a clot sometimes! Remember when we saw *The Mark of Zorro*. You said any halfwit in the hacienda could tell Don Diego and Zorro were the same person. That mask didn't even cover Fairbanks's grin.'

'The teeth and the moustache,' Amy admitted.

'Unmistakable! But even if he wore a mask to cover his 'tache and gnashers, they'd know him by the way he stands and holds his sword... or the pong of his hair oil, or any number of other tells. Imagine if flickers could speak. Don Diego would have to spend his whole life as a lisping weed, then put on a low, growly voice as Zorro. Even then, anyone who wasn't an utter Dim would recognise him. Who knew it was Amy straight off?'

Speke and Little stuck their hands up.

'We don't know another floater,' admitted Speke.

Amy didn't want to bring up Stephen Swift. She also wasn't sure about 'floater' and hoped the expression wouldn't catch on.

From now on, she'd admit it. She could fly.

One vote on the mask had yet to be counted.

Knowles was fiddling with her gyroscope. Cloak spread

dramatically, Amy awaited her verdict.

Granting Amy a sliver of her attention, Miss Memory said 'Oh yes, it's you, all right. There's a thing you do with your bottom lip when you're fed up but don't want to make a fuss... and you're doing it now.'

Amy could have swallowed her lips.

Even with her mind in a muddle, Knowles saw through the mask.

'Exactly,' agreed Frecks. 'The Thomsett pout. Much admired in certain quarts, I can tell you. A correspondent writes you were recently voted Third Most Spoonable Girl in the Great Game. Modesty forbids mention of who came Second... and the sort of cold fury that leads to abrupt cessation of correspondence prevents me from naming the Draycott's tart who tops the poll. Oh, the pout's evaporated. Now you're just a grump. Unspoonable in all quarts.'

How this all came to be about spooning was beyond Amy.

The debut of her new look wasn't going as hoped. Light Fingers had talked Amy out of the glow-in-the-dark motif, but otherwise fulfilled the customer's requirements without offering advice or criticism. If Frecks were Moth Club seamstress, she'd have been blunt. Amy realised she'd seen the expression on Light Fingers' face during the costume-making before. On shop assistants who sold Mother dresses she wound up wearing only once. They all mysteriously shrank two sizes between fitting and delivery.

Any crest Amy's death's head might have was fallen.

Her cloak hung heavy. It took mentacle muscle to puff it out. She let it settle and slumped, round-shouldered.

Spotting Amy's dejection, Frecks – perhaps a little late – back-pedalled.

'That smart tunic is a huge improvement on the lumpy waistcoat,' she said.

Amy used to stick things into whichever pouch they almost fit, the way Knowles distended her pockets with anemometers and the like. This time she selected the items she wanted to carry and had Light Fingers modify a leather jerkin – worn by Handsome Helena Mansfield as principal boy in *Dick Whittington* two pantomimes ago – with sleek, concealed pockets for each. She'd added a Sam Browne belt with hooks for larger gear, including a medical kit, a clip-on lamp and her battered old hip flask.

'Please take off the scary face,' said Little quietly. 'I know it's you but I want to be sure.'

Reluctantly, Amy undid the cord and pulled off the domino. Gummy from perspiration, it hurt a bit coming off. She felt cool air on her face.

'*Ay caramba*, 'tis that spineless milksop Don Diego!' said Frecks. 'Surely the dashing daredevil who carves Zs wherever he goes can't be that powdered prawn! Who'd have thought!'

'Stop talking like an intertitle, you ginger nit,' said Amy.

'Zounds! Fie! Gadzooks! Amidships!'

Amy couldn't help laughing.

She rolled up her mask and slipped it into its pocket. She'd have words with the costumier about modifications to the modifications.

Light Fingers was 'off' this evening. When Amy called on the Sewing Room, the girl handed over the new outfit as if she just wanted rid of it. Light Fingers had been in a mood since her afternoon *tête-a-tête* with Miss Kratides. Amy couldn't recall her friend being as quiet since the time when Ziss *whispered* at her. Frecks and Kali, whose appointments were set for noon and four o'clock on Wednesday, were agog for details, but Light Fingers was close-mouthed. Experiences of the tutorials varied.

Knowles had been seen after Bizou De'Ath. She'd gone in almost recovered from her dose of Dyall but came out babbling worse than ever. Like feral Gould and shaken Light Fingers, Miss Memory was deeply affected by an hour with the teacher. Little and Speke didn't seem fussed either way. Mostly, they were happy to be given lollipops as if they'd been brave at the dentist. Amy tried to picture Miss Kratides as a kindly young auntie.

Handing out sweets with fake blood on her shoes.

Frost, Paquignet, Bok, Devlin and Harper had also been out to Windward. Amy hadn't seen them since. At least Miss Kratides must have talked Paquignet down from her tree.

No one was talking about the famous secrets.

The prep now seemed meaningless, though Amy knew Miss Kratides didn't just throw rocks in a pond to admire the lovely splashes. There was a point to each secret. Sharpened and dipped in asp venom.

While Amy and Frecks bantered about masks, Knowles paid closer attention to the skirting board. Her gyroscope whirled. She got down on her knees to investigate and rolled a bass drum into a stack of cymbals. Everyone froze at the crash.

'Have a care,' said Frecks. 'You'll wake the whips in their dorms. This night watch is a hush-hush mission…'

Knowles couldn't seem to remember whether shaking or nodding meant agreeing or disagreeing and in any case wanted to do both at the same time.

She opened a leather valise and exposed a contraption. A music box crossed with a conjuring set. Leaves folded out to reveal a twisted shape of incandescent tubes. Miss Memory twisted a key several times. The shape glowed like an advertisement. A five-pointed star in a circle, electric blue and pulsing. The device pinged and whined and crackled. Amy smelled roses and ash.

Knowles' hair stood on end like spun candyfloss. Amy's scalp prickled too. Little laughed for a moment, then got scared again. The girl needed to get a grip on her fraidy cat tendencies. Speke's hands stilled. Dogs alert to a silent whistle.

'What's that when it's at home?' Frecks asked.

'An electric pentacle,' said Knowles.

'Of course it is,' said Frecks, flapping her hand over her head. 'No wiser now. Elucidation would be appreciated.'

'It's a pentacle,' said Knowles. 'But electric.'

'Spook-spotting equipment,' said Amy.

'For spotting spooks, naturally,' said Frecks.

'Not only that,' said Knowles. 'For safety. Ours. This Broken Doll is a malign entity… an oddity entity and trippety trumpety entirety malignity of malicious magnitude. The pentacle inhibits the ability of enemy entities to alter eternities.'

Amy didn't see how the pentacle could ward off evil any more effectively than crossing your fingers behind your back and saying 'white rabbits'. She supposed it couldn't hurt. Unless it gave the operator an electric shock. Or exploded and set fire to something. Which, thinking it through, meant it could hurt quite a lot.

'Does it have to make that noise?' asked Speke, pained.

'What noise?' asked Little, concerned.

'That!' said Speke, clapping carapace palms to her ears. 'Can you really not hear it?'

Speke practically shouted, as if trying to be understood over a cacophony.

Amy listened hard. Maybe she heard a faint screech. Wind scything through pampas grass.

Frecks and Little strained too.

Knowles was so taken with her toy she didn't notice any ill effects. Her attention still inclined to the skirting board. Half her hair frizzed like a dandelion clock.

'I have a bonnet trimmed with purple,' she keened. 'Shall I wear it with my kirtle? I shall wear it like a noose, going to the butcher with my fat goose…'

'Knowles,' said Amy, 'Miss Memory…'

Amy stretched a mentacle towards the crackling device. She could reach so far and no further. She came at it from the side, but was still stopped. From above – the same thing. Less confident about working blind, she stuck a mentacle through the floor, feeling past dangling light fixtures, and sensed the curve of a barrier around the pentacle. Spongy but resistant. A sphere around Knowles' gadget was proof against her mind's touch. She'd not come across that before.

'I have a bonnet trimmed with red,' Knowles went on, 'shall I wear it when I'm dead? I shall wear it for bad luck, going to the blazes with my young duck... '

With trepidation, Amy walked across the room.

She stood over Knowles. She touched her shoulder.

A tiny shock stung her fingers. Miss Memory looked up.

The bluish, crackling light of the pentacle was in her eyes too.

'There's someone else here,' she said, not sounding like herself. 'Someone not... at all... kind... Someone *cruel*!'

II: Infernal Cakewalk

ON A GHOST conductor's cue, a phantom orchestra started tuning up. Brasses burped, strings twanged, woodwinds wheezed. No human hand was involved. Lid firmly shut, the piano produced unnatural chords. Eerie glissandi emanated from the harpsichord. Gongs bonged and triangles tinkled.

Little and Speke had reported night-time sounds.

All around the Music Room, instruments levitated. A trombone stood in its velvet-lined case, then wobbled aloft, aiming its slide at Amy. Mr Moony-Face Minstrel unhooked from the wall and plunked.

Ducking to avoid a cor anglais, Little backed into the waddling double bass. It fell over and sprang up again like a roly-poly doll.

'Is this you?' Frecks asked.

'No,' said Amy. 'Some other geist is poltering.'

She extended mentacles and tried to still the instruments. She anticipated the firm resistance she'd met in Stephen Swift. This was more like trying to make a hole in water. With her Talent, she could do that better than most but still not well. She easily moved the levitating instruments around but couldn't make them stay put. She wore out mental puff swatting piccolos and recorders. Amy was forever telling non-entomological friends that flapping in a panic didn't make bees go away but did make them more likely to sting. She should listen to her own advice.

Frecks fished her coif out of her satchel.

The relic protected her from evil, but not from looking like a medieval lamp post. Wearing her magic helm for any length of time resulted in frightful hat hair. That was not the least reason she kept it tucked away most of the time.

The double bass hopped at Frecks and stabbed her toes with its spiked endpin. She winced and let go of the enchanted silver.

'Creaking crocuses,' she exclaimed.

Amy reached but the silver mail dropped through her mentacles as if they weren't there. A new, uncomfortable sensation. Amy considered picking the coif up normally, but held back. She didn't want burned fingers. The Lady of the Lake might not approve of her Death's Head look. Frecks was right about that personage being excessively hard to please.

Meanwhile, the bass aggressively bumped Frecks, pushing her against the old joanna. She couldn't draw her legs back far enough to kick it in the belly. Her opponent dodged from side to side. A thin-necked boxer avoiding jabs.

Amy got a mentacle hold of the instrument and tripped it up.

Frecks took a good swing and punched the bullying bass, slicing her knuckles on the strings but smashing the bridge.

'That's for my foot, you fat fiddle!'

The bass went down. Frecks didn't give it time to bounce back again and stamped, crushing polished wood under her heavy heel. When the instrument was spread on the floor in pieces held together by strings, she realised her hand was bleeding badly. Gouts spattered the carpet.

Amy fought across the room, swiping a darting flute with a cloak fling. Reaching Frecks, she took out her first-aid kit. No time for liniment. She wound a bandage round her friend's bleeding paw and tied it off. Not a top-marks dressing, but up to battlefield standard. Nurse Humph would understand.

Even in the middle of this infernal cakewalk, Amy gave

herself a head pat for adding medical supplies to the Kentish Glory gear. She instantly regretted the twinge of smugness. Of course she hadn't *wanted* Frecks hurt just so she could show off her forward thinking, but still...

Something bashed the small of her back. She wheeled around to face it.

Mr Moony-Face danced in the air and twanged.

'Is that "Deutschland, Deutschland"?' asked Frecks.

'Or "Glorious Things of Thee Are Spoken",' said Amy.

Whatever words went with the tune, it was not a natural minstrel number.

Amy lashed with her fists, her mentacles and her cloak but couldn't land a blow. The banjo's mocking aerobatics flustered and frustrated her.

This wasn't poltergeist phenomena. This was *directed*.

Some Wrong 'Un – Stephen Swift? an unknown Talent? – was nearby, puppeteering. Probably spying on the scene. Were there peepholes in the walls? Eyes cut out of one of the portraits of frowning composers?

If Amy set her mind to it, she could do this. She'd experimented with mass floating of objects in other rooms. But it didn't seem sporting. A paladin should show her face to the foe. Even when she'd bashed them with A.H. Wax's prop crutch, the Draycott's girls could see her. They had a chance to fight back. Miss Steps might pull off this sly attack – the Orful Orchestra! – but Amy judged the boastful thug wouldn't conduct her sinister symphony from concealment. She'd stride through it all, showing off.

'Gloria stings of tiaras poke in...' muttered Knowles, along with the possessed banjo.

'Miss Kratides made a row sing that song,' said Speke. 'Dyall, Laurence, Bok and Harper.'

'Well remembered, but not terribly useful,' said Amy.

The trombone advanced, hiding behind the banjo, stabbing out the slide when it had a chance.

Knowles' electric pentacle glowed and fizzed. The animated

instruments kept shy of it. They couldn't touch the dropped coif either. Totems of mystic or scientific protection did a good job of looking after themselves. Meanwhile, the invisible band belaboured the living members of the team. Amy got bopped on the nose by the slide several times.

Music stands pranced on tripod feet to surround Knowles, but were too flimsy to do real damage. Penned in with her crackpot box, Miss Memory recited nonsense hymns and bowed her head as sheaves of sheet music poured on her.

Little covered her face with meaty arms. Cymbals flew at her like discuses, but bounced off her sturdy shoulders.

Speke's hands put up a fight. Speke herself was on her feet but in a daze. She'd been thumped on the head by a guitar, which let her hands off the leash. They tore drumskins, wrestled keys off flutes, snapped strings.

Frecks wielded the neck of the smashed bass like a cricket bat. She always was one for a good old slosh. When she connected, smaller instruments were knocked for at least a boundary.

The racket would have started a riot in a pre-war Paris concert hall. Amy would love to see Nijinsky dance to it.

If they lived through the night, they'd be Black Notched for this.

Extensive destruction of School property. Major Infractions all round. A whole term of scrubbing the Heel.

What would Speke's hands make of that gritty task?

At least they were holding up against the foe.

Only that drat banjo and its trombone familiar stayed in the game.

The puppeteer was concentrating on them.

Amy tried to discern a personality in their dance. There must be clues.

Or was this the Broken Doll? The delight in smashing things… The musical anarchy… The capricious cruelty. All Broken Doll traits. Knowles had mentioned the cruelty most of all. The nasty-minded scorn of the attack bothered Amy more than cuts and bruises.

She was still sparring with the banjo and dodging the slide.

The plunking pest wasn't carrying its tune well. One string snapped, so every fourth or fifth note was silent. The swinging trombone couldn't fill in. No breath went through it.

'You can tell a bogus spirit medium from a real one by musical instruments,' said Knowles, almost coherently. 'Gifted psychics have spirits bang drums, because ectoplasm can thump but not blow. Fakers toot trumpets, because an assistant with lungs and a mouth does it for them.'

Interesting, but not immediately helpful.

Then she saw the leaf. Mr Moony-Face Minstrel bobbed up and down, but always jumped aside at the end of the verse to give Mrs Slidey-Bones a clear shot at her head.

Amy hummed under her breath, trying to synchronise with the plunking.

'Fading is the worldling's pleasure,' she mumble-sung,

'All his boasted pomp and show…'

The banjo tensed, ready to make its move…

'Solid joys and lasting treasure

'None but Zi… on's… child… ren… *know*!'

Then Mr Moony-Face Minstrel feinted…

Amy, seeing where it was going, matched its sidestep and stretched out her cloak. Remembering Valentino coaxing a bull into killing range in *Blood and Sand*, she made a curve of her body and a curtain of her cape. The tooting trombone charged and slid past her side. She trapped the slide with her arm, then wrapped her cloak around it. Yanking the instrument free of the unknown fluence, she whirled like a dervish. Toes six inches off the floor, she floated, shifting most of her weight into her arms.

The trombone smashed the banjo.

Amy threw the wrecks of both instruments away.

'Goodnight, ladies,' she shouted. 'No encore!'

'Well played, that girl,' said Frecks.

They almost had a moment to catch their breaths.

The lid of the double bass case was flung upwards from

the inside. Scarlet velvet lining glistened like an open wound. A stocky sylph in a mauve body stocking leaped out of the makeshift coffin and bounded across the Music Room, singling out Frecks and pressing her cloth-covered face to her chosen victim's throat. Clinging tenaciously to the struggling Frecks, the Purple Peril chirruped like a frenzied bat. Amy stepped towards them, but was driven back by a *flash!* of violet light and a *pop!* that hurt her ears. Knowles' pentacle fizzed and the light tubes shattered, making a smoky stink.

In the embrace of the Purple Peril, Frecks went cross-eyed and slack-mouthed then slumped. Unprepared for total victory, her assailant buckled at the knees and collapsed with a panicked squeak. Frecks' unconscious deadweight pinned the Peril. She thumped the carpet, grunting in fury as she failed to shift the heftier girl off her.

Amy had a tiny stab of relief. Wrong 'Uns made stupid mistakes too.

Then she was overcome by worry and concern.

Who was this and what had she just done?

III: The Purple Peril – Unmasked!

'THAT WASN'T SUPPOSED to happen,' said Knowles, poking broken tubes with her pentacle key. 'I have the manufacturer's guarantee.'

Pages of sheet music strewn around the device caught light. Regarding the potential inferno with mild interest, Knowles nudged a smouldering sheaf of score closer to the fire until it burst into flames. Miss Memory had now forgotten her first nursery lessons about playing with coals fallen from the grate.

Amy had to leave Frecks and the Purple Peril to their pickle while she tried to stamp out the flames. As she vigorously trampled burning paper, her flapping cloak fanned the fire.

Dr Swan kept a degree of Supreme Infraction – vastly more serious than a Black Notch – on the rule books covering Arson, Treason and Unlicensed Assassination. A girl who burned down a school building would be expelled without refund of fees, but only after a succession of imaginative punishments. Dosson, Chappell & Co. of Tite Street still had Amy's measurements on file. Her arrow-emblazoned ensemble would be ready when she had to report to Lobelia Draycott.

Little ripped the backcloth down and used it to smother the fire. Coughing on dust and smoke, Amy saluted the First for her quick thinking. As Miss Kratides said, the Little Girl was young not stupid.

The Arcadian scene was ruined. No tragedy there. A less gloomy vista might be an inspiration to play better. A pity one or two frowning composers hadn't fallen off the wall in the excitement. Replacing craggy Beethoven with dreamy Chopin would add oomph to the orchestra. She *could* give Ludwig Van Beetlebrows a mentacle nudge...

'Walmergrave doesn't half weigh a ton,' said Speke. 'Does she wear chainmail undies too?'

Speke tried to hoist Frecks off the Mauve Mystery Menace.

The crab-hands scrabbled all over Frecks' back, failing to get a purchase. Did that tickle or just make flesh creep?

Frecks was still breathing.

She'd been sent to Bedfordshire, not Gravesend.

The Purple Peril wasn't Aurelia Avalon. That unpleasant Unusual also had the habit of jumping out of cases like a jack-in-a-box, but her party piece was different. She sent folk to Bedfordshire with her hands, not her face. Nightcap was small and lissom, not small and thick-waisted.

This girl might be *imitating* Nightcap. If responsible for the levitating instruments, she might be imitating Amy too.

Familiar Talents manifesting in unfamiliar ways.

Amy and Little knelt with Speke by Frecks and her pinned assailant. Fight squashed out of her, the Purple Peril glared through mesh-veiled eyeholes. Her featureless hood shaped into a peeved, resentful expression.

Knowles was still playing with the pieces of her bashed-in, burned-up box.

'I have a bonnet trimmed with black,' she hummed. 'Shall I wear it like a sack? I shall wear it thin or fat, going to the dogs with my young cat...'

Amy tried to rouse Frecks.

It was usually the other way round. Frecks and Kali were the bound-out-of-bed-before-the-bell brigade, given to boisterous exercise and hearty pre-breakfast conversation. Amy would happily swap any number of bowls of Drearcliff porridge for twenty extra minutes in her cot – not even asleep, just lying quiet and warm. Frecks would whip off Amy's coverlet. 'Stir your socks,' she'd say, 'wonders await.' Even on Monday mornings, when the only wonders awaiting were French tenses.

'Wonders await,' said Amy, shaking her friend.

'Unhand me, varlet,' mumbled Frecks.

Relieved, Amy hugged her.

Added weight made the Purple Peril squeak again.

That mousey noise was familiar. Amy began to have more suspicions.

Not fully conscious, Frecks started to come round. She opened her eyes and Speke waved sixteen crab-leg fingers over her face. That made her open her eyes wider and bump her head cringing away from the dangling spiny tips.

'What bounder slipped a Mickey Finn in my cocoa?' Frecks asked. 'I've got the woozes.'

She sat up and held her head. The Peril yelped as Frecks' full weight shifted onto her.

'This Wrong 'Un did something to you,' said Amy.

'I feel like Bro Ralph after a three-day Gay Paree bender. Have I got engaged to a *poule* from the Follies Bergère and gambled away my gaiters at *ecarté*?'

Frecks heaved herself off the Violet Viper. She staggered in a small circle and sat down again, cross-legged. Her head was still foggy.

'I didn't think to bring smelling salts,' Amy admitted.

'You should carry miniatures of brandy for occasions such as this,' said Frecks.

'I am *not* a St Bernard,' huffed Amy.

Frecks chucked her under her chin and made 'good doggie' noises.

Little and Speke laughed.

'You're not just woozy,' said Amy. 'You're... *squiffy!*'

Frecks giggled inappropriately.

The hooded girl was still laid out flat, breathing heavily. She must be bruised under her body stocking. Serve her right.

'This is Knock-Out Nora, then?' said Frecks.

Amy nodded.

'Not too impressive now.'

'Someone who weighs a ton fell on her,' said Amy.

'I do *not* weigh a ton, St Bernardette.'

'You in the mask,' said Amy, 'do you surrender?'

The Peril mumbled urgently. She had inhaled a patch of her hood and gagged herself. If choked, that was no worse than she deserved.

'You could be sat on again,' said Amy. 'Little…'

Startled eyes swivelled behind the mesh and took in the looming Gillian Little.

'Fancy a nice sit-down on someone squashable?' asked Amy.

The Little Girl made great play of stretching and yawning.

'I'm *sooooo* tired,' she said, smiling – almost sinister.

The Peril spat out her mouthful of wet mask and cried a high-pitched 'Pax!'

'Surrender accepted,' said Amy.

She found the seam between hood and body stocking and took hold, peeling cloth back from an inch or so of undistinguished neck.

'Returning to an earlier discussion,' said Amy, 'can anyone here say *which* Wrong 'Un we have at our mercy?'

Shrugs all round.

'Search me,' said Frecks.

'Knowles,' said Amy, catching the girl's attention, 'using the observational methods of the great Guilbert Phatt, can you name the maid behind the mask?'

'It's never a maid. Papa says the one who done it should never be a servant. It's always the nice friendly fellow.'

'Not in this instance, obviously. But do you know who this is?'

'Not a clue.'

Amy wriggled the hood off the Peril's head. The culprit's hair was pulled loose. She had to spit and shake to get it off her face.

'Good gravy, it's Shrimp Harper!' exclaimed Frecks.

'Who you didn't recognise because she was *wearing a mask*!' said Amy. 'Point proved!'

'That's not a mask,' pooh-poohed Frecks, 'that's a *hood*. Quite different thing.'

'Oh yes,' said Speke, stroking her chin disturbingly, 'quite.'

'I've never seen that girl before,' said Miss Memory, forgetting Harper had been in the Remove with her for four terms. 'The murderer shouldn't be a new character brought on in the last chapter. Mystery readers would vandalise library books and send nasty postcards to the publisher. Mystery readers are unreasonably demanding, if you ask me.'

Amy was disposed to give up entirely.

Harper sat up defensively and looked at Frecks and Amy, then at Speke and Little, then even at Knowles. No easy escape route.

'You could try the window,' said Amy helpfully. 'There's ivy. It's not *too* loose. And the wall might hold off crumbling for a few minutes.'

'Though we're awfully high up,' said Frecks.

'And you're no floater,' put in Speke.

'We're not using *that word*,' said Amy. 'Ever again.'

Shrimp was puzzled by Amy's flash of anger at someone else.

Amy was too. Was she still disturbed by Speke's hands? Light Fingers would frown on prejudice against a fellow Unusual. Amy would too, especially in herself.

'You can't fly, Harper,' she said calmly. 'And that get-up does not suit you.'

'Not at all it don't,' said Frecks. 'Unflattering in the nether regions. Baggy around the ankles. And the *colour*! Did you use beetroot juice to dye it?'

Amy felt the prickle of Harper's leeching touch.

'Don't do that,' she insisted.

Harper set her mouth in a determined line and exerted her Talent.

Speke slammed Shrimp around the head, smacking her shelled palm against her cheek and scratching with spines.

'She told you not to do that,' said Speke.

Harper screamed and held her face. She stopped trying to drain anyone.

'My hand tingles,' said Speke, examining her pale palm. 'That's funny. I usually only feel hot or cold.'

She'd slapped Harper quickly enough. It wasn't just her hands that were hard-shelled. For a Second, Harriet Speke was a tough little egg. Fifteen minutes, at least. Amy wished she could warm up to her.

'Who put you up to this?' Frecks asked Shrimp.

'Not telling,' she said, shaking her head. 'Code of Break.'

Amy was iffy about the prohibition against snitching.

Telling on a girl to a beak was not done. Telling all to a paladin was the lot of any apprehended Wrong 'Un. When the debutante of the year was tied to an anchor in a tank that gradually filled with water, Dr Shade strung Bizou De'Ath's father from the undercarriage of his autogiro and took a sightseeing trip over the Thames to persuade him to cough up the location of the Ghoul Mob's Aquarium of Abduction. Amy could imagine the splash Blake De'Ath would have made if he'd plead Code of Break as an excuse for being unforthcoming.

Amy stretched the hood between her fists and rolled it into a strangling cord.

Harper was defiant. Amy wound the cord round her neck.

She wished she were still wearing her mask. Harper should see the death's head glinting in the blurry light as the blood stopped going to her brain.

Harper was certain Amy wouldn't throttle her.

She didn't know the same went for Death's-head Hawk.

Amy tightened the cord.

Maybe Harper wasn't as certain now.

Shrimp began gurgling.

'Steady on, Amy,' said Frecks, touching her arm. 'No need to break her windpipe.'

For a few seconds, Amy *didn't* relax… and Harper's eyes popped. Then she let go. Frecks was right. No need.

'You had us worried for a mo,' said her friend.

Amy brushed away a gnat of guilt. Was she ashamed she'd started to strangle Shrimp or ashamed she'd stopped?

Harper unwound the rolled-up hood from her neck.

'You're all in trouble now,' she said. 'Multiple Major Infractions.'

'So *you'd* peach on us,' said Amy. 'Code of Break or no?'

'You said it – I'm a Wrong 'Un. We follow no code. I know that now. I shouldn't even try to play by rules. Anyone's rules. You'd never notice if I did, anyway. Every other bungler or blighter gets chance after chance. But not Jackie Harper. Not the perishing Shrimp. I am reminding you that you're not like me. You never let me forget it, so it's only fair you can't either.'

'*Fair!*' exclaimed Frecks.

'Yes, *fair*. You go on and on about being fair and codes and just causes… but it's only hot air.'

This wasn't how Shrimp usually talked. Someone had put ideas in her head. She'd had the last tutorial of the day with Miss Kratides, only a few hours ago. What had they talked about? The teacher was a great one for letting wolves off the leash.

'You can't snitch on us without snitching on yourself,' she told the wriggling Shrimp. 'You're Out of Bounds after Lights Out too.'

Harper smiled slyly. Here was the familiar, unmasked, unstrangled Shrimp. Smug in her own parasitical way, feeding off her own bitterness when cheated out of feeding off others.

'It'd be worth it to see you punished. *Expelled*.'

Speke went for Harper with both hands.

Shrimp screamed and shrank away from the chittering crab-fingers.

'I'm not doing this,' said Speke. 'They are!'

Harper was terrified by Speke's hands.

Amy felt the draining prickle again, but it was ripped away. Shrimp got half to her feet and scrambled across the Music Room. Her body stocking ripped under her arms and her pumps slipped on the worn carpet. She went flying face-first into Knowles, who held her up...

'Harper, no,' shouted Frecks. 'Leave her be!'

Shrimp pressed against Knowles, bending her over the half-column on the dais. She put her face close to Miss Memory's and breathed in. That was how she drained folk, getting near and inhaling the air around their bodies. She stole sap and spirit. She licked her lips as she did it.

Despite the ridiculous costume, the Purple Peril was a true monster.

A fluke.

Frecks and Amy strode across the room, Speke and Little at their sides. They gathered sternly round the dais, surrounding Shrimp.

Harper snarled, 'Stay back or I'll take *everything*!'

Knowles muttered about bonnet trim and flapping bats. She was grey in the face. The electric frizz went out of her hair. She wilted.

'You will anyway,' said Frecks making fists.

Throttling a Wrong 'Un was wrong. Punching her in the face was fine and dandy.

Amy was becoming impatient with rules written and unwritten.

When a deb was drowning, Code of Break was suspended.

With mentacles, Amy lifted small objects – twisted triangles, broken brass keys, flute shards – and angled them in the air, aiming them like daggers. With a *snap*, she could riddle the Shrimp with such shrapnel... and Knowles shouldn't get too badly hurt, though she could expect a slight piercing.

She was a moment away from that *snap*.

Harper looked up from Knowles and smiled. Her pallor gave way to a healthy glow. When infused, Shrimp seemed oddly innocent. A clean, happy postcard princess.

She held up her hand, palm out.

'Unsteady on your feet, Walmergrave?'

Frecks wobbled. She wasn't recovered from her dose of Shrimp.

Amy steadied her friend. Her cloud of sharp missiles vibrated in the air.

'Keep back, you lot,' said Harper. 'Especially you with the I-don't-know-what hands...'

Speke clacked her fingers but didn't pounce.

'This is lovely,' said Shrimp, enjoying her meal, enjoying her audience. 'And this is *a lesson*...'

The Purple Peril Triumphant!

Then Harper burped...

Little laughed.

Shrimp burped again and her glow rapidly vanished. She looked ill.

'What's the matter?' asked Speke. 'Milk gone down the wrong tube?'

Shrimp staggered, letting go of Knowles.

'No, really, I... This isn't *fair*... This is...'

'Is she going to be sick?' asked Little. 'Shall I fetch the bucket?'

Harper clawed the air like Count DeVille exposed to direct sunlight. She wasn't just physically ill – her convulsing stomach showed through the body-stocking – but addle-pated. She'd drained Knowles not of her pep but of her discombobulation.

'*I have a bonnet*...' shrilled Shrimp. 'I don't know what comes next.'

'Trimmed with blue,' sang Little. 'Do I wear it, yes I do! I will wear it when I can, going to the ball with my young man!'

Harper's brows knit. She was afraid as well as poorly and confused.

Amy let her makeshift weapons drop unnoticed.

Knowles unbent, alert and focused. She stood up refreshed, like Frecks first thing in the morning, eager to extol the joys of a bright fresh day.

Discombobulated no longer.

Indeed, supremely combobulated.

Shrimp crumpled in a heap, twitching.

'Did I miss anything?' asked Knowles.

'We know who has Light Fingers' second secret,' said Amy.

Miss Memory toe-prodded Harper.

'"She could use her Talent to heal the sick – but won't",' she quoted. 'Dearie me, what a wretch!'

'How do you feel?' Frecks asked.

Knowles tapped her head, did mental arithmetic, was satisfied, and smiled.

'Better than you look.'

Frecks was weighing heavier on Amy's shoulder.

'I'll be buttered,' said Frecks, 'I'm going off again...'

Her eyes fluttered closed.

Unlike Harper, Amy was prepared. She braced her back and legs, then gently let her friend down.

IV: Blessings and Curses

FRECKS WAS SNOOZING soundly. Amy hesitated to wake her.

'Best let her sleep it off,' suggested Knowles.

Miss Memory was probably right. Frecks was done in.

They all were, but the vigil wasn't over. The Purple Peril was unmasked, but other hands were against them.

The hour of the Broken Doll was yet to come.

Knowles' torch and Amy's lamp were running dim. The rest of the Main Building was quiet. Whole floors of dark, empty rooms. Amy wouldn't get a wink of sleep in so lonely a place. Silence would keep her awake.

'I could carry Walmergrave next door,' said Little. 'She can kip in my bed.'

'A kind thought,' said Amy. 'But we're supposed to be watching over you, not keeping you up all night.'

The Music Room was a smoky ruin. No hope of setting it straight before morning and no undoing damage done. Miss Dryden would get a shock. When annoyed, the music teacher was the scowling image of Beethoven in a bonnet.

'We'll take the Black Notches,' Amy told Speke and Little. 'No need for you to get infracted for all this.'

Speke's hands played with the smashed double bass, fitting the pieces together in new configurations.

'I can't think of a yarn to explain it,' said Speke. 'No one will believe the truth but no one will believe anything else either. Anyone good at fibs? I can't tell a whopper to save my life.'

'Oxenford is our champion liar,' said Knowles, 'but her "exaggerations" are of the Munchausen variety. More entertaining than convincing.'

Knowles crouched over Harper, who was curled on the dais. Unconscious, but in pain. She hugged her stomach. Her knees were drawn up tight.

'Shrimp's out for the count,' said Miss Memory.

'She's *not* invited to the Green Room,' said Speke.

Knowles patted Harper's back.

'Poor idiot,' she said. 'I know how she feels, because it's how I felt.'

'What was that about her secret?' asked Speke.

'"She could use her Talent to heal the sick – but won't",' said Amy.

'She healed me,' said Knowles.

'By accident,' insisted Amy.

Knowles looked at Harper from several angles, not without sympathy.

'Many of Miss Kratides' secrets tell the *what* but not the *why*,' she said.

Amy remembered hers. *You are right to be afraid of the Broken Doll.*

In that case, the *why* was obvious… *because she's dangerous.* Which was little help. Crucial details were withheld. Formless fears were hardest to overcome.

'I can guess why Shrimp won't use her Talent to heal the sick,' said Amy. 'She's a nasty, selfish girl.'

'There's more to it,' said Knowles. 'You don't have to be a saint to work miracles. In fact, if you *aren't* a saint and can make sick people feel better, there's a fortune in it. Laying on of hands, aches and pains relieved, ten guineas please, call again soon. It's not just the l.s.d. Think of patients dependent on Harper's whims and moods. She'd sit on a plush divan, wearing a turban or a white coat. Folk all around petitioning, desperate to keep on her good side, straining not to dislike her so they can get what they want – what they *need* – out of her. Shrimp's usual party piece is as much a nuisance for her as anyone she battens onto. She only gets one chance with most people. Everyone avoids her after the first fainting spell. Even in the Remove, we make her sit in the corner. So she makes out she doesn't want – or need – friends. She's very lonely. No wonder she's twisted.'

'Are you making excuses for her? After what she did to Frecks? What she tried to do to you?'

'No, Amy. I'm doing what you suggested. Applying observational methods. I have an advantage. Harper has done her worst to me, and – by accident – her best too. It cost her dearly. I understand how her Talent works. Because it's like mine. She harms by inhaling the vitality of healthy folk and heals by inhaling the malady of a sick person. When I bone up on a subject, what goes into my head doesn't stick. After a while, I'm ignorant again. I don't think the confusion Harper pulled out of me will last either. But it'll be horrid for her until it wears off. She's cramming weeks of brain fever into a single night.'

Amy still wasn't sympathetic. Harper had picked her path.

'Could she help Devlin get back in shape?' she said eagerly. 'Or fix Bok's knee?'

Knowles considered it. 'At the cost of going rubbery or limping for a bit? Probably.'

'Then we'll make her do it,' said Amy.

'I can make her,' said Speke. 'With my hands.'

Knowles looked at them. With Dyall Dizziness sucked out like adder venom, she seemed more grown-up than before. She was like the word portraits of her mother in the early Guilbert Phatt mysteries. Knowledgeable *and* thoughtful. At this moment, Knowles was saddened by what she saw in Amy and Speke.

'Are you sure you want to do that?' she asked. 'Make a slave of Harper?'

'Stretch is your friend,' said Amy. 'Don't you want her better?'

'Of course. I want us all better. You too.'

'I'm not ill,' said Amy.

'But you are *worse*. You should see your face at the moment. It's more frightening than your mask. Look at your new cloak. It's black.'

Suddenly self-conscious, Amy wasn't sure she liked this new Miss Memory.

'Zorro wears a black cloak,' she said defensively. 'He's not frightening.'

'You're not dressed like Zorro,' said Knowles. 'I was turned upside-downsey in Villa DeVille but I know who you got the cloak from. Not El Zorro, "the fox so cunning and free", but El Murciélago, "the Black Bat Night". You've picked your costume to scare people.'

'Not people... Wrong 'Uns. They *should* be scared.'

'What's a Wrong 'Un?'

'Them,' said Amy. 'Those who do wrong. The girl who chained you and Dyall, knowing what it would do. Whoever or whatever's out there in the china mask playing puppets. We can't let them have it all their own way. We can't let the Broken Doll laugh at us because we follow a chalk line on the floor and won't step off no matter what.'

'You sound like Harper. Where do you suppose she got it from?'

Amy instantly thought of Miss Kratides.

Is hurting wicked people so wrong?

'If you're in it for the *goodness*, Amy, be sure you know what *goodness* and *badness* are. Moreover, be ready for the time when those terms aren't useful any more.'

Ask yourself if you've done that much good as School Paladin.

Shrimp had spent an hour with the tutor too.

Amy recalled the persuasive, funny, sympathetic Moria Kratides but also the small, pettish, shrill child who said 'I won't be told not to be horrid...' All these girls – in Draycott's as well as Drearcliff Grange – had been taught the same lesson but learned different things from it.

Miss Memory came out of her tutorial more muddled than she went in. She was only clear-headed now Harper had blown away all her cobwebs. Gould was running wild… Light Fingers wasn't talking… and Speke and Little had sucked the pops off their lolly sticks.

Knowles pressed her point. 'Is making someone do things they don't want to right or wrong?'

'Depends on the person; depends on the thing,' Amy replied.

Knowles picked Frecks' coif up off the floor and held it out.

'Could you put your hand in this and say that?'

Amy hesitated. She *did* see Knowles' point… but Harper *deserved* a limp, or floppy limbs, or a bad cough. She should *atone*. Suffering would be good for her in the long run. But should she be ill for the rest of her life so others could be cured? How badly sick should she be? How much punishment – really? – would be a fair reckoning for her many sins? Mumps, hives, runny nose, splitting head, weeping boils, leprosy?

If forced to think about it, Amy felt sorry for Harper. After giving birth to twins, Mrs Harper was struck by a wasting disease that baffled doctors. The invalid recovered when she and baby Jacques took a long voyage without baby Jacqueline. Since then, Harper had barely seen her family. They knew exactly what she was and took measures to avoid the ill-effects of having her in the house. While she was sent away to school, her brother was coddled at home. His Talent ran the other way. Everyone who met Jacques Harper came away full of vim and perked up no end.

So…

Amy didn't take the chainmail. She slipped her hands under her belt, reaching for pockets her costume didn't have.

'*I'll* clutch the silver,' said Speke. 'Happily.'

She reached out, but her fingers tucked up tight, withdrawing into the shells of her hands. Only the nails peeped out. She hesitated to touch the coif.

'They've never done *that* before. The blessed things have minds of their own.'

'Blessed?' asked Miss Memory.

Speke considered her hands.

'Blessings aren't always all good,' said Amy. 'That's why Frecks isn't wearing hers. Maybe curses aren't always all bad. This isn't *that* cloak, Knowles. The Count's. I know what that was doing to me and got rid of it. This is a Light Fingers special.'

'After all we went through last year, I wouldn't have thought you'd ever wear black.'

'Black is flattering,' said Amy. 'I like black. I've *always* liked black. This is a costume. I can take it off.'

'Be sure you can, Amy. You, of all of us, can go so far.'

Miss Kratides had said something similar.

'Just be careful,' said Knowles.

'Boldness *and* mistrust?' said Amy.

Knowles smiled wryly. 'I admit it didn't work out last time. Best to find a balance, but err on the side of boldness. Prefer silver to black. You too, Speke. You've a heart as well as hands.'

Miss Memory put the coif on the piano lid. She wasn't that comfortable holding the blessed thing, but also reluctant to let go of it. After smoothing the mail into the shape of a flattened crusader's head, she found the strength to leave it alone.

Speke's fingers slid out of their shell-sheaths.

With their little brains, her hands *knew* things. If only the things all small creatures knew – fingers out of the fire, don't bother anything that bites or stings, put up a fight if you have to.

Harper groaned but didn't wake.

'Is *she* the Broken Doll?' asked Speke, nodding at Shrimp.

'No, but she *listens* to the Doll,' said Little.

They turned to the First. She didn't often pipe up.

'The Doll tries to talk to me too,' she explained. 'I don't listen. You shouldn't talk to ghosts. It encourages liberties. The Doll lives in the cupboard that smells of tennis balls. It has other homes. Places I don't at all like one tiny bit. A tin in the larder which says biscuits on the lid but has dried figs in. Cook put it out for orphans because the figs went funny and no one eats them anyway but it was at the back of the shelf the next day. A railway carriage where the light doesn't work if the train goes into a tunnel and the clickiticlick goes faint so you can hear her voice in it. That path through the copses no one walks if they can help it. Upper-School girls call it the Runnel. An attic in Windward Cottage where an anchor on a chain swings like a pendulum though there's no window to let in the breeze. You can tell where the Doll lives because the doors are all the same. Even the lying lid that says biscuits is the same door only smaller.'

It was the most Amy could remember Gillian Little saying at once.

'That girl listens,' Little went on, meaning Harper. 'She was led up the garden path. She does what the Doll wants. Things I wouldn't do. She wanted to hurt you anyway but she'd stay in her dorm if she wasn't talked to.'

Amy agreed, but didn't think the voice in Shrimp's ear was a ghost.

'The thing with the musical instruments wasn't her,' said Amy.

'Are you *sure* it wasn't you?' said Knowles.

'Why does everyone think that? I'm not the only poltergirl in the world...'

Behind Knowles, Beethoven came away from the wall. Amy had thought of using her Ability to get rid of the ugly picture. *Was* she doing this? Speke's hands ran away with her. Harper didn't mean to heal Knowles. She used to float in her sleep. Could mentacles develop a mind of their own? Act on ideas she only toyed with?

No. This wasn't that.

The picture didn't fall off a hook, but folded out on a hinge. One of Little's doors. A Wrong Door. Beyond it was the Broken Place...

A cracked white face appeared in the square behind the picture. High forehead, tiny chin, blood-kiss lips. Live eyes like unshelled eggs – raw and wet, not poached – fixed Amy with a gaze she recognised at once.

The voodoo stare.

Larry Laurence was the Broken Doll!

On her, a mask was no disguise. It was hostile display. Not to hide her identity, but to add to it.

Larry had lifted the instruments. Had she kept an Application secret like Harper, saving the surprise for when she could do the most harm? Even an angry, hurt, hurtful Larry wasn't that calculating. Was the Talent in the mask? Laurence wasn't the first Broken Doll. The face and the name – and the Abilities? – had been around for a long time.

Where was Larry? Drearcliff Grange was riddled with secret passages, but she was further away than inside a wall.

Knowles caught sight of Amy's expression. The others noticed violet light spilling onto the carpet. Slowly, reluctantly, they turned to look at the wall, the light, the Doll.

Speke's hands hid behind her back. Little's fist went up to her mouth.

Knowles was too stunned to check her spook-spotting gear.

'She's not a ghost,' said Amy.

No one listened.

The wall rippled. Shimmering light filtered through patches where the plaster was thin. Fleur-de-lis designs on the wallpaper – long since faded in daylight – sprang into relief against the glow. Paper flowers bloomed darkly.

The corners of the Music Room grew ill-defined. The walls might have been close as the sides of a cupboard or a hundred yards away. The floor undulated. Quicksand under carpet. The harpsichord played a slow, tinkly 'Funeral March of a Marionette'.

Amy felt weak and rubbery.

When Larry wanted to post large items, the Purple reached out. Objects squeezed and the pocket stretched. Laurence said things turned to jelly before she put them away.

Amy was jellying.

A fissure opened below the Beethoven door. Larry's pocket extended into the Music Room. A seam in the wall unbuttoned like a shirt. The edges pulled apart. Millions of cilia wiggled inside.

The soles of Amy's feet felt wrong. She tried to wiggle her toes. She was inches off the floor. Lifted, but not by her own Talent. Off-balance, she couldn't right herself in the air. Her jellied weight was unevenly distributed. Her ears roared as if seashells were clamped over them.

She was sucked towards the Purple.

Larry would do to her on purpose what she'd done to Polly Sparks by accident. Kentish Glory or Death's-head Hawk – it wouldn't matter. After a dip in Larry's pocket, she'd be Ordinary Amy. Light Fingers would call her a slowcoach. Without her Abilities, what would be left of her?

For the first time, she really *was* afraid of the Broken Doll...

V: She Will Blame You...

EVERYONE WAS FLOATING.

Frecks and Harper hovered in their sleep. Knowles, too surprised to take notes, turned in mid-air like an hourglass – refreshed brain heavier than her dainty feet – and flapped her hands to right herself. Speke and Little were torn between panic and delight. Amy remembered how that felt. Little struggled to hold her nightie down over her knees. Speke's hands lunged ahead of her like pilot fish.

Larry's open pocket exerted a steady pull. Amy lashed mentacle grappling hooks to the walls and tried to fly backwards, fighting the drag. Inch by inch, she was drawn to the Purple. Looking into the cold, pulsing fissure hurt. She shut her eyes but still saw it. Numbness spread up her arms and legs. Flesh become fluid.

The Purple hummed soothingly. And spoke with a human sound.

Not Larry's voice. Or not *only* Larry's voice.

Amy heard the coaxing, wordless lullaby of the Broken Doll. She wanted to let go and disappear.

The wall was translucent now. A magic lantern slide projected on fog. The peephole eyes of gnarled composers were small exploding stars. Fleurs-de-lis burned.

The Broken Doll stepped through the wall, lurching with

shoulder and hip. She and the bricks were jellied. The wall swelled and popped, then re-formed behind her. Solid and with her feet on the floor, the masked girl stood in the Music Room. Hands apart, she stretched the sides of her pocket like a cat's cradle.

'Larry,' said Amy, struggling to speak, 'you don't *have* to be broken.'

'*Larry?*' exclaimed Knowles. 'That's Laurence?'

Miss Memory found handholds on the wall.

'I didn't guess,' she admitted. 'I was *sure* it was you.'

Amy had thought as much.

'Larry,' she shouted. 'I'm sorry. Frecks is sorry. We're all sorry.'

The Broken Doll's old-fashioned dress was thick lace with big stitches and a floppy bow. Marionette clothes made to a human scale. Her long midnight-black skirt flared to a dragging train. A dancer's thigh slit showed a rind of scarlet. Larry wore Count DeVille's cloak, belted around her waist with its wolf's head clasp.

Amy had left the bat thing in Number 347 Piccadilly and thought good riddance.

But here it was. Turning up like a bad penny.

The Broken Doll kinked her neck sharply... then kinked the other way... then angled up at the coving where Knowles clung. The voodoo stare was undimmed, but a tear crawled out of the crack in her cheek.

'But you have to stop,' Amy said. 'You're hurting people who don't deserve to be hurt. You're hurting *yourself*.'

The Doll *aimed* her pocket at Amy. An invisible octopus in the Purple gripped her with arm after arm and hauled her towards its beaked maw. The force was too cold to feel, too strong to resist.

One by one, her mentacles failed. The waves in her ears pounded shingles.

The choir of lost girls called to her.

It would be easy to let go. To let it all go.

Mother would be pleased, at least. To have her grounded.

Nothing would be Amy's fault any more. Her responsibility. Her duty.

She could let others take care of the just causes.

Who knew? Maybe Ordinary Amy would be happy…

The pull was overpowering. The octopus was a small planet. She was a falling meteor. Tyrant gravity reasserted its rule over the rebel who so often defied God, Newton and propriety to soar free of its iron shackle. She lost her grip, lost her hold on the air, and tumbled top over tail towards the dazzling rift… but bumped into something.

Someone – Harriet Speke – was diving like a seabird, hands ahead of her, aiming at the Doll's bread basket, determined to get in the first strike.

Amy opened her mouth to warn her. No words came out.

Speke shot across the room. Her crab-hands punched into Larry's pocket.

Indoor lightning struck again.

The pull of the pocket was suddenly gone. Amy shot backwards and slammed against the wall, then fell towards a tangle of twisted music stands. Instinct took over and a mentacle mattress formed between her body and the metal tines. Knowles landed with an 'oof' – but on flat carpet rather than spears.

The violet flash seared Amy's vision.

She blinked away squiggling light-worms.

Larry screamed, full-throated and high-pitched. Her unmoving mouth shook with the noise.

Speke was down on one knee, arms sunk up to the elbows in Larry's midriff, trapped by a shining seam. The pocket had closed on Speke's hands. The girls were locked together. Speke didn't scream, *per se*, but sang in terror, '*Oh oh oh oh oh oh… no John no John no John no!*'

Awake again, less chirrupy than her usual sprung-up-from-a-sleep wont, Frecks mumbled, 'Eh what, now, what's this, what?' Little got Frecks' feet on the floor and was there to be leaned on.

Amy floated herself upright – the trick was to imagine her head as buoyant and her feet as weights – and stepped down to the floor. The carpet was springy. She worried that her knees might give out. She needed to do more bicycling exercises, to maintain strength and flexibility in her legs. Flying too much could lead to atrophy of the leg muscles. She walked unsteadily over to Larry and Speke.

The Doll mask was attached like a limpet. She couldn't remove it without ripping Larry's face off.

Larry, Amy perceived, was in a right state. Which was no excuse.

Amy took gentle hold of Speke's shoulders. The girl was held firm. The pocket closed like a vice. Speke didn't pull for fear of hurting herself.

'Larry, please let go,' Amy said.

Her bones weren't fluid any more, but the feeling of jelliness lingered. It would take a while to get used to being unstretched. Her voice didn't sound right in her ears.

The mask angled down. She saw Larry's angry eyes.

'Are you all right, Speke?' Amy asked. 'Does it hurt?'

'I can feel my hands.'

'Phew, what a relief.'

'No. It isn't. I've *never* felt my hands.'

'Ah.'

Amy was fascinated by the mesh of Speke's arms and Larry's middle. They could have been born like that, clothes and all. They fit together like the puzzle of the twisted nails. She saw no way of disentangling them.

'What's this?' asked Frecks, starting to focus. 'Who? Where's Larry?'

'That's Laurence,' said Knowles. 'The Broken Doll.'

'No,' said Frecks, scornful. 'That's never young Larry. That's an apparition, an apport, an abomination...'

'You shouldn't have listened to the ghost,' Little told Larry. 'You shouldn't have opened the wrong door.'

Amy felt along Speke's arms, all the way to where they vanished. She avoided brushing Larry's new skirt.

She understood how Larry floated things. The cloak had leeched Amy's Abilities. Whoever put it on next inherited a portion of her Talent just like Amy had been infused with the senses and desires of the unspeakable former owner. It wasn't a gift, but a bad bargain. No one could wear the cloak and stay as they were. You weren't you with a new Talent, you were a Talent with a new you. A you who wasn't entirely you any more.

'What's happening to my hands?' Speke asked quietly.

'Ah,' said Amy, understanding her second secret at last. 'I should have told you. What I know about Laurence. I told some of the Remove, but not you, Speke. I'm sorry. I know you'll blame me.'

'It's letting up,' Speke said, not hearing Amy. 'I'm coming loose. Give us a haul, fellows.'

Amy didn't, delaying the fulfilment of prophecy by moments...

Little stumped over and gripped her friend's waist. She tugged her away from the Broken Doll.

Speke's arms pulled out of the pocket.

The violet seam pressed shut and disappeared.

Larry relaxed and staggered back.

'*Oh oh oh oh oh oh*,' exclaimed Speke, '*no John no John no John no!*'

Her crab-hands were gone. Her arms ended in glazed stumps.

The Broken Doll was impassive. Amy was seized by the horrors.

Then – another *flash*!

VI: A Final Moment's Dream

WHEN A. LOOKED up, she saw not ceiling but sky... She was accustomed to the Purple House... outdoors was as alien to her as dry land to a sailor after years at sea... Without walls, the world was too big to take in... Her legs couldn't remember how to walk on uneven, uncarpeted earth.

The moon was a mauve circle in the violet sky.

Night-time eternal... Day had forgotten to break for longer than she could remember.

Sensing danger at her back, A. pressed on... With her senses of up and down and forward and back scrambled, she was torn between urgent haste and excessive caution... Boldness and mistrust... Though she knew the notion foolish, she was afraid that if she lost her footing she would fall upwards, tossed to the winds... Up in the air, she would be torn apart.

She walked a straight path through twisted woods... Treading on powdered chalk spread on beaten earth... Eyes turned in knotholes as she passed... Her pace picked up.

A motto popped into her mind... A precipice in front and wolves behind... That was written on the Coat of Arms of the Purple House... She did not know whether the Broken Doll was the precipice or the wolves... Was she close behind, gaining on A. as she tottered, tiny steps punching black sole outlines into the pink chalk? Or in waiting by the side of the path ahead, sharpening china finger-shards on iron-hard bark?

Worst of all, the Doll might be inside A. and swelling, evicting her from her own body... A bud of malice sprouting inside her skull, extending tendrils through the meat of her mind, stealing her thoughts for its own.

A. was not alone – would *never* be alone – in the woods... The masters and servants and dependents returned, not as themselves but as Broken Toys, playthings of the Broken Doll... John Nohj, Ogrette, the Oracle, the Lady Knight... and others, fresh to the Grave Game... the Girl Who Grew on a Tree, who had a flower for a face and branches for limbs... The Girl Who Takes and the Boy Who Gives, Twin Heirs of Hugo Ape... And the Assassin's Small Daughter, new Mistress of the Purple House, who set the rules and chalked the lines.

The path she trod led back to Seaview Promontory... There, the Purple House stood high above Shark Shingles, propped and braced on iron poles and support girders added as the foundations crumbled... Old cellars were now open to wind and surf, as the cliff fell away rock by rock... Dreaded staircases were now exposed paths... Where maids once walked the chalk line, seabirds fought and fed and fouled.

Her crime haunted her.

A crime of omission... All her time at the Purple House, A. had been cautioned to keep mum... She was not to gossip or spread stories or volunteer information or even comment on the wallpaper or the food or the looks of that one particular under-footman with the curly hair and no nose... Like all the other maids – like her long-departed friend Millie – she had struggled against an instinct to chatter... but just once, when she should have spoken out, she had been silent... The chalk line was interrupted and she didn't know where to walk.

She had seen the brave girl – John Nohj – walk ahead into peril, approaching the ghost of Princess Violet when the coal behind her eye was white hot... The Mad Spectre Princess bit off

John Nohj's hands and spat them out alive... A. knew this would happen, but called no warning... She had opened her mouth, but did not know what to say... no, she *could* have spoken, but chose not to... and John Nohj suffered for it.

With sharpened hooks instead of hands, John Nohj was on the track, intent on vengeance... Ogrette strode by John Nohj, bending branches out of the way so her small, angry friend could pass... Their tongues clicked in the insect language they had worked out between them.

The Lady Knight and the Oracle could not help. A. must take her medicine.

She stumbled across a long sign, fallen off its struts, and made out part of a name... UFFLER's HAL... then ran down a cracked station platform, beside a railbed overgrown with eight-foot weeds... The Girl With Green Thumbs had passed this way – the Girl who was and yet *was not* the Girl Who Grew on a Tree... A stack of polished coffins were piled by the Lost Luggage Office... bat-crests on their sides like the coats of arms on the doors of a distinguished family's best carriage... A Broken Railway Porter stood on a circular base, whistle raised but unblown because his head was missing – the buttons on his wooden uniform were fist-sized blobs of gold paint.

Beyond Uffler's Hal was a meadow where night flowers bloomed... A. stumbled into fogbanks of heady perfume... moths the size of her apron flitted from flower to flower, spreading pollen... The stinging scent got into her nose and forehead and behind her eyes... She saw light bursts as she staggered through long, sharp grass that scraped her shins.

On the horizon was the Purple House.

Stationed by the front door Jimmy Wood, the Old Campaigner astride his charger... He was missing an arm and a leg and his horse's head... An axe-cleft divided his helmet and opened his forehead... His wood flesh was green and a shrub sprouted from his wedge wound, sporting a concerned floral face and twigs waving a caution.

'Amy, no,' said the flower...

Amy? Who? A. for Amy?

Nearing the front door, A. looked at the face that had spoken... The flower was lovely, but the stunted little shrub was ugly and had a strange smell... a bitter, poison smell she could taste... She had tasted it before and not liked it...

'Do not go in there,' said the Girl Who Grew on a Tree. 'She will hurt you.'

'I am already hurt.'

'She will hurt you *more*!'

A rustling across the meadow made A. turn...

Others were out of the woods and past Uffler's Hal. Ogrette strode through the meadow, skirt slashed by scythe-grass... John Nohj hooked moths out of the air, skewering them... All Broken Toys had white masks, blanks without feature or imperfection... The Broken Doll hung back on the platform, wanting the shade of the awning and a vantage point for a view of what came next.

The grass was agitated like choppy water... Out of sight, dozens of small, clicking creatures scurried across the meadow.

The door of the Purple House opened.

A. had passed through the front door once before, a long time ago, when first sent to the kitchens... It was different now, reddish and rusted and Wrong.

She had no time to think.

Creatures scuttled out of the grass onto the gravel drive, eyestalks waving... A dozen little voodoo stares drove A. up the steps and through the door...

'Amy,' said Paquignet, '*don't*.'

VII: In the Doll's House

IT WAS THE Hour of the Broken Doll. A thin promise of night's end pinked the wooded inland horizon.

After four steps and a jump into indoor gloom, Amy pranged her hip bone against a desk. Before her eyes adjusted she knew where she was. Windward Cottage. Electric lights came on. Seaview windows became midnight mirrors.

At this precipice, Amy must turn and face the wolves. In this classroom, she'd learn her lesson.

Had she run or flown from the Music Room?

She'd been dreaming but awake. There had been woods... the Purple House... and Broken Toys.

Seeing herself reflected darkly in the portholes, she realised she needed no mask. Her face was death's head enough. Her wings were torn, scratched by claws or twigs. She was a fright.

Fleur Paquignet had switched the lights on. She'd told her not to go into Windward.

An army of Sleeping Bettys must be winding down in the dorms. Had anyone gone to bed last night?

Paquignet shut the door behind her and leaned against it.

'That won't hold long,' she said.

Why was Paquignet talking to Amy as if they were best friends? The Ariel Fifth sat three desks away from her and was on intimate terms only with plants. She'd been acting out of character for weeks. Something was off about her flower-perfect face. A little *too* green?

'What are *you* doing here?' Amy asked.

'You won't believe this, but I'm trying to make it up to you.'

'Make what up to me?'

'Tell you later. We've other worries now.'

Amy wasn't satisfied, but...

A scratching began. Rats chewing through the doorsill?

'What *is* that?'

A chunk of wood was punched in, at the bottom of the door. At the same time, a window smashed. Two small, nippy creatures crawled into the classroom.

Speke's hands.

On her wrists, they'd looked like crabs. On their own, they were disturbingly more like hands. Fast and determined. And after her.

Amy rose off the floor and swatted with her mentacles.

She made the hand-crabs feel it. She *could* now use her Talent as a big fist. When threatened, she responded. She developed Applications by instinct, more like remembering than learning. In a return bout with Stephen Swift, they'd be equally matched. Death's Head Against Draycott's Damsel. She'd settle Miss Steps' lie about letting her win last time. She'd break any Duck Press, Iron Maiden or Cosy Coffin. She'd put the Wrong 'Un in her place.

The hand-crabs scuttled in circles under Amy's feet. At eighteen inches off the floor, she was out of scrabbling reach. Their finger-limbs pushed like grasshopper legs, and they leaped higher and higher. She took a few more steps up her imaginary staircase. The hand-crabs jumped and skittered, but couldn't pinch her ankles.

Was it Speke who blamed Amy? Or her hands?

Those sharp-tipped fingers could gouge and slice.

The door was pushed in, knocking Paquignet over. She

grunted in an unrefined, ungirlish manner.

Little stumped into the classroom like a coalman hauling a half-hundredweight bag. Frecks was slung over her stout shoulder. With an oof of relief, the Little Girl dumped her unresisting burden on the teacher's desk. She was under the violet sway of...

Who?

Larry Laurence or the Broken Doll?

Larry floated through the doorway, legs dangling inside a skirt half again as long as she was.

Amy assumed a mid-air fighting stance. Larry couldn't best her with stolen Abilities. She wouldn't have the measure of them yet. But she had a Talent of her own and reached deep into her pocket for Applications. Like Amy, she was learning in the field, becoming more dangerous.

Speke came in, towel wrapped around her stumps. She saw her disembodied hands. Returned from Larry's pocket, they were more and more agile and dextrous. They sprang up onto desks and ran across the lids, jumping the chasms between them. For an instant, Speke was proud of her hand-crabs. A mother cat watching her kittens torment a shrew. Then she looked up at Amy, angry and hurt.

Couldn't she at least *try* to blame Larry?

Or herself, for barging in?

No. Speke had saved Amy – if only temporarily – and bravery had cost her dearly. She couldn't blame Amy as much as Amy would – given a few moments to reflect – blame herself.

The Broken Doll's crown – a stiff horsehair wig – scraped the ceiling. Count DeVille's cloak trailed on the floor. Larry was like a circus performer on stilts. Not a jolly-on-the-outside/crying-on-the-inside clown, but a *punchinello* with hot red coals of rage for eyes and three stilettos in each fist.

Little prodded Frecks, who was conscious but not properly awake. She groaned.

Amy wasn't happy the Broken Doll had brought her best

friend to Windward. Larry had a list of people she took issue with. Amy was at the top, of course. Frecks, who had scorned her worship, was on it too. Love turned to hate was merciless. Most crushes ended this way, but most girls didn't respond to an offhand rebuff by turning into Lady Caliban.

Frecks' coif was in her pocket not on her head. The mail had to be worn for the charm of protection to work. Having spiky hair for days would have been small price to pay for living past the dawn, but Frecks hadn't thought that far ahead.

Larry alighted on a desk edge, cloak underfoot. Perfectly balanced, she steadied herself with mentacles. Amy had never thought to use her Talent to make a perch less precarious. Was Larry using her stolen Abilities more imaginatively than she did herself? That'd be irritating.

Larry put clawfingers against her stomach and prised her pocket open.

It was a rip – a wound! – in reality. Unpleasant to see. Worse to think about. Inside, fluorescent worm-things writhed and knotted obscenely.

Amy tensed to resist the pull of the Purple but Laurence didn't repeat the trick.

Larry's thin body was racked with spasms, as if she'd swallowed a jar of electric eels. She bent this way and that, Broken Doll fashion. Spurts of light came from her pocket. A chittering, chewing, clicking began... and grew louder and louder. Small objects popped out, one after another. Soft cannonballs shot from the void. Fist-sized rolled-up woodlice. They struck walls or the ceiling or the floor – or wary Paquignet, cringing Little and aghast Speke – then fell and scrabbled and righted themselves.

Purple duplicates of Speke's hands. More crablike than the originals and marked by their maker. Their cracked carapaces were miniature doll faces. Blue flame-gems burned in eyeholes. More hostile display.

The torrent of hand-crabs continued.

Paquignet and Speke got up on desks, tucking their legs under them. Hand-crabs blanketed the floor. They hopped and climbed over each other to get up at the girls. Insect-swarm behaviour. One locust was a specimen. A hundred thousand were a plague. A sharp-nailed pinch would be painful. A hundred thousand might be fatal.

It wasn't lost on Amy that Speke was afraid of the duplicates too.

Little was too big and clumsy to get up on a desk. She wore nightie and slippers. Her bare arms were goosefleshed and bluish from the pre-dawn chill. Hand-crabs nipped at her ankles. She grimaced and swallowed revulsion, too terrified to scream. Gillian Little would need a lot of kindness after this.

Larry convulsed and retched horde upon horde from her pocket. Her back arched as her pocket enlarged. Her cape-skirt rose primly from the floor to avoid being spattered with purple ichor. Amy hadn't seen Larry disgorge anything with a semblance of life before. Was that her original Ability or a new Attribute? Larry almost doubled backwards, spine bent like a longbow. Cobweb cracks spread across her mask.

How much of Venetia Laurence was left? The skin of the Broken Doll wrapped her like a china shell. Her mind – its tangle of loves and grudges, joys and pains – was mulched for compost. The cold, cruel cuckoo thrived in her skull. Count DeVille's cape sucked her marrow like ivy crumbling a stone wall. Hardy parasites smothering a weakling host. Child-brains swelling as the girl's shrivelled to the size of a pea. This Doll was new-born, a nursery tyrant princess. She only knew small words and simple sentences.

Spot is a dog. Chase Spot. Hurt Spot. Break Spot.

Amy remembered the Russian Doll. The centipede in the middle – whatever that had been, lost to history and undiscovered even by Knowles – was the seed of the Broken Doll. Something new was added as each bulbous face slotted over the last. All earlier dolls were contained, but each onion layer had its own particular nastiness. This time, it was the cloak… and all that came with it, the powers and hunger and traces of Amy she'd let the thing steal. Over a week after she'd worn the cape for less than an hour, she still had the taste of blood on her tongue.

Amy is a girl. Chase Amy. Hurt Amy. Break Amy.

Speke's white hands were lost in a raging sea of purple duplicates.

Amy tried to sweep them back with mentacles. It was her experiment with making holes in water again. If she concentrated, she stemmed the tide. A flicker of distraction and the hand-crabs swarmed back in.

A desk collapsed. The thorn-tips of a thousand fingers tore through metal and wood. The desks were still in use after all these years because they were almost indestructible. But only almost.

She picked her fight and flew across the room, landing in front of Little. The big, bare-legged First was in the most immediate danger. Amy didn't dare look down at what crunched under her feet. Summoning every ounce of mentacle muscle, she extended her arms and held her palms out. She focused, imagining her own hostile display, a Death's Head in the dark. Black flames wrapped around the skull. She swallowed coppery spit and tore through her own cocoon, emerging as something truly *fearsome*. She *pushed* – throwing back and turning aside surging waves of crab-hands.

Flipped on their backs, they scrabbled like real crabs. A few lifted off the ground, fingers dabbling like tiny galley oars. They only kept aloft for a few seconds before falling back into the crowd. Amy recognised more locust behaviour. The next fliers would be more skilled. Then the whole swarm would fill the air.

'Larry, I'm who you want to punish,' Amy said. 'Please stop hurting the others.'

The Broken Doll didn't hear. She floated from her perch, cloak-skirt flaring. Larry's feet – in grubby bedsocks – dangled. Her legs were covered in recent bites and scratched scabs. The cloak's scarlet silk lining was fresh and shiny.

Larry stopped spewing hand-crabs. The last two or three purple duplicates slipped through the pocket's lips. The hand-crabs slid down the folds of the cloak and dropped onto the floor, where they got lost in the throng.

The more duplicates Larry made, the cruder they were. The fourth or fifth outpouring of hand-crabs were jellying already. Mask-marked shells came to pieces. Caught fingernails bent and snapped. Clayish meat sludged off the bone. Scratching, scrabbling things covered the floor.

Recovered, Larry snapped up straight. Her eyes fixed on Amy.

She floated over to the teacher's desk. A flap of Count DeVille's cloak slapped onto Frecks' face like a wet flannel. The cape fit her features like an eyeless mask, undulating slightly. At its touch, Frecks woke. She tried to unpeel the stinging cloth. It wouldn't come unstuck. The little hooks had her. She opened her mouth to catch her breath. That gave the cloak a wider hole to fill.

Speke, nearest to Frecks, reached to help… then froze. Seeing the ends of her arms as if for the first time, she let out a single, agonised sob.

That stabbed Amy. This was her own fool fault.

The Broken Doll stood in mid-air, voodoo stare exclusively for Amy. She didn't even glance down at Frecks as the cape fed.

Amy took a mind-grip on the china mask.

Fluencing the cracked white china stung. Amy's antennae prickled. Then spasms of pain shot through her forehead. She kept hold and increased pressure. Laurence's mad eyes watered. The Doll's face was still firmly attached to the girl's skin. This parasite had hooks too, sunk deeply into the host. Amy couldn't get the mask off without breaking Larry.

Was there a Larry left to break?

It would all be over if Amy just snapped her neck. The Broken Doll was a terror. The Broken-in-Bits Doll would be no such thing. A Death's Head solution. Simple and final. Best for everyone. Frecks and the others saved. Even Larry would be thankful. She was no better off than Palgraive. No matter the provocation and the promises, Larry must regret opening the Wrong Door and inviting the Doll into her head. If Amy were in Laurence's place, she'd be grateful – wouldn't she?

No, of course not. She'd be dead.

Still, others would be saved. Frecks, Little, Paquignet.

Even Speke – whom Death's-head Hawk would have to tackle next, lest she pick up the mask and the name. Unforgiving Speke. Then her friend, Little. Terrified, but angry and strong. Not to be taken for a Dim. Once they were done with, Harper deserved worse than she'd got so far.

Shrimp is a Pest. Chase Shrimp. Hurt Shrimp. Break Shrimp.

Crowninshield II, Nobbs, Ziss, De'Ath, Inchfawn. Wrong 'Uns all. They should be broken. Stamped with the Death's Head. As a warning to the rest. Sidonie Gryce beckoned. Amy couldn't just leave that witch to Moria Kratides. Their difference was personal. Other rotters she didn't know personally were begging for a breaking. Spring-Heel'd Jackanapes, the Gaiety Ghoul, Stepan Volkoff, the Slink. They deserved no mercy. The Lady of the Lake would want them cast down. Their lot was the Mausoleum or the Morgue. Despatched by the Death's-head Hawkmoth.

First, there was a neck to snap. Wires and strings to cut.

Amy's mentacles coiled around the Broken Doll's throat.

The edges of the crack in the mask ground together.

Just a little more pressure... and...

'Amy,' said Paquignet, '*don't*. You won't only break her. You'll break *yourself*.'

Amy heard Paquignet, but didn't relax her grip.

Just causes were all well and good, but *unending*. A paladin strives nobly and clears a patch for honour, but in the end must falter and fall. The unjust swarm back across the beach, tear down the monuments. Innocents are put under the yoke or to the sword. A fresh paladin eventually rises to the challenge, but the Great Game is played at the expense of those on the sidelines. Their lot was to be trampled, lashed or forgotten. Being rescued or avenged was no recompense for the suffering.

The line wasn't always chalked where you needed to go.

Amy kept up the pressure.

With additional mentacles, she scooped hand-crabs and tossed them at Larry. They thumped against her thin chest and arms, tore her sleeves, burst on the floor when they fell.

The cloak flipped off Frecks' face. Frecks sat up, blood on her forehead.

Amy's friend was saved. For the moment.

Amy could save her for all time. With just a little effort.

Dolly is a Wrong 'Un. See Dolly. Chase Dolly. Hurt Dolly. Break Dolly for good.

Not the Broken Doll, but the Beaten Doll.

The cloak rose around Larry, folds animated. Tendrils slapped Amy's mentacles. Larry folded her arms over her chest and let the cloak fight for her. The Doll could animate or shift objects with Amy's stolen Abilities by hiding inside Larry's mind and concentrating. Amy should learn that trick. She still relied on conjuring gestures, exerting her will like an orchestra conductor.

Amy held up her hands and made tight fists. Her arm muscles were taut as cables. Her mentacles constricted. She forced pain out of her head and into the cloak. Despite its recent feeding, it grew weaker as dawn neared. Amy mind-wrestled the shade of Count DeVille. She outstared a voodoo master. At last, the cloak stiffened like a batwing kite. It collapsed, heavy cloth slapping Larry's legs, no more dangerous than a kilt of curtains.

DeVille was down... but the Doll still stood.

Amy sensed Larry's larynx being compressed... vertebrae straining, pinching a nerve.

One sharp *snap* and it would be over.

'You're a Glory not a Death's Head,' cried Paquignet.

Amy *squeezed...*

VIII: Results

THEN *STOPPED*.

Amy caught herself in time.

She couldn't claim she didn't know what she was thinking. No ghost mask or parasite skirt whispered in her mind, urging her to be Doll or DeVille.

Death's-head Hawk was her own idea.

Amy let Larry go, but the girl still choked and struggled. Stripped of stolen Abilities, she fell like an unstrung marionette. She landed on Palgrave's front-row desk, rolled off the lid, and got jammed in the seat. The cloak wadded around her legs like a too-big blanket. She tried to free herself, stamping and twisting. The more she shook the more stuck she got. She slammed her face against the desk in frustration and lay there, china cheek to ink-stained wood. The girl inside the mask was exhausted. Her voodoo stare dimmed. But she wasn't dead.

'Good show, Amy,' said Paquignet. 'Well done, girl.'

Paquignet had nagged her at the crucial moment.

Amy had opened a Wrong Door but not stepped over the threshold. Being a Death's Head was easier than being a Glory... at first. Larry was a pointed illustration of how that ended. A suit of armour could turn into an iron maiden.

Amy stepped down to the floor. Hollow doll-face carapaces

crunched underfoot. The purple duplicates congealed, jellying *en masse*. Larry had made too many too quickly.

Frecks, fully awake, dabbed her bloody face with a hankie.

'Have you enough sticking plasters for this?' Frecks asked Amy.

She handed over the medical kit.

'You'll need to wash first. You are a sight.'

'Thank you, nursie.'

Little held Speke. Both were wary of Amy now.

And no wonder.

Was that blame in Speke's eyes? Resentment? The towel had unwound from her stumps. Little hugged her friend protectively. Perhaps *too* protectively. Little should be careful. She wasn't just big. She was big and strong.

Paquignet stood over Larry.

The Girl With Green Thumbs had elected herself Lady of the Lake for the night. She didn't look or sound like herself.

'You'll thank me,' she announced.

'More likely she'll thump you, Floradora Girl!' said Frecks. 'Explanations had best be forthcoming forthwith!'

The door of Miss Kratides' study opened. *Another* Fleur Paquignet stumbled out, wrists bound behind her.

The old Paquignet, the one from last term... smaller, greener, spryer.

The *real* Paquignet.

Who was the new girl? A duplicate from the Purple? No – she wasn't puce in the face.

'Venetia,' said the imposter, close to Larry's shaking mask, 'I'm trying to make it up to you too.'

The false Paquignet spoke to all the girls in the classroom.

'We were playing the Game. To win. Drearcliff Grange are no different. It was never meant cruelly. I speak for the school. The Capt might have a qualm or two about the Finish. He understands how you might feel the final moments of play were less sporting than the ideal. I was sent here as an exchange student. Moria knows all about it. We had a jaw-jaw session yesterday. Geoff Jeperson sends his regards, by the way. Especially to Serafine. If you want to know a secret, the Capt is a tiniest bit sweet on the Seraph. That's why he's gone a bit soft. He's told me to make it right. It's an obligation. The School Charter demands it. I swear on St Cuthbert's honour, such as it is.'

The shammer unhooked a wig and wiped off his greenish face.

'This isn't what I look like,' he said. 'I can't show you that. I don't really know myself.'

'Alfred Henry Wax!' said Amy.

She should have known.

Among other annoyances and astonishments, Amy was irked by his casual reference to a teacher by her first name? *Moria*, indeed! Humblebumblers treated all women – no matter title, accomplishment or status – as maids or shop girls. They high-handedly called females to heel with a sharp, coaxing or familiar 'Millie' or 'Gretchen' or 'Florrie'.

Aside from that, in general and with specific regard to Amy… *how dare he!*

'H'At your serveece,' he said, scraping her nerves. 'No, sorry. He's faded to nought. They always do. My Paquignet's gone already. I sometimes miss them. Isn't that funny? They're real people to me.'

The true Paquignet eased herself into a desk seat and rubbed her wrists together behind her back. What must she think?

One of Speke's hands was crawling through purple sludge. Amy nudged it towards Paquignet. The fingers might still be good with knots.

Speke shuddered as she saw her severed hand nip behind the desk. No, she didn't *see*… she *felt*. Stealthy and purposeful, the crab-hand climbed to Paquignet's bonds and fiddled. Speke was *using* her detached body parts. If anything, she had more control over her free hand than when it was fixed to her wrist.

Her hands were handier.

Speke saw Amy notice her new Ability and regarded her coolly.

Mentacles of a sort extended from her stumps to her hands. She could puppeteer them into all sorts of mischief. Another girl, another Application discovered *in extremis*. Would that change how she felt about Amy? Miss Kratides expected them to be at daggers drawn. Kentish Glory was still in the market for an arch-nemesis. What had Amy thought to call her – Miss Stumps? Daisy Dextrous? The Punch and Judy Girl?

Paquignet's wrists were freed and she made and unmade fists to get the sap flowing again. She wasn't disturbed by Speke's crawling hand. It clambered onto her desk lid and waited for approval. Paquignet stroked its carapace as if it were a healthy ficus. Speke and Little gathered. Another triad in the making. Handy Hands, Strong Girl, Green Thumbs. Paladins or Wrong 'Uns? Or just an End of the Pier Show?

The purple mess was almost dissolved, leaving only streaks of dried scum.

Amy tried to see H'Alfie 'Ampton in Wax. He hadn't taken off his Paquignet disguise but rearranged it. She had another heart twinge of fury at the random unfairness. The rat had worn make-up in school for *weeks* and not been infracted. A real girl dabs on the merest speck of rouge and is scrubbing the Heel come Sunday. A fellow plasters his face with Leichner and gets away with it. A greater injustice than the Dreyfus Case! It must be taken to the House of Lords!

She caught herself getting distracted – by his impertinent use of first names, by his profligate application of make-up. A dozen irritating particulars provoked disproportionate ire. None were why she was really angry with young Master Wax. It was the other thing. Their last encounter. The betrayal at the Finish.

Amy would far rather snap *his* neck than Larry's. Was that why he'd intervened? He could get round Kentish Glory but feared a Death's Head.

They might pass it off as 'playing the Game' at Humble

College, but gulling a girl was low and callous. Amy felt hot shame that she had been *taken in*. Wax had made her think less of herself, perhaps permanently. No matter how appealingly he chased his tail, she was not ready to stroke the dog that bit her. A.H. Wax – Culprit of a Thousand Faces. Just being in the same room made her dream up revenges. Would he enjoy being upside down in the air? Slammed against the ceiling? Dunked in the Bristol Channel?

'Are you a boy?' asked Little.

'Mostly,' said Wax.

'Eek,' said Little, stepping behind Paquignet and Speke to hide her bare legs.

Wax pulled a toggle on his belt. Trouser legs rolled down from under his skirt, which he undid and removed. He took a few steps, getting the measure of a new walk. At first, he overdid the masculine effect, heaving shoulders like a knuckle-walking gorilla. He toned it down and got proper balance. Amy doubted this slouch was any more natural than the fairy-steps he'd taken as Paquignet.

'I was sitting next to a boy all along,' said Little, cheeks crimson. 'Uck!'

'It's all right, Gilly,' said Speke. 'You can't really get *germs* from boys.'

Amy wasn't so sure about that. Girls could get germs *and worse* from A.H. Wax.

His Talent – if Talent it was, not just a diligently acquired skill – was deceptive. Now his Paquignet was finished, Amy saw there had been screaming tells. He resembled the real girl, but hadn't her knack with plants. Vines saw through him and withered no matter how much he used a watering can. He never got the voice right and called Amy by her first name when Paquignet wouldn't. The flaws came to mind only after the curtain. H'Alfie was the same. Convincing when limping around, but ridiculous in retrospect. It wasn't just acting. Wax *was* an Unusual. His Talent clouded the mind, lulling folk into falling for his acts.

He might be able to pull off his personations without wigs or costumes. He made you *want* to believe in his disguises.

Of the girls in the classroom, only Larry could explain the extent of Wax's perfidy – and she was lost inside herself. Another thing Amy was blamed for that was really his fault. Frecks, Speke and the real Paquignet were more puzzled than annoyed by the strange, exotic creature – a boy! – who had popped up among them. Only Little was properly appalled, and she'd have been the same about anyone in trousers.

Only an hour ago, Amy had worn a mask. Now she came down on the side of being barefaced. A paladin might conceal their true name, but never their true self.

Wax must know she was still furious with him. Even Humblebumblers weren't *that* insensitive. He demonstrated courage just turning up – if not exactly showing his face – at Drearcliff Grange.

He *said* he wanted to make it up to her.

Her instinct was to tell him his unwanted intervention didn't make it up to her – or the school. Not by a considerable length of limestone calcite.

He had only reminded her who she was.

Which was the right thing to do. Sloshing Death's-head Hawk on the head with a flowerpot would have saved Larry. Letting Amy make her own decision was riskier, but saved them both. She shed the Death's Head of her own free will.

Still, she wasn't ready to thank him.

'I'm not your enemy, Amy,' said Wax.

'Then who is?' she demanded.

The question hung in the air. Frecks darted a glance at Larry, who still lay over her desk. Speke looked from her hands to Amy. Little tried her – pretty poor – best to shrink so there were girls between her and Wax. Paquignet alone was above it all. Her only enemies were spring frost and clumsy lawnmowing.

Moria Kratides came out of her study. She took tiny Japanese steps, as if hobbled by a kimono. Thick-soled shoes and piled-up hair drew attention to her short stature. She sat behind her desk.

Mouths fell open. Including Amy's.

Wax tutted at the interruption.

'Now, *children*,' said Miss Kratides, 'what have we learned?'

The teacher was outwardly calm but *buzzing*. She'd been up all night too. Amy's antennae jangled. Miss Kratides gave the impression of knowing more than she was telling – and, through her red-lettered cards, she'd already told a lot.

Her manner was odd. She knew the Remove had long since grown out of the 'now, *children*...' stage. Drearcliff Grange was not a nursery. Even Firsts didn't need to have their hands held.

But it stung. What *had* they learned?

Amy was annoyed, exhausted and confused... but had to admit she was thinking more clearly. Prompts and hints had been necessary, but the working-out was her own. She was Kentish Glory. She understood her choice. Though proud of herself, she felt a pinprick at the loss of Death's-head Hawk. If this was growing up, she didn't much care for it.

Others had suffered far worse from the Kratides Method. If Knowles, Speke or Larry declared the result – Top in Cleverness for the Term and Gold Stars for New-Found Abilities – worth the Ordeal of the Broken Doll, Amy would eat her now-superfluous Death's Head mask.

Miss Kratides cast an eye around the classroom. The purple residue was all but vanished. No damage done. That wasn't so back in the Music Room. Miss Memory had stayed behind and was stuck with tidying things as best she could before the Yeoman Lute Quartet ('The Peasant Pluckers') arrived to practise madrigals.

Miss Kratides was fascinated by Speke's hands. They cringed on Paquignet's desk as if the small woman were a roaring spectre with a raised chopper. Speke got a mental grip and her hands sat up to attention. They had become expressive.

Frecks finally asked the question. 'Did you do all this, Miss?'

'I *did* very little,' said the teacher. 'I oversaw and encouraged, where necessary. But you must learn for yourselves. Which you have.'

'What she means,' began Wax, 'is that she's delighted you're all alive. Because now Headmistress won't push her over the cliff.'

Miss Kratides' frozen cheek twitched.

Amy squelched her outrage at the outsider's impertinence. Drearcliff Grange girls could mock a beak or carp at a rule – the Code of Break practically required that they do so – but if anyone else spoke ill of the school or any of its staff they'd jump to the defence. Her immediate instinct was to round on Wax and give him a stern talking-to. But she wouldn't be distracted. She had her own bones with Miss Kratides. Which needed picking this exact moment.

'Where did Larry get the mask and the cloak?' she asked.

Miss Kratides didn't immediately answer.

'Tell them, Mori,' prompted Wax.

Mori?! This was too much!

'You've met our exchange student, I see,' said Miss Kratides. 'Sorry about him, by the way. Alf-and-Alf isn't easy to get shot of. I've been trying for years. You tear off one face and another appears, twice as annoying.'

Wax spat out a laugh.

'She's my sister,' he explained. 'I can't believe she's allowed to be a teacher. She shouldn't be in charge of cats, let alone girls. Not with her shabby, sorry record. *Mitéra* thinks it's a hoot. She says Mori'll join the Women's Auxiliary Police next and clap us all in the Mausoleum.'

'*That* is not likely,' said Miss Kratides, glaring.

Girls with brothers didn't need nemeses. Amy had noticed that before.

'You've ducked Amy's question,' said Frecks. 'Cleverly. So I'll ask it too. Mask and cloak?'

'I furnished one,' said the teacher, 'but Laurence made the other... or found it, or it found her.'

Larry hadn't *made* the cloak, so that was the item provided by Miss Kratides. Venetia Laurence – last in the Remove's register of first names – hadn't yet had her personal tutorial. She and the teacher must have had private meetings. The Broken Doll had been busy for at least a week. Small, unthinking cruelties put cracks in Larry's heart. Amy, Wax and Frecks were only the latest guilty parties. Her family had been mistreating her all her life. In the end, Larry chose a mask to fit how she felt. Broken, not whole. Then someone cunning 'oversaw and encouraged'. Amy could imagine. Smaller even than Larry, Miss Kratides would sit next to her like a friend – not with a desk between them like a beak. A drip of sweet poison in the ear. A helpful stir of the bubbling cauldron. Then a shyly presented gift. The teacher had suggested tactfully that Amy become a Death's Head. She'd urged Larry to become a Worse Thing. Miss Kratides was the maker of this Broken Doll.

Amy pinched a cloak fold. It was unpleasantly oily between her prickling thumb and forefinger. She dropped it quickly. The cape was up to its old tricks.

'You know what this is,' she said. 'Yet you let Larry – not a well girl, which is my fool fault as much as your beast of a brother's – wear it as a skirt, knowing what it would do to her? That she couldn't just take it off?'

'Why couldn't she?' responded Miss Kratides. 'You did. Even after you understood the benefits. That's when you first impressed me, Amy. When I knew what you could be.'

'You were in the Villa DeVille?'

Miss Kratides admitted it. 'I wasn't even hiding particularly well. You weren't looking for a small person.'

'Did you cuff Knowles to Dyall?'

'There was a good reason for that. If Knowles hadn't had a dose of Dyall you'd never have found out Harper's secret.'

'I doubt Knowles is grateful.'

'Are you sure? She's a new Miss Memory. Dyall has siphoned pandemonium from her mind. Her Talent is unbound. She's come out of this stronger and better. Most of you have. Including you.'

'Most,' said Frecks sternly. 'Not all.'

'What's the point of an exam everybody passes?' said Miss Kratides.

'You've never passed an exam in your life,' said Wax.

'Not so,' his sister responded. 'I've never passed an exam as a girl. I was never set one worth the bother. In my life – that's different. You said it – Dr Swan won't throw me off a cliff. That's a test I've passed.'

Amy still thought of the house in Piccadilly.

'When we were all gone you picked up Count DeVille's cloak,' Amy said.

Miss Kratides' half-smile was knowing.

'Is *that* what the thing is?' said Frecks. 'Ugh and faugh!'

'Funny story,' said Miss Kratides, '*Mitéra* met the Count's wives. Yes, wives plural. Fancy! *Mitéra* called them Flopsy, Mopsy and Coffintail. You see why stalwart Englishmen wanted to hoist the goaty old bat on bits of wood.'

'Why didn't you use the cape yourself?' Amy asked.

'Not my size,' said Miss Kratides. 'I was careful not to get bitten. I picked it up with coal tongs and wrapped it in yards of brown paper.'

'What were you doing in the Great Game?'

'Cheering silently from the sidelines and hoping – in vain, thank you very much – your year would do better than mine. I was tempted to tattle on H'umble H'Alf and let you string him up by his braces from the Statue of Eros, but that'd have invalidated the Finish. Old Girls can't take active part in play. Helen Lawless had already stretched that rule. If I'd taken a hand, we'd be in for something worse than the Disagreement of Eyas and Annwn.'

'You were in lessons when we were in the Conservatory,' said Little. 'I took you for a girl. I said it was funny Miss Gossage never asked you questions. Speke said I was seeing a ghost. But I wasn't.'

Speke shrugged. Her hands spread their fingers in a matching gesture.

'Well noticed,' said Miss Kratides. 'Gold Star for attentiveness in class. Black Stains for the rest, for being utterly blind. I was with the Remove for weeks. I stood quietly at the back and took notes. Dr Swan had me shadow Miss Gossage for a term. She wanted me to get the measure of each of you. You go a long way standing quietly at the back and taking notes. Headmistress and I devised a programme to bring out the best – or the useful worst – in all of you. We used a principle you are familiar with. Not School Rules, but the Code of Break.'

'No snitching or sneaking?' said Frecks.

'Share tuck if there's tuck to be shared,' put in Little.

'No, but that's a kind thought. You are a kind girl.'

Little beamed at the approval. Amy wasn't sure Miss Kratides thought kindness a virtue.

'Does anyone remember Mrs McMichaels?' asked the teacher.

Mrs McMike was before Little's time and Speke – then a First – wouldn't have had her Advanced Maths lessons. But Amy, Frecks and Paquignet remembered the Test to Destruction. It was all over the school. After the poor woman was packed off to Craiglockhart for her nerves, Crowninshield II strutted the halls like the victor of Towton. She bragged she would collect mortar boards the way Geronimo collected scalps. She only shut up about her mean-spirited victory when Lamarcroft took her out for a cross-country run. Lungs brought Crowninshield II back with a squashed nose, supposedly sustained by smacking into a face-high tree branch.

'"If a teacher can be broken, she should be",' said Miss Kratides. 'It's the duty of the girls to give her the Treatment.' She broke off and *hummed* for a few seconds. 'Any beak who can't take it should pick another profession. Best weed out the oversensitive early on. Else time and effort is wasted. A teacher who *can* take it learns to give it back. Her steel is the stronger for being forged in fire. Yes, it's harsh... but no one ever says school shouldn't be.'

'But that rule's for *teachers*,' said Speke. 'Not girls.'

'Oh, it's for girls, Harriet,' said Miss Kratides. 'It's for everyone. If a girl can be broken, she should be. Consider my example…'

'Yes, do,' put in Wax. 'She first tried her theory out on dolls. Bet you can guess how that went.'

Wax indicated Larry slumped over her desk.

'I didn't *invent* the Broken Doll,' said Miss Kratides. 'Knowles told you the history. We all have to dance with the Doll at least once in our lives.'

'Does this poor girl look like she's dancing?' said Wax, prodding Larry's back.

At his touch, Laurence screeched, sat up, and flung her arms out. Wax was knocked over and Little caught him. He was embarrassed to be rescued by such an unlikely paladin. She was aghast to land a boy in her lap. She'd probably caught *germs*.

Amy was more worried about Larry. Evidently, she *could* be broken – too easily.

The screech continued, issuing from the mask's unmoving lips.

Blood pooled around the runners of Larry's desk. Her cloak-swaddled lower half contorted like a rabbit being digested in a python's coils.

The mask – whether made or found or grown remained a mystery – came loose. She shook free of it. Her wig fell off, to reveal an uneven self-administered bob. Her drawn, white face was streaked with tears. She was no longer staring, but imploring. She looked like an eight-year-old in pain. Her screech dwindled to a whimper.

The cloak-skirt twisted around her like tight leggings.

'You'd better get that off her,' said the teacher.

The girls – and Wax – hesitated.

That Larry was in this state was Miss Kratides' fault. It was the class's duty to get the girl out of it. Amy saw the reasoning. Teacher sets the prep. Girls solve the problems.

'Come on, Remove,' said Miss Kratides. 'Gumption is now

required. What was it your old teacher prescribed? *Boldness!*'

Wax eased away from Little but was unsure about taking hold of Laurence again. If Amy hadn't forgiven him, what could he expect from the creature who'd suffered most from his play-acting?

'Someone else best do this,' he said. 'Seraph...?'

Frecks knew her lot was to give succour.

She enfolded Larry in a hug and cooed, 'Stay still and be brave, young Larry. I fear this will sting a bit.'

'My legs have needles and pins,' said Laurence.

Amy wasn't surprised. She remembered.

She tried to get a mentacle grip on Count DeVille's cloak.

Speke's hands, acting in concert, crept up and nipped the hem. The cloak shrugged them off.

'Oh,' said Speke as her hands flew apart. 'Ah,' she said, as they righted themselves in the air.

The finger-oars worked. The hand-crabs stayed aloft. The originals bested the duplicates. A smile spread across Speke's face. *Many* Applications came to mind. The hands zoomed like fighter planes, circling Larry and Frecks.

'Pickled conkers,' gasped Frecks.

Everyone was amazed, but the miracle had no obvious immediate Application.

Laurence's face was deathly. The cape wouldn't leave an ounce of blood in her. Amy suspected she had often imagined herself dying in Frecks' arms. When everyone got over being distracted by flying hands and paid attention again, Larry fluttered her eyelashes and dribbled daintily. Without benefit of soap and Stanislavski, she made a meal of the last act of *Camille*.

'Grab-hands didn't work,' said Miss Kratides. 'So, next approach. Think, girls, think!'

'It's her own fault,' said Little. 'She shouldn't have haunted Harry and me. She's no better than Nobbs and that lot. She deserves it.'

The First had a stern, unforgiving streak. Amy was the same at her age. A well-intentioned prig. She should have told Mother to stick with Uncle Cedric of the toy soldiers. He was *nicest* of the uncles. Instead, she'd harped on about how *babyish* he was. The worst thing an eleven-year-old could say of anyone. After three weeks, the poor man packed up his cuirassiers and retreated.

'Maybe Laurence does deserve it,' said Miss Kratides, 'but do you want the cloak well-fed? Stronger? More cunning? Treating the register as a menu, selecting its next supper? It's not a dishcloth, it's a menace.'

'Larry *doesn't* deserve it,' said Amy. 'This isn't her fault.'

'Could have fooled I,' said Little.

'You mean it's *your* fault?' said Speke, stare approaching voodooness.

'Don't be obtuse,' said Frecks. 'And don't fret on whose fault it is.'

With great effort, Larry raised her hands. Violet threads glistened as she prised her pocket open.

'Let me go into the Purple,' she said. 'No pins and needles there.'

'No *anything* there,' said Amy.

The sun was above the horizon. Beyond the portholes, the long shadow of the ship-shape weathervane lay on the sea. Dawnlight didn't spill into the sea-view room. Windward Cottage faced sunset, not sunrise.

'Amy, Alf, what's the problem?' asked the teacher.

Amy and Wax eyed each other.

'We have no problem,' said Wax. 'I've said I'm sorry and we've agreed to put it behind us.'

That was news to Amy.

'Not that problem,' said Miss Kratides, impatient but amused. 'The *immediate* problem.'

Amy looked at Larry.

'Count DeVille's cloak,' she admitted.

'And what does that have to do with the price of tea? Come on, numbskulls. Knowles or Naisbitt would see it at once!'

'They're not here,' said Amy.

'So do your own prep for a change. You can't always crib.'

'That's not fair.'

'Fair comes once a year... Widdecombe or Scarborough or the village fete. What do you do for the other fifty weeks?'

Amy considered the pernicious black bundle around Larry's legs. The thin cape had ambitions to be a plump shroud.

'That's not just a swishy way of keeping the fog out while strolling back from the opera,' she said. 'It's a *cursed thing*. The Count was an evil man. Everything he owned is – was – *is* tainted by him. He's in the cloth, the way Speke is in her hands.'

'I say, I've just tumbled,' said Frecks. 'Count DeVille. Not *of town* in French, but the Devil in any lingo.'

'Devil *en Français* is *Diable*,' said Speke, top in French in the Second year.

'It could also be Count *de Villainous*,' said Little.

'Or D'*Evil*,' said Speke. 'Or de *Vile*!'

'Bloody silly handle,' said Frecks. 'Dead giveaway. He might as well call himself Mr I-Am-Going-To-Kill-You or Baron Drink-Your-Daughter's-Blood! And handed out cards with his evil plan written in big print. No wonder he got found out. He should have written his real name written backwards. That'd be clever.'

Larry suffered less nobly now. She scratched herself as if her camellias were infested with nits. Frecks hugged her shoulders.

'You're haring off up a garden path,' said Miss Kratides. 'Remember the important thing Amy said. This is a *cursed thing*. What's the cure for that?'

Amy saw it. Yes, Miss Memory or Light Fingers would have got it yonks ago.

'A *blessed thing*!' she said.

One of Speke's hands leaned back on its stump and waved all its fingers at Frecks' sagging blazer pocket.

'Clouds part,' said Frecks. 'My silver knitting!'

She pulled out her enchanted coif. The links glinted under the electric light.

The item was dipped in purity by the Lady in the Lake. She probably bathed in holy water and powdered her cheeks with crumbled Catholic wafers. They were all Romans in Olden Days. Her light trumped the Count's dark any day of the week and twice on this particular Tuesday.

Amy had an idea the cloak knew its number was up. It writhed, winding tighter around Larry's legs.

Frecks dropped the coif...

Larry's pocket opened a rip, and a diamond-nailed twice-life-size purple hand reached out to grab the silver... The charm tore through the apparition's fingers, turning it to a puff of violet smoke... and fell on to Larry's black-covered lap.

Salt on a slug. Pepper on a tail.

Frecks picked up the coif and slipped it over Larry's head like a big sock. She got it the wrong way first. With her face covered in crinkly mail, Larry was a well-polished Egyptian mummy. Frecks adjusted the shining hood and settled it properly to frame Larry's face. She fondly pinched the girl's nose. Larry responded with a brave, weak smile.

'There, you're protected by the Lady,' said Frecks.

They all stood away from Larry and waited long moments.

Amy had a second of worry. What if the Lady of the Lake judged Larry harshly?

Frecks said that if a truly evil person wore the coif, her head would catch light.

Larry shivered a little. She'd lost her china hands and her bloodless fingers fiddled with the tiny bone buttons of her doll dress. The links shimmered and spat out sparks like Knowles' pentacle thingumabob. In the wire-wool wimple, Larry looked like Joan of Arc.

'It's angry,' she said. 'And upset.'

The cloak unwrapped with a wet, slick sound and reared up, collar flaring. Panicky bat squeaks vibrated Amy's antennae. The cape took off with a flap, spreading more like a manta ray than a big bat. Speke's hands harried the cloak like Pendragon

Squadron on a Zeppelin hunt, driving it up to the ceiling.

Amy propelled herself off the floor and got her hands on the cursed thing.

The material was cold and slimy, ghastly to the touch.

The cloak remembered the taste of her – and wanted her back! She flew at a window, mentacles outthrust like a big fist, bursting the glass. Making herself skinny by tucking in her elbows, she let the cape enfold her as she pushed through the punched-out porthole. She was protected from protruding shards, but glass daggers raked its black hide. Soaring over the cliff edge, she rolled over to prevent the cloak from getting its hooks in her and headed out to sea. Her lungs filled with fresh early-morning air. The cape caught the wind like a sail and was ripped loose. She held its trailing edge with mentacles and grabbed its collar points with her fists. She lay back and let herself fall, stretching the cloak above her like a parachute. She saw sun through the smoking scarlet lining.

Blessed light of day scourged the cursed thing. A loathsome smell – worse than London fog and Drearcliff liver – stung her nose. Amy halted her plunge so close to the grey waves she could feel spray on her back. Above her, the cloak flapped into a hundred burning leaves. For an instant, a fire-and-ash ghost held the shape of a man. The wind tore it apart. Amy executed a swift aerial backstroke to avoid an expanding cloud of particulate matter. She held her breath until she could be sure she wouldn't inhale specks of DeVille dust.

Red powder sprinkled the waves. Crimson froth smashed on the shingles.

Exhilarated, she looped the loop. The manoeuvre had eluded her until now. The Sausage would have been proud. She inhaled healthy, salt-sea air and felt sun on her face. A small metal object was grasped in her paw. It didn't burn or bite.

Her return to the classroom was more dignified than her exit. She fixed her course by the weathervane and dived slowly at the smashed window. She slipped through feet first.

'That will not come out of my salary,' Miss Kratides was saying.

Amy alighted with a ballerina flourish. Paquignet and Wax applauded.

Frecks and Speke's hands were wrapping Larry's legs with strips of Speke's towel. Speke stood by with her arms folded. Larry was lucky she'd worn the long old doll's dress under the cloak-skirt. It was shredded below the belt where the silk lining had scraped like sandpaper. Better a dress in tatters than skinned shins. Larry still had the coif on. It would help her heal.

'Is the bad bat gone?' Little asked.

Amy opened her fist and showed them the blackened wolf's head clasp.

She flipped it like a coin. Miss Kratides caught it.

'Might make a nice souvenir,' she said, polishing it on her blouse.

'Might pay for the window,' said Amy. 'That's old gold.'

'*Cursed* gold,' said the teacher.

'Purified by sunlight?'

'Maybe.'

Larry was a poor patient but enjoyed the attention. She winced archly as her wounds – bad rashes rather than death bites – were tended. She should watch the habit of milking a situation for sympathy. The Lady of the Lake could still scorch her ears.

'Young Larry's taking a turn for the better,' said Frecks.

Amy was suddenly tired. She hadn't slept all night... again

At least this Game had a happier Finish than the last.

'What about that?' said Little, toeing the discarded Doll mask.

On the floor, it seemed a flimsy thing. Plaster. Perhaps just paper. It didn't shrivel in sunlight, as a shed snakeskin. Someone – preferably Fre – should quiz Laurence on how she came by and the *idea* of the Broken Doll.

Amy picked the mask up with mentacles. It didn't sting any more.

Little was still unnerved by the floating face.

'It's all right, Gillian,' said Wax gently – though that was probably part of his latest disguise, not an actual admirable trait. 'It's only Amy showing off.'

She had a good mind to clap the mask on him and see how he liked the role of Broken Doll.

But she didn't. All Wax's faces were masks anyway. Including this one, which was more detailed every time she looked his way. He'd dug out Harold Lloyd spectacles. A new dot by his nose was more pimple than beauty spot. A forelock stuck up like an unwashed paintbrush. His Drearcliff tie was swapped for a flashy job with a St Cuthbert's crest.

Other hands took the mask. Speke's.

Amy had known this was coming. She flicked a glance at Miss Kratides, who was watching Amy and Speke closely. The flying hands put the mask down on a desk.

Speke raised her stumps. Her hands circled the room, fingers fluttering, and came back like birds to a nest. They settled on the ends of her wrists. A clicking sounded, like bony plates meshing. Speke was pleased. She twisted one hand off and let it fly away and back. She caught it as if playing with a rubber-stringed cup and ball toy.

'You're her who I'm supposed to blame,' she said to Amy. 'For not telling what you know?'

Amy agreed.

'That annoyed me,' Speke said, half-turning to the teacher. 'I think it was supposed to. Other girls' secrets were different. *She is right to be afraid of the Broken Doll.* That's not just true. It's sensible. Can't argue with it. My secret wasn't that was *right* to blame Thomsett for not telling what she knew. said I *would.* That's not a prediction or a suggestion. That's ing me what to feel. Which you can't, Miss. No one can. It's when you had Frost and Thorn's seats mixed up. You are only *mostly* right... and you're wrong this time.'

Amy raised the mask off the desk and turned its face to Miss Kratides.

'I *don't* blame Thomsett. She didn't mean harm. She'd have warned me if she'd had the chance. So I don't blame her for what happened with my hands, Miss... I blame *you*. Thomsett *knew*, but you knew *better*.'

Amy settled the mask on the desk.

'Not exactly an apple for the teacher,' said Miss Kratides, picking it up.

'Put it on, Mori,' said Wax. 'You know you want to.'

Miss Kratides didn't immediately rise to her brother's bait.

Amy squeezed Speke's shoulder. The younger girl laid her crab-hand over Amy's for a moment. Amy didn't cringe.

The girls approached the teacher's desk. It was ridiculously large for such a small person. She had to have pillows on her chair to get her elbows above her blotter.

'You're wrong about us all,' said Amy. 'None of this was necessary.'

'Wasn't it indeed?'

'It was futile and cruel.'

'You are improved, Thomsett. You are closer to what you can be – what you *will* be. You'd fly rings around the Aviatrix. Knowles can remember what she crams. More than that, she *understands* what she learns. Speke – you are a marvel, not a fluke. Harper can do something useful for the first time in her life. Light and De'Ath are new best friends. Laurence has been saved from herself. That's all in *my first week* as your teacher.'

'*Please* don't tell us we'll look back and thank you,' said Amy.

Miss Kratides shrugged tensely. 'I'm here to bring out your potential. It's not my job to be your friend.'

'Good thing too,' said Wax. 'Mori's not much of a one for friends.'

'Which runs in the family,' snapped Amy. 'I'm not thanking you either, you sneak!'

He was hurt. Or, rather, the boy he was pretending to be was hurt. That imaginary lad would be stung by such a remark. So he simulated a wounded expression. Beneath the mask, he was carved ice.

'You've put us on our guard, Miss Kratides,' Amy continued. 'Your *method*, such as it is, won't work any more. We shan't let it. We shan't be broken.'

Frecks and Speke stood by Amy. Little hesitated. Miss Kratides hadn't claimed all this was good for *her*. She was learning Dr Swan's old lesson – *mistrust*. Larry was still serene in the aura of Frecks' blessing. Paquignet thought plant thoughts. Wax was halfway between the girls and the teacher's desk.

'From now on, you won't Test to Destruction… for we'll stop you. We'll make up our own minds about whether we *want* to be improved. You're on notice, Miss. Mend your ways or else you'll get the *Full Treatment*. When you were here as a girl, you only had the staff and the whips against you. Now you've us. Girls. This isn't the Count's trainset or the Broken Doll's house. We won't let you hurt any one of us. We want none of your little hints that we should be what you want us to be so you can feel better about who you are.'

'Thomsett, you are a *wilful* girl,' she snapped, not looking at Amy. 'Impertinence Infraction. Mark it in your Time-Table Book.'

'See, *now* you're a beak,' said Amy.

Miss Kratides, sly and proud, paid her attention. The fixed side of her mouth tried to complete her smile. She pressed the Broken Doll mask to her face. When she took her hands away, it stayed put. She was a new Doll, with different cracks. One of her eyes was glass and green. The dull white cracked visage perfectly fit with her glossy black upswept curls and crimson hairband. Her slender neck wasn't up to supporting the disproportionately heavy mask, so her head hung to one side as if she'd survived the gallows.

Girls sat at their desks. Others filed in, fresh from a night's sleep and breakfast. Kali and Light Fingers sat behind Frecks and Amy. Devlin and Knowles – who wasn't quite as fresh as the others – sat in front. After some shuffling – and giggles at the presence of Wax, who had no desk to himself and had to bunch up with Paquignet – every place was occupied.

Miss Kratides looked at the class through her mask. There were murmurs of disquiet. Everyone knew who the alarming apparition was though. No doubt about the identity of this Doll.

She winked her unconcealed eye at Amy and opened the register.

'Aconita Gould,' she called. Her voice was deeper and issued from unmoving lips.

'Present,' barked the Scots girl.

'Alfred Wax.'

Laughter and amazement all round, quadrupling at his 'present and correct'. Hubbub continued. De'Ath launched a paper plane, which Amy deflected before it speared onto Wax's head. She'd no idea why she bothered.

Miss Kratides raised a hand for silence. She wore old white lace gloves with ruffs. They were new. The Remove settled.

'Amanda Thomsett…'

Amy let the moment linger.

'Still here,' she said, at last. 'Still *glorious*.'

Coda 1: A Week Later – Break

AMY HOBBLED OUT of the gym, aching from indoor flying. Stopping short to avoid bumping into a wall or the ceiling was more of a challenge than weaving between climbing ropes or zooming through hoops. Miss Borrodale had devised a system of aerial exercise to develop her Talent. Miss Kratides helpfully suggested weaving hooks into the ropes and setting the hoops on fire. Fossil baulked at that.

Outside the gym, a louche girl leaned against a wall. She beckoned Amy.

Heike Ziss. No fear.

Amy would not be *whispered* at.

'Hop off, Ziss,' she said.

The menace wasn't offended. She went back to her leaning, eye out for less wary souls.

Ziss was a future cause for concern. She wasn't in the league of Antoinette Rayne, Ariadne Rinaldo or the Broken Doll. Yet. But she bore watching. Miss Kratides had said as much. Though suspicious of any intelligence from that source, Amy suspected it made sense to suggest Miss Memory investigate Whispering Ziss and share anything worrying that came to light.

School was the same as ever, yet completely changed.

Alfred Wax caused an unprecedented stir. Interest in the

sudden, strange appearance of a boy in their midst tapered, then flared again when he changed his face – and indeed, everything about him, including his height and weight – and seemed a completely different boy. Amy was tired of him all over again. At least he stuck to his own name for now. He was on the register of the Remove and sat at one of the five exchange-student desks added to the classroom. The other four places prompted useless speculation. Some in the Remove had far-fetched notions of who might be joining them.

Miss Kratides didn't wear the mask in lessons, but the Broken Doll was active by night. Knowles collected and collated sightings. A spate of mysterious vandalism – which began with the red paint tipped on the Heel – continued. Moustaches appeared on portraits of distinguished Old Girls. Soap mixture was poured into organ pipes, so bubbles filled Chapel when Miss Dryden played 'Nymphs and Shepherds' – not, as Amy recalled, Miss Kratides' favourite ditty. Whips sought the phantom culprit, but no one in the Remove was inclined to snitch on their beak. Not even Harper.

An underground trade sprang up in contraband items like itching powder, coal soap, marked cards, and wickedly potent sherbet. The epidemic of not-terribly-amusing practical jokes led to vendettas, accusations and ill-feeling. The Moth Club were sure their teacher was behind it, but had no proof. The name of the Broken Doll was invoked by all sorts, but mostly as a mythical creature who could usefully take the blame for unattributed infractions. Miss Kratides might not even be the only Broken Doll at Drearcliff Grange.

Stories circulated about what happened on the Night of the Broken Doll. Light Fingers, over her moodiness but now a fiend for finding things out, kept pressing Amy and Frecks for details, alternately interviewing them together and separately like a policewoman intent on breaking an alibi. The fact of Alfred Wax's presence was so colossal everything else – including the sorry state of the Music Room the next morning – was swept under the carpet.

The whole school had an epidemic of the giggles. Which only served to make Amy not see the funny side of anything. Especially japes involving itching powder and coal soap. Make-up infractions were on the rise. The most unlikely girls – Inchfawn, Pinborough, Marsh, Spikins – painted themselves like flagrant houris and contrived to be in the way whenever Alfred Wax was out and about. Others were so crippled with blushes and shyness they fled his presence. Amy sympathised more with the second faction. She had to tolerate the sneak's presence in lessons, but otherwise could well do without him. Infuriatingly, he found a place, invited by the newly hussified Inchfawn, at the Desdemona Fourth table.

He was perfectly civil but she didn't believe anything he said.

His latest appearance was rumpled and athletic, with a slight hesitation before certain words as if he'd conquered a stammer. He was suddenly a demon stamp collector – which got him in with the Philately Phellows – and full of yarns about relatives who sent mysterious missives from far corners of the world, with fabulous rarities gummed to their envelopes. If Amy had Miss Kratides for a sister, she'd make up relatives too.

A cold spell had come.

Amy reached the Quad. The rest of the Moth Club were milling about with hands in their blazer pockets, breathing plumes of mist in an attempt to talk with smoke signals. The project wasn't going well. Kali and Light Fingers were still at odds over a basic vocabulary.

Light Fingers puffed 'hello' at Amy and Kali told her she wasn't doing it properly.

Frecks shrugged. Amy noticed her I've-got-a-secret air. Her beauty mark was newly applied. Her hat hair was tamed and smoothed. Using only water and a mystery ingredient, Frecks managed a fair approximation of a permanent wave. She looked more flapper than ragamuffin. Her coif was locked up in a tin box and shoved to the back of a drawer.

Wax, as ever, loitered nearby – exciting more interest than a one-legged juggler but less than a Martian Giant Squid. Among Firsts, a craze for pestering him had caught on. He was surely getting fed up with it. Every few minutes, some tiny girl would boldly dash close to him. The aim was to grab his knobbly male knee then run off screaming. No one outside the year understood the game, but it was great larks to the infants. Amy was weary of telling Wax to push off and wearier still of being told he wasn't such a bad sort and should be given a second or third or eleventh chance to *make it up*.

He tried to catch her eye. She turned away and huffed, exhaling a signal that made Kali laugh.

As long as the play-actor was lurking, Laurence stayed away. Still vaguely attached to Bok, she sometimes drew Frecks out of the Moth Club circle for precious moments *à deux*. Amy and Larry hadn't exactly become friends, but several things drew them together. That they were the only girls not willing to mark 'forgive and forget' in Wax's Time-Table Book gave them common cause. Yes, excusing Larry's Broken Doll doings while holding Wax's trespasses against him was inconsistent. But it made sense to her. And to Larry. They also shared the cloak. No one else understood what wearing the thing was like. What it made them find out about themselves.

'Do you miss it?' Larry would ask.

'Crumpets, no,' Amy would respond.

'Me neither.'

Then they'd look at each other and mouth the truth.

They both still had disturbing dreams. The cloak would be on them again, stifling and demanding. They woke up terrified, relieved it was only fancy. Then they missed being able to see in the dark. The nap of the collar against their throats provoked a sickly elation which reoccurred at odd moments. They crooked little fingers together and swore to be resolute if the cape reconstituted and came for either of them.

Frecks nudged Amy and pointed at Muriel Lavish. The excessively ineffectual Viola Third Captain didn't know why a pack of Seconds were hopping up and down around her and braying. Lavish had 'lick me' chalked on the back of her blazer. Amy presumed the japester was either in too much of a hurry to get her message right or had a peculiar idea of fun. The mocking mob stuck out their tongues but didn't actually go so far as to lick the victim. Amy would have gone over and patted the chalk off the poor girl's back, but Lavish's cellmates Featherstowe and Phair reluctantly stirred themselves to defend the honour of their Captain and told the perishers to push off.

A kite drifted across the Quad, pursued by Speke's hands.

Second only to Wax as an item of interest were the flying hands. The little miracles made Speke the Star of the Second Form. She accrued an active coterie – sly-eyed minx Alison Hills, peppery scrapper Hazel Hood and chirrupy intellect Yung Kha. The Magic Hand Gang had Little as a mascot and a Secret Lair in the Green Room (which everybody knew about). Young, intrepid, enthusiastic, the Magic Hand Gang were forever rushing around having their own adventures. The sophisticates of the Moth Club were jaded by comparison. A baton had been passed. Again, Amy felt loss and pride in equal measure.

The Magic Hand Gang, not the Moth Club, were in the front-line of the battle against the Plague of Not-So-Funny Japes. They had acquired an arch-nemesis in the Tamora Third Stuckey, *ducesa* of the Club Mussolini. An admirer of the Italian Prime Minister, Stuckey and her shrill mollies were given to marching around the Quad in black jodhpurs and peaked caps, constantly declaring the complete success of a phase of her master plan. Stuckey's aim was nothing less than domination of the school by the time she was a Sixth. The Moth Club would have passed out by then, so it was as well the Magic Hand Gang were joining the fray. Experience taught Amy that if someone had a master plan, someone else jolly well better thwart it.

Knowles and Devlin walked up to the Moth Club.

'Rattletrap's back from the station,' said Knowles.

'With the other exchange students,' explained Devlin.

Miss Kratides had announced that the four remaining exchange-student desks would soon be taken, as part of a programme Dr Swan had negotiated with other schools. All anyone wanted to know was whether that meant more boys. The presence of a solitary specimen created an appetite for variety. Amy said the one boy they had was quite enough. He was variety all by himself. Did Wax ponder the loss of his unique status with dread or relief? Or both, depending on who he was that day?

No one wanted to be the one to suggest it, but they would have to go to the gates to eye up the new arrivals.

Word spread and the Quad emptied. Whooping girls swarmed away.

Speke's hands flew in circles then took after their owner.

The Moth Club ambled along in the wake of the exodus, making a point of not showing too much interest. Amy noticed Larry creep out from behind the Heel – where she had been playing jacks with Bok and Dyall – to join the throng.

An assembly of Thirds and Fourths broke and ran, leaving Stuckey stood on a plinth, fired up to make a speech. Few *fascistas* were committed enough to listen to her announce Phase Omicron rather than nip off to goggle at new arrivals. Unhappy with the desertion, the little *ducesa* hopped down to scurry after her followers. She hadn't got the hang of goose-stepping in jodhpurs. Amy hoped she'd have a better reason for devastating a continent within the next ten years.

A cheer went up from in front of the main building. The brass band played 'Entrance of the Gladiators'.

Gawky Gifford ran at them, so excited she blurted out the news without asking to be paid for it.

'Another boy!' said Gifford. 'A *dreamy* one!'

'Hear that,' Kali snapped at Wax. 'You're a back number.'

Wax shrugged.

Amy noticed Frecks being ostentatiously diffident.

'You knew,' Amy accused her friend.

'I might have had a postcard,' Frecks admitted.

Light Fingers whirred her hands to make a passage through the crowd. The Moth Club followed her to the driveway.

Geoffrey Jeperson stood by the charabanc, shaking hands with Dr Swan.

'The gallant Capt,' said Wax.

Jeperson caught sight of Frecks and smiled wider.

There was a mass outbreak of sighing and semi-swooning. Wax's moon was eclipsed by this bright star. Jeperson wore crisp, baggy Humble College cricket whites. He tossed his cap to the crowd like a bride bunging a bouquet in the general direction of a foaming pack of envious bridesmaids. Berthaiume II – who retained her numeral, though her older sister passed out years ago – snatched the thing and hung it on Pendill's head.

'You'll have competition,' Amy told Frecks.

Frecks snorted. 'Much you know, young Glory. This toby is in my pocket. It's just a question of whether I want to give the gruesome object mantelpiece space.'

Jeperson was waving at Frecks now. A thicket of girls pressed around him.

Frecks didn't seem that fussed. Which showed she was serious.

'The others are coming out now,' said Devlin, who'd stuck her neck out to get a better view. 'They're... not boys.'

No one was so rude as to groan, but the crowd's interest cooled.

Girls drifted away. A phalanx of whips frog-marched Jeperson to their hut – where he would be plied with cream tea and have rules against fraternisation impressed upon him in no uncertain terms. That had happened to Wax. It would go double for a more glamorous fellow. For the moment, the newcomer needed the protection. Frecks smirked the smirk of a fellowess who has an assignation after supper and is confident enough in her co-assignatee to be half an hour late to the designated secluded area and claim the trifling appointment had almost slipped her mind.

Dr Swan moved on to greet a dumpy, dithery middle-aged

woman. She must be a chaperone. Amy would have bet her charges ran rings around her.

'Know who that is?' said Knowles. 'Lobelia Draycott.'

Amy saw the dumpiness and ditheriness were a pose. Anyone who tried to run a ring around her would trip over a scythe.

Miss Kratides was presented to the Dragon of the Disapproved School.

With dread, Amy looked at the open door of the charabanc.

A three-girl crocodile marched down the steps.

Primrose Quell. Aurelia Avalon. Stephen Swift.

They wore immaculate Draycott's uniforms, with shining arrow-pins in their berets. They had matching tight smiles. Quell was back at Drearcliff Grange. Nightcap was in line – but for how long? Miss Steps was here for a rematch. They all saw Amy at once. The tight smiles grew tighter.

The Break Bell rang.

'Back to the salt mines,' said Frecks.

'You know those girls,' said Light Fingers.

Amy nodded. 'New chums,' she said. 'New challenges.'

Coda II:

Thirteen Years Later – the Mausoleum

THE MAUSOLEUM – pronounced 'mouse-o-lay-um' not 'maws-o-lee-um' for no reason she could ever determine – appeared to be a Tudor manor. It stood in the middle of Egdon Heath, a thousand acres of iron-red bracken unclaimed by Devon or Dorset. Architecturally, it was unremarkable – but the location was perverse. Manor houses, as a rule, are built on natural or artificial elevations, so the nobs can look down on the surrounding countryside and the yokels therein. The Mausoleum, however, skulked at the bottom of a depression. Its chimneys barely poked above the level of the very flat landscape. Millennia before the Undertaking posted their 'Keep Out' signs, Egdon Heath was a shunned place. The dent in the land was an ancient meteor crater, ringed with standing stones. The Mausoleum was prison, museum, menagerie and oubliette. Here, Great Britain kept things – and people – it wasn't safe to keep anywhere else.

The Rolls-Royce cruised along a cart track. Amy would have to get the car serviced and cleaned before returning it to Jonathan. She could have borrowed the autogiro, but needed to arrive in something more impressive to pass muster with the Undertakers. The ShadowShark drove like a dream, but she wasn't in a mood to enjoy it.

'You've been in a fret all morning,' said Emma, who was curled up in the passenger seat.

Amy shrugged at the wheel. Her old friend was right.

This was not a place she cared to visit or even think about. If she offended the wrong people, she would be added to the Mausoleum Collection – with ribbons over her wings and a silver pin through her breastbone. The Undertaking barely tolerated Kentish Glory and she'd never warmed to them. Taking up with Jonathan made her unpopular in certain circles. Dr Shade was the least clubbable of paladins.

Emma – Inspector Naisbitt of the Women's Auxiliary Police – spoke up for her, and she had been entered in the *Shadow Chronicle*, which was the equivalent of being 'mentioned in despatches' in their line of work. She had served with distinction in the Weird War. For the moment, that kept the 'men in black crepe' off her case. No butterfly nets and killing jar for her yet.

'They'd let you in without me to hold your hand,' said Emma. 'They asked you, remember?'

'*Somebody* asked for me. It's not the same.'

'Please yourself.'

She might not need Emma to get into the Mausoleum. She might need her to get out again.

They seemed to have been driving across the heath for a long time.

'I spy with my little eye something beginning with…'

'B,' said Amy. 'Bracken!'

'You *are* a mind-reader.'

'I spy with my little eye something beginning with…'

'S,' said Emma. 'Sky!'

'I was going to say C…'

'Clouds! Same difference.'

The journey was so desolate pub cricket was out. They hadn't passed a sign that didn't warn them not to go any further on pain of dire consequences in half an hour.

'Do birds eat bracken?'

'Not if they don't want to be poisoned. Some moth larvae like the stuff... the Map-Winged Swift, for instance.'

'Always moths, eh?'

Amy was used to being teased. She'd never grown out of moths.

She had too little time to cultivate a proper secret identity, but 'Amanda Thomsett' was becoming moderately well-known in lepidopterist circles. She was proud of her articles in *The Entomologist's Record and Journal of Variation*. 'Rannoch Looper – Is it Breeding in Sussex?', 'In Search of the Blind Peacock – an Aberrant Form of *Inachis Io*' and 'Winter Damselfly in Glamorgan'.

'What I was getting at, though,' said Emma, 'is whether birds eating your bracken would be a problem.'

'I imagine there's enough bracken hereabouts to spare.'

'Thought so. Then why are there so many scarecrows?'

They had passed several – flapping black coats and pierced top hats, shirts and britches stuffed with straw.

'It's a retirement plan,' Amy suggested. 'When one of the Undertakers goes to his or her just reward, they hang him up to watch over the path.'

Amy and Emma laughed.

Light Fingers – not a handle much heard these days – was still her best Unusual friend or Unusual best friend. She was glad Scotland Yard could spare Emma for this outing.

The ShadowShark was a step up from good old Rattletrap.

She thought about the circumstances of the summons.

'It'll never be over,' Amy said.

'Sentences to the Mausoleum are for life,' said Emma. 'Even longer, in some cases. No one – and nothing – has ever escaped. This case is wrapped up and you don't need to worry any more. Whatever she's done, it's finished. The Broken Doll is a common or garden criminal...'

Amy snorted.

'Yes,' Emma insisted, 'she is. She's not a Talent. Never has been.

I don't know why she's here and not Holloway. She's not Colonel Zenf or Billy Beetle. That's not to say she's not formidable. Or dangerous. But, you know, I was always *disappointed* in her crimes. She had folk quaking in their britches with the masks and costumes and toys and tricks. I think she was always more interested in frightening people than anything else. All she really did was run a disreputable nightclub, steal a few jewels, and print her own money. After the fanfare, I expected her to replace the cabinet with life-like electric mannequins or dissolve the Rock of Gibraltar like an Alka-Seltzer. Not water drinks and rob trains…'

'Steal trains whole. They still haven't found them.'

'They found the drivers, guards and passengers.'

'Who were no wiser. It's an unsolved mystery.'

'You can ask her to explain her workings-out. She always used to do that to us. "I know how I know the answer – I want to know how *you* know it."'

Amy could still hear that.

'Did you ever go to the Broken Doll's House?' Emma asked.

Amy shook her head.

'We raided it last year. Oversized furniture. "Hostesses" dressed as dollies. The clientele – all rich, all men, all ghastly – liked to be put in oversize cribs and be "played with". Naughty boys could be spanked by Nanny, for a fat fee. Oh, the Doll collected snapshots. For her blackmail portfolio, we presume. The detail they get with infrared plates is remarkable. You wouldn't want to look at the pics. I've not been back to a church since I saw the Archbishop in his big nappy. Guess who was stood outside as bouncer? Gillian Little. A foot taller with a pinny the size of a circus tent. Same hairdo, with all the curls. Like a gargantuan Shirley Temple. Funny how we Old Girls turn up, isn't it?'

'I'm not sure the common or garden crookery is the whole story,' said Amy. 'I think it's another cracked mask. It's what we're supposed to see. A distraction from what she's really been up to.'

'Should I check the Prime Minister for a winding-key in his back?'

Ahead, Amy saw the standing stones – shadows long in the late afternoon.

'Nearly there,' she said.

'Does it annoy you that she wasn't even your special friend?' asked Emma. 'I know you crossed swords a time or two, but she *fixated* on Ghost Lantern Girl. The *Shad Chron* has *pages* about their spats.'

Grace Ki was one of the stranger paladins. A professional dancer – chorus girl, basically – who inherited the skills of the women who were Ghost Lantern Girl before her. Their spirits were bound to her lantern. So long as it burned, she was proficient as a boxer, sharpshooter, justicer, chef, calligraphist, gambler and a dozen other specialty acts. A one-woman war party. She finally brought in the Broken Doll.

Emma was right. The crimes of the Doll were too petty for Kentish Glory.

Jonathan wasn't interested either. Dr Shade had other concerns.

'Any word on Doctor Eismond?' asked Emma.

'I have the report Lottie Knowles sent you. Something will have to be done. The man can't hide in the German Embassy forever.'

Werner Eismond was supposedly a long-lived retainer of the Ziss family. He had special responsibility for their Miscellany, which filled half a dozen chateaux scattered across Europe. The family collected rooms, reproduced in every detail with all the original fittings – and sometimes inhabitants – intact. Charlotte Knowles said the idea was not to own physical things, but to own events that took place in the rooms. Births, marriages, deaths. The theatre box where Lincoln was shot. The drab lodging where Mary Kelly was cut to pieces. The cabinet where Faust conjured Mephisto. The asylum cell of the Marquis de Sade, complete with his polished bones. Interested parties – including the Diogenes Club of London, the Opera Ghost Agency of Paris and Mr John Bronze of Harlem, New York – believed Eismond the true head of the Ziss Family. He, or someone with his name and face, had cultivated the line since the fifteenth century, amassing one of the great fortunes of Europe. What transpired in the basements of Zisshofs from Amsterdam to Bucharest was done in his name. Whispering Heike was the least of it.

Jonathan took the Eismond-Ziss case personally.

Recently, the Ziss Miscellany had added many more outlandish items – as if the Devil were on a shopping spree with God's chequebook. The last time that damned cloak came back, it was snapped up by agents of Dr Eismond and shipped to Frankfurt in a coffin sealed with garlic. Amy couldn't say she was sorry that particular rag was off the market. Eismond often sought things owners were reluctant to part with. Some collectors were so attached to curious works of art – not just tattoos – that surgical operations were required for a change in ownership.

Eismond hired a cat burglar to scale the Tower of Big Ben and break into Dr Shade's Laboratory. Siam Slim got his tail clipped for the impertinence, but several of Jonathan's souvenirs went missing. Miss Memory – on the retainer of the Diogenes Club, who took an interest in such things – reported that the loot was in the Embassy along with other stolen goods Eismond was preparing to smuggle out of the country. Dr Shade wouldn't recognise diplomatic immunity. He'd declare war on Hitler to get his baubles back. In that conflict, Amy would not bet on the Nazis.

The Eismond-Ziss shopping list must include several prizes kept in the Mausoleum – not that any were for sale or any thief could be persuaded to try to lift them. They'd get more than a tail lopped off if they tried.

The Rolls passed between megaliths.

'Here we are,' said Emma redundantly.

Men with long black overcoats, bowler hats and dark glasses raised shotguns.

'This season, it's black again,' said Amy.

Emma laughed.

Amy rolled down the window.

An Undertaker ambled over. A woman with her left arm in a black silk sling.

Amy recognised her. She'd known what the girl did after passing out but was still surprised to see Shrimp Harper in dark glasses and a black hat. It suited her better than mauve.

'Miss… Aitch?'

No smile – not that Amy would have expected one.

'Arre,' said the Undertaker, like a pirate. '*Mrs* Arre.'

'Congratulations,' said Amy.

No flicker of emotion. They bled it out when you signed up. When they did the thing to your eyes that made the glasses necessary. Amy remembered the Undertaking was never in the Great Game. They were the linesmen, referees and blowers of the final whistle. They totted up the scores and ruled on fouls. They didn't play. They didn't care who won or lost.

'It's been a while,' she said to Mrs Arre.

'Jackie,' said Emma, leaning over and waving very fast.

'Inspector Naisbitt,' she acknowledged, touching her bowler brim.

'You've pranged your arm,' said Emma. 'Nothing serious, I hope.'

'Mr Arre had an altercation with one of the… resident items. I've made him better. You remember how it works.'

When Harper took away someone's hurt or illness, she experienced symptoms – felt *pain* – but sustained no lasting harm. She healed from injuries which would lay a person up for weeks in a few days. Very uncomfortable days.

'Are you all right, Jackie?' Emma asked sincerely.

'I'm useful here, Inspector. That's all we can ask.'

Amy wondered how frequently Mrs Arre bore Mr Arre's burdens. She had an idea it was often.

'You know who's asked to see me?' Amy said.

Mrs Arre nodded.

'How is she?'

'Quiet. We like quiet.'

Mrs Arre waved them through. The ShadowShark purred down the gentle incline towards the manor house.

'Funny how things turn out,' said Emma.

'Funny for some,' said Amy.

'Remember what a horror Shrimp was... until, well, until Aurelia Avalon and Noxiter Hume made her look like a kitten...'

Amy shuddered at the names.

She parked in the shadow of the Mausoleum. It was gloomy in the crater.

Mr Eye, the Warden, was waiting in the library. He did not care for visitors. Once an item was added to the Collection, it should pass from view. Not only should it never be seen again, it should never be thought of. He shut doors with nails not keys. Amy didn't know why this request, of all he must receive, had been approved. His charges must howl in vain for all sorts of things.

Emma was happy to be out of the car. If cooped up for more than an hour, she got itchy. It was her Talent, manifesting unhelpfully. If she put her hands in her pockets over and over again, as she did when she got the fidgets, she could set fire to her uniform. She more often thought fast than ran quickly these days, but was still a speedy little thing.

Her friend was also still curious enough to want to poke about the Mausoleum. She'd like to make sure the items Dr Eismond would love to get his black gloves on were safely behind silver bars. Isidore Persano's worm unknown to science. The heads of Don Felipe Molina and Sir Timothy ffolliott. The Angel Down Changeling. The sarcophagus of Queen Tera. The Clohessy diadem. The Amersham aelopile. The sole unpulped copy of Vol 2, No 11 of *British Pluck Magazine*, containing the interview with the Mystic Maharajah where he Said Things That Should Not Have Seen Print.

Amy understood Emma's concern but was impatient to hurry to the main attraction.

'The Broken Doll is quite comfortable,' Mr Eye explained. 'She has a private room. There is no lash or wheel here. We are not Dartmoor. Those who need to feed are fed well. Guests can order books from the library. Even gramophone records. Within limits.'

'And she wants to see me,' Amy prompted.

'She said she wanted you here.'

'That's not the same thing.'

Emma's ears pricked. She looked at an opening door.

An Undertaker came in – the old-fashioned top hat that denoted seniority tucked under his arm – and told Mr Eye a fire was spreading on the bracken. There was nothing to be worried about.

Something buried deep under the house began screaming.

Amy slipped on her mask. She sensed hectic activity.

'Take us to her, now,' she said.

'I thought you might like some sherry first,' said Mr Eye.

'*Now*,' Amy insisted.

He saw her mask and knew she was serious. 'Very well.'

He pulled a sconce and a section of bookcases swung open like a bank vault.

A steel lift-cage lay beyond. An Undertaker sat on a stool, surprised reading *Komic Kuts*. He rolled the periodical into a truncheon and pressed a button.

As they descended, the Warden told them this was the only way in or out.

Amy and Emma looked at each other, knowing that was no longer true.

The screaming continued.

Seven floors below the house, the lift stopped. Mr Eye waited for the door to be opened from the other side.

'Whoever's on duty won't be at his post,' Amy said.

'Mr Vee has been with us for some years. He has never...'

Amy wrenched the door open with her mentacles. She saw a door-lined passage, nicely carpeted and not at all institutional. It had curves, not corners. A hat rolled on the floor, ribbon undone...

The Warden called for Mr Vee.

One door was open.

Amy and Emma crowded around it.

The room was windowless, but comfortable. Oak panelling. Musty Victorian furniture not to modern tastes. Potted plants and bowls of flowers. Pictures of previous wardens, all in hats and specs. The recent tenant must have *hated* it.

A hefty fellow sprawled by an overturned divan, face pressed into tasselled cushions.

Alarm bells sounded from other floors. Amy knew what that meant.

No one had ever escaped from the Mausoleum. No one had ever stolen items from the Collection.

If you were of such a mind, facts like that could be construed as challenges.

No wonder the Broken Doll surrendered so meekly. Amy was flattered that Ghost Lantern Girl had been chosen to make the arrest. The Doll didn't think she could pull the wool over the eyes of Kentish Glory so easily.

The screaming stopped, which – somehow – was worse.

Emma searched the room, moving so swiftly she became a whizzing blur. Cupboards seemed to open and shut by themselves... Papers flew up but were sorted and stacked neatly when they came down... Carpets flipped then smoothed back in place and were properly tacked... Every panel was sounded for hollowness... The divan was righted, slit open and gutted of stuffing... A canopied bed was served the same way... Every place where a person could be concealed was turned out.

In impossible escapes, always make sure the prisoner isn't simply hiding so they can stroll out of the cell when jailers follow that useless old saw about not bothering to lock stable door after the horse has bolted. Amy and Emma knew from a Guilbert Phatt mystery that it was a sound idea to lock the stable, in case the horse has turned invisible.

'She's gone,' said Emma, not out of breath but standing still.

'She wants us to follow,' said Amy.

'She wants *you* to follow.'

'Not Grace Ki?'

'You were *always* her favourite, Amy.'

'She had – *has!* – a strange way of showing it.'

The hefty fellow sat up. Clamped over his face was a white china mask. A crack ran diagonally from forehead to chin.

'She left that behind,' said Emma, reaching for it.

Amy raised a broken pair of spectacles from a wastepaper basket.

'Don't take it off,' she warned. 'His eyes.'

Emma shuddered at the floating specs and took her hands back quickly. She tucked them into her armpits.

Amy looked at the familiar mask.

'Mori, Mori, Mori,' Amy said, approaching the Undertaker, flexing her fingers, 'what do you want us to learn now?'

Drearcliff Grange School Register

Ariel

First Form

Rebecca Coates
Faye Device
Veronica Golden
Rachel Knightley
Vivienne Landau (Captain)
Ines Rodrigues
Jean Thomas
Sally Ward
Katrina Worthington
Jasmine Wilder

Second Form

Susan Ah
Hilda Courtney (Captain)
Jane Dogge
Phaedra Hunt
Demeter London
Lydia Marlowe
Jean Orfe
Ivy Prosser
Anne Sercombe
Janet Thaw

Third Form

Maria Biddlecombe
Martina Bone
Emily Dace
Anne D'Arbanvilliers-Cleaver
Georgaina Fell (Captain)
May Forrest
Monica Frensham
Venetia Laurence
Lucia Maunder
Valeria Mrozková

Fourth Form

Hannah Absalom
Chastity Banks
Octavia Benjamin
Catherine Bourbon
Chloe Catchpole (Captain)
Bizou De'Ath
Natalie Laverick
Evelyn Lowen
Catherine Trechman
Sybil Vigo

Fifth Form

Christina DeManby
Isabella Fortune
Arabella Hughes
Idominea Lescaulles
Titania Mondrago (Captain)
Sally Nikola
Fleur Paquignet
Cassandra Wilding
Heather Wilding
Priscilla Wilding

Sixth Form

Seras Bubastis
Susan Byrne
Thomasina Campbell
Dorothy Dungate
Alexa di Fontane
Prima Haldane (Head Girl) (Captain)
Marion Keith
Sonali Shah
Charlotte Teller
Rosina Terrell

Desdemona

First Form
Chiara Barbo
Sarra Doke
Carolina Fasolo
Ellen Gall-Augure
Marika Gallman
Fionnuala Halligan (Captain)
Katharine Hart
Hannah McGill
Madeleine Searle
Cinnamon Trundle

Second Form
Elizabeth Chick
Jennifer Dawes
Pearl Dennison
Gawky Gifford
Louise Hartley
Ruth Hipgrave (Captain)
Taff Jones-Rhys
Helen Knight
Avril Parrish
Ellaline Terriss

Third Form
Janet Blake
Nancy Dyall
Philippa Farjeon
Dorothy Fulwood
Elisabeth Gaye
Kathryn Hall
Lillian Hyson
Cynthia Moul (Captain)
Violet O'Brien
Polly Palgraive

Fourth Form
Maude-Lynne Arbuthnot
Kali Chattopadhyay
Clodagh FitzPatrick
Thomasina Hoare-Stevens
Lydia Inchfawn
Emma Naisbitt
Verity Oxenford
Amanda Thomsett
Serafine Walmergrave
Alice Wright (Captain)

Fifth Form

Janet Aden
Ella Bowman
Honor Devlin
Nicola Helfrich
Charlotte Knowles
Rosanna Kyd (Captain)
Lucinda Leigh
Aurora Martine
Clare Saxby

Sixth Form

Dorothy Abbott
Theresa Crockford
Fiona Fergusson
Dilys Frost
Rosalind Kaveney (Captain)
Saskia Kriegsherr
Amelia Lipman
Winifred Rose
Pamela Soon
Doreen Wychwood

Goneril

First Form

Margaret Davis (Captain)
Anastacia Dooks
Manon Fargetton
Melanie Fazi
Patricia Kearney
Marysia Kolodziej
Gillian Little
Pamela McCleave
Leah Moor
Kiriana Walden

Second Form

Jane Addey
Selina Briss
Maureen East
Marina George
Julie Godfrey
Julianna Keddle (Captain)
Kiime Rickord
Sabine Saussure
Tzara Tetzlaff
Millicent Trundleclough

Third Form

Margaret Carmichael
Wilhelmina Fudge
Muyun Ker (Captain)
Louisa McClaren
Freya Outerbridge
Annie Pridhaux
Ruby Raven
Tabitha Spikins
Lillie Stevenson
Jane Thicke
Emily Usborne

Fourth Form

Katherine Berthaiume
Rachel Cray
Miriam Ellacott
Joycelyn Hilliard
Hermione Jago
Priyanki Khalsekar
Isabel Loss
Ekaterina Pendill (Captain)
Jemima Sieveright
Linda Thiele

Fifth Form

Sophie Calder
Helen Davisson
Cara Fielder
Aconita Gould
Mary Jones (Captain)
Netta Kinross
June Mist
Dorothy Ooms
Ninja Sundquist
Phoebe Wellesley

Sixth Form

Hjordis Bok
Roberta Hale
Janice Marsh
Euterpe McClure
Helen O'Hara
Sarah Pinborough
Emilia Pitt-Patterson
Annabel Portillo
Susan Su
Alicia Wybrew (Captain)

Tamora

First Form

Abigail Blackmore
Pandora Boxe
Marie Femm
Olga Godofsky
Thelma Guildmar
Glumdalclitch Hayley
Aelita Konigen (Captain)
Virginia Kreaper
Giulietta Nefaria
Monica Richards

Second Form

Sarah Ackland
Mary Candlewick (Captain)
Vera Claythorne
Olivia Duel
Damaris Gideon
Louise Gilclyde
Laura Harvey
Iris Overton
Felicity Quilligan
Carlotta Smith

Third Form

Cleopatra Cotton
Elaine Finn
Cecily Garland
Miramara Ghastley
Siobhan Grimm
Clara Mill-Carston
Cunegonde Quive-Smith
Victoria Silk (Captain)
Tanya Six
Esther Stuckey

Fourth Form

Allegra Bidewell
Barbara Bryant
Selma Head
Mary Jarvis
Faith Merrilees
Bridget Mountmain (Captain)
Silja Mueller
Louise Sawley
Sarah Stallybrass
Francesca Stone

Fifth Form

Zenobia Aire
Sarah Carnadyne
Ottilie Churchward
Miranda Crowninshield
 (Captain)
Humphrina Jarrott
Gwendolyn Nobbs
Mara Rietty
Susannah Thorn
Phyllis Thorpe
Ruby Wool

Sixth Form

Lucia Bewe-Bude
Erica Boscastle
Caroline Cowper-Kent
Flora Griffin (absent)
Jacqueline Harper
Margaret Hume
Sylvestra Phillips
Sylvia Starr (Captain)
Clementine Talbot
Heike Ziss

Viola

First Form
Clara Amias
Jamila Birkett
Sarah Cleary
Valerie Edwards
Johanna Fletcher
Rosamund Fletcher
Larushka Ivan-Zadeh
Samantha Leigh
Virginie Sélavy
Theresa White (Captain)

Second Form
Carol Coker
Alison Hills (Captain)
Hazel Hood
Yung Kha
Margaret Ring
Monique Soutie
Harriet Speke
Marianne Toulmin
Cecily Wheele
Jemima Williams

Third Form
Marie Adkins
Annabelle St Anne
Karen Featherstowe
Emanuelle Gotobed
Joan Hone
Eve Lapham
Juliet Lass
Muriel Lavish (Captain)
Helen Oakes
Marian Phair

Fourth Form
Heather Beeke
Theosopha Busby
Simret Cheema-Innis (Captain)
Ann Dis
Sarah Ladymeade
Abigail Pulsipher
Angela Stannard
Morgana Vail

Fifth Form

Kitten Carnes
Barbara Chess
Isola Doone
Daphne Gallaudet
Philippa Hailstone (Captain)
Unorna Light
Harmony Meade
Sara Paço
Laura Tallentyre
Susannah Thorne

Sixth Form

Ida Acreman
Ellen Eyre
Sally-Anne Flyte
Sheila Johnstone
Oona Kite
Doris de Marne
Holly Queenhough
Mary Thompson
Lavinia Trent (Captain)
Kathleen Vaughn

The Remove

Aconita Gould
Amanda Thomsett
Bizou De'Ath
Charlotte Knowles
Dilys Frost
Emma Naisbitt
Fleur Paquignet
Gillian Little
Harriet Speke
Hjordis Bok
Honor Devlin
Jacqueline Harper (Captain)
Janice Marsh
Kali Chattopadhyay
Nancy Dyall
Polly Palgraive
Serafine Walmergrave
Susannah Thorn
Unorna Light
Venetia Laurence

Staff

Dr Myrna Swan

Dr Ailsa Auchmuty
Miss Violet Borrodale
Miss Elizabeth Downs
Miss Jennifer Dryden
Mrs Alexandra Edwards
Miss Clemency Gossage
Miss Moria Kratides
Mademoiselle Myrtle Hobbs
Miss Millicent Tasker
Mrs Rosemary Wyke

Hilda Percy
Louise Humphreys R.R.C.
Nellie Pugh
Joxer Chidgey

The Great Game

Drearcliff Grange School for Girls

Hjordis Bok
Kali Chattopadhyay
Honor Devlin
Nancy Dyall
Prima Haldane (Captain)
Charlotte Knowles
Venetia Laurence
Emma Naisbitt
Amanda Thomsett
Serafine Walmergrave

Lobelia Draycott's House of Reform

Aurelia Avalon
Jennifer Fire
Rebecca Kensington
Alexandria Purdie
Primrose Quell (Captain)
Deidre Simons
Pauline Sparks
Allison Sterlyng
Stephen Swift
Alicia Vickers

St Cuthbert's School for the Sons of the Humble and Pious

Basil Biddlecombe
Jackson Bullett
Neil Devonshire
Jolyon Goodfellowe
Geoffrey Jeperson (Captain)
Malcolm Killick
Pericles Pfister
Vikram Singh
Alfred Henry Wax
Hugh Weald

The Brain-Boxes

Three Addams
Bazeley Barraclough
Richard Cleaver (Captain)
Soren Dart
Xtopher Fowler
Barrington Forshaw
Jonathan January
Andrew Mosse-Mowbray
Rhys Rodgers
Gertrude Smarthe

Secrets of the Remove

Aconita Gould

You shave.

She wears a wig.

Amanda Thomsett

You are right to be afraid of
the Broken Doll.

She will blame you for not
telling what you know
about Laurence.

Bizou De'Ath

You are what you wish to be.

She is not a white witch.

Charlotte Knowles

Your father makes plans to
murder you.

She can't feel anything.

Dilys Frost

You froze a dog to death.

She burned a cat to death.

Emma Naisbitt

You refuse to visit your father
in prison.

She could use her Talent to
heal the sick – but won't.

Fleur Paquignet

You are not Fleur Paquignet.

She is not the only worm.

Gillian Little

You don't think your name is
half as funny as others do.

She shaves.

Harriet Speke

You will blame her for not
telling what she knows
about Laurence.

She is right to be afraid of the
Broken Doll.

Hjordis Bok

You should be grateful Laurence broke the girl who hurt you.
She knows how to turn down her Talent.

Honor Devlin

You can't feel anything.
She doesn't think her name is half as funny as others do.

Jacqueline Harper

You could use your Talent to heal the sick – but won't.
Her mother is alive.

Janice Marsh

You wear a wig
She refuses to visit her father in prison.

Kali Chattopadhyay

Your mother is alive.
Her father makes plans to murder her.

Nancy Dyall

You know how to turn down your Talent.
She should be grateful Laurence broke the girl who hurt her.

Polly Palgraive

You are not the only worm.
He is not Fleur Paquignet.

Serafine Walmergrave

You hate your blessing.
She has cause to hurt you all.

Susannah Thorn

You burned a cat to death.
She froze a dog to death.

Unorna Light

You are not a white witch.
She is what she wishes to be.

Venetia Laurence

You have cause to hurt them all.
She hates her blessing.

Acknowledgements

T HANKS ARE DUE to the Titan team of Cath Trechman, Jill
Sawyer Phypers, Martin Stiff, Lydia Gittens, Vivien Cheung
and Nick Landau.

About the Author

KIM NEWMAN IS a novelist, critic and broadcaster. His fiction includes *The Night Mayor*, *Bad Dreams*, *Jago*, the Anno Dracula novels and stories, *The Quorum* and *Life's Lottery*, *Professor Moriarty: The Hound of the D'Urbervilles*, *The Secrets of Drearcliff Grange School*, and the critically acclaimed *An English Ghost Story*, which was nominated for the inaugural James Herbert Award, and *The Vampire Genevieve* and *Orgy of the Blood Parasites* as Jack Yeovil. His non-fiction books include the seminal *Nightmare Movies* (recently reissued by Bloomsbury in an updated edition), *Ghastly Beyond Belief* (with Neil Gaiman), *Horror: 100 Best Books* (with Stephen Jones), *Wild West Movies*, *The BFI Companion to Horror*, *Millennium Movies*, *BFI Classics* studies of *Cat People* and *Doctor Who* and *Video Dungeon: The Collected Reviews*.

He is a contributing editor to *Sight & Sound* and *Empire* magazines (writing *Empire*'s popular Video Dungeon column), has written and broadcast widely on a range of topics, and scripted radio and television documentaries. His stories 'Week Woman' and 'Ubermensch' have been adapted into an episode of the TV series *The Hunger* and an Australian short film; he has directed and written a tiny film *Missing Girl*. Following his Radio 4 play 'Cry Babies', he wrote an episode ('Phish Phood') for Radio 7's series *The Man in Black*. Most recently he has co-written with Mark Kermode the BBC4 series *Mark Kermode's Secrets of Cinema*.

Follow him on twitter @annodracula. His official website can be found at www.johnnyalucard.com